LOVE'S TOUCH OF JUSTICE

LOVE'S TOUCH OF JUSTICE

Flynn's Crossing Romantic Suspense Series

Book 7

Yvonne Kohano

Nanokas Press

A Division of Kochanowski Enterprises

Also by Yvonne Kohano

FLYNN'S CROSSING ROMANTIC SUSPENSE SERIES

Pictures of Redemption, Book 1
(Serena & Dane)

Flashes of Fire, Book 2
(DK & Vince)

Naked Intolerances, Book 3
(Gabby & Rick)

Tastes and Consequences, Book 4
(Mac & Roxy)

Blooms on the Bones, Book 5
(Tess & Powers)

Wine Into Water, Book 6
(Marguerite & Deke)

Love and the Christmas Tree Nymph, A Flynn's
Crossing Seasonal Novella

Love's Touch of Justice, Book 7
(Jake & Marlee)

This Proposal Between Us, A Flynn's Crossing
Seasonal Novella

Measure Twice, Love Once, Book 8
(Geno and Agnes)

And more to come!

**Learn about upcoming releases at
www.YvonneKohano.com.**

Subscribe to Yvonne Kohano's enewsletter to be among the first to learn about new releases and special offers. Visit www.yvonnekohano.com for more information.

Follow Yvonne at www.yvonnekohano.com, on Facebook as Yvonne Kohano, and on Twitter @yvonnekohano to learn what tickles her about being a writer, and at www.GooseYourMuse.com for creativity tips.

LOVE'S TOUCH OF JUSTICE

Prologue – Labor Day Last Year

The two men exchanged words that looked harsh and contentious. As they scanned the crowd, she caught sight of their faces. She couldn't avoid recalling the last time she'd seen them. They were older, but no less intense. She'd wanted to escape those memories, but dark thoughts were impossible to avoid. Ducking deeper into the doorway of the shop behind her, she couldn't pull her gaze away.

She wasn't stalking them, not exactly. Besides, it wasn't as if they would recognize her anymore. He'd taken care of that years ago.

"You stupid bitch, how could you get caught? All you had to do was drive down the road, stop where I told you to stop, and hand packages to people. How could you fuck this up?"

The sharp cracks of his fists to her face had not been as painful as the fear that clutched her gut. Curling into a ball and wrapping her arms around her knees so tight she heard tendons pop, she'd given up pleading with him. When he knocked out some of her teeth and blood ran into one eye, he'd finally seemed to be satisfied.

"Just remember we're married, you and me, and you can't implicate your husband." *He'd sneered the words in her ear before throwing her to the floor of their squalid apartment. Through swollen eyes, she'd watched his huge silhouette stomp to the door, slamming it open. It bounced against the wall before snagging on the dingy shag rug. He'd left it hanging there, wide open for anyone to peer in and see her. Not that anyone would care. Even after she'd heard the rattle of his car's holey muffler driving off, she'd stayed in her tight little knot.*

Her hands went to her face now, tracing its rebuilt bones. Her tongue ran over straight front teeth. She pressed a steadying hand to her belly. Everything had come at a price, but one she'd paid gladly. A single tear escaped, and she swiped it away. She could do nothing about her past stupidity. She only had the future, however hopeless and empty. Shaking off the self-pity, she resolved once more that things would be different.

She pulled her cap lower and adjusted her large sunglasses, wishing they could conceal the evidence of her fear and mistakes as easily as her make-up and long sleeves. People would judge her and find her guilty. Distancing herself was for the best. Even in a crowd, she stood alone.

From the number of people milling around, it seemed that everyone in the surrounding countryside had come into Flynn's Crossing for the Labor Day parade. Parents hoisted children on to their shoulders to see decorated vehicles and marching bands. Dancers tapped up the street. The lawn mower brigade followed the tractor team. High school teens cheered from home-designed floats. Horses pulled coaches and wagons with waving people on top. For most, it would have been an enjoyable and captivating scene of small town USA. But not for her.

The two men she'd been watching stood back to back now, turning in a tight circle and scanning the late summer crowd. Both equally tall, they looked to be the same age, though she knew years separated them. The older one carried his beefier body with an aggressive fluidness, fitting for someone who'd spent his career in construction. Leaner with the grace of a jungle cat, the younger man barely showed the extent of injuries that almost killed him, the only scars visible to the public carved into his face. The structure of their faces marked them as brothers. She knew they shared bold determination and stubborn independence as well.

When their gazes passed over her without stopping, she let out the breath she'd been holding. It was the closest she'd come to them in years, and she couldn't tear her eyes away. Their watchfulness didn't end, and they continued to turn in a tight circle. Covering each other's backs. That's what they did.

Their watchfulness didn't change when a sheriff's deputy strode over in long steps and questioned them. Their negative head shakes and the older one's gestures indicated frustration. She thought about melting into the crowd, but the exchange made her linger.

The deputy was almost as tall, appearing leaner but just as strong, even under the cover of body armor. His wide-brimmed hat hid most of his expression, but she sensed his alertness as his hands stayed at his waist, close to the belt weighed down with equipment and a big ass gun. He wore it as easily as the authority in his stance. She should be afraid of the danger he represented. She'd already spent too much of her life inviting trouble. Staying on the right side of the law was critical to her success. She doubted he'd understand.

When he added his scrutiny of the crowds clustered on the sidewalk, she froze, willing them all to glance over her in their search. The two civilians did. She was not surprised. Her disguise blurred their perception of her. The deputy's concentrated gaze paused as if searching her area. Through his mirrored sunglasses, she swore he looked right at her, but it was probably a trick of the light. Her heart beat a little faster and she wanted to run. Willing herself not to move, she waited. His gaze lasted five seconds longer before his face turned away.

She was again invisible.

Chapter 1 – January, Present Day

Jake pulled into his driveway after another long double shift to find her seated in the old pick-up, lying in wait for him. She pounced as soon as he unlocked his front door.

"You live like a monk."

She followed him inside, taking two and a half steps for one of his, continuing her rambling monologue. He didn't understand what was wrong with his house. He wasn't overly fond of clutter, which he thought she understood.

"I'm comfortable here. It's fine." He glanced around, seeing nothing out of place.

"Jake Kermarrec, this is your mother you're lying to. You need some stuff, you know. Pictures, other than those three of the family, and maybe some nice throw pillows on that couch, or on second thought, maybe a new living room set altogether, and – "

His mother Emie was shorter than the mirror on the side of his patrol vehicle, with bird bones and not an ounce of spare flesh on her, and still she wore him out. Her never-ending smile hid the iron will she used to rule everyone in her domain. No one could deny Emileen Kermarrec, or at least, not for long.

But Jake tried. "I don't need new furniture, Ma, but thanks for the offer to redecorate."

He brushed a tired hand over his closely cropped hair. It made long days and required headgear easier to handle. Lately, his mirror told him it seemed to be thinning on top, or maybe he was only imagining it. And maybe his forehead was getting bigger too. He didn't want to worry about it, since he couldn't control it.

"You're not paying attention. I said, Eugene Kermarrec the Second, you aren't getting any younger. How do you expect to entertain a nice young woman when you live such – why, I don't even know how to put this kindly – such an austere life? You used to laugh more, and you were always the life of the party. I raised you to have more color and zip than this." Her fluttering hands swept in an arc encompassing his home.

He liked his simple design scheme. If it wasn't regulation khaki and black or denim, what was the point? It made choices easy, just like his job. Either you were on the right side of the law, or you were on the wrong side. Any cop worth anything would agree it all came down to the law.

"Ma, thanks for coming over. I appreciate the pot roast and I'll make sure to reheat it just like you said." He stood in front of her, trying to redirect her to the door.

Emie reached up and patted his cheek, then paused with her head cocked to one side as if considering something that amused her, right before she gave his ear a quick twist.

"Ow! What's that for?" He rubbed hard at the tweaked skin already beginning to tingle and burn.

She smiled, as angelic a look as you could expect from a former hippie who handled a gruff husband twice her size, raised five rowdy boys, and played substitute mother to countless men and the occasional woman on a huge ranch for most of her life. Emie had probably seen everything and heard every story, real or imagined.

"You might be a big fearsome sheriff's deputy and all that, but you're still my second born. If I want to keep you in line, I will." Giving him a quick hug that meant her arms wrapped around his waist, she looked up at him. "Remember about Sunday supper. Deke is bringing his Marguerite. You're welcome to bring any of your young lady friends."

He ignored the subtle interrogation in her words and turned her toward the front door, glad he hadn't taken off his thick jacket. January in the Northern California foothills was cold. He didn't respond to her continuing chatter as he followed her down his front path and dutifully opened her door, waiting until her seat belt clicked and she started the engine. At his quick peck on her cheek, she gave him an impish grin as if she knew he was trying to kill that line of questioning.

"If you can't find anyone, I could fix you up, you know. Sunday's two days away, plenty of time."

God forbid. His fingers tightened on the pick-up's faded doorframe. Her kind heart would likely suggest one of the strays she often took on as personal projects, women who often carried secretive and checkered pasts, but in her estimation, were trustworthy and full of potential. They were never his type.

"I'll think about who I could bring, Ma. Okay? Now please drive safely and please, please, obey the speed limit, at least in Flynn's Crossing. I can't stand the ribbing every time you get another ticket."

She squealed like a girl caught in her undies in public. With a finger wave that ended in the two-fingered vee of a peace sign, she backed out of his driveway, changed gears, and crept forward. He watched, wondering how long it would take before she was back to her customary ways. She made the corner turn at a sedate speed, complete with blinker. As he turned back to his bungalow, he could almost count the seconds until he heard the engine in the old truck rev and rubber squeal on asphalt.

God bless Ma. She exasperated him, but she also made him smile. When his eyes fell on the covered dish on his kitchen counter, he couldn't resist lifting the aluminum foil and sniffing deeply like an addict with a line of coke. The need for sleep won out over the need for food, though, and he crimped the foil back in place and shoved the dish in the empty refrigerator.

How she had been able to get along with their father, he wasn't sure. The old man was as rough as they came, with no patience for anything he considered foolishness. The fact that he married a woman whose primary colors were psychedelic mystified their sons. And yet, she claimed it had been a love match until he died a decade ago. His passing hadn't kept Rock or the twins from leaving home. Jake's smile faded as he thought about those dark days, before he compartmentalized his mind and shut off the memories.

Five paces brought him from his kitchen to the living room, where he secured his service weapon in the small safe at the bottom of the entry closet. Seven more steps took him down the hall to his single bathroom. One bedroom made up the remainder of the floor plan. The layout wasn't cramped, but it wasn't fancy either. Keeping things simple had become a mantra for him, along with keeping things under control and always, always following the rules.

It made life easier.

If Ma or one of his brothers remarked occasionally that his life now was very different from his wild youth living on the edge, he merely shrugged and said it was high time he grew up. His older brother Deke, in particular, watched him thoughtfully, and while he didn't ask about the change often, Jake knew what was on his brother's mind. He tried not to think about it either, but sometimes, faced with the stark contrast of the past and the present, it was hard to avoid.

When had this urgent need for control won out? Why did his need to challenge the rules morph into rigid acceptance of the law? What made the brother who laughed the most and played pranks as often as possible become this sober, restrained guy? The questions were written on Deke's face, and often.

He wished he could explain it to his brother. Hell, he wished he could decode it himself. The thought drained away his little remaining energy after too many long workdays in a row, and he only managed to shove off his boots as he sat on the bed before dropping into an exhausted sleep, still dressed in his uniform.

Chapter 2

Jake felt his teeth rattle a little as the heavy-duty shocks of the patrol unit bounced over ruts in the gravel drive. He'd stuffed himself on cold pot roast for breakfast, eating too much and too fast. Maybe all this jiggling would help that settle. He'd have to thank his friend for that, though some of these holes were large enough to swallow a small country.

It seemed that as fast as Dane Ashland added more rocks to the surface, another delivery truck with a heavy construction load carved a new set of grooves. Dane's truck was sturdy and didn't mind the bounces, but his wife's SUV wasn't nearly as rugged. Nothing was too good for Dane when it came to keeping Serena comfortable. Dane probably had the rock delivery service on speed dial.

The thought made Jake grin as he pulled into the clearing. On this winter Saturday with no clouds on the horizon, Dane had called on his unlikely group of friends, the wolf pack, to help button up the roof and sides of his new workshop while Serena took a much-needed day off. The fact that she was spending this time with her girl tribe wasn't unusual, as most of those women were in relationships with one of the wolf pack men in attendance. It was interesting how everyone else's lives became intertwined.

It wouldn't be for him, of course. He didn't have the time or inclination to work at a relationship, and from his perspective, all relationships required work.

Shutting down the engine, he did a head count of the guys who'd already arrived. Vince Cassidy's little red foreign coupe was almost hidden, dwarfed by larger vehicles. The fact that Vince had two left thumbs he would probably hit with a hammer more than once today would only add to the amusement. Geno Altimari's carpentry truck blocked in the convertible. Deke's shiny pick-up filled the parking spot closer to the house, evidence his brother was taking a day away from the ranch to lend a hand.

He wished he could stay. Long hours made committing to anything difficult these days. Or had it been months?

"Hey, you better watch where you park. I hear there's a sheriff's deputy around here who's a real stickler for regulations and he might write you up."

Jake turned toward the voice, already smiling. Dane wasn't always the first one to speak in their group, nor was he the most voluble, but he did have a knack for coming up with a good one now and again. Jake missed hanging out with him.

The man coming toward him was lean, as lean as Jake was himself, and about the same age. They shared a few things in common, like having over-protective big brothers and their appreciation for the simpler things in life. But Dane's journey had taken him to points far away from Flynn's Crossing, to some of the hot spots around the world, and he had the scars to prove it. When he'd settled on this cliff, he'd been a recluse. That was, until Serena pulled him out of his comfort zone.

Jake, on the other hand, had been born and raised in this area, part of a legacy that went back seven generations. The only time he'd spent away was four years of college, funded by a partial scholarship he earned running track. He couldn't get back to his hometown fast enough once he graduated, and luckily, the sheriff's department was hiring when he was ready to return.

Eyeing his friend, Jake noticed the pronounced limp. Most days, the only signs of past battles were the deep scars on Dane's face. Those were bad enough. On the one occasion when he deigned to mention it, he reported his leg looked a whole hell of a lot worse.

"Rough day?" Jake flipped his gaze down at Dane's leg, then back up again. This was the closest the men came to expressing sympathy. It wasn't something they did. Most of the time, a hard pat on the shoulder letting another wolf pack member know you cared and had his back was enough.

Dane leaned a hip against the SUV and seemed to groan, though Jake wasn't sure over the racket made by men out of sight. The work party had begun.

"It's been a rough few weeks, trying to finish up construction before the weather sets in. Serena's doing everything she can, but she's at work morning until night. More service men and women return home each day, and almost to a person, they need counseling and support. At least Balance now has the funds to continue to serve them without any immediate threat of closing."

Dane had a hand in that, too. He'd used his photographic skills to tell the story of Balance in such a compelling fashion that the agency had been spared government budget cuts while bringing in new funding. The nonprofit's counseling and support services for military men and women provided a vital asset to the community. Jake respected his friend's courage and his willingness to break out of his hermit existence to help people he didn't know.

It wasn't too different, in some ways, from what Jake did in law enforcement. His commitment was to protect the people of his county to the extent of the law. He knew many didn't see it that way, but that was usually because they were breaking the law at the time.

Both men turned to watch a sedan make slow lunging progress up the drive. The car barely stopped before its back doors popped open. Two gangly boys poured out, along with a large blonde dog of uncertain parentage. A tall dark man rose from behind the wheel, looking as if he'd just done five rounds with a champ and lost the bout.

"Hey Rick, thanks for coming, especially since you have kid duty today."

Dr. Rick Chagres, engineer and university professor, paced toward them. Worry and resignation warred on his face as he watched the boys race for the edge of the clearing. He only cringed a little when one of the boys yelled at the dog, and when said dog barked uncontrollably as a ball shot past the men into the trees. Jake thought he looked more than a little stressed out.

"Hey guys? Make sure you stay away from the edge of the cliff when you play, okay?"

The boys raced back in response to Dane's words, coming to a dead stop in front of the men and adopting a similar cross-armed stance. They eyed the men for a moment, glanced at each other, and raised their shoulders in the same careless shrug.

The boy on the right, Jeremy, said, "We're not here to play, Dane."

Will finished, "We're here to work. So put us to work."

Jake smiled, not even trying to hide it. These boys might not be brothers by birth, but they'd come to be brothers in every other sense of the word. Where you saw one, the other wasn't far away. They often seemed to finish each other's sentences and communicate without speaking. And when they hung out with the men of the wolf pack, they were all business.

Dane pointed to a messy pile of scrap wood and asked them to stack it out of the way. The boys walked over in the loose-limbed amble Jake remembered from his pre-teen years. The dog licked their hands as they crossed the clearing. They stared down at the wood, consulting in low tones. Then they yanked matching work gloves from jacket pockets, pulled them on, and rummaged through the pieces.

The men watched them, Dane now joining Jake in an open smile, and Rick looking pensive and exhausted.

Jake directed his comment to Rick, though he guessed the answer already. "They're a handful, aren't they?"

Rick let out a deep sigh. "Yeah, that they are. They're always into projects, whether it's designing and building something or doing a science experiment to test one of their theories, though I use that term science loosely. They make up a system for everything. We have to keep a close eye on them, though thankfully, they are using their powers for good most of the time, and they haven't blown anything up – yet." He chuckled when he finished, shaking in mock horror.

Dane asked, "How's Gabby feeling? Serena said she's having a rough time with the baby."

"Yes, though from my perspective, my wife seems to be handling the pregnancy like a champ. I'm the one falling apart at the seams. All I can think of is, what if it's another boy? I know the guys would dote on a baby sister and watch over her. But another turbo-charged handful of mischief in the house? God help me."

Jake joined in as all three men laughed loud enough to draw suspicious glances from the boys. Dismissing the adults, they turned back to their work, occasionally stopping to debate, a piece of wood in one or the other's hands.

"How's my brother coming along on the addition to your house?"

A yell from Will punctuated Dane's question as the dog grabbed an end of a length of wood to play. Will wrestled it away and threw it for the dog, who barked and chased after it with her tail a wagging blur in the air.

"Powers and his crew are doing a great job. In fact, he'd be here today, except they're trying to complete our siding before the snow. That means I should pull double duty on your place in gratitude. So, as the boys said, put me to work."

Dane clapped a hand on Rick's shoulder, and they both turned to the building taking shape at the edge of the clearing, a short distance from the main house. They called back a goodbye to Jake as the dog bounded after them, her game of fetch forgotten.

His uniform and the cruiser were sure signs he wasn't staying, something they'd probably come to expect. He would have liked to pitch in. It seemed he rarely had time for anything that wasn't work or his degree these days.

Jake's radio hummed but remained quiet, and he took a moment to enjoy the warmth of the sun on his face. Out over the canyon, a buzzard screeched, gliding on the wind. Rock outcroppings broke up the heavy forest, adding texture to the view. Dane had selected a picture-perfect spot to build his new life, Serena by his side. Jake reassured himself the feeling settling into his gut was his unusual breakfast and not envy. Marriage and kids were for his friends. His career came first, though that idea didn't give him the buzz it usually did.

Uneasy with his thoughts, he glanced around the clearing for a distraction. His curiosity got the better of him as his eyes settled on the boys. Jeremy handed a piece of wood to Will, who eyed it carefully before placing it on one of five stacks.

"Hey guys, what are you doing?" He kept a hand on his equipment belt as he crouched down for the stick the dog had dropped a few feet away. Coming over to the boys, he tossed it casually on one of the five stacks.

"Jake, that's not where it goes." The exasperation in Will's voice was clear.

"Yeah," added Jeremy, "it's not the right place."

Jake hoped his expression looked serious, even as he chuckled on the inside. "Why, exactly, is that not the right place?"

The boys exchanged glances, and when their eyes returned to him, he figured their estimation of his brainpower just dropped a few points.

"We're sorting them by size and type of wood. That pile over there," Jeremy gestured to the far right, "is for wood that's in bad shape and should be burned."

Will continued without a pause, "The rest is still good, and the guys can use it if it fits right. So we're keeping the pieces together. See?"

Well damn, they sure had a system. Rick was right. These two would require watching. Who knew what kinds of interesting situations they'd get themselves in to as they got older?

And Jake would be on the outside of their lives, watching, as he was with everyone else. That idea made the sun feel colder and the pot roast toss in new discomfort.

Three identical workstations lined the wall of the spa, and women crowded every corner of the room. The noise level was intense, no doubt helped along by the bubbly in some of their glasses, and Marlee Cruiz wondered how they had so much to talk about when they seemed to see each other all the time.

It wasn't the noise that bothered her. In fact, she welcomed the hubbub of activity. In this environment, she could disappear. Happy talking to each other, clients needed little input from her.

But today, the identities of the clients increased her unease.

"What a great idea, a pedicure spa day, but I do wish it was summer so I could show off these toes."

In front of her, Tess Willowspring wiggled those toes, and Marlee couldn't help herself. She grabbed Tess by the ankle and squeezed gently.

"Please stop twitching. The polish needs to dry. Give it a few minutes."

Tess chuckled, even as she looked suitably chagrined. Beside her in the next chair, Serena Williamson Ashland joined in the laughter with more enthusiasm.

Serena said, "Goes to show how rarely we get our toes done. We don't even remember that we need to keep still."

Seated across the room, Marguerite Devereaux took a sip of sparkling wine and tsk-tsked. "You need to get out more, you two. Spend time and money on yourselves. Your men will appreciate it. I know Deke does."

The suggestive purr in the delivery of that last sentence made the whole room burst into fresh laughter. Marlee struggled to join in, cracking what she hoped was a semblance of a smile.

These women had it all, in her opinion. Good men loved them to distraction. Rewarding jobs filled their days and a community embraced them. Their friendships were strong. Children, either in hand or on the horizon, were reasonable parts of their expectations, and none of them seemed to be concerned about how untold events might change their lives. They didn't look over their shoulders, expecting tragedy to strike at every turn. They were lucky on so many levels.

She had so little in common – in fact, maybe nothing in common. But she couldn't tear herself away from Flynn's Crossing, no matter how much she felt the urge to run overtaking her again.

Spa owner Bliss, a highly styled woman with generous curves on her short frame, guffawed along with her customers. As things quieted, she gave them each a sly, considering look.

"You all do need to pamper yourselves more, ladies. Why, you haven't even tried Marlee's massages. An hour under her hands, and you'll feel so peppy and hot, you'll march right up to your men and do'em on the front porch."

"What makes you think we need a massage to make that happen, Bliss?" With Marguerite's expression of sly delight, the room burst apart in laughter once more.

"On the front porch? As in at home, on Main Street? My business license would be revoked." Tess's startled exclamation mixed with the laughter and made the raucous noise louder. Marlee bent her head to hide her blush. After so many months at the spa, she should be used to her boss's outspokenness, but she still colored when the subject of sex came up.

It wasn't a virginal blush, not in the least. She'd had sex, lots of it, and much of it wasn't something she was proud of. That past was far behind her, though, so maybe she qualified as a virgin again. And as she often assured herself, she had no desire to break the dry spell.

"Let me tell you a little about my nickname, and how I named this spa. It's racy, and you'll get a kick out of it."

Bliss didn't need any encouragement from the group to launch into her explanation. Their rapt attention gave Marlee the perfect opportunity to shake off her thoughts and grab the towel holding her used pedicure tools. The back room shared a wall with the nail area, and while it wasn't thick, it blocked the women's view of her. With the door closed, Bliss's booming voice was muted and her words indistinct as the laughter continued. On edge and unsettled, Marlee wondered how she'd get through the rest of her day.

The news hadn't been good, not for weeks. It made her doubt her direction. What if she was following the wrong path again?

"Marlee, the ladies are leaving. Where'd you wander off to?"

Straightening her back, she pushed her tired thoughts away and opened the door to see Marguerite, Serena and Tess admiring each other's feet. While they would be cold in their flip-flops on this winter afternoon, no doubt they would consider it worth the discomfort. Their distraction gave her one more chance to observe them up close, envy and sadness warring inside her as she blinked and looked away, busying herself cleaning the pedicure stations.

"Marlee, I will come back for that massage, I swear it." Coming up beside her, Serena gave her arm a light squeeze, pausing on her way to the door. "By the way, do you do couples massages here? That would be a fun thing to treat Dane to as a Valentine's Day gift, don't you think?"

Tess stopped next to them and added, "Yes, that would be the perfect gift. I'd love to do that with Powers too."

Bliss said, "Sorry, ladies, but we don't have the space for that. But you can get your men gift cards for solo massages. They'll thank you for it, since Marlee is the best."

The women turned toward the counter as Marlee tried to hide her shock. This wasn't something she'd ever considered, and she wished she had. Watching the men from a distance was one thing, but up close and personal was too risky.

She took fast steps sideways, ignoring curious glances. When she reached the safety of the back room, she closed her eyes and willed the wild beat of her heart to slow.

>>>>>

Her heart still felt unsteady when Bliss later told her that Serena and Tess decided to think about massages as gifts for their men. What could she do? If they had certificates, they'd expect the service. She hadn't thought of this possibility.

"That's a really sore spot. Do you think you could dig a little deeper?"

Marlee's mind snapped back to the muscles under her hands. Her pregnant client sat at a computer for long hours each day, and her tight back and knotted shoulders were testament to that. Usually this kind of bodywork took Marlee to a Zen kind of place, allowing her to help release stress for her clients while emptying her own mind. She was good at massage.

It was the rest of her life she wasn't so good at.

"How's that? Better?"

The woman on the table gave a happy groan in response.

"I wish I'd had you around when I was pregnant the first time," Gabby Cooley Chagres said. "It would have made carrying Jeremy so much easier."

Marlee didn't respond. She didn't need to. Often her clients talked while she worked on them. Sometimes the repetitive movements and the release of their body's tension was enough to put them to sleep, and she'd listen to their light snores while she kept untying their knots.

It was the closest she let herself get to any human being now. Even as she cared about how they felt, her touch on their skin remained as impersonal and distancing as her words. The fewer questions about her personal life she answered, the lower the risk. Perhaps she should move again, since more people seemed to be getting curious about her, but she wasn't ready.

"You don't like to talk much, do you, Marlee?"

Under her probing fingers, Gabby didn't appear to be inclined to doze off today. She was often too observant, a fact that made Marlee cautious. As a romance writer, Gabby also loved to talk about her work, where she got her ideas, and the resulting happily-ever-afters. Her real life romance with Rick Chagres had its own happy ending, one that produced this baby already treasured by both parents and doted on by the blended family of little boys who'd become brothers.

What did Marlee know about romance? Nothing. And if her personal experience with ever-afters was anything to go by, she didn't care to learn more.

To her client, she said, "No ma'am, I don't."

The woman chuckled. "I really can't get used to you calling me ma'am. I'm Gabby, okay? 'Ma'am' makes me feel like I came in for a rinse and comb-out and you need to rub cream on my hands to cover up the liver spots."

Marlee couldn't help herself. She chuckled.

"That's better. I've been coming to see you every other week for a massage for what now, over three months? You did my nails for my friend's wedding. And in all that time, I've barely learned a single thing about you."

Marlee never broke her rhythm, her hands on autopilot. "You've learned that I don't talk much."

Gabby laughed, and then moaned when Marlee hit another particularly good spot between her shoulder blades.

"Okay, uncle, or maybe aunt. I give up. People say I can get rocks to talk, and I will get you to tell me something about yourself yet, Ms. Marlee, I swear I will." Gabby sighed in continuing bliss.

Marlee knew she was good at her work. Her hands were strong and artful, and her ability to match nail styles with a client's personality won raves. At least that's what the last salon owner told her. After six months at Bliss Day Spa, she figured she was doing okay, since Bliss had long since stopped making any noise about a probationary period.

"Time to turn over, ma'am."

She held up the privacy sheet with one hand so Gabby could adjust to the side of the massage table, with Marlee giving the extra cushions to guard the baby bulge a practiced twitch to the floor. Gabby resettled on her back with a hum.

"I so appreciate those magic fingers of yours, Marlee. Who knew carrying a baby at my age would take such a toll on my body? Jeremy wasn't an easy pregnancy, but I don't remember feeling quite so ungainly this early."

Gabby laughed at herself, and Marlee felt compelled to smile as well. She liked her clients here, especially Gabby. Who knew when she chose this little town that she'd find the closest thing to friendship she'd felt in years? That wasn't the reason she'd come, but it was a pleasant bonus.

"I've been raving about you constantly, so expect all of my girl tribe to come to you for massages. I'm sure Serena's going to bite any day now. She and Dane have been building a studio on their property, and she's been complaining about how sore she's getting, hauling lumber and boards after an already full day of work. She swears once they get the framing and drywall finished, she's going to treat herself."

That idea gave Marlee a momentary pang of alarm. But another client was good, right? And who it was didn't matter.

She felt Gabby's eyes on her as she paid extra attention to the wrist and forearm in her fingers. She could massage a client's body with her eyes closed, since her skill drew from how things felt under her hands. But Gabby didn't know that there was no reason for Marlee to pay unflinching attention to her work.

"You're a deep well of still water, aren't you?"

The soft question caught her by surprise. Usually, Gabby didn't probe after her initial foray. But today, she seemed intent on knocking down walls.

Marlee shrugged, trying to appear nonchalant. "I just don't have much to talk about. My life is pretty boring and ordinary." At least, that was her cover story.

Gabby made a rude noise, a cross between a snort and a squeak, drawing Marlee's attention. When their eyes met, Gabby's sober gaze made her squirm at her protective lie.

"Everyone has a life story, Marlee, along with baggage and secrets. We have a choice. It can weight us down and limit our future, or it can serve as the foundation for growth. I think you've been lugging your stuff around by yourself for so long, you've forgotten you need to share it to lighten the load. And to be happy in life, you have to solve the mystery of how to let all of that make you stronger, not sadder."

If only she knew how. Happiness was a concept so foreign to her, she almost laughed aloud. Marlee knew work. She knew worry, which meant she checked over her shoulder often. She knew to keep her head down and her confidences to herself.

She turned away so the other woman wouldn't see the pain her words caused. She wanted to be happy. In her mind, there was a picture of what that would look like, one she didn't take out and examine too often or too closely. It only made her cry.

Chapter 3

It wouldn't be hard to consider Valentine's Day a complete failure before it even started. Marlee's coffeemaker sounding a death rattle instead of its comforting gurgle this morning was enough to turn her day dark and stormy, kind of like the clouds that threatened outside.

She had few vices left, but coffee was one of them. Tinkering with the machine did no good. It had seen better days half a decade ago, and on the way to her car, she tossed it in the apartment complex's dumpster. As she parked in her slot at the city lot, she hoped Bliss had stocked up the client station inside.

There was no way Marlee could function without caffeine.

Unlocking the spa's back door and punching in the security code, she hit light switches as she moved down the hallway toward the client waiting area in front. The heater had barely kicked on, and the space held an early morning chill that would take another quarter hour to let go. But she liked this time of day, when she was the only one here and she could prepare her stations and her mind for the appointments ahead.

The refreshments area held a fancy dispenser with individual serving selections. She sorted through the little cups. Decaf. Decaf. Tea. More decaf. Next to the machine, she found a scribbled shopping list. At the very top, the note to buy regular coffee was written in red and underlined.

Great. She could do without milk and orange juice. She might even forgo her treasured cereal. She would not go without coffee. The day would be ugly.

Sighing, she reversed through the spa, punched in the security code once more, and locked the door behind her. Ignoring the threatening clouds, she walked up the street to the bakery. This would be a treat, one she deserved. Her money was too dear to spend on fancy coffee every day, but on this occasion, it was as close as she would get to a personal Valentine.

"Hey, look who's here, little Marlee."

The beefy man behind the counter greeted her before the tinkle of the door's bells finished announcing her entry. She wasn't sure why the owner decided she was little. Her height belied the title, but he used it whenever she came in.

"Hey Sarge. Can I have a medium mocha, extra shot, please?" Even she heard the desperation in her voice.

"Well, and a happy Valentine's Day to you. But you don't look very happy. Stuart, does she look happy?"

Marlee wanted to sink into the tile floor, or maybe crawl under one of the polished metal tables. Sarge's reed-thin partner came out of the back and stared at her in a considering manner with a tilt to his head, a small frown coming to his face.

"No, she doesn't look happy. What do you say, little Marlee? What kind of pastry can Sarge get for you?"

The two men moved like a well-orchestrated team behind the counter, Stuart working on the mocha, Sarge waiting with tongs in one hand and a pastry bag in the other.

She thought about the contents of her wallet and the upcoming expense of a new coffeemaker. Hopefully, today's tips would be generous, with women pampering themselves for a big night with a significant other. But you couldn't buy a pastry on hope. Adding mocha to the coffee was already an indulgence. Her fingers tightened on the strap of her big purse.

"Just the mocha, guys, thanks." She turned toward the street to avoid drooling over the baked goods. The growl of her stomach wasn't audible to the men behind the counter, right?

"Just pulled some Danish out of the oven. You know, the ones you like, with the lemon curd filling." She heard rustling as something hit the bag in Sarge's hands. "On the house."

She spun around. She didn't like being beholden to anyone. Favors given meant favors expected. It was what those favors turned out to be, precisely, that always seemed to work against her.

"That will be four-thirty-five, and not a penny more, for the coffee and the pastries. Looks like you could use some meat on your bones, little Marlee, and a smile in your face." Stuart beamed as he pushed her items across the counter. Sarge crossed his arms over his barrel chest and grinned, as if waiting for her to deny the gift.

She wanted to argue, to turn the bag away. The top was open, and out of it, a wonderful rich aroma of butter and lemon wafted up. Her mouth watered as, without warning, her stomach rumbled loud enough to bring bigger smiles to the faces of the men.

She handed a five-dollar bill across the counter as Stuart passed coins in change back into her reluctant hand. Sarge pushed the coffee cup and bag closer, and her stomach growled again. She felt the blush rise under her make-up and hoped the men wouldn't notice.

"Thanks, guys, really. Thanks. I guess maybe I do need that pastry. I would like to pay you for it." She fumbled in her wallet, trying to hide her embarrassment.

They shook their heads, Sarge making shooing sweeps with his hands to send her on her way, and Stuart smiling an even bigger grin. She argued and they laughed, until she couldn't say no.

"Happy Valentine's Day, little Marlee. You have a good one, you hear?"

When she pushed the door open, the jingle of the bells sounded almost merry.

Sun peeked out from behind the clouds overhead and a gentle breeze caressed her face. The shops on Main Street looked bright and enchanting to her eyes all of a sudden. Few people strolled along at this early hour, but each one she passed wished her a good morning. Inside a couple of the restaurants, people she didn't know waved at her in such a friendly way that it was impossible not to smile and wave back.

She strolled back toward the spa, unwilling to rush as she took small savory bites of the pastry. Crumbs stuck to her lips as the lemon curd exploded on her tongue. Concentrating on the flavors, Marlee allowed her eyes to close on a low groan of satisfaction.

"I heard that," a female voice said with a chuckle.

Marlee spun around and found herself staring at the exotic Native American beauty of Tess, her dark hair with its signature white streak hair pulled back and her arms full of flowers, standing in a shop doorway.

"Ah, good morning. You caught me enjoying one of life's few true pleasures."

"I know. Pastry from Brew Bank Bakery should be illegal." Tess shifted the flowers, staring more closely at Marlee until she felt herself squirm under the scrutiny.

"I rarely see you wandering on Main Street. Want to come inside and visit? I'd stay here to chat, but today's the busiest day of the year and I have a ton of orders left to fill."

Marlee hesitated at Tess's invitation. The older woman's eyes were too knowing, her smile too bright. It was as if she sensed Marlee's secrets. Not that she would guess the biggest ones, of course.

Tess headed inside the shop as if she expected Marlee to follow. She shouldn't. She didn't have the time. She didn't want to be found out for the fraud she was. But the flower shop had always intrigued her, first in its original place at the end of Main Street in the old Victorian, and now in a new building that looked as authentic as if it stood in this spot for a hundred years. Powers Ashland could claim credit for that.

Her thoughts snagged. Powers had come to Flynn's Crossing to add a building to Main Street, and he'd built a life here with Tess as well. From what Marlee heard, he was well respected, both for the work he'd accomplished, and for the man he'd become. He and his brother Dane had settled in, becoming pillars of the community. Getting close to Tess would give her insights into their lives. She couldn't walk away from that opportunity.

She closed the bag on the remainder of her pastry and crossed the threshold, her nose immediately flooding with the scents of hundreds of flowers. Every level surface seemed to hold bouquets of buds, primarily roses, but also lilies and other plants she didn't recognize. There hadn't been much room for flowers in her life.

"Please excuse the mess. It's not usually like this, but today is different from every other day in the year." Tess moved behind a long table that might have once belonged in a dining room, setting down the stems in her arms and dividing the flowers into two piles.

Marlee drew closer, unable to resist reaching out a finger to caress a rose petal that looked like silk. She expected it to be fake, but it was real, the surface as soft as well-tended skin.

"Sniff that one. Too many of the commercial growers aim for long vase life, but not a lot of scent. That one, though, has both."

Marlee hesitated. It looked too fragile, and she didn't want to break it. But its incomparable beauty drew her closer, and when her nose neared the barely unfurled bud, the heady spice was intoxicating.

"That's a great rose, isn't it?" Tess carried two in her hand and returned to the front door, peering down at them closely. "They sent me two batches that are close in color, but slightly different. I don't want to mix them up in different bouquets. Their colors could clash in certain kinds of light."

Wow, who knew building a bouquet of roses was so exacting?

Setting down the rose with as much care as she could, Marlee wandered around the shop, appreciating the casual placement of bric-a-brac and pedestals. It might look haphazard, but from what she heard about the owner of Buds and Blooms, she suspected everything had been situated to set a mood. And it worked.

A young woman emerged from a back room carrying containers full of daffodils. They seemed to be sleeping with their buds firmly closed. With a pang, a memory jumped out of the past before Marlee could avoid it. Her mother had loved daffodils and insisted on bringing in the first tight buds each spring as a sign of the new season. Together, she and Mom fashioned bouquets in little vases and her mother let her pick where they should stand around the house. It was personal time Marlee always treasured.

"Thanks, Jan. Do you know Marlee? She works at Bliss."

Pushing the past away, Marlee nodded at the introduction. Jan launched into an explanation about the lack of space in the back room. Tess glanced at the young woman from time to time while her busy hands seemed to prepare two flower vases at once.

"Powers will be back with the van in a little while and he can load the completed orders. Then you'll have space.

I'm glad we ordered extra daffys. Some people aren't keen on roses today."

Powers was coming back soon? Before she realized it, Marlee took two steps toward the door, nearly spilling the coffee cup clutched tightly in her hand.

"I need to get back to work. Nice to meet you, Jan. See you, Tess."

"Hey, wait a second." Tess's voice followed her out the door and three rapid paces down the sidewalk.

"Wait up, Marlee."

It wasn't an order, exactly, but she stopped anyway. She turned, expecting to see big questions on Tess's face, or maybe anger for her abrupt departure.

But instead, Tess held out a bunch of daffodils. Her smile was as sunny as those buds would become. She all but shoved the cluster into Marlee's hand.

"Happy Valentine's Day," she said as she gave Marlee a quick hug. "Enjoy your day."

Marlee watched her quickly retreating back, the black and silver braid swishing in time to her rapid movements. She was about to call out her thanks when her glance fell on the Buds and Blooms van lumbering up the street. There was no doubt who was behind the wheel. And on that signal, she fled with her hat pulled low, the flowers clutched in her hand.

A Hallmark holiday on a Saturday night. He wasn't sure which bugged him the most, the fact that it was a holiday he had no reason to celebrate, or the fact that he was going to pull a long night when there were sure to be multiple cases of driving under the influence – though which influence was most powerful would be the question.

Love? Wine? Or maybe, according to Ma, chocolate? She swore it was an aphrodisiac.

He drove up Main Street, enjoying the morning's quiet. Few people were out and about yet since most of the shops weren't open. Except for the flower shop, of course. Tess even had Powers on delivery duty today.

As he slowed to peek in the doorway, a woman dressed in black rushed out of the shop's door followed by Tess. If his friend hadn't been smiling, he would be suspicious. But she shoved flowers in the other woman's hands and turned back inside without losing her grin, so he relaxed.

He'd noticed this woman before on Main Street and around town, dressed in black year round, a hat always pulled low. He'd come to think of her as Goth Girl. If this was his beat, he would have followed up and tried to get a line on her, because her behavior was odd. She was constantly nervous. In his experience, only people with something to hide acted this jumpy on a regular basis. But even as he wondered what she was up to, she haunted him. He'd had a dream or three about her, and none of them would be suitable for viewing by boys the age of Jeremy and Will. They didn't even like the idea of girls yet, much less kissing them.

Maybe someday he'd follow Goth Girl and see where she rushed off to. But today, he had plans he couldn't break. Pulling into a parking space at the corner, he glanced up and down the street, the watchfulness so much a part of him that he didn't even need to consciously catalog the people and vehicles in his view. Satisfied that peace would reign for a few minutes, he pushed into the coffee shop and nodded to the men behind the counter.

His older brother Deke, closest to him in age if not temperament, stood at the cash register of Brew Bank Bakery and paid for coffees and pastries piled high on plates in front of him. The owners, Sarge and Stuart, exchanged good-humored ribs with him about his current affair.

Not an affair, not by a long shot. If Deke had his way, sexy winemaker Marguerite would be tied up as tight as a steer for branding, and fast. He undoubtedly had a big night planned for his ladylove, based on his sappy smile. Accompanying that wine and chocolate would be lots of hearts and flowers.

Jake wasn't sure how he felt about that.

Weaving between the tables and setting two coffees on the metal surface, Deke's face held that smile as Sarge asked him in no uncertain terms what his intentions were toward one of the girl tribe. Sarge and Stuart were mightily protective of those women. In fact, almost anywhere in this town, the girl tribe was akin to royalty.

And by association, the wolf pack basked in their glow. One by one, each man found a woman who turned their lives upside down. One by one, they lost control and changed the directions of their lives. Jake didn't necessarily like that either.

Deke returned, shuffling plates of scones and other pastries between the cups of coffee. The scrape of the chair's legs as he took his seat across from Jake sounded shrill in the small shop. Jake gritted his teeth.

"You look like the meanest bad-ass criminal just cut a path of destruction through your county and escaped. Do you need to go arrest someone so you'll feel better?"

Jake glanced around to make sure no one observed their exchange before extending his middle finger behind the cover of their mugs. It made him feel marginally better.

Deke chuckled, taking off the ball cap that made him look more like a mechanic than the rancher he was. Long hair pulled back in a ponytail made him look younger than his years. Or maybe it was love. His eyes twinkled with good humor, eyes that mirrored Jake's own in color. It was a legacy all of the Kermarrec boys shared, the mix of green, blue and gray of their family's Breton roots.

His big brother's face grew serious as he stared at him, saying nothing for so long that Jake began to grow uncomfortable. He wasn't up to an inquisition today.

Letting his gaze sweep the street outside the window, he steeled himself for the questions to come. Deke felt he needed to smooth everyone's way. He'd want to know what was wrong, why Jake felt even less like joking than he usually did. And damn if he knew how to respond.

What was wrong with him?

"Has Ma been visiting you?"

Jake's eyes swerved from the SUV inching into a tight parking space outside to Deke's face.

"Why? Did she say something?" Another thought grabbed him, and he was sure his face paled. "Is she planning something?"

Deke shook his head, grinning once more. "Not that I know of, but who's to say? It's about those Sunday dinners, isn't it? You haven't made one in, let's see, a month. Always working, that or studying, according to Ma. You have her perturbed, little brother, and Ma perturbed is a scary thing, as you well know."

Jake grimaced at the concept. Their mother had a mind of her own, every good aspiration in the world, and a tendency to complicate things when she put those two traits together.

To Deke, he replied, "Doesn't she have enough to bug you about, what with Marguerite in your life and all? I'm betting she would love to see you married to that wonderful woman, providing the next generation of Kermarrecs to take over the legacy."

Deke's scone-filled hand stopped halfway up, his mouth hanging open a little. A goofy expression came over his face, followed by a lazy smile as the hand descended slowly back to the plate. He dropped the scone and brushed off his fingers. Then he glanced around the shop as if looking for spies. Satisfied, he dug into his pocket.

Jake had a clue he knew what was coming next.

A small black box hid in the cup of Deke's large hands when he put them back on the table's shiny surface. A look Jake took for reverence crossed his brother's face as he looked up from the box, his eyes full of determination and pride.

"I'm going to ask her tonight, after I cook her a fantastic dinner. She's bringing the wine, of course. I have flowers all over the place, and plenty of candles, because she loves to be romanced. I even memorized some poems, in the tradition of St. Valentine."

"Well of course you did." Jake snorted. His brother loved to study anything that engaged his curious mind. Evidently, the language of love was the present topic of interest.

Deke opened the little box with a distinct pop, and Jake's eyes traveled down to the simple diamond sparkling in a plain silver-white band. It was one honking huge rock.

"It's two carats of the highest quality. The band is platinum. Marguerite likes bold colors and wears gold too, but from what I've observed, she likes silver things best. What do you think?"

What did he think? His confusion wasn't about the ring, or even his brother's choice in a bride. The jolt to his gut was a sensation of uncertainty he seemed to be feeling more and more recently.

His mind flashed forward a few years, to a Sunday dinner. Ma ruling the table, with Uncle Rowan, who seemed to be hanging around a lot these days, at her side. Deke and Marguerite, along with a riot of kids sharing the mixture of her dark good looks and his brother's blond surfer-dude features. Hell, maybe even the three younger boys would have returned home from wandering the world and be there with wives and families of their own.

And he'd be there, sitting solo at a corner of the table, his chair kicked back away from the party. His hair would have the same buzz cut, thinner on the top with even more forehead showing. His uniform would be pressed and his radio cackling at his shoulder. And at the end of the afternoon, he'd either head out to work, or home to his cold, empty house.

"Jake? Are you okay?"

"Hey, is that a ring we see?"

Jake wanted to kiss Sarge and Stuart for interrupting the conversation. Okay, not kiss the guys, but he was grateful they distracted Deke. His brother's warning glance meant he still expected an answer to his question. But then, Deke might think Jake didn't approve, and that wasn't a concern he wanted to let fester.

"Yeah, guys, Deke bought Marguerite a ring, hearts and flowers all around. I'm happy for them. Bro, I'm very happy for the two of you. I really am."

Jake put all of the rough emotions he was feeling into his words, and Deke's small nod let him know they were okay. There was a warning in the glance too, though. Deke wanted to know what was bugging him.

Stuart threw a skinny arm over Sarge's beefy shoulders as the two of them asked in minute detail how Deke planned to propose, making suggestions and arguing like a married couple about the best options. Jake leaned back, content to watch Deke take in their ideas, nodding his head as if he welcomed every one.

But Jake knew Deke, and Deke would do things his own way no matter what anyone else said. They'd shared this trait since they were boys.

His radio sparked to life, his badge number coming through loud and clear. He was on his feet before he'd even responded, already in motion toward the patrol SUV. For once, he welcomed the timing.

Sarge and Stuart called good luck after him. Deke told him to be careful as he always did, and Jake waved over his shoulder as he hit the door. Putting his hand to it, he turned long enough to meet his brother's eyes. A wise light shone back at him.

"And Jake? We're not done with that discussion yet."

Like there was any doubt about that. Deke with an idea that something was wrong was like a dog with a favorite bone. He just wouldn't let it go.

"I know, Deke. Believe me, I know."

Chapter 4

The call that pulled him from the bakery was a winner, one that would bring a smile to his face for weeks. An older woman, one Helen Sinclair, living alone at the end of the road and out of sight of any neighbors, whispered to the dispatcher that a strange man in weird clothes was lurking outside her house, making odd noises. She thought he was crazy.

Jake approached as he did any unknown but suspicious situation, parking a distance from the house and creeping nearer for reconnaissance with a hand on his gun just in case. As he drew closer, he spotted the man.

The old man was dressed in an outfit with ruffles and a big white wig. He pranced around, though how, Jake wasn't sure, considering the heeled boots he wore. He had a book in his hand, and from it, he appeared to be reading out loud.

Jake moved closer, careful not to startle the man. He saw the curtains inside the house twitch, parting wide enough for him to see the frightened face of its resident. When she saw Jake, she waved in obvious relief.

"Excuse me, sir?"

The old man stopped his dancing and whirled around, freezing when he saw Jake.

Jake asked, "Can I help you with something, sir? The occupant of the house is concerned you might be having some sort of problem."

The old man glanced toward the house, back at Jake, and then to the house again. Closer up, Jake could see make-up on the man's face, as if he was dressed for a costume party. He must be in his seventies. What hadn't been visible before was a bouquet of red roses clutched under one arm.

"No, sorry, officer. I'm not having any problem, I mean. At least, I didn't think I was." He dropped his head, grabbing at the roses as they slipped out of his grasp. He caught the ends, and the buds hung toward the ground, looking as defeated as he did.

"You see, officer, Miss Helen said she wanted to be courted. I been trying to convince her to go out with me for months now, ever since last summer. Her husband's been gone a long time, and my wife died over a year ago. Miss Helen and I, we went to high school together and we been friends all these years. She was my first love, you see. So since she wanted to be courted, I'm courting her."

The radio crackled to life, requesting an update. Jake keyed the mic and notified the dispatcher that he had the situation well under control, trying to keep the grin out of his voice. Based on her response, he knew he wasn't successful and would be explaining this one later.

"What's your name, sir?"

"I'm Desi, Desi Barzetto, Deputy," he leaned forward and squinted at Jake's nameplate, "Deputy Kermarrec. Hey, you one of the brothers from Three Rivers Ranch? My dad and granddad worked there from time to time."

Jake nodded, walking around Desi to stand between the man and Miss Helen's front door. He heard it creak open behind him, and a woman's voice called out, "You going to arrest him, deputy?"

"Ma'am, do you know a gentleman by the name of Desi Barzetto?"

"Course I do, known him all my life. Why?"

Jake gestured to the older man, who executed a commendable bow. The woman took a step out on the creaky porch, bending as if to get closer and squinting. She patted her apron pockets, pulling out a pair of glasses and setting them on her nose. After she squinted again through the lenses, she straightened and clapped her hands.

"Desi? Is that you? What the hell you doing all dressed up like a fool?"

The man blushed under his make-up, waving the flowers at the woman.

"Miss Helen, I been asking you out for months now. You said you wanted to be courted, so I looked up what that meant and I rented this getup. I even found some poetry and crap to read to you. Crazy woman, if you want me to dress like this all the time, I don't think I can do it."

"Now why the hell would you think I'd want you to dress up like some kind of clown? I swear, when that horse kicked you in the head years ago, he broke something."

She stopped, tilting her head to the side as she looked at the roses. A shy little smile lit up her face, and Jake forced another chuckle into a cough behind his hand. She asked, "Those flowers for me?"

Desi took three eager steps forward.

"Yes they are, milady." And he bowed again.

Her smiled got bigger as she laughed a girlish giggle, and she opened the door wider. "Oh, you damn fool, get in here. I got some coffee on and cookies fresh baked out of the oven."

Desi stepped gingerly across the sparsely grassed front yard, walking up the steps with care as if the boots killed his feet.

Helen peered at Desi's clothes, her gaze stopping at ground level. "Them boots on your feet have heels on them. There something I don't know about you, Desi?"

She ushered him into the house, clucking and tittering over his clothes. And just like that, she shut the door in Jake's face.

Jake knew he was grinning from ear to ear when he knocked and asked for confirmation that Miss Helen felt safe, and she looked at him as if he was the crazy one before thanking him and dismissing him with another snap of the front door. He'd felt a little silly asking, but procedures needed to be followed, and he needed to know that the woman no longer had concerns.

Yeah, that was a good call for a change, and thinking back on it, he laughed again. Ah, what people did for love. It served as more proof that it made you demented. That would never be him. But he couldn't help but continue to grin when he pictured Desi in his weird outfit.

He swung the SUV from the black top to a wide turnout in the road, the gray light matching the well-beaten gravel. Finishing his brief report on the incident, he left out the more humorous parts. Stick to the facts, and the facts alone. No law had been broken. Only people being silly. If this was the extent of Valentine's Day craziness, maybe this shift wouldn't be so bad. But it was early yet, and those clouds looked more like snow than rain. The forecasters had waffled about what kind of wet stuff could fall from the sky. A shift of a degree or two would be all it took.

If the weather wasn't enough of a concern, the memory of Deke's warning glare wiped what remained of the smile off his face. His brother's implied threat hung with him all day. Deke would want to know what was wrong, and once he did, he'd want to fix it.

And what exactly was wrong, anyway? It wasn't like Jake was unhappy with his life. He worked in a rewarding field, helping and serving people. His career would continue to advance, thanks to the master's degree he was short months away from completing. He had good friends and a family that loved him.

It was enough, right?

An engine rattled loudly enough to shake his SUV, cutting off his darkening thoughts. An ancient sedan came to a full stop at the intersection as its left blinker came on. The driver checked both ways twice. The car lurched forward, and a medium-sized cloud of smoke belched out from underneath. Jake watched it leave a trail of black exhaust, and as it crept past him, he noted that the muffler hung low, barely clearing the asphalt.

Now this was an accident waiting to happen. If – no, when – that muffler fell off, he'd be called out when the next vehicle ran into it on the roadway. He hit the lights, checked to make sure the traffic was still clear, and pulled in behind the hiccupping monster. Someone needed a warning.

One flower in the small bouquet of daffodils unfurled its petals in her makeshift vase. A soda cup from the gas station was the only thing she could find to bring the buds home safely. At least it fit in the cup holder in her car so she didn't have to try to hold them while she drove. Marlee needed both hands to maneuver this beast.

That pastry this morning and the bunch of flowers bobbing next to her were the only high points in her day. Her last two clients were no-shows, one without even a message of cancellation. This ride to fill her empty time by enjoying nature was a mistake too.

The tempting view had beckoned her, and she'd pulled over. Sitting on her car's warm hood and watching curtains of rain advancing across the river canyon was a balm to her nerves. When big drops drove her back inside the musty interior, she'd felt better. Not calm, but less down.

That was, she'd felt that way until she pulled back on the road with a hard bump, and black smoke immediately poured out behind her old beater. Driving a few miles hadn't made it better. In fact, as she glanced in the rear view mirror at the stop sign, it looked like a black cloud followed her. Just like her life.

If she could get back to town, she'd leave the car with the mechanic at the end of Main Street. She stopped there so often, people must think they had a thing going on. But the only thing she had was a piece of crap car that required an almost weekly dose of costly care. Maybe it was time to ditch the car and spend the money for something more reliable. If she couldn't get around, she couldn't follow up on her leads. But money for a better car meant less for her pursuit, and that delayed the achievement of her goal. Based on today, though, she might be out of options.

As she made the turn, a distinct metallic scraping sounded from under her car. A new belch of smoke hid the rear view from her. She glanced at the mirror again, and through the smoke, she saw lights. Flashing lights. Red and blue flashing lights. When the smoke momentarily cleared, the vehicle bearing the lights became visible. A cop car.

Great. Without a doubt, her day was now officially flushed down the toilet.

The man behind the wheel didn't look pleased. Hell, she wasn't pleased either. If she had a way to get around town without this monster, she would gladly leave it on the side of the road with the keys inside.

No shoulder graced this stretch of road, so she waited for almost half a mile before she found a spot wide enough to pull off. The cop's lights rotated in sequence, creating a kaleidoscope that blended to purple in her rear view mirror. Or maybe she was seeing purple through her tears. She'd learned to keep her anger in check, but disappointment and fear rose on this occasion without any hesitation.

She bumped off the asphalt on to gravel and dirt, put the car in park, and shut off the engine. It coughed three times, accompanied by a fresh blast of dense black with each sound. Its rattle to a complete stop sounded like the death throes of her coffeemaker this morning. A shrill squeak marked its final passage.

Reaching across the wide front seat, she slammed her fist against the dash to pop open the glove box and pulled out her registration, her other hand digging in the big purse on the seat for her wallet. Would he question anything? Card and paper clutched in her fingers, she put both hands on the steering wheel and stared straight ahead, waiting.

Jake tucked the patrol car in as tightly as he could to make sure he wasn't hanging out on the road. This stretch of county highway was notorious for people driving too fast on blind corners and the lack of a shoulder didn't help. There was space enough for both of them – just. The fact the driver put them both out of their misery by turning off the noisy machine, cutting off the black smoke shortly thereafter, mollified him only a little.

He punched the keyboard to record the plate and started the onboard video and camera clipped to his vest. The driver dipped out of view on the passenger side, then reappeared and stilled. Who would drive such a beat-up old clunker? He looked forward to finding out. Checking for traffic behind him, he eased out of the car and crossed to the passenger side, approaching slowly.

Shoulders hunched and paper gripped in hands visible on the steering wheel, the driver did nothing to acknowledge his presence. He had that dull sense in the pit of his stomach that this would be trouble, and he gave the car a wider berth, sinking his boots into the wet dirt along the shoulder.

It was a woman behind the wheel, a young woman dressed in funereal black on the part of her he could see. Pulling even with the passenger front window, he tapped on the glass and stepped back, in case she held a hidden weapon.

She started, the papers in her fingers flying in two directions. She hit a bunch of flowers in a cup holder as she dove after the smaller piece, her head ducking down to the floor. His fingers tightened on his holster as she sat up. She bumped her head on the steering wheel, and in an obvious fit of pique, she beat it with the palms of her hands.

He couldn't help the chuckle, relaxing into the routine. Clearly, she didn't see this as her lucky day. His smile was still in place when she leaned across the expansive front seat and tried to crank down the window. At first, nothing happened. With a sudden audible pop, the window dropped all the way into the door in one jolt. He heard the woman sigh, the ripple of it running down his spine. It was only then that he got a good look at her face.

Goth Girl. Her clothes were black, but they did nothing to hide the lines of her lean body. Black hair cascaded around her shoulders from under a black ball cap. Her face bore none of the extreme make-up he expected. Her skin was pale, but her eyes were unadorned. Thick lashes dropped before he could register their color. He realized he was staring, but he couldn't force himself to look away.

"I'm sorry, officer. Here's my license. Give me a minute and I'll pick up the registration."

She handed the driver's license across the passenger seat, and Jake reached to take it, leaning on the doorframe. Their fingers grazed, and he swore electricity shot through him. It was probably the car, shorting out or something, and he removed his other hand in case the battery was somehow linked to the metal. She stared at him for a few seconds, her fingers still on the plastic.

Her eyes were blue, the pale kind that looked iridescent. Against her white skin and the black duds, she should have appeared to be a ghost. He thought the depths of color gave her eyes a deep, mysterious glow.

Her fingers released the license abruptly, and she immediately ducked down, this time trying to reach the paper on the floorboard in front of the passenger seat. The glove box over her head popped open during her struggles, and she responded with a low curse as she slammed it closed with the back of her head. With her fingertips outstretched, she brushed at the page, trying to pull it closer by waving her hand.

He stared, captivated by the sight of her fingers. They were long, almost as long as his, and yet they looked dainty. Ligaments and muscles contoured the back of her hand, and her wrist, where it slipped clear of the sleeve of her black jacket and shirt, was slender and finely formed. No jewelry adorned this hand, and he suddenly wished he could see her left hand, the one that might hold an indication of her status. Was she married? And why did he care?

A flick of her pointer finger brought the paper closer, and she grabbed for it, giving a small mew he assumed was triumph. She held it out, her pale eyes locking on his again.

"Sorry. Here's the registration." She opened her mouth as if she was planning to say more, then shut it with a snap and put her hands on the steering wheel and faced forward.

He worked hard to ignore the desire to ask her to face him again, just so he could stare into her eyes. Shaking free of the urge, he examined the driver's license. A San Jose address, though he knew she'd been around here for at least a few months. Stepping back, he said, "Thank you, Ms. Cruiz."

He keyed the mic at his shoulder, providing her driver's license number and name. As the dispatcher acknowledged it, her face swung back to him, and he was pulled forward once more. She stared at him with a slight frown on her forehead.

"It's not cruise."

He caught sight of her left hand on the steering wheel. Empty of any ring. Distracted, her statement caught him off guard. "What?"

"It's pronounced crew-ezz. Not like a trip on a ship. Cruiz." Her fingers tightened on the wheel.

"I'm sorry. I find the simplest names are often the most complicated to pronounce." Now why the hell was he apologizing?

Because she'd pinned him with those pale blue-gray eyes and his airflow suddenly felt threatened.

He was a stronger man than this. The single look of some woman – no, girl – driving a car that should be condemned wasn't going to break him.

"You know you're driving a hazard, ma'am? Your muffler is nearly dragging and the smoke coming from your car is sure to be over the legal limit." He froze his face into what his brother called his serious cop stare, designed to indicate who was in charge. That felt better.

She stared back at him, her expression a mix of exasperation and dismay. The hands on the steering wheel flexed, and if possible, the skin of her fingers became even whiter. "It just happened, officer. I pulled on to the roadway from the turnoff over the river. The potholes are bad and impossible to miss, and something hit the underside of the car. That's when the smoke started. I haven't even had a chance to get back into town."

"There's a wider turnout up ahead another mile. Why don't you leave the car there, and call someone to come get you? You can have the car towed back to town. Find yourself a mechanic, someone who can fix everything that's obviously wrong with the vehicle."

If anything, she looked even more miserable. Her face shifted forward, her eyes blinking rapidly as her upper body lifted on an audible sigh. Stepping closer was instinctive. But she continued to stare straight ahead, finally giving her head a small shake. When her gaze returned to his, an unmistakable glisten shimmered in her eyes.

This would go on record as the worst Valentine's Day ever. Call someone? Who the hell would she call? There was no one to rescue her. She blinked back threatening tears and took a deep breath.

And it would have to be this cop who pulled her over. Jake Kermarrec, brother of Deke who was going out with Marguerite. He was part of that inner circle her clients Gabby, Tess and Serena called the wolf pack. Another bad coincidence.

Damned if he had to be even better looking up close than from afar too. His hair was an indeterminate color under a black and khaki cap. If she had to guess, she'd say dark blond to brown. His build under the required bulletproof vest lacked thick muscles, but he looked strong and powerful just the same. The skin on the back of his hands was tanned a light gold, and before she could control the thought, she wondered if he'd be as tanned everywhere else.

For the first time in way too long, she felt the thrill of electric recognition when their fingers touched. He stared at her out of eyes that reminded her of the turbulent Columbia River meeting the Pacific. She'd been on a fishing trip with her family to the point where the river churned into the ocean, and she had proudly been the only one not to upchuck over the side. The water looked like his eyes, a mix of blue and green and gray with no one color standing out for long. Staring into his eyes mixed her up more than those agitated waters.

She couldn't allow a ticket on her license. Her record needed to stay clean, absolutely and positively spotless, if her plan was going to work. As the officer pulled a pad from his pocket, her eyes filled further, and she couldn't turn off the faucet. To get so close, only to be faced with failure.

"Please, Deputy Kermarrec, I'll get it fixed, I promise. I'll drive straight home, and first thing on Monday, I'll drop the car off at my mechanic's to repair. I don't need a ticket to convince me to fix it. Like I want to be seen driving this fire-breathing dragon, right?"

She tried her best cajoling smile, one she hadn't used in so long that she wondered if her facial muscles remembered how. One errant tear escaped, drifting down her right cheek. She could feel its trail down to her chin, and she made a conscious effort to ignore it. If she did, so would he. He would not see her cry.

She noted the twitch of a muscle in his cheek. His eyes weren't on hers now, but followed a path down her face. Damn. She wasn't above using emotion to get what she wanted, but it felt low and demeaning.

His eyes shifted back to hers, assessing and thoughtful, as if he was trying to read her sincerity. She widened her eyes further, intending to assure him with her expression alone that she would do exactly as she said.

How she would pay for the repairs was another issue altogether.

The microphone attached to his uniform came to life, and she recognized her name in the noise. Kermarrec stepped back and turned slightly as if to hide his reaction to what he was hearing. She saw him nod. How much would there be to report? Surely there couldn't be anything. She'd been very careful for years and the past was in the past.

He spoke into the mic, his words and codes unintelligible. He didn't look like he was reaching for his gun as he approached her side window once more, though that didn't make her relax. She'd never feel completely safe. But there was no predatory tension in his movements as he glanced up at the sky, frowning.

She looked out the windshield and frowned as well. Big fat snowflakes fell, not a lot, but enough that soon the ground would be white. Her bald tires weren't going to be a help at that point.

"Ms. Cruiz, I'm glad you updated your record with your current address. That was smart, in case of any emergency. You should get a new license too. I want you to go straight home. I will follow you. I want to make sure the muffler doesn't fall off and cause another driver an accident. Please get the car fixed as soon as possible." He tore a piece of paper off his notepad and handed it through the window. "If you take the car here, tell him Jake sent you. He'll treat you fairly. He'll tell you how much it will cost to fix everything, and he'll be honest about it."

Her eyes pricked as she took the page from his outstretched hand. That unfamiliar zing carried up her fingers as they brushed his. Her eyes jumped to his, and she found his tense stare unnerving.

That stare locked for longer than it should have. She should thank him, start the car, and drive away in a cloud of smoke. The snowflakes grew thicker, and a few clung to impossibly long eyelashes that she hadn't noticed before. Rather than challenging his masculine appeal, the lashes made him even sexier. Why she was wasting any brainpower thinking about that, she wasn't sure.

He palmed the doorframe with a light slap. "The snow is about to get thick. Better get going so you don't get stuck."

He stepped back, his height diminishing. He must be standing down the slope of the road. He still looked formidable. His height had nothing to do with it.

She turned the key, and the engine cranked but did nothing. Closing her eyes, she prayed with her forehead against the steering wheel. Now would not be the time for it to give up entirely. She had to get home.

"How about rolling up your window?" Kermarrec's words were as clear as the bite of icy wind that brought fat white flakes spinning through the opening.

"It doesn't close once it's down. A mechanic needs to fix that too."

She wasn't sure, but she thought she saw him shake his head and grin when the old engine cranked to life, spewing out a new burst of acrid smoke.

Chapter 5

Those few fat snowflakes invited their friends along, and by now, the evening's flat light did nothing to make the storm look any friendlier. His night of corralling carousers had turned into enforcing icy road closures and pulling people out of ditches.

Jake shook off the latest layer of snow and stepped into the cruiser, grateful that the engine had been running and the SUV blew warm air. He'd been out on eight calls already and had done none of his paperwork, and the snow fell thicker. Before long, the roads would be impassable no matter what.

He pulled off the gravel on to slippery ice, considering the need for chains on his tires. Heavy-duty mud and snows were good, but only so good. Bald tires were even worse.

That brought his thoughts back to Ms. Cruiz. As the snow fell more thickly even at the lower elevations, the road went from bad to treacherous to hazardous, and he'd watched her car shimmy and slip more than once as she crept along well under the speed limit. Going slow was okay with him. The traffic piled up behind them should have been going slow too, given the conditions. Good to her word, she'd driven straight to her address, a shabby building on a less than desirable street.

In her face before they parted, he's seen something. Was it desire? Or maybe it was his imagination. Maybe Deke's talk of love and marriage made his brain play squirrely tricks on him. Or it could be his long dry spell.

Hell, he had no time for a relationship. Between duty time and training, his courses online at the university, and the little bit he spent with his family and friends, his days and nights were full to capacity.

But that didn't keep his mind from lingering on those pale glowing eyes. Why did she wear such drab dark clothes? The make-up on her skin was thick, and only her dense lashes decorated her eyes. In his experience, a true Goth wore heavy black and white with raccoon eyes. He needed to reassess his opinion of her.

"7-6-3-9, possible vehicle accident, M 13, CR 6."

"7639, copy, responding." He shoved thoughts of Ms. Cruiz to the back of his brain. County Road 6 was a twisting, turning two-lane climbing up and down canyon walls. Unsuspecting drivers often crashed into guardrails, in the few places the road had them. Take a corner too fast, and you headed down the canyon into the river four hundred feet below.

Marker 13. He knew that turn. It was a blind one if you were headed down slope. Upslope in this snow, it would be difficult if not impossible to navigate, with a hairpin turn at its end. Whatever happened there wasn't going to be good.

He hit the lights and increased his speed marginally. In this snow, a cop car under a lead foot would be in the ditch as fast as a civilian's. It would take him about ten minutes to reach the turn.

Ms. Cruiz invaded his brain once more. Her eyes were luminous, tears or not. When she shut off the engine, it gave the same cough and sputters as before, smoke still billowing from the rear end. As she got out, she looked in his direction, and he was tempted to douse his headlights so he could see her expression without their glare. She held up a hand to shade her eyes as if she was trying to see him too. No, that was wishful thinking. Then she'd pulled a big black bag from the front seat, grabbed the bunch of flowers he'd noted earlier, and disappeared around the corner of the building.

Unit 2-A, according to her updated driver information. He'd scanned the front, noting the letters on the doors, and placed her apartment on the second floor in the back. Faint puffs of smoke continued to come from her car, grabbed by swirls of wind and snow in the fading light.

Maybe he'd swing by on Monday and see if her car still smoldered in the parking lot. If it wasn't there, maybe he'd swing by his mechanic, to see if she took it in. He wasn't checking up on her, not really. Well, maybe.

His brain clicked back into work mode as he neared the road marker. His rotating dome lights and headlights caught a side view of an old blue van, two wheels off the road and the two that should still be on it tipped up. Immediately, the driver door popped open and a middle-aged woman stepped out, waving her arms and slip-sliding her way toward him.

"Oh thank god you're here." The woman's nose ran and her head wasn't covered. Snow gathered in her hair as she gestured at her vehicle in a panic. "I can't move the van. It's up against a tree, and then there's the canyon. And the kids are inside. I tried to get home, but driving up out of the canyon, I slipped all over the place. I thought I'd nearly made it when I got to this curve."

In the van, he saw two sets of eyes in small faces peering out at him. One waved, and he waved back. He frowned, looking at the van facing downhill.

"You were coming up out of the canyon, ma'am, when this happened?" The van was facing the opposite direction now.

She nodded hard enough to make the snow collecting on her face fall off. "Yeah, stupid, right? But we only need to get to the top of the hill and then we're home. I had to work late because of Valentine's Day and I had to get the kids from the babysitter's."

Valentine's Day, a day meant to be filled with love, hope and happiness. He wasn't feeling it. He doubted Ms. Cruiz was, either.

The woman next to him gave a small scream. That scream turned into a shrill shriek. They were lit up like a runway under jet lights, and a horn blared. He glanced over his shoulder to see a vehicle hurling toward them. If it hit the van, the kids would be in the river before a minute passed.

He didn't think, he reacted. Shoving the woman up the bank and away from the path of the oncoming vehicle, he yanked at the van's back door and reached inside. Fisting a child's jacket in his hand, he pulled hard and the little girl fell against him. Pushing her behind him after her mother, he reached back in.

It wasn't something he planned logically in the seconds available. Years of training and drilling took over, guiding his quick movements. A child screamed. As the lights grew bright and blinding and the horn shrieked closer, he felt a hard blow. He fell in the snow, momentarily dazed. He shook it off, standing and running on adrenalin. Words, voices young and old, fast movements. Someone cried out. He took a deep breath to steady and make sense of it all as he sat down. Then, darkness.

Everything hurt. He felt as bad as the time he went three rounds with that uncooperative bull when he was fourteen. He hated that animal with a passion after that. Damn bull.

Wiggling his toes followed wiggling his fingers. They worked, or at least, he thought they did. The pounding in his head kept time with throbs of pain throughout his body, the strongest sledgehammer beating at his lower back.

"Mr. Kermarrec, how are you feeling?"

The young doctor looked barely old enough to be out of high school, much less practicing medicine. Jake hoped that he was neither as young nor as inexperienced as his fresh face would lead you to believe.

"Like I've been hit by a truck, doc." He attempted a chuckle, but it brought a spasm to his back that put his whole body in a vise.

"Actually, it was an SUV, and you're lucky to come through it with only contusions and minor lacerations. Unfortunately, some of those bruises are deep, affecting your nerves and muscles. That's why you're having those spasms. I'll increase your pain medication."

"Doc, no, no more pain medicine. It makes me loopy, and I don't like that feeling. I'd rather tough it out, if you don't mind." He gritted his teeth, willing his body to release its deep cramps.

"What is it with you first responders? You're all the same. Big, tough, refusing something that will help you heal faster." The doctor shook his head in apparent disbelief as he tapped something into the tablet computer in his hand.

Not that it was any of the man's business, but cops too often found solace from their jobs in vices, and knowing how quickly a simple prescription for a necessary narcotic could turn into something bigger was the reason Jake wanted no part of it. A little rest and some ibuprofen and he'd be back to work next week.

"I suspect you'll be out of work for a minimum of eight weeks, though the specialist you'll see tomorrow might extend that. During that time you'll be in physical therapy, rehabbing those injured muscles. Once you're released to return to work, you'll be on desk duty for additional weeks, to make sure you don't develop long-term problems because of this injury. No lifting over five pounds until you're cleared by the physical therapist."

What the fuck? It seemed appropriate to say it, so he did.

The doctor looked up and grinned in response, a boyish expression so full of life that Jake thought he enjoyed this too much.

"Look, did I give you a speeding ticket or something and don't remember? If I did and you're considering this payback, I'm sorry. But the law's the law." He squinted at the doctor's identification. Kinkead. It rang a bell, but he wasn't sure why.

Dr. Kinkead continued to smile at him, saying, "And medicine is medicine. The body heals in its own time. There are things you can do to help it along, but really, the length of the healing process I'm recommending is brief, based on the extent of your injuries. And no, you haven't given me a ticket. My big brother Gideon, on the other hand…" He let the sentence trail off and if anything, smiled even wider.

It clicked then, and he immediately saw the resemblance. Gideon Kinkead was a local firefighter, frequently in one form of trouble or another. On the periphery of the wolf pack, Jake ran into him occasionally.

The doctor held out his hand with a now-solemn nod. "Noah Kinkead. I've only been in the area for two months, two very busy months, so I haven't had a chance to get into trouble – yet." And he grinned again.

Jake held out his hand to shake Noah's. "You're younger, huh? Me too. Jake Kermarrec, but you know that already."

Noah shook his head a little sadly. "What is it with big brothers?" He asked the question as he stood with his hand on the door. "I move my family here so that the girls can get to know their only uncle. But somehow, we never seem to be on the same wavelength."

"Ah, so you're married?" Gideon never spoke about a brother or family.

Noah shook his head, and his face took on a haunted quality. "No, divorced, and a messy one at that. I brought my daughters here to recover. All three of us need to heal." He seemed to shake off the sadness and waved an admonishing finger at Jake. "Remember that, will you? Everything heals, but in its own time."

The door swung shut before Jake had a chance to rebut the comment. It no sooner closed than it burst open again, this time bringing his lieutenant, a deputy, and his union rep. The lieutenant hung back, allowing the deputy to bump fists with him and the union rep to shake his hand solemnly. Rites of camaraderie concluded, his boss stepped forward and stood at the end of the bed staring down, and she didn't look pleased.

"I'm sorry I let this happen, Lieutenant. I should have been paying attention, maybe put out more warning flares. I didn't intend for this to happen."

The lieutenant's frown deepened. "Yeah, I bet. I'm sure you started your shift yesterday thinking, gee, what can I do to get a commendation today, and boom, getting hit by an out of control SUV while rescuing a woman with two small children who'd slid off the road in a snowstorm was the best you could come up with."

The lieutenant was like that. Bratty, abrupt, smart-mouthed. She was the first female to rise to her rank in the department, and the fact that she was drop-dead gorgeous had made it harder for her to earn her stripes. She made sure everyone knew she earned them the hard way, and she reminded them every day.

"Who was that little man who just left? I don't know him." She glanced at the door.

"Dr. Noah Kinkead. He's the ER doc who's been taking care of me since I got here. I guess I'm not getting sprung any time soon either. They're moving me to a regular floor in the next couple of hours."

The lieutenant shook her head, her hair in its tight braid swinging back and forth. "We heard. That's why Dakota is here, to assure you that any worries you have about your sick leave and recovery and eventual return to work when you're done slacking off will be taken care of." She flicked her hand at the man in civvies, who stepped forward again.

The union rep pulled folded papers from his jacket pocket. "Kermarrec, you pulled me away from a great Niners game in the middle of a Sunday, so I'll make this quick."

Dakota shot a quick look at the lieutenant. She flipped him her middle finger, and the deputy standing against the wall let out a brief laugh before he stifled himself and the union rep continued.

"Your medical bills and therapy and meds and so on will be covered, anything past your little deductible. You can thank the union for that great coverage. You got any questions, Kermarrec?" Dakota handed Jake a form with a sheaf of papers attached. "This says I explained your benefits to you, but you don't need that, do you? Just sign the form. You keep the rest."

Jake set it aside with deliberate slowness. "I'm a bit out of it right now, Dakota, so if you don't mind, I'll read it when I feel less impaired."

The wall-leaning deputy chuckled again.

Dakota frowned, opening his mouth as if he planned to argue.

"You need anything else, union man?" The lieutenant pinned the man with her deadly stare, the one you never wanted to be on the receiving end of. He shut his mouth and backed away from the bed, and was out the door before five seconds had passed.

The lieutenant sighed and shook her head, still looking at the closing door. "I swear, I know that man is just doing his job, but he is a pain in my ass. Every time, it's the same thing. What if you didn't understand your benefits and had questions? The asshole just doesn't care."

The deputy pushed away from the wall and approached the bed again, standing with his legs spread and his arms crossed on his chest. Lankowski had been in the department as long as Jake, and like Jake, he pulled extra shifts to help cover the vacancies the county couldn't afford to fill. They worked many scenes together over the years, and they'd been at the traffic accident together on Saturday night, or at least, that's what Jake had been told. Jake was a little foggy on some of the details.

Lankowski stared down at him, and Jake felt the pressure of that direct gaze. The deputy's usual laughing demeanor and practical joking were nowhere in evidence.

"What?" This being stared at thing was beginning to wear on him. Everyone seemed to be doing it.

Lankowski shook his head, then turned to look at their lieutenant.

"I swear, I never saw anything like it, Lieutenant. It was like Superman, come to life. Out of the snow comes this big black SUV, flying like the angel of death with a trumpet blaring. You could see he was coming sideways in a skid, control all gone, and right for the minivan. The woman and kids in the minivan were terrified, one of the kids crying while Kermarrec tried to get him out of his car seat, and all the while, the little tyke is screaming for his teddy bear as mom crawled up to hover nearby."

His boss shook her head in apparent amazement along with Lankowski, and Jake felt a flush of embarrassment rise in his face. He hadn't taken time to think about it, acting on instinct in the moment.

"Yeah, I heard about it so many times now, I could probably tell it as well as you. Kermarrec, seeing that the SUV is about to plow into the minivan, grabs for the mother and kid just as he's free of the safety seat, throwing both to safety in a snowdrift. Then the SUV hits the mini, and it careens into Kermarrec. The SUV comes to rest broadside against the mini, both vehicles moving toward Kermarrec, bouncing against him again, knocking him to the ground."

"Yeah, like that, Lieutenant. By then, I'm running over and calling for back up and an ambulance, because I could see how hard Kermarrec was thrown and he's lying face down in the snow. But what does our hero do? The idiot gets up, grabs the kid's teddy bear from inside the mini and tosses it to him where he's crying in the snow with his mama and sister, and jogs around the vehicles to yank the SUV's driver door open."

"Ah, I'm right fucking here, you know?" They were more than embarrassing him. They were annoying him to hell and back.

The lieutenant grinned widely now, like she knew he didn't want to be called a hero. "Yeah, he yanks the door open, pulls the driver out before the guy has a chance to utter a word, puts him face-down in the snow and handcuffs him, faster than he could rope and tie a steer when he was younger. Must have been all that fucking adrenalin."

The lieutenant and Lankowski laughed, and Jake closed his eyes, letting the pain wash over him all over again. He hadn't felt it at the time, bathed in what was surely high proof whisky fumes breathed out by the screaming SUV driver. Not when he read the guy his rights, jerking him to his feet to turn him over to the other deputy. Not when he jogged back over to the woman and helped her and the children up out of the snow, assuring they weren't hurt. Not when the little boy looked at him with big solemn eyes and thanked him for saving the life of Rufus, his toy bear.

Not until Lankowski urged him to sit down so the paramedics could check his injuries, and he passed out.

"Listen, the rest of the unit and probably most of the department will be in to check on you. PD and CHP too. They're already planning casseroles and all that shit. Expect to be driven anywhere you need to go, and if you try to worm your way out of PT because you can't drive, forget about it. That's been covered too. We take care of our own, you know?" The lieutenant's expression was fierce but proud.

Law enforcement was like that. Their community was tight, as tight as Flynn's Crossing.

"I know, Lieutenant. Thanks."

She approached the side of the bed where his arm wasn't full of IVs to do the customary fist bump that passed for a handshake in their department. Lankowski took his turn, and together, the two moved toward the door. Lankowski reached it first, turning only long enough to call him a colorful name that included lazy bastard. When the lieutenant put her hand on it, she closed it and turned back.

"Seriously, Jake, that was some hero bit. It worked out, but don't make a habit of it. I know you feel that there's only one right way in any situation, but you take it a little too far at times. You could easily have been killed. Accept risks. But don't take chances."

She waited, staring at him once more. They'd had similar conversations before, not that he went out of his way to play hero. But in a rural area with sparse cop coverage, you were flying solo more often than not in situations that could turn ugly or deadly in less than a heartbeat.

The lieutenant moved back to the foot of the bed and frowned at him. "Someday, we're going to have a little talk about where this hero inclination of yours comes from. You never let on about it in your psych eval, and I never heard any stories about you. I may be a newcomer in Flynn's Crossing, since I only got here twenty-five years ago." She smirked at this. "But the stories about your family make for big gossip around here. And still, I have no clue what drives you."

The silence of the room made the beeps and pings of the machines echo and take on a life of their own. The lieutenant sighed, an exhale meant to express her dissatisfaction. She'd been doing it so often lately that most of the squad did it too.

"You can't solve all of the world's problems by yourself, Jake. You know that. A second either way, and I'd be visiting your family in my dress uniform, delivering very bad news. So don't try to be a hero."

And she left before he could protest that he didn't see himself as a hero or even set out to be one. He did what he was trained to do, protect people within the letter of the law. He'd never change that part of himself, no matter what.

Chapter 6

Standing in the untidy garage on Monday morning, Marlee wondered if she should rethink her pledge to Deputy Kermarrec. She'd had plenty of time to think about both him and the condition of her car throughout the day yesterday. Admittedly, she thought much more about the man and less about her embarrassment of a vehicle.

"So here's the thing." The mechanic, Big Al, wiped the cloth in his hands across his brow, and Marlee saw grease and other stuff darken his already grimy features.

"What thing?" She knew it was a figure of speech, but waiting for him to respond got on her last nerve. Money spent here meant less for other, more important, things.

"So here's the thing. Your muffler's gone – poof. You got multiple places where you hit things, and each place has a problem now. You're leaking oil, by the way. That causes the smoke. Bottom of the oil pan – scraped. Plus you got hoses that need replacing so your radiator keeps working, and the serpentine belt needs replacing too. That's just normal wear and tear."

It sounded like so much. She thought of the money carefully saved for the next phase of her plan and cringed.

"Jake sent me." She'd said that already, but maybe he didn't hear her. He'd been irrationally fascinated with the smoke and the cough and the death rattle when she'd turned off the ignition. Maybe she should just donate it to him, in the interest of mechanical science. But then how would she get around?

He shook his head from side to side, grimacing. "It's a shame. A dirty, rotten shame. Of course, it could have been worse."

Maybe she should sign the pink slip in her purse and hand it over to him right now. Evidently, he didn't think the car was salvageable.

He clapped his oily hands, rubbing the grease rag between them as he did so. His runny eyes met hers, his mournful gaze settling on her as if he just noticed her. The smile he tried out let her know dental care wasn't his highest priority, and she shivered, not wanting to consider what the red stuff stuck in his teeth could possibly be.

"Tell you what I'm going to do, in honor of Jake and all. This little baby will be a challenge, but I'll only charge you parts. It'll need a lot of parts, mind you, but in honor of Jake, no labor. All on me."

This guy must owe Jake a whole long list of favors.

"How long will it take?"

He examined her more closely, his eyes moving from her ball cap to her boots and back. He smiled again, and she held back the cringe, but barely.

"It might take a couple of weeks, depending on what I find when I really get into it. You know, sometimes situations aren't obvious until you get in the middle of them. So, can I give you a lift someplace?" He leered at her, wiping his hands more slowly in the oily rag.

It made her skin crawl, so she said the words that seemed to work such magic. "No, that's okay. I have a friend picking me up. One of Jake's friends."

He raised his hands as if surrendering, his attention turning almost immediately back to her car. He caressed its hood, leaving behind a streak mark from his palm, and she kept the grossed-out exclamation to herself. Turning and pulling out her cell phone, she stepped to the door of the shop and called Bliss.

>>>>>

She stared at the cell phone as it rang in her hand. Luckily, she was available to answer it. Her next client had yet to arrive, a woman who had a weekly standing nail appointment for which she was chronically late. Then her nails were always a mess, though how she got them that way, week after week, was still a mystery to Marlee. Retired and inclined to do nothing more strenuous than watching TV and heating microwavable dinners, she usually came in with at least a couple of tips missing and the rest in ragged condition. Marlee suspected the real reason was she wanted to prolong the opportunity for conversation. The conversation was always one-sided.

Marlee knew more about this woman's bodily functions than she cared to consider. The woman knew next to nothing about Marlee. Like why the caller id on her screen brought twin feelings of dread and hope.

On the fourth ring, she dug her finger into the green receive button on the screen and lifted the phone slowly to her ear.

"Hello, I'm here."

The man at the other end delivered his information, brief and to the point.

"Thank you. I guess I don't know what to do."

The man offered more words. Her stomach dropped, and an ache settled low in her gut. It was the same. It was always the same. The man posed a question.

"I'm not sure. Do you have any advice for me?"

Gruff instructions followed, along with the standard disclaimer to seek an independent assessment. He wasn't licensed to advise her in this regard. Blah, blah, blah. She'd heard this before. He disconnected before she had a chance to thank him, though she knew the only way to really thank him was to pay his bill on time.

Her ache turned to an icy grip of fear. If she didn't find an answer soon, she should abandon this project. It was costing her a shitload of money to continue a battle she had very little chance of winning.

She thought of the two photos she guarded so carefully in the depths of her purse. If only – but then, she couldn't go there. History and her past prohibited it. Pride, stupid pride. Or maybe it was more fear. Who would forgive her after her past mistakes? She never forgave herself.

"Marlee, there you are my dear. Oh, what a week I've had. I've popped off four tips, can you imagine? And I have had the runs for four days straight. Let me tell you – "

Marlee pushed herself away from the wall, realizing that if she stayed there, she would sink to the floor and roll her body into a ball of despair. Her client settled her ample form at the nail table and placed her hands on it as if presenting proof of her travails for the last seven days. And she never stopped talking.

By the time her last client settled on the massage table, Marlee was on autopilot. The day had been nonstop. A call from Big Al didn't raise her spirits, particularly when he asked if she really, I mean really, wanted to continue the repairs on her car. He referred to its sounds as the rattletrap of death. And he wasn't joking when he said it.

"How much would the total repairs cost?"

He offered a figure, and she'd choked on the water in her mouth, nearly spewing the contents on the framed picture of a Japanese garden on the wall. It was more than she paid for her apartment, utilities, food and everything else – for two months.

"And if I simply pay you for your time so far? I'd have to get the car towed to the dump."

He named a much lower figure, one that was still ugly but affordable. He even offered to take care of the disposal of the carcass himself. His tone of sympathy dissipated when he asked her out, replaced by something that sounded distinctly like the leer he'd offered her as they discussed a ride into town that first day.

She ignored his question, merely saying she'd send him that amount plus the pink slip, and hung up as he began restating his date question, with much more force this time.

Marlee took a deep, cleansing breath, emptying her mind and focusing her energy on the woman who had turned into her favorite client. She checked the pillows, making sure the very pregnant belly was protected. The scent of lavender filled the small dark room as she scooped massage lotion into her hands and rubbed to warm it more thoroughly.

"Is there anything in particular that hurts today or feels more sensitive?" She ran her hands down the spine, seeking out areas of tension or stress.

Gabby let out a small groan. "Anywhere and everywhere. I swear, it wasn't this difficult at the end with Jeremy. Maybe it's because I'm more than a decade older, but this baby is wearing me out. It kicks and rolls and will probably be a world-class acrobat one day. The bets among the wolf pack are that it's a boy, and the girl tribe is split."

Marlee let the smile pull her lips, grateful to ease into the rhythm of her hands and her search for the knots in Gabby's back. She carried the baby low, pulling her muscles out of alignment and putting pressure on her lower back. It showed it, tight with tension.

What should she do? She needed a new car, not a brand new one, but something that provided reliable transportation. How she would pay for it wasn't clear. She couldn't afford not to buy one, though. Bliss had been wonderful about picking her up and dropping her off when her hours didn't coincide with the limited county bus service. That couldn't continue forever though.

And what should she do about the words she'd heard earlier today? It wasn't much to go on, and if she was honest with herself, there wasn't much hope, given what he'd learned this past week. But at least there was some.

"You're very quiet today." A low sigh followed Gabby's muffled words as Marlee hit a rigid muscle.

Could she ask for help? Who would she ask? The answer would appear obvious to anyone else, but not to her. And even if she involved them, the outcome wasn't assured. In fact, it might make things worse, given the need of the people in question to fix things. It was what they did, what they'd always done.

"Marlee, is anything wrong? You're a million miles away."

Gabby's question jerked her back, and she realized her hands had stilled on her client's back. She quickly added more massage cream with one hand, keeping the other on the skin under her fingers as if she had intended to pause all along.

Shifting on the table, Gabby turned to face her, and Marlee was suddenly glad the light in the room was so low. Gabby was as sharply observant and outwardly focused as her earlier client was self-absorbed. Maybe she wouldn't notice the tracks of earlier tears.

"I'd like to think that we have more than a customer service relationship, Marlee. In the last few months, I've come to think of you as a friend. What's going on?"

In the darkness, Gabby's expression carried enough concern and sympathy that Marlee almost – almost – unburdened herself. It had been a long time since she'd had anyone to share things with. But if others found out, it would be nothing but trouble.

"I have a lot on my mind today. I've been working a lot. I'm tired."

She massaged down Gabby's right arm, spending time on her forearm and wrist and hand.

"You don't want to talk about it. I can understand that. I've been accused of that a time or two as well. Just know that when you need to talk, I'm happy to listen."

It would be so good to have a friend again. But she resisted, moving to work on Gabby's left arm.

"So since you don't want to talk, I will. I'll fill you in on all of the girl tribe gossip. And the wolf pack too, by association. Let's see, Deke proposed to Marguerite on Valentine's Day, and as a matter of principle, or so she said, she strung him along for hours. Actually, I think she was simply scared to death she'll get it wrong. I know I'm not speaking out of school when I tell you that she was married before. She makes no secret of it, though her first husband – well, never mind. I'll let her tell you that story someday."

Marlee moved around to Gabby's head, working on tense neck muscles.

"Powers and Tess, now there's a story. It doesn't seem either one of them is inclined to formalize that relationship. Not that they'll ever be with anyone else. They're fused together so tightly, even her flowers couldn't grow between them. And Tess can grow almost anything."

Marlee's hands stuttered, her short fingernails nearly digging into Gabby's neck before she stopped herself.

Gabby shifted as if unaware how close she'd come to bruises. She continued her update. "And rumor has it that Serena and Dane have decided it's time to get pregnant. Looks like we'll have lots of babies running around soon. Now if DK and Vince decide to join the baby march, or Roxy and Mac announce wedding plans – "

Marlee backed away from the table, dropping her hands into fists. "I'm sorry, Gabby, can you give me a minute? I need to step out. I'll be right back, I promise."

She didn't wait to hear Gabby's response, slipping out the door and shutting it with less calm than usual. It snapped into place just before she covered her face with her hands. Breathing in the aroma of lavender, she sank to the floor and let tears flow.

Chapter 7

"Hey, a real sit-down table? Exactly what we need." Dane lowered his spare frame into the curved wood, nodding to Deke and Jake as he did so.

Jake hated this. Deke insisted he go out to Mallory's with the wolf pack tonight. He didn't want to. He wanted to stay at home and wallow in his misery.

Six more weeks until he could presume to return to any kind of duty. No one took any chances with cops and back injuries anymore. It was one of the most frequent causes of disability separations, a bigger problem than damage from a gunshot wound. The union rep told him there was no fighting it, and that it was for his own good.

But he was itchy and fidgeting, only finding relief in his online courses. e'd been able to devote his time

He'd be able to complete his final units much faster, simply because he had nothing else to do.

"Yeah, we thought it would be a good idea today. I mean, why do we always stand around a table? Why not sit down, like adults? Right, Jake?"

Deke delivered his joking words in a tone meant to keep Jake in line.

"Yeah, it's a good idea. Rehab's a bitch. I should know." Dane rubbed his leg under the table, the scars covered as they always were, even in summer's heat.

"You should know what?"

Dane's brother Powers dropped into a free chair, slapping his brother on the back and nodding to the men across the table.

"Rehab. It's a bitch. I was just telling Jake."

"Yeah, don't I know it. I thought my back would never recover."

Jake watched Dane swing to Powers in surprise, and the two men stared at each other.

"What, I never told you? I guess you were traveling. It was stupid. My boots were caked with mud in the middle of winter. I climbed a ladder without checking them, and I lost my footing. Fell from the second story to the ground, which luckily was also muddy and therefore softer than usual. My back took the brunt of it."

Dane smiled slowly, nodding as he did so. "That explains a lot. You must have bumped your head on the way down. You always were an oaf of a big brother, and now, you're even worse." He took the sting out of his words as he punched Powers in the arm and laughed.

Jake felt better, but only marginally. Others had problems that were as bad or worse than his. They'd conquered them. He would too. He squirmed in his seat, trying to find a way to ease the ache that never went away completely.

"You okay?" Deke's question was a whisper that no one else would hear over the blare of sports and clink of glasses.

"Fine. Just trying to get comfortable. PT was tough today. Thank god that's over." There was nothing more the therapist could do, other than recommend he keep doing the exercises at home, setting his own pace.

When he lifted his eyes, Deke locked on, eyeball to eyeball. Deke gave a knowing nod, as if he could sense every hesitation and doubt Jake carried. Could he ever go back to work? Would the doctor ever clear him? And what would he do about the continuing pain? He refused to take anything stronger than over the counter pain medicine.

Swiveling back so subtly that Jake doubted the other men even noticed their private exchange, Deke asked, "How did you conquer the pain? I mean, after you got done with rehab, what came next?"

Jake didn't want to discuss this.

Dane and Powers turned as one, and the fact they were brothers was clear in their shared expression.

"Massage," they said together, then laughed heartily and slapped each other on the back.

Seriously? These macho guys had a girly thing done to them?

Dane stopped chuckling first. Turning back to Jake as if he heard his thoughts, he sobered immediately. "Seriously, Jake, it's a miracle."

"What's a miracle?"

Their friend Rick dropped into another open chair, sitting forward and folding his hands on the table like he was a teacher in front of the class.

Dane and Powers, joined by Deke this time, answered in unison, "Massage."

Rick nodded vehemently as he leaned forward. "Yeah, agree. Gabby swears by it. She's carrying the baby so low, it's killing her back. If she didn't have that relief, I'm not sure what I'd do. I hate to see her hurting so much."

"Isn't she about – what – twenty months pregnant at this point?"

"Thirty-three weeks, my friends. Six weeks until d-day. Delivery day, I mean. And this time, I am absolutely going to be there." He lifted a hand to signal the waitress.

Jake arched his back and shifted the buttock he rested on, hoping that he could shrug off the ache. With the movement came incredible pain. The doctor and the PT warned him about this. They said it might never go away.

And if he couldn't put a brave face on things, he wouldn't be able to go back to work.

Law enforcement was his life. Making sure the bad guys didn't get away and victims were protected was who he was. Until he wasn't. Sidelined by his good deeds. He didn't want to think about it.

He stretched, trying to lengthen his spine the way the PT taught him. That man was brutal in his treatments, with a guarantee of aching hours after every session. Moving muscles that Jake swore he didn't need for any purpose he could fathom, each session and subsequent work at home only promised more of the same. When the PT said there was nothing more he could do, the pain turned into a different kind.

What if he could never return to full duty?

Reaching for the soda he usually drank when they were together, he paused. He had nowhere he had to be. Nothing he had to do. No call of duty. The emptiness that thought brought needed filling. He grabbed an empty glass and the pitcher of beer, lifting and filling the glass with more foam than liquid. All conversation at the table stopped as four sets of eyes locked on him.

Had he ever had a beer in front of them before? Probably not, because he had always been working.

Stretching again, he hoped the beer would help dull the edge of pain. As the silence lengthened, he took a long pull that brought mostly foam into his mouth, then another that was more successful. Without looking at his friends, he asked, "So, is there anything new with you guys?"

If anything, the silence became more pronounced. This time, the focus wasn't on him, though. Powers and Dane glanced at each other, then each reached for their beers and drank deeper than usual. When they put their mugs down, they nodded to each other as if in agreement.

Powers said, "You remember how we've felt like we're being watched every once in a while?"

"Like you did last Labor Day at the parade? You two were freaked out, but there didn't seem to be anyone stalking you." Jake knew, because he'd both scanned the area and notified other officers on Main Street that day. No one noted anything out of place.

Dane shrugged, a noncommittal movement involving little of his body. Quiet and still most of the time, he seemed even more restrained now.

"Like then, yes, and other times. Powers, you remember when we were shopping for the ladies at Christmas and it seemed like someone stared at us coming out of the Brew Bank? I bought Serena flowers from Tess's shop, and I felt it then again. And at the grocery store. It's happened a number of times."

"Who's watching you?" Jake leaned forward with a deep frown, his attention focused intently on Dane.

They had each other's backs, as members of the wolf pack. Related by blood or by friendship, the gang was tight. If something or someone threatened one of them, they all took on responsibility to make sure things ended well.

Powers answered, "We don't know. I didn't know you'd had that many other instances. I've felt like someone's been watching me too, but at different times and different places. It seems to happen most often on Sunday or Monday, in and around town, sometimes when I'm with Tess and sometimes not. There's no pattern to it."

Jake fought the urge to jump in and question them more closely. Maybe one man could become paranoid and think they were being stalked, but both separately and at the same time? Something weird was happening.

Dane and Powers stared at each other, both nodding finally as if in silent agreement. As one, they turned back toward the table and Powers flipped a hand palm up for Dane to continue. The sounds of the bar faded as Jake leaned forward to concentrate.

"You're correct, Jake, in thinking back to Labor Day, because that day, we both felt eyes on us. Who or why is unclear. Powers and I hadn't been close up until a short time before that. We disagreed on a number of things. But the sensation of someone tracking our movements was indisputable to both of us."

Powers reached for the dwindling beer and added, "Sometimes Tess picks up on it too. I credit her spiritual connections for that. What she's said, though, is that she doesn't feel like someone's watching her. She senses someone watching me, as if she can see them stalking me through their eyes."

Avoiding the urge to shake his head in disbelief, Jake considered Tess's special ability to communicate with those who didn't reside on an earthly plane anymore. Tess and Powers shared a special bond, one in which they could experience each other's reality in a spiritual sense. If Powers said Tess could feel it too, she did. Jake wasn't going to question it.

Dane turned his glass slowly on the scarred table, pushing the pool of condensation into a crack in the old wood. "Serena wanted us to go to the police with this, but we don't have anything concrete. We haven't noticed anyone specific following us. No threatening letters or phone calls or contacts of any kind point in the direction of a particular person."

Cop instinct overriding his attempt to keep silent, Jake jumped into the conversation. "Do the two of you have any enemies in common? Have you pissed anyone off or stirred up trouble?"

Powers said, "You mean other than our father being his usual total asshole self and taking every opportunity to remind us both that he isn't speaking to us?"

Dane added, "I doubt that will change. You see, he blames us."

Inhaling sharply, Powers looked away, and Jake sensed a lot of unresolved simmering anger. His friend's eyes smoldered, and his fingers twitched around his glass before tightening so hard, it was a wonder the glass didn't shatter.

Looking for a culprit and a motive, Jake questioned further, using his most neutral tone. "What does he blame you guys for?"

As Powers continued to stare out into nothing, Dane answered for them both. "At first we thought he blamed us for our mother's death, that the reason the cancer wasn't caught soon enough was because she was distracted by us. But one day, when Powers and I were at the house after I was already working and traveling, the truth became clear. He didn't blame us for Mom. He blames us for Mandy."

Powers slapped the flat of his hand on the table so hard the glasses and pitcher jumped, sloshing some beer on to the surface. Rick jumped, a hand in the general area of his heart. Deke, who'd been silent up until now, cleared his throat and glanced at Jake with worry on his face. Dane stared at Powers without moving, his nerves of steel earned on foreign battlefronts. Jake honed his at the academy and never seemed to go a day at work without something calling that stillness up for use. When Powers barked out a laugh, he waited to learn what the man found so funny.

"He doesn't exactly blame us for Mandy. He blames me. And since I chose to be here with you instead of in Oregon with him, by association, he now blames you too."

Dane frowned at his brother, the dense gathering of his eyebrows indicating that the brothers had covered this ground a time or two before.

"I thought Mandy left after high school." Deke finally spoke, ping-ponging his eyes between the two of them, his hands closing around his now-empty beer mug as his eyes settled on Powers.

"She did, but Dad blames me for not being attentive enough to what she was going through to keep her at home."

"Bullshit, Powers, and I am not going to repeat myself on this again. I've told you before, you did everything you could to be a parent to both Mandy and me when Mom died and Dad retreated even further into his work. You were in college keeping high grades, working for Dad and any other odd job you could get, and trying to keep wild child Mandy out of trouble and me from becoming a hermit. You went above and beyond. You were not to blame." Dane ground out the last words in slow syllables.

Jake waited for the tension to abate before asking, "Where is Mandy now?" He let the question hang in the air and didn't push, waiting to see who felt compelled to respond. As one, Dane and Powers finally turned to face him.

Powers answered, "We don't know, exactly. We've been trying to find her."

"You've been trying to find her," Dane broke in, his face in a tense frown. "If she wanted to find us, to come home, she could. Dad hasn't changed a phone number or address since the beginning of time. Powers is easy to find – just follow the Ashland logo on any of the construction trucks. And I've been back in the news enough to be traceable. Mandy hasn't been in touch because she doesn't want to be."

Chapter 8

"You have a new client today, Marlee."

That explained the appointment slot filled in as a therapeutic massage, with doctor's notes to review prior to treatment. The name of the client hadn't been entered.

"Who is it?" A massage brought her more income than a set of nails, a blessing she wouldn't question. She stared at the computer screen, wondering why the usually detailed Bliss hadn't bothered to enter a name.

Bliss only glanced up from the packing slips she perused with a distracted wave and said, "Our local celebrity, that's who. You'll enjoy it, I promise. Can't believe we're lucky enough to have – "

"Bliss, where's the color I ordered? I need it for my next client, and if it isn't here, I'll have to use the other stuff, and she claims it makes her scalp itch."

The hairstylist planted herself between Marlee and her boss, hands on hips and temper barely contained. The woman was a bitch of the worst kind, convinced that the whole world revolved around her and her issues. God forbid anyone else need anything when she was in the room.

Bliss shot Marlee an apologetic look at the same moment that Marlee's next client, Gabby's friend Serena, walked in the door. She was here for a pedicure, and Marlee sincerely hoped she was in a quiet, contemplative mood. Stories about Serena's wedded bliss to Dane were the last thing Marlee wanted to hear today. It hurt too much.

"Marlee, sorry I'm a little late. Problems at work. These new soldiers returning from lengthy deployments need every bit of support we can provide, and then some."

Serena dropped into a chair and waited for the bowl at her feet to fill.

"What are you looking for today? A basic pedicure or a spa special?" Marlee pulled the flip-flops from Serena's feet and looked up over the soaking bowl.

"I'm not sure – maybe something new? Dane loved the last one so much, when you drew little flowers on my big toes. It was all I could do to keep him from tickling my feet to death." She chuckled, with the faint stain of a blush high on her cheeks.

Serena's expression, a mixture of love and giddiness, moved her beyond belief. Marlee felt the pang under her sternum, the one she equated with her heart cracking a little more. With a forced smile, she said, "I'm sure Dane will tickle your feet no matter what. But I know he's a perfectionist, so I'll do my best."

Serena stared at her, her face puzzled and her eyes searching Marlee's. Realizing her error, Marlee ducked her head and fussed over her nail tools, pulling one of Serena's feet from the hot water and busying herself removing the old polish. Serena said, "I guess I raved about my husband the last time I was in. You describe him very well."

Marlee's eyes flew up to meet Serena's. The woman's eyes remained curious as they flickered across Marlee's face, a slow curtain of thoughtfulness falling into place as she said, "You remind me of someone."

A pedicure and manicure later, Marlee huddled in the back room. Serena's probing look haunted her all day. As perfect a hiding place as Flynn's Crossing was, at some point, someone would connect the dots. And she'd have to run again.

A pang of regret shot to her heart. The town had come to feel like home. Even when she didn't want to be noticed, the caring nature of the people made their support genuine and difficult to turn down. Here, even the cops cared.

Her thoughts snagged on her personal encounter with one member of the law enforcement community in particular. Deputy Kermarrec. A twitch of a smile transformed his face from ruggedly handsome to deeply appealing. He'd fueled a few dreams over the past couple of weeks, pulling her out of deep sleep and leaving her hot and yearning.

"Marlee? Your next appointment's here. Looking like a cross between a bewildered child and a gruff grizzly, I must say. If his friends hadn't convinced him to come in, I'm betting he would do the whole suffer in silence thing." Bliss put a hand to her heart and fluttered her fingers. "But I must say, even my heart goes pitta-pat when he walks across the room. Such a hot and hunky manly man, all the more so because of what he does."

Her last client was a man. She didn't mind massaging men, often enjoyed them in fact, since it was the closest she allowed herself to any male flesh. Not since before – well, before. The biggest benefit? They rarely talked during a massage. She could be alone with her thoughts while she concentrated on the flex and pull of tendon and ligament under her hands.

"Give me a minute, will you? I'll be right out."

Bliss waved her back. "Take your time. I put him in your room and gave him the particulars on what to do. Here are the notes from his doctor, what you need to work on and what to stay away from. I'm sure none of it will be a surprise to you, given who he is."

Marlee glanced down at the papers in her hand, running her eyes over the doctor's notes. A back injury. A huge thumbprint smeared the patient's name, obliterating the ink. She sighed. She wasn't fond of walking in blind, and she liked to think that while she kept emotional distance from her clients, she also made them feel welcomed and comfortable when she greeted them by name.

"Bliss, what's this client's name?" But her question echoed in the small space because her boss had already bustled out of the room.

Oh well, it wouldn't be the first time she'd needed to ad lib.

She washed her hands, careful to heat her palms under warm water. Putting on her massage apron and fastening the tie, she walked the short distance to the treatment room's door and knocked, waiting until a deep-voiced acknowledgement sounded from inside.

The room was dark, with the glow of electric candles and the scent of vanilla and lavender comforting her. After this new client, she could go home. Then she'd worry about her myriad problems.

Her eyes fell on the man's naked back. Even in the dim light, she could see his muscles flexing and relaxing, his arms extended above his head. He must be doing stretches his physical therapist prescribed. Watching the tensing and letting go, she had to admire his body. Just because she hadn't been with a man in a long time didn't mean she appreciated a well-made male any less.

Clearing her throat, she found she couldn't stop staring. What would it be like to be able to run a soft caress along those muscles? His buttocks under the sheet flexed with the rest of him, rounded and full the way she liked a man to be. His hair, which looked like it was growing out from a short cut, curled slightly at his nape as he laid his head back and cracked his neck. What would it be like to kiss that stubbled cheek and trail her tongue to his ear?

Shaking her head at her foolishness, she grabbed for the warmed massage lotion, adding a nut-based aromatic to make the scent more acceptable to a guy. It must be her hormones, or her emotions, or the fact that nothing, absolutely nothing, was going her way at the moment. She swore the air crackled with unspent energy.

"Hello, my name is Marlee. I'll be giving you your massage. I have your doctor's notes, but I'd rather that you tell me what hurts, what feels tense, and what you'd like me to work on."

She turned back to the table, and the man lifted his head, hands in fists under his cheek as he stared at her. The dim light did nothing to hide the brief incredulous expression, one that morphed almost immediately into a shuttered professional blank. But even as he hid his thoughts, nothing could hide the emotions in his eyes.

Eyes that seemed to glow with the colors of a deep sea. She stared, because she knew those eyes. She'd had dreams of them. Her hands started to shake and she nearly dropped the massage cream.

"You," Deputy Kermarrec said, even as his piercing gaze never left her face. The accusation in his tone made her feel like she'd been arrested, tried and judged guilty in the space of two seconds. His eyes pinned her in place, even as she felt the blush rising in her face. How could he know he'd become the prime actor in her overactive dream life?

"Ah, Deputy Kermarrec. I didn't realize that you were the client. Bliss didn't tell me. I'm sorry. I'll get her to reschedule you around other clients. It won't be today, but maybe she can give you a massage tomorrow." She backed to the door, feeling heat rise and fall, settling in places she hadn't thought about in a long time.

He continued to stare at her. Then he turned away with such deliberate motion that it felt like a slight.

"No. You. I called and asked for whoever gives Gabby the massages she raves about, and that brought me to you. They tell me you're the best. I want the best. I want to return to work, and everyone says you're what I need to accomplish that." He curled his hands and put his forehead on them as if the idea angered him.

"What do you mean by that?" The pang of uncertainty warred with the swell of pride that others saw her as the best.

His voice was muffled when he responded. "I injured my back. My doctor wants to give me pills for the pain and the physical therapist can't do anything more for me, but my back is still too compromised to return to work. My friends swear by massage therapy as the way to reduce the pain. That's what I need. I need the pain to go away and I don't want pills."

She must have remained silent too long. The man on the table shifted and she found herself drowning in the sea of his gaze once more.

"So what do you say, Ms. Cruiz?" He emphasized the pronunciation of her last name as if mocking her. "Will you be my saving grace?"

There was nothing saving or graceful about her, or her past. What would he say if he knew the truth?

She couldn't help but stare back at him. The kaleidoscope of colors shifted in his eyes, warming to a bright blue. They heated her as she moved forward, pulled by an invisible and insistent force. She found there was only one answer she could give.

"Okay, Deputy Kermarrec. I'll help you."

Why had he agreed to this? He should have known this would come back to fuck him over. He'd never asked for the name of the massage therapist.

"Gabby swears by her, says she's the only one who can make her baby aches go away. When she comes home, she's like a new woman." Rick's testimonial was enough for him. He trusted Gabby and he trusted Rick. He hadn't trusted his instincts, which told him to check out anyone who would be touching his body. He'd been that desperate.

When he called to ask for an appointment, the spa's owner tapped fingernails on a keyboard at her end of the phone, made a sound of triumph, and said she'd had a cancellation tomorrow at four. He would be the last client of the day, and he could have as long as it took.

He'd never asked for a name then either. Shit on him.

"Deputy, you'll need to put your arms at your sides and scoot up the table a bit so your face is in the cradle."

"The what?" This felt weird, both because he was lying somewhat helpless on a table, and because the woman who was about to touch him had glowing blue eyes that reminded him of the sky on a summer day, shimmering in the paleness of her face. He preferred being in control, and he was anything but at the moment.

A long finger tapped the round cushion extending from the end of the table. "The cradle. You put your face here in the ring so you can breathe."

The slight amusement in her voice, delivered in a hushed tone, reminded him of candlelight and teasing seduction. He shifted on the table, suddenly wishing that he'd gone against convention and kept his briefs on. Bliss said he'd be more comfortable naked. He doubted it now, even more than before.

He moved up the table, resting his face in the cradle and putting his arms at his sides. She pulled the sheet further up over his body. The woo-woo music, some weird combination of electric instruments, played low in the background. For him, it set the wrong kind of mood.

"Are you warm enough? I can turn up the heat in the table."

Hell no, he didn't need more heat. He grumbled a response, not trusting his words to bite, or worse yet, embarrass him.

He waited, wondering what would come next. Would her fingers dig into his back? He braced himself for it to hurt like the hands of the therapist did when he worked Jake over during each session. He could stand anything, as long as it got him back to work.

Lost in his own thoughts, he almost missed the light brush down his spine, hands separated from his skin by the sheet. It was almost a caress, or maybe that was his imagination. The hands returned again, one always touching him, running in slight circles around each of his injuries. One came to rest to the right of his spine on his lower back, exactly at the point of impact from the minivan on that fateful evening.

With a gentle prodding of her fingers, Ms. Cruiz said, "Too much pressure? You have to tell me, because I don't want to aggravate your injuries."

He swallowed, the lump in his throat accompanied by a bumping increase in his pulse. The guys said this was relaxing. He felt anything but relaxed.

"You seem a little tense, Deputy. You'll have to talk to me so I can help you."

He grunted a noncommittal response, shifting on the table to find a better position. That was hard, because one thing in particular was getting hard. Why did his friends not mention this part of the experience?

Her hands were on his bare skin now, firm but gentle, and he could feel each individual fingertip. Her knowledgeable strokes tested and released various spots on either side of his spine. Was that her elbow putting pressure below his shoulder blade? He should explain what hurt, tell her where she needed to make it better. A sudden vivid picture of her placing red lips on his back, to kiss it and make everything better, raged through him. He got harder.

He should tell this woman with bewitching eyes and jet black hair he didn't think she could help him. He'd pay for the session. Based on the condition of her car, she must not make very much money.

And he almost acted on the thought. Almost, until she pressed fingers into precisely the spot that needed to be released. He sucked in air, but her fingers didn't move, simply holding down some kind of magic button of a nerve. And suddenly, his back let go with the first relief he'd known since the accident.

She felt the moment the knot untied, heard his swift exhalation of relief, and with it, his body sagged under her hands. The shot of satisfaction she felt at his surrender was brief. She could almost read his thoughts and knew he'd been seconds away from jumping off the table, grabbing his clothes, and hauling ass for the door. Frankly, she couldn't blame him. She'd been seconds away from bolting herself when she realized who he was, and again when she'd placed her hands on skin that reminded her of smooth velvet over unyielding steel.

And yet, he'd been kind to her. He could have given her a ticket when he stopped her. Instead, he gave her advice. Ultimately, it made little difference. She and that car were ready to part ways. But he'd tried. Besides, he was a hero. Without his timely actions, a young family might be grieving. Making him feel better was the least she could do.

She worked the telltale spot of his injuries with care, feeling the tense knots of pain as if they were her own. Her connection to this man was more intense than she was used to. Every once in a while, he squirmed on the table, and she lessened the pressure to ease his discomfort. Then he grunted.

Her hands stopped, resting lightly on his shoulders. She was nowhere near his areas of impact, but that didn't mean pain couldn't be triggered from multiple places. He stopped twitching and exhaled in a loud burst of breeze blowing gently over her skin. It raised the hairs on her arms and made her nipples harden for no apparent reason. His hair, curling slightly and looking damp, brushed her wrists like a stroke of a feather.

"Deputy Kermarrec? Am I hurting you?" She hated the sound of her voice, breathless and airy. Clearing her throat, she tried again. "You need to tell me if I'm putting too much pressure on any area. What feels better? Less? More?"

She waited, surprised to find herself panting ever so slightly. It wasn't as if she was exerting herself. This was barely a two on a ten-point scale of difficulty for her. Except for that velvety skin, of course.

Listening carefully, she wondered if he'd fallen asleep. That she could subdue the big bad cop so easily was almost amusing. Almost, because she knew how terrifying a cop could be as well.

The back under her hands flexed and he pushed up on his forearms, bringing his gaze up to look into her face as she bent near his head. When their eyes met, a shock of energy pounded through her, and she felt her fingers tingle against his skin as if she'd plugged them into socket. His eyes were wide, wider than they should be and the color of turbulent ocean. His nostrils flared slightly as they stared at each other. Then thick lashes dropped as his eyes fell to her chest. As if on cue, her nipples hardened even more and seemed to thrust in his direction of their own accord as her heart rate exceeded the legal limit.

"I think, ah, I think I've had enough for today. Don't want to overdo it, you know?" His statement would have seemed nonchalant, if not for his continued shifting on the table, rolling his hips slightly from side to side, and the gruff tone of his voice.

Her fingers didn't want to let go, clinging to his skin as if attached with super-glue. She willed them to disconnect, leaving the tips of each pad with lingering tingles of electricity. Turning quickly on the pretext of putting the massage lotion on a side table, she kept her face turned away.

"Take your time getting up. It would be a good idea to drink as much water as you can for the rest of the day, because massage releases a lot of toxins. The glass on the side table should get you started. I'll be waiting at the desk when you're ready, Deputy."

Her hand was on the door handle before she heard his quiet words.

"Thank you, Marlee. I feel better."

Chapter 9

A week later, the previous trepidation he had about massages had changed to anticipation. He'd found relief, feeling better for at least a day after the last two. If twice a week made him feel so much better, how much more would three times a week help? With that schedule, he might be able to return to active duty early. But then, how would he have enough time for massages? And after only two sessions, he knew he'd miss it.

The fact that his fantasy life got a rise out of it didn't hurt either. Laying on the table was slow torture. And it wasn't only during massages that he felt as turned on as a pimply kid with his first girly magazine. Marlee featured prominently in more than one hot dream over the past week. Fighting the caress of her fingers on his skin had him searching for any distraction.

He imagined her evenings, sitting in her little apartment. She probably had a cat. She most likely listened to woo-woo music and drank herbal tea. Or maybe she was one of those raw food people who only ate things that weren't cooked. His mind wandered as she worked on him.

"What do you do for fun?"

Her magic fingers paused on his leg, massaging his right calf. Then they continued and she stayed silent. If not for the pause, he would have thought she hadn't heard him.

Wasn't it to be expected that women who dressed like dark witches and had magical powers in their fingers were supposed to be a little odd? Her professional demeanor was calming, different from her nervousness the day he stopped her on the road. He was curious about everything that made her tick. And analyzing her might distract him from his increasing problem. He shifted, attempting to reposition himself for more comfort.

He cleared his throat as the offending organ now throbbed in time to her hands' movements, and spoke louder. "You must not have heard me. What do you do for fun?" Maybe she'd tell him what kinds of weird magazines she liked to read.

"I work."

He frowned, and the cover on the face cradle of the massage table bit into his forehead. He huffed out a breath when her fingers dug deeply into the bottom of his foot, easing down to stretch his toes. God, even that turned him on.

He needed to think about crime statistics. The last thing he needed was to be told to turn over and being unable to move without his body giving him away. He shut his eyes tighter and willed his breathing to slow and his arousal to disappear. Yeah, like that was going to happen.

An image of her dressed in black lacy underwear, her pale skin covered in a sheen of excitement and her eyes on his as she stalked across a bedroom, danced across the inside of his closed eyelids. Would she have black sheets on the bed? Would she be into anything kinky? That wasn't his thing, but maybe he could talk her into other interesting activities.

He definitely needed to think about crime stats. There hadn't been a murder in the county in how many months? Eleven? Was that a record?

He couldn't remember, not when her fingers gently rubbed the tension out of his other thigh, then worked down to his calf and dug in.

"Damn, that feels good." The groan escaped before he could quash it.

Her fingers didn't stop, merely traveled down to his left foot and began digging and stretching. Something else was trying to stretch too as her fingers touched that magic spot in his arch. His erection twitched, even pressed as it was into the table at an angle that grew exceedingly uncomfortable.

How was he going to explain this? Would she think he was hot for her? No, she was a trained professional. This probably happen to guys on her table all the time, right?

Her hands left his body, smoothing the sheet over his back. Her voice sounded low and slightly hoarse when she asked, "Any pain in your back that you need me to continue to work out?"

Not his back, no ma'am, but his front could use some attention. What the hell was wrong with him?

When he didn't reply, he felt the sheet lift. "Time to roll over, away from me and on to your back."

No way, no how.

"I'm fine. I think we're done." He shifted on the table to release the pressure, which only brought his significant organ up against his belly. Ah, relief of one kind, and pain of another. He tried to hold his body off the table, and a cramp seized his lower back. He couldn't hold back the hiss of pain.

The sheet dropped back into place. "Sounds like we're not done yet. I'll spend the rest of our time on your back." Her hands rested on his lower back, her fingers gently probing and testing.

And pressing. More pressing, and he was even harder. Was this normal?

Who could he ask? Guys didn't talk about things like this, at least not the wolf pack. Yeah, they all swore by massages to relieve aches and pains and he could understand that now. But did they all get hard during the process?

"You have tension in your lower back that wasn't there a few minutes ago. Is anything wrong? Am I hurting you anywhere?"

Her voice held that roughened quality that reminded him of torch singers in smoky clubs. She probably smoked. That was a big turnoff for him. That should do it. Concentrate on her smoking. Or murders. Or bloody vehicular accidents.

"Deputy Kermarrec? Am I hurting your back?" Her hands stopped.

No, sweetheart, not my back. But something on my front is probably turning blue.

"I think we're done for today. That's about all I can take." He heard the raspy edge to his voice and wondered what she would make of it.

"Okay. I'll leave the room now. Take your time, and get up slowly. You might feel a little light-headed, so don't rush it. There's a glass of water on the table by your clothes, and as a reminder, drink as much water as you can over the next few hours."

He heard the door open and shut, the click so quiet he would have missed it if he hadn't been holding his breath. He couldn't roll to his side fast enough.

His erection jutted out, hard and expectant, pointing toward the door like it wanted to follow Marlee.

Increasing the massage schedule was going to be a challenge to his libido and might cause permanent physical damage.

Marlee felt her cheeks burning hotly, the blush evident in the mirror as she washed her hands in the bathroom. An hour of Jake Kermarrec under her hands created more zings of heat than she could take. A glance told her that her nipples had yet to recede from view.

Worse yet, parts of her were damp and aching and sitting on that pedicure stool for the next hour would be excruciating.

Breathing in and out deeply, she stepped out of the bathroom and moved toward the front of the spa. If she was lucky, Jake would be gone already. She would be safe for another two days, until his next appointment.

A deep voice sounded in a brief laugh, and she wilted, thinking that perhaps she could run to the back and compose herself as she cleaned the massage treatment table. Then he'd be gone, right?

"Oh, there she is. I'm sure she wants to check on you before you go." The suggestive tone of Bliss's voice carried over every other sound in the room, leaving Marlee with no choice but to continue forward, struggling to ease her breathing and exude the calm that was her trademark.

"Hey Marlee. Jake was just telling me how much your massages are helping him."

Her next client smiled warmly.

"Hi Marguerite. I'll be right with you." Damn, she sounded like she'd been running a marathon. A deep cleansing breath did nothing to slow the rapid syncopation of her pulse.

She forced herself to meet Jake's eyes across the distance, willing her voice to lose the breathy quality he seemed to bring out in her. "Deputy Kermarrec, how are you feeling? Any residual discomfort?"

A frown crossed his face.

"If you are experiencing any unusual pain, you need to tell me so that I can make sure I don't worsen the situation. I'm here to help you, Deputy, not hurt you."

Even frowning, he was sexy. The furrows between his eyebrows deepened and the look in his eyes did funny things to her pulse. His mouth, the same one she'd heard laugh moments before, flattened into a grim line. When he opened it, she wondered what the hell she'd done to make him so angry with her.

"It's Jake."

She blinked, not understanding.

He waved a hand in Marguerite's general direction. "You call Marguerite by her first name, but not me. I would like you to call me by my first name too."

He stopped talking but continued frowning. Then an expression that she thought was confusion crossed his features, gone before she could examine it more closely. "Please," he added, his tone coaxing but sounding a little unsure.

That one word made her tingle again, the delicious roll of lust spiking in her midsection and heading north and south. She felt lightheaded. And she couldn't look away from his face as his eyes grew brilliant in an almost unnatural shade of blue-green. When he suddenly smiled, she swore her heart skipped a few beats.

"Well Jake, we'll see you in a couple of days then. Always a pleasure to take care of one of this county's finest." Bliss finished on a giggly laugh. Marlee blinked, and she watched Jake blink too, as if recovering. He turned and gave Bliss a wave, then hugged Marguerite and headed out the door.

"Man-oh-man, what the hell was that?"

Marlee heard Bliss, but she was busy watching a very fine male rear end walk down the steps before turning the corner and disappearing. She fought the urge to sigh, and realized that she needed to clean that massage room to calm herself down.

Turning to Marguerite to explain, she bumped into a speculative stare. A smile on her client's features told her this pedicure was going to be one of those talkative ones, and she might not like the topic. She really needed to get her shit together and her mask in place.

"I'll, ah, be right back. I need to clean up first. Take a seat," Marlee said, waving in the direction of the pedicure chairs.

She spun and forced herself to walk, not run, back to the massage room. The dim lights made it feel more intimate, but then, the lights were always dim and it didn't feel like this after other clients. Worse yet, the room carried a subtle but unique scent, an earthy, woodsy one that ratcheted up her level of heat. Even without cologne, Jake carried a distinctive manly fragrance she would recognize at first whiff.

Her traitorous hands caressed the sheets, still warm from his body, and she stared at them, wondering why they weren't responding to her brain's command to rip the sheets off the bed and shove them, hard, into the laundry bag. Inhaling deeply did no good, bringing in more of Jake instead of chasing thoughts of him away. Did the lights just get a little dimmer?

"Well, well, well. I see that our favorite sheriff's deputy is enjoying his massages."

Marlee jumped. Bliss lounged in the doorway behind her, arms crossed and fingers tapping.

"He's like any other client, someone in discomfort I'm trying to help." She wasn't sure why she felt the need to defend herself. If Bliss saw her attraction to the man, there would be no end to the sly grins whenever he walked in.

"And he looked like he left in a whole lot of discomfort, if you ask me."

That stopped her, sheets bundled in her arms at the yawning mouth of the laundry bag. She sniffed one more time, thinking she needed to put this load in the washer as soon as she got home so she wouldn't be tempted to sit with the sheet in her arms during her lonely night.

Turning, she met Bliss's direct gaze and frowned in return. "You think he was in worse pain? He doesn't tell me what hurts and what doesn't, so I'm reading his body and its responses. He does get tense, but he isn't flinching or pulling away. Maybe I need to question him more closely."

Bliss let go a big booming laugh and clapped her hands. "Tell me, did he roll over?"

Marlee pulled back a little, surprised by the question. "No, he didn't."

"Then you didn't notice?"

"Didn't notice what?"

Bliss pushed off the doorframe and moved into the room, closing the door behind her. Lowering her head, she looked conspiratorial as she whispered, "Our favorite deputy was sporting a whole lot of action in his jeans, if you get my drift. I couldn't help but notice, given that I was eye level with said part of his anatomy as I sat at the desk. Yes indeed, he had a boner that would make a stallion proud."

Chapter 10

He squirmed even now, thinking about it. The sure strokes of Marlee's hands on his back ran dangerously close to his ass. If she'd touched him the wrong way – no, make that the right way – he would have exploded on the table like a guy copping his first feel. His thoughts raced alongside his runaway pulse. How could he know if this was normal or not? If he asked his friends, he'd have to turn in his wolf pack card and probably his macho guy club membership too.

The wolf pack had been at his side throughout this ordeal. Four weeks almost to the day. One of them was always willing to help him when he needed a run to the grocery store, or a visit to a doctor, or a ride to his physical therapy appointments. When massages with Marlee replaced PT, they were happy to help with that too.

But they couldn't answer a question like this. Even if he asked his brother, he'd probably hear raucous laughter and be the lifelong butt of the joke.

Maybe today, the doctor would clear him to drive. He'd pee in a cup to prove he wasn't taking painkillers, explain that he was feeling fine, and he might be free again. Since he wasn't taking anything stronger than over-the-counter stuff, he felt secure in the outcome. He would miss the male bonding time on these trips, though.

Some days, they didn't say much of anything as they drove back and forth, which was fine. Dane was generally quiet, Powers the same. Rick had a tendency to gab, requiring little feedback to keep going. It must be the professor in him.

Even the new guy, Geno, artisan of all things wood, had jumped in to help. With him, Jake was more inclined to discuss the general stuff guys talked about as they got to know one another – sports, trucks, and local politics. Having determined they agreed on football teams but disagreed on baseball favorites, enjoyed less amped up trucks, and agreed that the local politicos were out of touch, Geno had broached the next topic of general interest.

"There seem to be a lot of great women around Flynn's Crossing. Anyone I should stay away from?"

That surprised a gut laugh out of Jake.

"You want to know who to stay away from, not who to chase?"

"Well yeah. I don't poach, and I don't want to invite trouble. I figure that you being a cop and all, you'd know who would be trouble."

The blue glow of Marlee's eyes and the gentle but firm touch of her hands sprang to mind immediately. Trouble with a capital T. Geno didn't need to be looking in that direction. That day, when Jake headed the list of single available women with Bliss at the spa, Geno frowned and didn't ask anything more, accomplishing the remainder of their ride in silence.

"So, after today, maybe you won't need any more rides."

Dane's statement brought Jake crashing back to the present. Back to the interior of the recent model pick-up truck that still had a new leather smell. Of course, the truck bed looked like it had heavy construction miles on it, which it did. But like his beloved camera gear, Dane the perfectionist kept all things mechanical neat and tidy. Content to turn up the music and let the blare of country rock pound the windows, Dane left Jake to his thoughts. That wasn't necessarily good, since his thinking single-mindedly circled back to one topic he'd be better off ignoring.

Marlee. Every time the woman laid her hands on him, his body reacted. Sometimes in tortured agony, he was still unwilling to scream uncle. He was a cop, after all. He could do inscrutable, even if his body flooded with a tsunami of lust every time he even thought about what happened in that dark cocoon of a room.

She touched him in a way no one had ever before. Of course, he'd never had a massage before. Her hands on his body – they felt fucking incredible. What would sex with her be like?

"Jake? You getting out or what?"

Dane's words brought him out of his viscous haze of horniness. If he wasn't careful, he'd get a hard-on right now. Then what would the doc think?

He shifted in his jeans. Yeah, half-mast with the mere thought of Marlee and her magic hands. He needed to get himself in the waiting room, busy peeing in that cup and examining the masses waiting to see the doc.

And yet, he waited. Dane, of all the men, was least likely to create a never-ending joke out of what Jake was about to ask.

"You had a lot of rehab and you swear by the benefits you got out of physical therapy and massage."

There was no question in the statement, so when Dane only nodded, eyeing him with curiosity, he expected nothing more. Jake moved as if stretching in the confines of the truck, a normal kind of position for a man recovering from a back injury. It did little to relieve the tight press of flesh to zipper.

"Were your therapists men or women?"

If Dane was interested in why Jake was asking, he didn't show it. In fact, he settled back in his seat as if expecting a good story to be coming soon.

"My PTs were a mix, mostly men though. The massage therapists were women. Why?"

Straight and to the point.

"Just curious if you had any sort of – ah – reaction to the massages."

Dane frowned, his eyes flicking front to stare through the windshield as if thinking back. There was a momentary flash of emotion, a wrinkle of pain crossing his features. Jake nearly told him to forget it.

"I remember the pain being worse before it was better, if that's what you mean. It took a few sessions before I felt any benefit. But then once I did, once the pain started to release for hours, then days, I couldn't wait to stretch out on that table and have them do their magic to me."

Magic, like Marlee's fingers.

Jake waited, hoping for more. Dane shrugged as if dismissing the memories, then turned back to face Jake. "Why? What's up?"

His overactive libido, that's what. How long had it been for him? Maybe that was his real problem. Maybe he needed to find a willing woman and –

"Is Marlee not working out for you? If that's the case, let me know and I'll ask Serena for another recommendation. I know she and the girl tribe probably have others they've used in the area. But according to Gabby, Marlee is the best."

No, he didn't want anyone else. He simply wanted to know what to do with his rising problem, so to speak.

"She's working out fine, just fine. The massage really helps. It's only that – " He bit off his next words. What would he say? That her magic fingers turned him on? That the sight of her aroused nipples in the black t-shirt at his last appointment made everything worse?

Jake shook his head, suddenly wishing he'd kept his thoughts to himself. It wasn't as if Dane would ever probe for more details. But he'd know something wasn't right.

"Listen, thanks for the ride. Deke's picking me up afterwards, and I'm sure I'll get cleared for duty today. Maybe we can all meet up for a celebratory beer tonight. I'm sure everything's going to be fine."

Everything except his reaction to Marlee, that is.

Three hours later, he was angry and ready to lash out.

Deke said, "Listen, it will be fine. What's another month, if you have a chance to heal fully? The doctor said you've made terrific progress, more than he would have expected based on the damage, and given your age."

"What the hell does my age have to do with it?" Jake banged the glass of soda down in frustration. To prove to himself and the world he was in great shape and didn't need to wait another four weeks to return to work, he decided beer was again a thing of the past. Straight and narrow for him.

"There are various ways to approach recuperation, you know." His big brother leaned back in his chair, his ponytail half-hidden under a ball cap. Their contrasts were marked, and yet, Jake suspected that if he let his hair grow out, it would be the same dusky hay color.

But that didn't fit who he was. He was a sheriff's deputy, and projecting the appropriate image was critical. Let Deke be the laid-back rancher. Not that the man didn't take on causes of his own and could be damned fierce about them, but there was a fundamental difference between them. To Deke, if the law said something but he didn't think it was right, he might ignore it.

Not Jake. Never him. No, justice and the law were firmly entwined, as deeply massaged into his psyche as Marlee's fingers had been in his muscles.

Now why the hell was he thinking about her? About the magic in her firm hands as they cruised over him? About the torment of sadness he glimpsed on rare occasions when she met his eyes? Even thinking about her idly like this, he needed to shift in rapidly shrinking jeans. Those massages were working on him in more ways than the intended healing.

"Jake? Earth to Jake?" The humor in Deke's voice reminded him he was in a public place, sitting across from a brother who could read him like the proverbial book most of the time.

He cleared his throat and looked across the bar as if examining the crowd. "I'm just thinking about what the doctor said."

Deke hesitated for a moment, then said, "Maybe you need to consider what your options might be." Pity in his brother's voice made Jake snap his head around in a sudden wave of anger.

"My options are doing whatever it takes to heal completely and return to work. Period. End of story."

His back picked this moment to twinge and cramp as a reminder of the doctor's warning. "You may face some permanent impairment as a result of your injuries, Deputy. The extent of those limitations is uncertain. I can't release you, even for light duty, until we understand what those will be. Give your body time to heal. Take these instructions to your massage therapist and have her give my office a call with any questions. See you in a month."

Permanent impairment his ass.

"Listen, all I'm saying is that you always wanted to be a cop, but maybe life has other plans now. You know, like a career change. That's part of the reason you're finishing your master's degree, right?"

"I will not need a damned career change. What is this, job placement counseling? My back will be fine, is fine." Until it cramped like a mother as it was doing now. If he had been forced to stand up at that moment, he would have crumpled like a dried leaf in a fist of pain.

Deke regarded him with an unwavering gaze, wearing his compassion in the crinkles at the corners of his eyes. His brother knew what Jake's chosen life's work meant to him. Giving it up was out of the question.

"I don't want your pity." It burst out of him before he could control the words.

Deke shook his head slowly from side to side, one corner of his mouth rising in a grin that was sympathetic. "You don't have my pity. Pity is for people who don't have choices and are stuck in intolerable circumstances. Now sympathy, that I have. You feel stuck. You feel like life's dealt you a bad hand. You feel like you have no control. You feel like your body's betraying you."

Bingo on all counts.

"I think I should go. At least I've been cleared to drive. That means I won't need your taxi service anymore. Just drop me back at my place. Come on."

But when he pushed the chair back, intending to stand, his back had other ideas. The sharp slice of white heat made him gasp and curl into the seat.

"What did the doctor say about those shots of pain?"

Was he that transparent? The doctor had said that these, too, were normal, part of the process of healing nerves and tissue. Massage helped the healing, he'd said. Muscle relaxants and pain meds might speed things along too, but Jake refused to go down that road.

He waved off Deke's question, sinking more deeply into wood worn to fit a slumped body through years of use. Marlee's black hair and too-pale face that rarely seemed to smile swam into his mind's eye. Something about her intrigued him, and he didn't want to fight the urge to know her better. Her quiet voice, designed to make her fade into the background as much as her looks, rang in his ears. And thoughts of her magic fingers on him even more frequently than they were now made his blood surge until the throb of pain in his back kept time with a more disconcerting throb of life in his jeans.

Chapter 11

How had this happened again?

"Go to dinner with me."

Jake's request had carried a touch of command as he waited after his appointment. Marlee felt his forceful pull even as she denied his request.

"I can't." She'd busied herself straightening the already perfectly organized desk, her eyes downcast. He waited, patient and unmoving, and she felt herself weakening.

"I know a great place you'll love." His coaxing tone made her insides heat, until she remembered the truth, her truth.

"No, you don't want to be seen with me. You're a cop. I'm, I'm –" She stopped and bit her lip hard, because she'd nearly said it.

If he heard her fumble, he chose to ignore it. He leaned forward, and his unique aroma of forest and man made her sway. Why he'd suddenly decided he wanted to spend more time with her, she wasn't sure.

Jake said, "This place is old-fashioned and quaint and fun. We'll talk. You'll be able to relax."

When she'd lifted her eyes and stared at him in surprise, he quirked an eyebrow as if to say he thought she really needed to relax. Was it so obvious?

"I can't tonight." It was Friday. She had a phone call to wait for.

"Fine, then tomorrow. Even better, because you don't work on Sunday, do you? You won't have to get up early for work the next day."

How the hell did he know? Maybe she wanted to work on Sunday. Maybe she needed to. But no, he made assumptions about her without a thought about the consequences. Because there were consequences, at least for her.

"Jake, I can't. Don't you realize that – "

"That you need time off? Of course I do. I'm not trying to fill up your dance card. It's just a meal. Here." His hand extended across the counter between them, and in his palm, his cell phone rested with an expectant lit screen.

"Put in your phone number. Give me your phone and I'll add mine. Do you text? You don't even have to talk to me beforehand. I'll send you directions. Come on. I'm a cop and you know almost every one of my friends. They'll vouch for me. I'm not a bad deal."

His skin seemed to tighten and his eyes darkened. The smile on his face held both promise and danger. He leaned forward like a co-conspirator, bringing the phone closer.

"Please, Marlee. I'd really love it if we could spend casual time together. Have dinner with me."

It was the please that did it. Few people ever said please to her. If she expected him to look triumphant when she keyed in her number, she was disappointed. He merely smiled a little wider and took her phone.

She'd had plenty of time to reconsider this decision over the last day. Even as she got in her car and followed the directions he'd texted her, she thought about bowing out. She could plead work, or illness, or – something.

The ping on the seat next to her drew her attention. She stopped at an intersection and glanced down, noting

Jake's name on the screen. No one waited behind her, so she picked up the phone.

The message was simple and direct. *'Please don't stand me up.'* As if he read her mind. Dropping the phone back on the seat, she kept driving.

When he'd said the place was outside Flynn's Crossing, she hadn't thought he meant they would cross state lines. She felt like she'd been following the winding two lane roads for hours, and only now did she think she was approaching the country corner his directions led to.

In the fading daylight, she saw him before the sign for the crossroad came up. He leaned against an SUV, his hat at the perfect angle to hide his expression. He seemed to notice her coming from a distance as well. His deliberately casual stance, arms crossed over his chest, eased a bit. Did he really think she'd stand him up?

She pulled her old sedan in next to him, waiting for the hiss and whine of the engine to settle into idle before turning it off. While it was less temperamental than her last ride, if she didn't shut it down just right, it didn't want to start. But it was the best she could afford. She'd even taken it to Big Al, who, despite his disreputable appearance and lecherous ways, seemed to know what he was doing when it came to cars. Even he hadn't been able to explain it. But she figured the car was like her in many ways. It fought the world around it every day to survive.

Jake pushed away from his car and leaned toward her open window. "Right on time. Any trouble finding the place?"

She frowned up at him. He blocked the sun. His sunglasses masked his eyes, and the mirrored reflection of her own face and big dark glasses threw her for a minute. They were stuck in a reflection of a reflection of a reflection, like those fun house mirrors. What was real?

"No, your directions were precise, down to how many minutes it would take me to get here." She heard the snap of anger in her voice. She was trying to be social, except she'd long since lost any social skills where small talk and men were concerned.

He frowned at her as if he heard the anger too and was confused by it. Then he dropped his professional mask in place and put a hand to the door handle to give it a tug. It didn't move. He tugged again with the same result.

"Your door appears to be stuck. Are you sure you're not just making life difficult for me by keeping it locked?"

The undertone of humor in his voice got to her. There were a lot of things about this man that got to her. Why was she here again?

She pulled the handle on the inside and the door popped open, the hinge squeaking in rusty protest.

"The outside handle doesn't work." She slid out and rose to stand next to him. In her tall heels, she was almost on par with him in height. She'd worn these boots on purpose, like body armor. She needed to keep herself on equal footing with him in any way she could.

He looked between her and the door as it swung shut. "How do you get back in?"

"I climb in on the passenger side."

His face turned quizzical. She bet that if she could see his eyes, they'd be sparkling with curiosity right now. What color would they be? Would the blue or the gray or the green be more evident?

"So this is your replacement for the car Big Al towed to the junkyard." It was more of a statement than a question.

She nodded, feeling his judgment and wanting to crawl back inside and drive away. At this point in her life, this car was the best she could do.

"Why don't you get the door fixed?"

She barked out a laugh in response. "Get it fixed? Do you know how much that would cost? The part alone costs twelve massages. The repair time is another eight. That price is too dear."

She needed to keep reminding herself of that when it came to rugged blond cops too. They didn't ride in on their trusty steeds, or in black SUVs, to save the day, at least not for women like her.

Why was she here again?

She turned toward the building to hide her confusion. It didn't have a traditional sign with the name on it. In florescent colored neon, big letters spelled out 'Eat Good Food Here' and nothing else. She wouldn't have pegged it as his kind of hangout.

"Why did you call this place the diner?"

He waved a hand toward the building and she started walking toward an old wood door in the center as he fell into step beside her.

"It's always been the diner. It's been around since I was a kid, changing hands a few times over the years, but the menu never varies and who knows what happened to the original name out front. It's a favorite place for the ranchers and farmers south of town, which means I usually meet my brother here. I patrol this area too."

He took off his shades and hooked them in his shirt pocket as he pulled the door open for her, waiting as she passed inside with a hand resting lightly at his waist. She bet he often stood like that, hand in casual position where his gun usually rode, just in case a bad guy happened by. Too bad she hadn't had someone like him in her past to rescue her.

The idea made her mad all over again. She should never have agreed to this. Mr. Almighty Sheriff's Deputy Kermarrec wouldn't want anything to do with her if he knew about her past. And she didn't need rescuing.

A waitress about their age bustled over, her well-endowed body filling the vintage diner uniform to overflowing. "Why Deputy Kermarrec, what a nice surprise. Haven't seen you since your accident. So glad you're better. Your usual table?"

"Hey Poopsie. Thanks, that would be great."

Wow, that was rude. Marlee let her anger tick up a few notches.

One laminated menu hit the corner table by the window with a swish, and she hesitated, waiting to see which side of the narrow booth Jake claimed as a regular. He stood behind her, waiting too.

"What can I get for you, hon? Coffee, tea, soda?" The waitress stood with a hand on her hip, and Marlee met her expectant stare.

"Ah, coffee please."

The woman nodded once and flounced off.

Marlee turned and frowned at Jake. "She didn't get your order."

He grinned, suddenly looking less fierce and a whole lot younger.

"That's because I always get the same thing. She's long since given up on getting me to try anything different." He waved at the table as if to say, pick a side, and she shrugged out of her black denim jacket and slid into the one facing the wall. He was a cop. He'd want to be able to scan as much of the room as possible.

He slid in across from her with a smile that said he approved of her choice. Shoving his leather jacket into the seat next to him, he pulled up his sleeves and rested well-muscled forearms on the table. The sight of his skin made her heart rate pick up, even when she wanted to stay mad at him.

The waitress returned with two mugs of coffee and table settings. Paper napkins hit the table first, followed by the hollow clatter of silverware, and finally, the mugs.

"You want to know the specials, hon?"

Marlee shook her head.

"Give her a minute. Thanks, Poopsie." Jake gave the woman a genuine smile that she returned with her own big grin.

Marlee seethed again.

"I can't believe you did that." She didn't bother to hide her anger.

"Did what?" Jake looked honestly confused.

"Why do you call her that?" She suspected her face was turning red. It always did when she got agitated. And any disrespect to women made her agitated.

"Because it's her name?" Jake responded with the question like he thought it was a test.

She couldn't help it. "What do you mean, it's her name? Who would name a girl Poopsie?"

He smiled as if he suddenly got it. "Her hippie parents. They had interesting names for all of the kids. Like Disco, and Thunder, and Dirt. Those were the boys. Poopsie went to school with my brother Deke, and her little sister DearGirl was in with the twins. It's probably a good thing her parents stopped having kids after that."

She met his smiling eyes, more than a little on edge. Sincere humor shined back at her, tensing her further. She picked up the sugar dispenser and poured in a heavy serving. Stirring vigorously, she contemplated setting down some rules. Better to know the rules now, so that no one got disappointed later.

"Do you want some coffee in that mug?" His teasing voice pulled her out of the depths of her thoughts.

She met his gaze as if defying him to criticize her choice in beverages.

"Is this a date?"

His eyes narrowed in surprise as they flicked across her face. She could feel each second of scrutiny like a slap. Around them, the clatter of plates and silver, chattering of people, and call of orders from the kitchen made their booth feel more intimate. Parts of her long ignored tightened and heated as he continued to stare at her.

"Because I don't date and I don't do relationships."

He watched her eyes flash with her words. She grew more fascinating by the minute, like getting upset when she thought he belittled their waitress.

"Okay." He heard himself draw out the single word to buy himself time.

"Just so you understand." She leaned back in the booth, not that she could go far in the narrow space. Crossing her arms in a protective gesture only drew his attention to her breasts. He liked the lean look of her body, even though he knew that her spare frame hid amazing physical strength.

"Why don't you?"

She frowned at him. He realized the pseudo-Goth thing didn't work for her. It made her look like she was masquerading as someone she wasn't. Every once in a great while, she let out some charm that seemed more in line with her real self than this persona she wore to antagonize him. Each time she shifted positions, his nose caught the scent he'd come to associate with her, a rich combination of lavender and vanilla.

He clarified his question, since she didn't seem inclined to answer. "Why don't you date or do relationships?"

One hand snaked out to grip her coffee mug and the other resumed stirring, though the pile of sugar she'd added should have long since melted into syrup. After four turns, she met his gaze head on. Those eyes of hers did crazy things to him. He felt that stir of memory, like he knew her from someplace.

"Relationships make you trust. You trust the flowery words coming out of the guy's mouth and then you do stupid things before you realize you should never have trusted him in the first place."

He waited for her to say more, but she stared at him instead. Something about the grim line of her mouth and set of her chin tickled his memory too.

"Wow, that's harsh." He waited for her to respond, but she only raised her chin a little higher, so he asked, "Who made you that way?"

She huffed and turned her eyes to the window before answering, a typical evasive technique. That was all right. He'd learn the truth sooner or later.

"A man." She examined the parking lot and occasional vehicles passing on the road as if watching the most interesting show imaginable.

"Is that the whole truth?" He wondered if she would bother to lie to him.

She looked back at him, her face now serious. Her arms extended on the table in front of her, palms flat, and she leaned forward, her posture telling him that she hid nothing as she said, "Whatever I tell you will always be the truth."

He paused, considering her careful choice of words. "But you won't always tell me everything, will you?"

She nodded once, one corner of her mouth curling up as if pleased that he understood.

"What I choose to tell you will be the truth." The other side of her mouth joined in the smile. "I may not choose to tell you everything."

He sat back, regarding her steadily. She didn't flinch, didn't back down, and didn't even change her expression. This stronger, powerful side of her turned him on, and he had no idea why.

"I'm a cop, Marlee, so I appreciate the truth. Most times, I have to make do with lies. The whole truth, now that would be a hell of a lot nicer."

Poopsie returned to the table, coffee pot in her hand. She turned to Marlee with a bright expression.

"What can we get for you, hon? Don't let him pick. He never gets anything different."

Marlee glanced down at the menu she'd never opened, and her lips parted as if she was about to ask for more time. He had a sudden flash of covering that open mouth with his, dancing tongues, and taking the kiss as deep as Lake Tahoe. When she met his eyes, she seemed to read his thoughts, because a slight blush started at her neck and climbed to her cheeks, making her make-up stark in contrast.

"What does he usually have?" The sudden huskiness in her voice made him wonder what she'd sound like in bed. Would she be vocal? Would the blush drop to her breasts? Their gentle rounded shape pressed against the cloth of her t-shirt, and he tried to avoid staring at her nipples.

Poopsie giggled, answering, "The burger with blue cheese and grilled onions, medium-well. Fries with a side of mayo, if you can believe that. And a chocolate shake."

Marlee continued to stare at him, her lids falling halfway over her brilliant eyes. "I'll have the same," she said, "but medium-rare and vanilla, please."

The waitress gave a harrumph of apparent disappointment and spun, her shoes squeaking across the tile floor.

"You could order anything you want. Would you like a glass of wine, or a beer?"

Marlee shook her head. "I don't drink, but thanks." Her eyes swept around the room, stopping to examine each customer in her line of vision briefly before moving on. He recognized the movement. She swept the space as easily as he did to dismiss any possible threats.

"Why don't you?"

Her eyes snapped back to him.

He clarified, "Why don't you drink?"

She shrugged. "I have my reasons. Maybe someday I'll share them."

Ms. Marlee Cruiz was full of mysteries, and he found himself smiling. She looked anything but delighted to be here, and yet, here she was. She didn't seem to be inclined to break their silence, so he stared back at her, daring her to make the first move.

Poopsie delivered their milkshakes with a sweeping gesture, and Marlee reached for her straw, running it through her fingers until Jake thought he might need to grab her hand in a desperate move to get her to stop the motion. He worked hard to blank his expression as she put the straw in her glass. When she sucked on it, he blew out a deep breath and shifted in his seat. Heat fired in his blood and he inhaled sharply through his nose, which drew her eyes to his face with a concerned frown.

"Are you okay?"

He couldn't look away, though each passing minute made his jeans feel more uncomfortable. Across the table, he could see Marlee's pupils dilate, and a quick check down let him know her nipples had become hard. At least the discomfort was mutual.

Platters clattered to their table. Their burgers were huge, dripping juice and melting cheese, with a mound of fries large enough to frighten a teenager. When she dropped her eyes and reached for her sandwich, he did the same.

He wondered why he couldn't think of a single thing to say to her. He didn't usually lack for conversational skill, but he wanted to act, not talk. He knew that alone should tell him how much trouble he was in.

Mopping ketchup with a fry, he tried for a safe question. "Tell me about being a massage therapist."

She shrugged, as if her answer didn't matter. This woman had her hands on him many times, and the touch was almost intimate. And yet, she didn't want to talk to him.

"Marlee, I really am interested. What made you pick this profession?"

She looked back at him, scrutinizing him as if judging his sincerity. Evidently satisfied with what she saw, she dropped her eyes and played with the straw in her shake. He wished she wouldn't do that.

"I gave people massages to earn money. I found I was good at it, so I went to school. I learned about cutting hair and doing nails too, so I can work in any area of a salon. It's a way to assure I can always earn a living. There are always beauty parlors or spas that need someone with my skills."

He nodded. The world would always need law enforcement too, unfortunately.

"Why are you a cop?"

She asked her question without guile, her posture more relaxed now as she continued to play with the straw and watch him. Her fingers ran up and down the plastic, and he wondered if her movements were deliberate.

"I'm the second of five boys, and the son of a man who made sure we all understood the difference between right and wrong. Dad wasn't easy to please, so we wanted to be right. Sometimes we got it wrong anyway, and usually it was because we were busy beating each other up over something. Being a middle child, I turned into something of a peace manager."

"A peace manager, not a peace maker?" She looked puzzled.

"Yeah, trying to sort out Dad's rules and where we screwed up. Trying to explain that to my brothers. I couldn't make peace, exactly. Deke and I, we were close growing up, and we tried to be right. Rock, who's next in age after me, rebelled the most, and he didn't care if he was right or wrong, as long as he got his way. The twins came along later. They're a self-contained unit, so whatever they did, they did together. Do you have any brothers or sisters?"

She jumped in her seat as if something bit her and her eyes widened. Her intense stare made him want to squirm almost as much as he did under her touch.

"We're not close. They wouldn't approve of the choices I've made in my life. What was it like growing up on a working ranch?"

Her brief statement made him pause, processing what she said. What kinds of choices? But she didn't look inclined to share, since her arms wrapped protectively around her body.

"Where did you grow up?"

She shifted in her seat and turned to stare out the window. He thought she wasn't going to answer, and his curiosity made him want to force a reply.

In a quiet voice, she said, "The West Coast. Please, I don't want to talk about me, okay?"

He stared at her longer, but she didn't look back at him. He met her eyes in the window, and her sorrow made him wish he hadn't pushed. He'd tell her more stories about growing up, anything to make her sadness go away. He launched into a long tale of the trouble he and his brothers got into when they let one of their dad's prize bulls escape, and when her lips lifted in a grin, he sighed in relief.

She listened with care, he realized. There was nothing casual about her attention, and when she laughed at his stories, the rare sound made him feel like he was a hero. She didn't laugh often enough.

That sound did other things to him too. It made him feel angry about everything that caused Marlee to distrust the world. His protective instinct roared into gear and burned alongside the anger, making him wish he could shield her from any future hurts. And his pulse continued its jungle tempo, until he realized he was staring at her and they hadn't said anything for quite a while.

He reached for something to cool his temperature and tried a slurp of his shake. Empty. He needed something to quench his thirst, before he reached across the table for Marlee instead.

Poopsie picked that moment to reappear, picking up their plates. "You all want some dessert?"

Marlee's eyes blinked as if she was trying to focus, and her face turned slowly toward the waitress. "Do you have any pie?"

Damn, a woman who loved pie. Why did he find that sexy too?

Her childish delight when a thick slice of apple a la mode appeared in front of her unwrapped a warm feeling inside him. He couldn't ignore his arousal as she smiled at him. When her lips opened for a full, lopsided grin after her first bite, his erection throbbed. He wanted to make her smile like that all the time.

Jake glanced around the room, surprised to find they were the only ones left in the diner. He started when the time registered. They'd been talking for over three hours. He still knew very little about her. She casually deflected any personal questions about her family or childhood.

When the check arrived, she insisted on splitting it.

"No, this one's on me. If it makes you feel better, you can buy dinner next time." He put his hand on the tab and pulled it forward, tugging a bit to release her fingers gripping the other side.

"What makes you think there will be a next time?" She regarded him with a hint of sadness in her eyes.

He wanted to put the smile back instead. Waiting, he tugged again. She released the paper with a huff, her eyes turning to the darkened window as she bit her lower lip.

All through dinner, she'd done things like that, and he swore the moves were unconscious. She couldn't even guess what they did to him. How the hell was he going to walk out of here without her noticing?

"It's dark out already."

The anxiety in her comment drew his eyes from their casual slide down her body. Her face pinched tight with worry.

"We've been talking a long time. Or rather, I've been talking. I feel like I know only a little more about you, Marlee."

She seemed to cringe when he said her name.

When they slid out of the booth, he tried to help her with her jacket, but she slung it around her shoulders, pushing her arms in fast without looking at him. Picking up her huge purse, she straightened and headed for the door. At least she hadn't looked down to see how much she affected him.

He held the door for her, giving Poopsie a casual wave as she wiped down tables and put up chairs. From the back, he heard the cook singing as pots clanged and the dishwasher whirled. He could smell the steam and leftover cooking odors. They'd closed the place. It had been years since he'd spent this much time getting to know a woman.

But Marlee wasn't any woman.

As soon as they stepped a few feet from the diner's door, the front lights went out. Marlee gasped, extending a hand, and he grabbed it.

"It's very dark out here." Her fear was obvious.

He squeezed her hand in response, and within seconds, she tried to pull it out of his grasp. He let it go, inhaling the cold night air in hopes that it slowed down the heating in his groin. Every pulse of his blood pulled him closer to Marlee.

"I'm not used to it, the dark. I don't like it. I'm used to city lights." The arm not clutching her purse tight to her side swung out in an arc as she walked. "It's so dense, like ink instead of night."

He put out a hand to steady her when she wove from side to side. When he connected with her upper arm, he tightened his hold. She gasped, not pulling away, but he could feel muscles twitch under his hand through her jacket.

"Steady, Marlee. Your eyes will adjust in a minute." He loosened his hold, sliding his hand down until he wove his fingers through hers and pulled her next to him. "Relax. I won't let anything happen to you."

Her body jerked from head to toe, and she tried to pull away. When he turned to look at her face, her eyes shone with panic in the dim light.

"I, ah, need to leave." She yanked out of his grasp and walked the wrong way. Their cars were the only two vehicles in the lot set back from the diner, shadowed and hidden now that the front lights were out. Getting her bearings, she changed direction, her steps choppy over the uneven ground. He followed, giving her space as she increased her pace. He thought he heard her sob.

In the final steps to her car, she tripped, falling hard against the passenger door. She wrenched it open and started to crawl inside, and the idea that she'd be hidden from him soon made him sprint forward and grab her waist. A shiver ran through her body and into his hands, as potent as every touch on his back when she massaged him.

"Hey, slow down. I'd like to have the chance to say good night to you properly. Marlee, what's the problem?"

She reared back, stepping on his right foot in the process and driving the heel of her boot into his instep. He chose to think it wasn't intentional as he swore, pulling back.

"Oh god, I'm sorry. What did I step on? I'm so sorry!"

Marlee backed out of the car, spinning and grabbing his shoulders, her eyes wild as she looked him up and down. If he wasn't hurting at the moment, he'd comfort her. His hands wrapped around her arms in return without conscious thought.

"It was only my foot and I have another one, so don't worry about it. What has you spooked?"

She stopped moving so quickly, it was like a freeze frame in a video with her face hidden in the dark. He released an arm and stepped closer to put fingers under her chin and tip her face up to the limited light.

Her eyes filled her face, huge and round. Unable to stop himself, his fingers traced her cheek, and she jerked. A huge sigh lifted her chest, and his eyes traveled down even as his fingers found their way under her ponytail and massaged her neck.

"I need to go, Jake. This was – this is a mistake. Not you, but me. I, ah, I can recommend someone to continue your massage therapy. I think it's best if we don't run into each other again."

What the hell? All he wanted to do is hold her in his arms, the urge to comfort and care for her growing with each passing minute. He pulled her forward against his body. Her eyes grew wider, if that was possible, and her face lifted to his.

"Nothing will happen to you that you don't want, Marlee, I swear it. I'll protect you. I'll take care of you."

Bewilderment filled her features, driving away the panic and terror filling them before. She examined his face as if looking for the right answer.

He could only think of one response. He lowered his head slowly, giving her time to pull away. The fact that he gripped her arms and held her closer with every second gave her a choice, right? But she didn't fight him.

Her lips held in a tight lie, and he took advantage of her stillness and lowered his lips to rest on hers, breathing her in. His cock hardened and his mind emptied, and for a moment, he swore his feet left the ground.

Chapter 12

Damn, why did Jake have to taste so good? He kissed like an angel and the devil in one. Marlee couldn't resist tangling her tongue with his, his lips persuasive and full. His hair ran under her fingers like silk. His body pressed against her, and the hard length of his erection nudged her belly and made her blood pound an insistent beat.

She shouldn't do this, though she was hazy on why at the moment. He ran his lips across her jaw and down her neck, nestling his lips on a pulsing vein that made her shiver. Just a moment more, and she'd break out of his arms. He was gentleman enough that he'd let her go.

She wished he wasn't.

The stakes were larger than her needs, though. What if he found out? He might stop her, and then the efforts of the last few years would be lost. That idea gave her the strength to push him away.

His rich lips were open, his eyes burning into hers as if she was the only anchor he had. And she recognized the sentiment, because she shared it. Regretfully, she had bigger considerations.

Her hand caressed his cheek, and he turned that amazing mouth into it, kissing her palm and sucking on the skin of her wrist. The jolt of electricity ran up her arm and down her body, settling in the pit of her stomach and lower. Much lower. The lower part that hadn't seen any action, well, since before.

She forced herself to tap his cheek, getting his attention. The colors in his eyes tossed like a kaleidoscope, and his breaths came quickly. She didn't dare let her gaze drift down his body, afraid it would weaken her resolve.

"Jake, I'm sorry. This was a mistake. I need to go."

His eyebrows met in the middle in confusion. Those lips she'd been savoring moments ago pulled into a thin line. He continued to watch her, his expression slipping into that detached cop glare she hated.

"I'm serious. I don't think we should see each other anymore. This is wrong. Or at least, it's wrong for me." She stepped back.

He let her go, and she felt a momentary pang. For once, she wanted to matter enough for someone to step forward when she asked them to stand down.

The open door of her car slammed into her thigh, and she let herself sink into the seat of the sedan, backing up on her butt. She could be kissing Jake, but instead, she was in full retreat. And he never took his eyes off hers, standing with his feet apart and his legs stiff. And another part of him was stiff too.

Oh god.

Scooting across the front seats, her fingers relaxed. She was almost there. Almost behind the wheel, and if there was a god, the car would start at once and she could drive like hell to her apartment and hide.

The clatter didn't completely register. Jake watched her retreat without saying a word, his cop mask of objective indifference all the more chilling because of the heat in his eyes. His body was primed, and so was hers. She gripped her hands and kept moving backwards, and it hit her with sudden clarity.

Her hand was empty. Her keys had fallen off her fingers when she wasn't paying attention, between the seats of yet another ill-willed car.

"Damn."

She dug madly for her keys, and over her shoulder Jake leaned into the car. "What's wrong?"

"Nothing, I'm sorry. God, I'm doing that a lot, aren't I? I dropped my keys. Don't worry, I'll find them. They're down here someplace."

Her hand strained. She felt something metallic, but if it was her keys or part of the front seat, she wasn't sure. Her fingers grazed the metal again, and she swore colorfully.

"Wow, that was quite a mouthful. I've never heard you swear before, and it is impressive. Need some help?"

"No, damn it, Jake. I don't need your help."

"Don't need it, or don't want it?" She heard the amusement in his tone and hated him for it.

"Neither. Or both. What the hell – I don't know. Oh shit!"

She couldn't reach them. Wherever they'd gone, they were beyond her grasp from the front seat. But the back seat might work – if only she could get Jake to leave.

"Jake, please, I've got this."

A chuckle sounded outside the car. She could no longer see his shadowed face. His crotch, on the other hand, was at eye level. Enticing, but not as much as before. His rough laugh sounded again, with more bitterness this time.

"What kind of peace officer would I be if I left you, a lady in distress, alone in the darkness? Where are your keys, Marlee?"

She pulled in a hard breath when his voice caressed her name, even if he was pissed off with her. Pissed off men were a big problem.

"They're under the front seat. I dropped them. I'm sorry." Shit, she was apologizing again. She didn't mean to do it. It just popped out. Habit.

He ducked down, meeting her eyes. The sight of his face calmed her. He wasn't angry. Frustrated perhaps, and she couldn't help the quick drop of her eyes to his jeans again. Still tight, but not as much. But enough to make her yearn.

"Maybe I can reach them from the back. I'll look for them. Relax."

Easy for him to say.

He opened the back door, crouching down and looking at the floor. It was a shame he cut his hair so short. Longer as it was now, it carried a wave that invited stroking and burrowing, while his mouth was –

Damn. She ordered her imagination to stop, but her body already knew. Her mouth already felt it. The full body shiver ran through her, so powerful that she swore the car tilted.

But it was Jake getting into the backseat. He crawled on his hands and knees. At least she kept the vehicle meticulously clean. One embarrassment avoided.

"Can you turn on the dome light?"

She sighed, mortified again. "It doesn't work."

"Why the hell do you have another crappy car? You had a crappier car before, and you know what happened. Why didn't you get a decent car?"

Because she couldn't explain why. Not now, and never to him. He wouldn't understand.

"Shit! Fuck!"

"What happened?"

"Back cramp." He swore, painting an array of colorful images with his words, and she almost smiled. He was very imaginative, though some of those physical activities weren't humanly possible.

She also heard the pain. He wasn't faking it.

"Damn it, Marlee, I need you." The force in his voice made her scramble out of the front seat and slam the door, then lean over him in the back.

>>>>>

"Where are you cramping up, Jake? Talk to me. I can make it go away." Marlee leaned above him, a shadow in the darkness of the car's interior.

"My lower back."

Over the pain, her scent made him heat up all over again. Up and down and sideways, he had no idea what direction he was heading with her around.

"God, I'm sorry. You're hurting and I'm the cause of it. Stay still now. Let me try to help."

He inhaled, swore, and blew out a breath. One hand traveled up his back, starting at his hip and working up his vertebrae until she reached the clench of muscle at his lower side. He cursed again, because the intense pain made it almost impossible to breathe. Kneading the tender area, she let her other hand follow the same course. He sucked in air, even as she continued to work.

"Can you get up on the seat? On your front. I can work the cramp out for you." Her soft words sounded as pained as he felt.

He grunted as a reply because that was all he could manage, moving to his left and lifting himself up on the bench of the back seat. When he got his body on that level, he groaned in relief.

Her fingers dug deeper, and he wanted to moan in response. Pressure increased and held firm, with her knuckles weighing heavily near his spine. When something released, another moan nearly escaped his lips. He wouldn't allow it. He was a cop, after all. He could do pain.

Soon, though, he knew she'd make him feel better, and then they'd both be on their way. Regrets on his side.

While the evening didn't exactly start out on a friendly note, it improved the more they talked. Everything he heard intensified his interest. There were secrets to Marlee, and he looked forward to learning all about them.

He shifted as she prodded tense tissue, and she paused.

"Am I hurting you? I'm sorry."

"Stop apologizing." The guttural tone of his voice changed to a stifled moan as she pressed deeper, and he cringed.

The knot he'd tied in his back throbbed under her fingers.

"You must be in terrible pain, and all because you tried to help me. I feel guilty, which is why I keep apologizing. I make your life worse on so many levels."

"Isn't that for me to decide?" He softened his voice to match hers, trying to reassure her that she wasn't at fault for anything. "Besides, we haven't even begun to explore those many levels. I want to get to know you better, Marlee."

She stilled over him, the heat of her body penetrating his jeans. Imperceptibly, her body relaxed into his, changing the motion of her hands. And damned if his groin didn't tighten, even in their uncomfortable position.

He heard no reply, and he wished he could watch her face to try to read her thoughts. When she pulled his shirt free from the waistband of his jeans and worked her hands under the fabric, deepening the massage, his blood flowed south at a faster clip. The knot in his back loosened further, and the gradual change lulled him. Rhythmic movements and elevated breathing gave the interior of the car a sultry air, even with the open door.

What would it be like to wrap his arms around her and hold her, listening to the sounds of their rapid heartbeats? Would her skin taste like vanilla and lavender?

If he tangled his hands in her dark hair or ran his fingers over her body, would he be able to stop?

He found he could breathe deeply again, which was useful, since he needed to feed oxygen to his rapidly beating heart. He gave up any hope of easing the pain of his arousal digging into the seat. Her body heat as she straddled him drove him crazy, and he wished more than anything they were in a bed, where he could explore her.

She interrupted his musings when her left knee, propped between his body and the seatback, slipped on the old vinyl and pushed her body down more fully on his. She squeaked in surprise, then braced the other foot on the floor and cursed the faulty overhead light. The darkness made it impossible to see much of anything outside. Night air blew in through the open back door, and he felt her shiver.

Or maybe that had nothing to do with the cold. If she slipped again, she'd be lying on him, and if his little brain had anything to say about it, that would be exactly right. He got harder at the thought of the aching part of his body against her feminine softness with only denim to separate them. Years had passed since he'd wanted a woman this much.

He felt her lean away, lightening her touch on his back. He wanted to protest, even as he realized it was for the best. His hot thoughts would only scare her away.

"I'm going to figure out how to climb out without injuring your back again."

"No hurry." In fact, he enjoyed her squirming on top of him. It brought all sorts of ideas about how to get them in a more compromising position.

She braced herself on the front seat and shifted.

"Do you think you could shift a little to the left, toward the back of the seat? Maybe I can then get my leg straightened out."

He knew what would happen. She'd give him time to recover, help him stand, and make sure he could drive. Then she'd dig out her keys and leave. Damned if he was going to let her go.

Without giving Marlee any warning, Jake shifted under her, rolling to his side against the back of the seat, and with a thrust of his hips, completed the maneuver until he lay on his back. His quick actions didn't give her time to brace herself, and her foot slipped on the floor. With a surprised gasp, she fell forward, and he caught her upper arms as she landed with the cushioning softness of her breasts against his chest. They were nose to nose, her body pressed down on his, and it was exquisite torture.

"Jake?" She uttered his name in confusion. He wished he could see her face more clearly. In the filtered pale light from outside, the glitter of her eyes and the occasional flash of white teeth was all that was visible. She was smiling at him.

He thought about pushing her off his chest, which would the gentlemanly thing to do. But he wasn't feeling well mannered. Each touch of her, his angles to her curves, his hard to her soft, overrode every command to his muscles to move.

Instead of pushing her away, Jake settled her more closely, his fingers loosening and running up and down her arms slowly, mesmerized. If she felt his cock growing under her belly, she didn't seem to mind. All he could feel was the quickening rise and fall of her breasts as they pressed against him and the heat at the apex of her thighs warming him to the point of combustion. She shifted, and the action lined things up even better. He felt her breath whisper across his face as she let out a weak groan.

"Marlee?" He would give her the choice, stay or go. He badly wanted her to stay, but he wasn't sure how she would answer. Stay, and learn more about each other for a couple of hours of bliss? Or say no, stumble away, and leave him living with the cold nights of regret it would bring?

He took the decision out of her hands when he pulled her face closer, cupping a hand to her cheek and angling her mouth to align with his. Then he set his lips on hers, and he lost any ability to second-guess himself.

Her lips were soft and pliable, and as he ran his mouth over hers, she began returning the favor. Tentatively at first, she seemed to grow more accustomed to him, her lips opening and allowing him to explore inside. She tasted like the best sugar cookies in the world, rich and buttery with sweetness and decadence. With each gentle pass, he felt her quake, and his desire zoomed through him at illegal speeds.

God, the woman could kiss. Sweeps of her tongue added another layer of eroticism to their linked mouths. One of his hands worked its way into her hair, massaging her neck to persuade her. The other swept down to her hip, then up under her jacket to caress her spine. Every nerve ending, the ones she touched and the ones she might soon, lit on fire. The throb between his legs grew stronger, as her hardening nipples rubbed against him through their clothes. He shivered this time with a rampaging need unlike anything he'd felt before. He was far from a virgin, but this time, it felt different.

She disengaged their lips and pulled her face away from his. In the scant light from outside, he read the emotions in her expression. Arousal. Fear. Worry. He felt pissed off and turned on at the same time, knowing he should let her leave, wanting her to stay.

"I didn't plan this." His voice was rough and unsteady as he held her against him, immobile.

"I know. Jake, I'm not sure this is what we should be doing. I'm not just talking about sex. I mean the whole friendship thing. You don't know me."

She bit her lip, and he sucked in air. If this is what she felt like, what she looked like, ravished by kisses alone, what would she be like naked in his bed?

"I know a lot about you already, and what I know I truly appreciate. You can tell me more about yourself, your truths, when you feel more comfortable with me. As to talking about sex, I'd much rather be doing it. Conversation is highly overrated at times."

Jake quirked a grin as he nestled his throbbing length against her, glad when she smiled back, a self-conscious giggle rolling out of her as her fingers loosened their death grip on his shirt. Sliding up against the back of the seat until he was upright, he kept an arm around her. She straddled his lap, and when she attempted to shift away and off to the side, his arm tightened around her and held her in place. His other hand, still wound in her hair, pulled her face closer. His eyes stayed open and on hers as he kissed her, and a flash fire ignited inside him, consuming what little sense he had left.

His mouth moved across her face, kissing and licking and pressing everywhere until he settled at her ear lobe, sucking. She panted and he tried to slow his heart, but it raced ahead, unwilling to listen to reason or wait for conscious thought to return. He wanted. It seemed she wanted too.

A kick of wind blew into the car, distracting Jake for a moment with its frigid interruption. He shifted her only far enough to reach over and pull the car door shut, closing them into a warm cocoon of privacy.

"You remember when I called this a crappy car?"

She leaned back to look into his face, good humor in her eyes and in that very kissable quirk to her mouth.

"Yes." He couldn't resist kissing that uneven spot and she hissed out a breath, thrusting her hips downward until he felt every inch of the zippers dividing them.

"Forget I said that. This is an American classic, and as such, it has a wonderfully roomy back seat. And you and I are going to make great use of it."

One hand settled at her waist, fingers tracing the line of her jeans before traveling up under her shirt to cup the bottom of one breast. She arched into it, crying out when he traced a nipple begging for his attention.

"God, Marlee, if I'm not inside you soon, I'm going to explode. Feel what you do to me." The hand cupping her face dropped and grabbed hers, moving her palm to the long form of his erection pressing between them. He felt her heat increase a few degrees, and felt a fleetingly disappointment that this first time with Marlee would be in darkness.

"Condom?" He didn't recognize her voice, rough and edgy.

"Wallet." He reached into his pocket, the movement making his body arch harder against her, and his eyes nearly rolled back in his head. He might ignite from this much sexual overload.

His wallet flopped to the seat, and a crinkle announced his fingers had found their prey. His eyes dropped from hers for a moment, and he froze, staring. Shit. How long had that condom been in his wallet? His emergency stash, just in case he was ever ass over backwards with lust. This situation qualified. But condoms came with expiration dates, didn't they?

Her patience seemed to evaporate, and she grabbed the package from him, tucking it into her jacket pocket as she ran her hands down his chest, leaning forward to kiss him as if her life depended on it. Whatever thought he might have had next raced out of his head when her tongue met his and her hands locked behind his neck, tugging at his hair. She wriggled over him, and he nearly lost it. Yeah, it had been way too long.

Her fingers did amazing things to the muscles in his neck, his body tensing to the point of pain. Her mouth locked on to the vein under his ear, and he swore as stars appeared in front of his eyes. When her fingers walked their way down his chest and opened the buckle of his belt, he forgot to breathe.

The car grew hot and steamy as they both panted. He had a fleeting moment of regret, that they were doing this like a couple of teenagers instead of responsible adults. She deserved a bed, a big soft one. He wanted to lay her out and savor her. When she pulled down the zipper on his jeans and her hand wrapped around him, he felt like he'd been branded, and any thought about savoring dissolved.

It was impossible to rein in the desire washing over him. How she got his jeans down his legs enough to free him, he wasn't sure. He reached for her jeans and eased them down her shaking legs, throwing the denim over the headrest to the front seat. He wanted to peel off her shirt and run his open mouth down her arms, tasting her skin, before traveling back up to suck each hard nipple into his mouth.

"No time," she panted, pushing against him, only her panties and his briefs between them. She shoved his cotton down as far as his jeans, trapped around his knees. When he ripped off the thong covering her, she kissed him hard enough to draw blood.

The crinkle of the condom wrapper. Her strong fingers running it down the length of him. Her round breasts filling his hands as she settled on top of him with a cry that made him thrust into her without any finesse. Her scent wrapping around him as he covered her mouth. Two bodies moving in unison toward a release that felt as inevitable as the sunrise.

Marlee reared back in his arms, her eyes huge and her mouth panting. He wanted it to last longer, to give them both so much pleasure that they'd go insane with it. Her orgasm, soundless and squeezing him so intensely that he nearly passed out, drove him over the edge right after her. When he could see past the lights flashing in front of his eyes, her shocked expression filled his vision.

His hands, numb from the strength of his release, began to tingle. He ran them over her, loving the strength beneath her curves. Her slender frame belied the muscles it took to do her work. As he caressed her, he grew hard again. Or maybe it never stopped. She certainly could wring everything out of him. He wouldn't mind.

Marlee suddenly whooshed out air, blinking a few times and shaking her head.

"I'm hearing ringing. Or angels singing."

He smiled at her words, pulling her down for a quick kiss, then lingering. When he was temporarily satisfied, he leaned her back only enough to respond.

"I'm seeing flashing lights. Or maybe they're stars."

She giggled, pressing her own kiss to him in response. His jeans, halfway down his calves and in a bundle, cut into his skin. She still wore that skintight shirt, the long sleeves twisted, her unclasped bra, her socks, and nothing more. What a pair, in the back of an ancient car. Thank god for that roomy backseat.

He blinked, still trying to clear his vision. He heard those angels too. Was it possible to share post-coital visions? He might have to ask Tess about that, if he got up the nerve.

He pulled her forward again, his mouth finding a special place behind her ear. Pressing his lips there, he enjoyed the way it made her wiggle and squirm against him. He couldn't wait to push her back and cover her.

The lights shone brighter, and the angels' voices grew louder. This time, it would be even better than before.

"All right, kids, it's time to zip up and come out. Slowly, please, and keep your hands where I can see them."

An authoritative knock accompanying the voice sounded on the roof of the car, and Jake felt everything shrink in response. Marlee jumped, and stark terror spread over her features until she was paler than any ghost.

>>>>>

"Fuck, I'm sorry, Jake. Really sorry. I didn't see your personal vehicle, and I didn't recognize this one. With all that fog on the inside, I thought it was just some kids." Lankowski grinned, and he didn't look in the least bit apologetic.

Jake felt the redness creep up his face. This was so damned embarrassing. To be found by a fellow deputy, making out behind the diner.

Thank god he hadn't shown up a few minutes earlier.

He glanced across at the old sedan where Marlee sat in the front seat, her hands on the steering wheel like she was about to tear out of the parking lot. Luckily, she couldn't. He had her keys in his pocket. Along with her torn thong.

At least Lankowski had given them time to yank clothes on, politely turning away as Marlee pushed open the back door on the far side to tug on her jeans. Jake shoved open the opposite door, directly into the bright lights from the patrol vehicle. He'd been able to get his jeans pulled up in the back seat, shoving the condom in his back pocket because he couldn't think of what to do with it.

Thankfully, Lankowski was willing to let things go, no questions asked other than an inquiry about whether or not Marlee was okay. He was curious about her, but when he didn't ask her name, she jumped into the driver's seat as fast as a bullet. Jake saw the moment she realized her keys were still missing. She all but slammed her head into the side window.

This would be the stuff of legends. He couldn't wait to see how much ribbing he'd get over this. His ten-year-plus reputation of being the squeaky-clean one, the one never caught in stupid or compromising positions, was officially over.

But damn, it had been worth it. He stared at Marlee, wishing she'd lose the end-of-the-world stare and turn to him. He could reassure her that everything would be okay.

"Seriously, Jake. You have a house with a bedroom. I assume it has a bed in it. You're not a teenager. You're nuts." Lankowski turned to look at the object of Jake's interest. "But I can understand the inspiration. Who is she?"

"Listen, Paul, can you please lose all memory of this? Like, this never happened? The lady would appreciate it, and I'd owe you."

Lankowski swiveled his head to look back at him, grinning from ear to ear. "Owe me, like how much? Like working my shift during the big game? Or maybe on crazy night?"

Jake nodded, sighing inside. Oh yeah, he'd never hear the end of this.

Lankowski slapped him on the shoulder. "Consider it done. Though I can't speak for Dolores, since she heard it all on the dispatch feed. Or the lieutenant, who, I'm sure, will read it on the night report. And you know, anyone else who was working tonight who heard the calls too." He smiled again, even wider. "But me? Not a word."

He laughed out loud, drawing Marlee's attention to them. Jake gave her what he hoped was a reassuring smile. In the bright searchlight, he was sure she could see it. She did not look reassured.

The squawk of the radio sent Lankowski in the direction of his patrol car. He responded to the call, then looked back at Jake.

"You know, Kermarrec, if you're feeling good enough to," he made a crude gesture, the pantomime of which there was no question, "you should be able to come back to work. Just saying."

He laughed again, killed the searchlight as he climbed into his vehicle, and drove away with a friendly wave in Marlee's direction.

Not that she saw it, Jake noticed. Her head was down, pressed against hands clutching the wheel in front of her. She didn't appear to be crying, but Jake wouldn't blame her if she was.

When she didn't raise her head, Jake walked over to her car, leaning over to pull on the driver door, which, of course, didn't open. But it did make her look up at him.

Pools of grey-blue stared back at him, full of sorrow and tears. Did she regret this? He was sorry about the lack of finesse, but not about the act itself. Making love with Marlee Cruiz was spiritual as much as physical. And he wanted to experience it again, and soon.

Chapter 13

The digital display flicked off and darkness settled back in. Three twenty-one in the morning. Again. Early Monday morning like today or on any morning, it was the same. Would it ever get any easier?

Marlee's eyes readjusted from the brief burst of the clock's light and traced the vague patterns in the popcorn coating of the ceiling. Enough illumination seeped around the blind from the weak security light to cast shadows and form faces.

Her mother. Her father. Her family. And later, the one face she swore she'd always treasure and one day again protect, unlike before. She didn't need to look at the pictures to know that face as well as her own.

The echoes of empty promises and futile actions made her loneliness more profound. There was no one she could trust, no one she could reach out to, and no shoulder for her to cry on. A nagging voice in her head reminded her that it didn't have to be this way. One phone call and she'd be surrounded with support, or at least she'd like to hope so. But what if her family didn't forgive her? They were paragons of virtue with high ideals and standards.

Worse yet, what if they'd forgotten all about her?

She wouldn't think about that now. Couldn't afford to think about it. She had her work, her life, and sometimes, she had hope. She had to focus on the hope. A picture of Jake's face flashed in her mind, and she pushed it away with regret. He wouldn't be a part of her future.

Sleep would never return, fleeing on rapid wings as it did almost every night around this hour. Tossing and turning was a meaningless exercise. Pushing back the covers with more resignation than anger, Marlee got vertical before she could wallow in self-pity. At this time of night, the apartment closed its walls in tight around her, suffocating in their stark emptiness, and the only thing that pushed them back was light. Flicking on the switch in the bedroom as she passed the doorway, she moved through the small unit, hitting every light until the place blazed like midday. At least the walls receded.

The bathroom came last, its overly big mirror commanding the wall over the sink. Usually she tried to avoid it at any hour, but with the stark overhead light blaring, her face was impossible to miss. Without make-up, so were the scars.

"You're a worthless bitch, you know it? And ugly too now. Hey, I guess you'll always remember me. Remember this too, bitch. I'll always get even."

He'd laughed harshly as he said the words, taking pleasure in her pain. She'd never forget the sadistic glint in his eyes or the way he'd lunged at her, as if he could have shaken off his guards and killed her without any remorse. His brutality knew no limits, and that memory would live in her mind forever.

Her eyes stared back at her, overly huge and their usual light blue appearing more washed out in the brilliant light. They almost matched the smudges of gray coloring her skin from lack of sleep. Disappointment did that, robbed you of sleep and hope and life.

She wouldn't think about that. She'd vowed that she'd make it right, and she would. If only she could catch a break.

"You look like hell."

Talking to her reflection in the mirror didn't seem to help. Would her family recognize her now? She turned to the side, trying to get a true picture of her profile. It too had changed, she suspected. Only her eyes looked the same, and she took care to hide those behind dark glasses whenever she could in public. Examining the roots of her hair, she realized it was time again to get out the hair dye. Bliss would be happy to color it for her, trading nails or a massage for the work, but she might ask questions. And Marlee hated those kinds of questions.

Backing away from the mirror, she turned for the only other room, the combined space intended to contain living and dining room and efficiency kitchen. Her limited furniture was utilitarian and multipurpose. The table and two chairs she'd bought at a big box store could be folded to fit in the trunk of a larger car. Other furniture was rented. She cooked in one pot and one pan, ate off one place setting of dishes, and used one set of flatware. The walls were bare. There was no television.

Spartan, adequate for survival, and easy to move. Her only extravagances were her laptop with its small printer, her cell phone, and her coffeemaker. She turned on the first, picked up the second from its charging station, and pressed the button to heat water in the third. It was the same routine for her most early mornings, working, searching, debating, until frustration or her first client at the spa required her to turn away.

She spent her money where it mattered, though recently, progress had slowed to almost nil and the news hadn't been good.

"Are you sure you want to continue this, Ms. Cruiz?" The gravelly voice on the other end of the phone had asked this same question almost every week when he called. She'd only met him in person once, and she suspected the rasp was due to years of chain-smoking, a habit he evidently replaced with chain-gum-chewing. He punctuated the question each week with a pop of the wad currently housed in his cheek.

"Yes, please keep looking." At some point, it had to pay off, right?

Tangy and sharp, the aroma of brewing coffee drew her, even as the laptop whirred to attention. Her fingers ran over the cell phone, activating its screen of notifications. Though why she bothered, she wasn't sure. Few people knew how to reach her. It wasn't like she had any friends.

Today the phone mocked her once more. Jake said he wanted them to be friends, or that's what he said before disaster struck. What if he had forgotten all about her too? After Saturday night, she wondered if he'd seek her out. Sunday passed, and to distract her wandering thoughts, she dug deeper into her computer research. No call from Jake cut into her day. After twenty-four hours, she felt resigned. The embarrassment of that evening was more than he wanted to think about, and he dismissed her along with it.

Her work schedule for the next day popped up on the phone. Jake was still on it. Things had changed between them, and she couldn't trust the feelings he generated in her. Even if he was more than willing to have sex with her.

The humiliation of that night made her cringe, even now. His friend, the cop who stopped them, all but took a picture of their compromising position. Even from a distance, she could hear the ragging Jake got, and he didn't look pleased about it. He was even less happy when she hit the road afterwards, following her all the way back to her apartment and idling in the parking lot until she rounded the corner, out of sight. When she looked out her window in the dark, he still waited. It wasn't until she turned on the lights that he finally drove away.

Would he have followed her up the stairs to express his displeasure? She didn't think he'd be like that, but she didn't trust her own instincts when it came to men. Look at how wrong she'd been in the past. She couldn't afford any more mistakes in her life.

But Jake was different, she was sure of it.

A mocking little voice silenced her thoughts. She was developing a serious case of the hots for a cop. Could the world get any stranger?

Now that the idea was out there, she couldn't help but explore it. The coffee burned on the first sip, and she blew on it, thinking about the soft exhalations of Jake's breath as she told him to breathe through any discomfort. Her hips shifted against the abrupt edge of the kitchen counter, mimicking the shifts he made on the table as she worked on him. The heat of the mug made her fingers tingle, not too unlike how they tingled when she touched the coarse hairs on his arms and legs. Would there be a light dusting across his chest as well? She never had a chance to check.

Maybe it was purely sexual. If it was, a good roll in the back seat should have burned him out of her system. His cowboy-lean body wasn't her usual type, not that she'd been discriminating enough to have a type in her younger years. In the past eleven years, there'd been no type whatsoever. She'd worn out celibacy, if the low burn of lust racing through her body was any indication.

And the man kissed like a demon. He tasted like raw energy, spicy and dangerous, the flavor like his scent, heady but controlled. He drove her to an orgasm that still left her vibrating at the mere thought of it. Assuring herself it was just self-imposed celibacy that made it so spectacular wouldn't work any longer.

That dinner had been a bad idea from the beginning. She'd sensed it, but still, she went. If he saw her for the fraud she was, the consequences would be tragic. It was harder and harder to hide her true self behind the mask of her everyday existence, and she found herself longing to be real again, without the artifices she'd adopted for survival.

Jake's megawatt smile flashed in her mind. That smile hinted at the easy-going guy he probably was when he was with friends and family. She saw some of that charm on Saturday. His name came up often and with great affection when the girl tribe discussed the wolf pack. It seemed that the whole community respected and appreciated him, if the comments about him since the accident were any indication. A homegrown boy, doing good in his 'hood.

Damned if that wasn't sexy too. Her audible sigh echoed off the walls and bounced back, mocking her. The t-shirt she wore to sleep suddenly felt too tight on her breasts and heat made her wonder if her panties would combust. Yeah, she had it bad. And now she had empty hours of alone time to ponder how good the bad things were between them.

>>>>>

"Marlee, are you sure you're not coming down with something? You look – funny."

Bliss frowned at her, and Marlee shook her head, putting a serene smile on her face. It did nothing to calm her on the inside, but at least it might fool her boss.

If only she could fool Jake into thinking that whatever was between them didn't matter. How long before he saw through her carefully constructed façade and learned the truth?

"I still think you look different, but I can't put my finger on it. Tess, don't you think our girl looks different?"

Of all of the customers to have today. She could yell at the fates for this, but it wouldn't do any good. Tess wanted a pedicure, and she wanted Marlee to do it. If she kept her head down, Marlee hoped to avoid eye contact and with it, conversation.

No one said anything, and she hoped she'd skated by for now. She knew Bliss would continue to push it, but she could hold firm and not respond. If she said anything, she knew it would only reveal her problem.

Jake's next massage was at the end of the day today. She'd left him a polite voicemail yesterday, giving him the name of another therapist and reminding him that she planned to cancel his appointment. He didn't respond. When she tried to erase him from the schedule, Bliss had a fit and reminded her that the customer was always right. Unless he cancelled, she would have to wait for him. Maybe she could talk sense into him when they were further away from the heat of the moment.

She was more afraid that he would convince her otherwise.

She buffed Tess's bare toes, grateful if surprised no one had continued their interrogation. When the front door's chimes jingled, a collective sigh ran through the women in the spa, and Marlee glanced up to see the reason.

"Powers, I didn't expect you to meet me here. I'm not done."

Marlee froze for a second before gently putting Tess's foot down and rising. She turned toward the back of the spa. She could buy herself a few minutes. The man wouldn't stay long.

Silence reigned behind her, a passionate kiss, no doubt. Powers and Tess were in love in all caps, and you only had to look at the two of them together to realize that nothing would break that bond.

"Darn, I wanted you to meet Marlee. She's terrific."

"I came to see you. Getting buffed and polished again, my love? Is this for me?"

The playful exchange made Marlee pause out of sight in the back corridor. She could hear the smile in man's voice, echoed by Tess who was all but purring in response.

"I used to get my nails done regularly and a whole lot more before you."

"You had a life before me?" Teasing tone, evident smile.

"Ah, but that was mere existence, my love. My life began when I met you."

Around the spa, women chuckled. Powers laughed outright, along with Tess. They sounded so perfectly happy. The man continued the repartee, and his delight rang in every tone and word.

Marlee sighed. What did that feel like, to be settled and happy? Powers could tell her if she was brave enough to ask him.

"And you are here because? I mean really, why?" Tess queried her other half and he chuckled.

"Serena and Dane want to have a barbeque this weekend, since the weather is supposed to be nice. I told them I thought it would be a great idea, but I wanted to check with you first."

"You could have texted me, or called on this handy little device called a cell phone."

"Ah, but then I wouldn't have the opportunity to do this." Silence. He was probably kissing her.

More chuckles and sighs from the peanut gallery. Even Bliss simpered. Marlee traced the seam on the arm of her shirt, up and down in a steady rhythm. Lucky woman. Lucky man.

She was the unluckiest person on the planet, and she only had herself to blame.

The clock stood at three minutes to four. Jake was usually here by now. She wasn't sure how she felt at the moment. Should she be glad that perhaps he took her advice to see someone else for his massages? Her body revolted, clenching in pain. No, profound disappointment was more like it.

"I don't agree with your action, Marlee. He's a customer here. Why would you send him across town to the competition? I don't get it." Bliss rapped a pen on the desk behind the counter in obvious disappointment.

She didn't need to explain herself, but Marlee did anyway. She wasn't ready to move on yet, and she needed this job.

"I believe Deputy Kermarrec's recovery will benefit from someone else's therapy. I may have overstepped my abilities on this one."

"Bullshit." The word came out of Bliss's mouth so fast, Marlee blinked. "This is about Saturday night, isn't it? It was you."

Marlee wondered if the blood draining out of her face made the shadows more obvious under her make-up. She opened her mouth to respond, but the other woman already waved away her denial.

"Don't even pretend. I heard. Hell, half the town's heard, and the other half just hasn't because their hearing aids are turned down low or they're on a cruise. Jake and his mystery woman. Her description sounds exactly like you."

Marlee glanced up, realizing terror had settled in the pit of her stomach. She'd made a bigger mistake than she thought.

Instead of carrying on, though, Bliss leaned across the high desk and patted Marlee's arm. "Don't worry about it, dear. I'm not going to give you up. No one knows your name. Jake was all macho mysterious about you himself that night, and while the other deputy could probably pick you out of a line up, I doubt he'll do it. He's loyal to Jake. They all are. If he's keeping a secret, they'll keep it for him too."

The bile rose in her throat, threatening to bring up the yogurt and cereal she'd tried to swallow for a late lunch. A line up. The idea made her wish she'd stayed home in bed today.

The door chimes jingled, and the man they were discussing stood in the frame, the sun lighting him from behind so he looked larger than life. His sunglasses still covered his eyes, but Marlee had no doubt about where he was staring. Directly at her. She felt the drill of energy in every nerve of her body.

"Jake, so good to see you. I heard you had a little bit of an adventure on Saturday night. Care to share with me who the luck lady was?" Bliss put on her most coquettish smile, tucking her chin into her palm and staring at him with feigned innocence.

Damn. And this would be it. He'd confirm it, and that would be that. She'd be mortified. She'd be moving on again, though where she'd go this time she had no idea.

Jake walked up to the tall counter, leaning his elbows on it as he swept off his sunglasses with a flourish. His devilish smile focused on Bliss, but Marlee knew the show was for her benefit. Bliss leaned forward expectantly, and Jake did the same as if he was sharing a great secret. He smiled, wide and wolfish.

"Ah, Bliss, I wish I could tell you. But you know how it goes. A gentleman never kisses and tells. The lady in question is mine to protect, and that's exactly what I'm going to do." He waggled his eyebrows, and Bliss gave a surprised laugh.

Marlee stood in shock, waiting for the truth to come out. Her poker face was in place, she made sure of that. When Jake swung in her direction, he gave her a fast nod.

"Marlee, good to see you. Did you have a nice weekend? Any excitement in your life? Sorry I'm a little late. Let's get this massage on the table."

And he strode past her down the hall to the treatment room, whistling.

Damn the man.

Chapter 14

Marlee rubbed lotion on Gabby's forearms, massaging muscles as she went along. With her baby due in less than a month, her serenity made Marlee yearn for that same kind of peace.

How long would her suffering continue? Massaging wrist and fingers more deeply, she thought about the report she received last night. It made her heart beat faster, even now.

"I think we have the most promising lead so far." The man on the phone didn't bother to express any personal excitement at the news. Maybe he was getting tired of this hunt. Marlee never would. To her last breath, she would forge ahead, even if it took the rest of her life.

The man had continued, "I was able to get some information that points us to a house in San Jose. It's in a not-so-great neighborhood, which means I need to get in there without being noticed, and I'll stand out. Give me a little time."

When she didn't respond, he continued as if he didn't expect her to argue. "Not a lot of time, but some. I should have something for you, say, by Friday at the latest."

When she belatedly thanked him and agreed that this was, in fact, great news, his tone dropped in grave cautious warning.

"Ms. Cruiz, I need to remind you that identification is only that – confirmation of location at that time. I can't guarantee the person you're interested in will remain at that location. I also can't help you make contact and in fact, I would discourage you from doing so, given the circumstances. You need legal help at that point, ma'am, not a private investigator."

An involuntary shiver ran through her at the thought. She didn't trust the legal system, and why should she? But what options did she have? She thanked him and hung up before he could continue his explanation about how he would get confirmation of the target's identity, as he put it.

She didn't care how he did it. She just wanted results. And now, maybe she would finally have some. The next steps would be up to her.

"You seem keyed up."

Marlee snapped her eyes to Gabby's face, finding the woman staring up at her with open curiosity.

"I'm so sorry. I wasn't paying attention to you. I'll focus now."

Gabby laughed, waving a dismissive hand as she resettled herself in the nail chair. "No problem. You're always so focused. Quiet, but focused. I was wondering what, or rather, who put that glow on your cheeks."

Emotion put it there, but she couldn't reveal what was behind it. People would want to understand why she was feeling this way, a mixture of trepidation and budding hope, and that was another thing she couldn't talk about. She buffed nails, repeating the action on both of Gabby's hands, letting the actions calm her.

"Of course, perhaps thoughts of a certain male client are the reason for that color, huh?" Gabby met Marlee's eyes with a full grin lighting her features.

Marlee's thoughts of her news last night slipped away in a flash, replaced by the looming presence of Jake. At his last massage, he'd asked her common questions about where she did her training and where she'd worked. When delivery of her vague answers took all of thirty seconds, he hadn't say anything for a time. Then he talked about his profession of law enforcement and how he always wanted to be a cop, saying that the line between right and wrong was clear, drawn by the law.

What would he say if he knew her real reason for long hours and tight guard on her privacy? His stare probed like the sharp point of a dentist's tool as he paid for his session. She didn't respond, controlling her features and offering a faint fake smile that made him frown. Even in that casual conversation, the sparks flew between them.

The touch of his skin lingered on her skin for hours after each massage, no matter how many times she washed her hands. That never happened to her. Only Jake brought out those sensations, but he wouldn't understand her motives and drive. Chemistry aside, they had nothing in common other than hot sexual attraction. The fact that he would walk through the front door and lay on the table for his next treatment mere minutes from now did nothing to help the pounding of her heart.

"And now you're blushing, if that's possible. Why do you wear so much make-up, anyway? You have such gorgeous features."

Marlee closed her eyes against Gabby's words, hiding the one thing that could still give her away. Her eyes shot open in surprise when strong fingers closed over her own and stopped her.

Gabby squeezed once but didn't let go, and Marlee could do nothing but stare back at her. What could she say? How could she explain any of it? This woman wouldn't understand. No one did.

"We're friends, right?" Gabby squeezed the hand she held once as if confirming the answer she assumed she knew.

Marlee lifted her shoulders in a shrug, but never completed the gesture. Sharp tears pricked her eyes and she turned away for a damp towel as if she intended to all along.

"You know you can talk to me about anything. Trust me, I'm never going to think the worse of you. I feel a great sadness in you, and Serena sensed it too. Sometimes you look scared, as if you expect the world to explode around you at any moment. Tess mentioned that your spirit is heavy with worry, and she would know, being connected to that other world so closely. You know that any of us would be happy to help you, if you confide in us. The men too, I'm sure. Dane and Powers and my Rick are the best, and with all of us come the rest of the girl tribe and the wolf pack. You have people on your side."

Disengaging her hand and using the towel to wipe excess lotion from Gabby's arms, Marlee let the lavender fragrance flow in and out with each breath, hoping it would calm her. Yes, they would all judge her if they knew the truth. The women would disapprove of her weakness, but it was the men she feared even more. They would convict her without benefit of a judge and jury, not that having those made any difference. And Jake would be standing at the front of the pack, hot sex or not.

The room closed in on her dark thoughts, and she spun abruptly and slipped her hands into the pockets of her work apron. The need for escape was overwhelming, from this place if not from her turbulent mind. Tight fists helped her to focus on getting out with a minimum of theatrics. Gabby would want to know what was wrong, and she could say without lying that she felt more than a little ill right now. Her stomach heaved and it was all she could do not to break into a run for the bathroom.

"I've upset you. I'm so, so very sorry. Marlee, please. Are you in trouble? Tell me what's wrong."

But she couldn't. Didn't Gabby see that? Ducking down the hallway, she registered the instant surprise on the face of her boss. The area where staff kept their purses was blessedly empty of anyone other than Bliss, and she grabbed for her bag and dug for her keys even as she whirled back to make her escape. Bliss blocked her exit, though, curiosity turning to concern as she examined Marlee's face.

"Hey, what's wrong? You look like you've seen a ghost. What can I do for you?" Bliss put out a hand as if to help support her, but all Marlee could think was that this hand would slow her down. She needed to get out of there.

What was she doing here, in this town? She all but ran past Gabby on her flight through the spa, grabbing the door to the street and yanking it open as Miss Helen Sinclair tottered up. The old woman let out a surprised yelp, which was enough warning for Marlee to avoid bowling her over as she made her escape.

"I'm sorry, Miss Helen. I'm so sorry." Her words came out in trembling gibberish, and the old woman called after her in confusion.

She couldn't run fast enough, couldn't get her feet to move at anything past what felt like slow motion. The heaves of her stomach increased, and with them, her cravings for all things bad and her sense of panic that she would fail grew. She needed support. She needed help.

Her car sat three blocks over in a city lot, and she crossed the street between cars and dodged traffic. Someone honked, and she heard her name called out in an incredulous male voice. But nothing would make her stop. Jake would demand to know why she ran out on his appointment. He wouldn't know how deeply she'd miss caressing him.

Her key added more scratches to the scuffed and abused door before she got it in the lock. Her hands shook as she cranked the engine to life, and she tore out of the parking lot as if the cops were behind her. Glancing up as she headed out of town, she saw an SUV match her turns and speed up as if trying to reach her, and it took her only a second to confirm who was behind the wheel.

Taking the entrance ramp to the freeway and tucking in front of a logging truck that would slow him down, she put her foot to the floor and felt the old car rattle and give her everything it had.

Maybe there was another beaten-up rundown old gray sedan with a scratched dark green driver door in town. But Jake doubted it.

Maybe she just ran out to do an errand. She was rigidly punctual for every appointment, a trait he appreciated. Maybe she wasn't going far and would return in time for his massage. Too many unknowns always made him wary. Today, a pang of unease for Marlee overweighed his scruples about chasing after her.

The logging truck accelerated slowly, almost as if the driver knew that an officer of the law was behind him, even in a personal vehicle. He had yet to reach cruising speed, and as a view of the road in front of the logger opened on a curve, it was empty. He'd lost her.

Slowing to pace the truck and pull off at the next exit, disappointment ate at him. She'd run across Main Street as if a monster had been after her, ignoring his call as he drove toward the city lot to park for his appointment. Panic filled her features as she glanced at his SUV, her legs churning beneath her.

What did he know about her, anyway? He'd made a point of checking what kind of vehicle she bought after her junker hit the metal scrap heap, purely for professional reasons. But checking into more of her background was against the rules. More unknowns raced around in his brain, none of them making him feel better.

What was it about this woman that distracted him so much? Doing his master's homework last night, his mind kept drifting to her pale complexion, the hair that he was sure she dyed falling in a dark curtain. The layer of make-up did nothing to distract from features that weren't symmetrical but made more intriguing by their differences.

Pulling off the ramp for Flynn's Crossing, he cruised down Main Street and found a big parking spot in the city lot. The thought of Marlee made his heart picked up its pace as he walked toward Main Street. The door to the spa loomed ahead of him and his heart rate sped up in anticipation.

"…but I'm not sure what I said to make her bolt like that. Honestly, Bliss, I have no idea."

He stopped two steps inside the door, letting the wave of misgivings wash over him. He'd been right. Something had happened to Marlee.

"What's wrong?"

Turning toward him, Gabby wore her pinched worry between her eyebrows, but said nothing.

"Jake, I'm sorry. Marlee just ran out." Bliss paused, her professional expression collapsing into apparent confusion. "I don't know if she's coming back for your appointment."

It wasn't an errand. She'd taken off, and he hadn't been able to catch up to her. And the fact that no one seemed to know the reason made it even worse.

"What happened?" The gruff tone in his voice surprised even him, and both women eyed him with sudden care. Gabby, who knew him better, wore a slight smile with her puzzlement, but answered first.

"She was doing my nails, and we were talking about trust and friendship. Or actually, I was talking and she got upset. The next thing I knew, she'd flung open the door and ran out like she was wanted or something." She stopped as if jolted. "She's not wanted for anything, is she, Jake?"

He hadn't broken any rules by checking to see if there were any open warrants. Maybe he should have looked a little harder.

"No, she isn't wanted for anything to my knowledge." He put a comforting hand on Gabby's back. "I'm sure it's nothing. Maybe she suddenly didn't feel well." But then why had she been going the opposite direction from her apartment?

"I tried calling her cell phone, Jake, but it goes straight to voicemail. I'm sorry about your massage. We'll comp your next visit, okay? I have two standing appointments next, or I'd take care of you myself."

There was nothing wrong with Bliss. She was an attractive if mouthy woman who ran her business with efficiency. She knew her stuff, he expected. But the idea of her touching him, massaging him the way Marlee did, left him feeling mildly ill.

"That's all right, Bliss. I'm sure there was a very good reason. Will you please call me when you hear from her?"

His mind whirled in growing frustration. Where would she go in that direction? Abandoning a client seemed out of character for her, as was leaving without any explanation to her boss. As he backed away from the spa's front desk, he processed options for finding her, and none of them felt right.

Gabby turned toward him, her face worried as she ran comfort-seeking hands over her baby belly.

"Jake, will you check on her? Someone has to. She's all alone, you know."

He barely heard her, pulling the door open with more force than necessary and catching it just before it banged into the wall. Reassuring Gabby with quick words thrown over his shoulder, he strode toward his SUV at a fast pace that didn't favor his back for the first time in two months.

>>>>>

Jake drove for hours without conscious effort, the activity so much second nature to him as he scanned the road ahead and the mirrors behind out of years of habit. If something looked amiss, he would notice it immediately. At least, he thought he would. His active mind was busy with Marlee.

He'd driven from one end of town to the other, by her apartment, by the city lot, and around again. On the off chance her new set of old wheels had broken down, he followed the freeway for a few miles until he got to the county border without seeing her on the side of the road. Too many arteries exited the freeway, and he had no clue where she might have gotten off. Hell, she might have driven all the way to Sacramento or beyond. He had no way of knowing what she was thinking. He doubted she acted without considering her actions.

They had this bond, though, and he was damned if he could figure out why. Her blushes colored one cheek brighter than the other. Her wide blue eyes often carried a startled expression, like she'd bolt in a second. When her breathing accelerated, he watched the rapid rise and fall of her breasts. They were the perfect size, in his opinion, matching her slender frame.

But then she was thin, too thin. He'd only caught a quick look at her bare forearms while she massaged him, her customary long sleeves back in evidence by the time she came out in front, and they looked as fragile as bird's wings. It was interesting that such delicate limbs carried so much strength when her hands worked on him.

And there it was again, another twitch of agony. The mere memory of her touching him, and his zipper pressed too hard against equally hard flesh. He needed a cold shower for about an hour. Discouragement drove him home. He figured he could continue to check her apartment throughout the evening until she came back. Where else would she go?

He pulled into his driveway, turned off the engine, and stared at his little house. What would Marlee think of it? It probably would seem like a castle. He'd been called out to that lousy apartment complex for domestic disputes and felony violations more times than he cared to think about, and the units were small and dark and poorly maintained. Some of the tenants were less than savory too.

She should move out of there. It was a dangerous place in a less than good area. She should move into town. He'd help her find a more suitable place.

"What are you thinking, idiot? You get horny for the woman, and all of a sudden, you want to take over her life?"

His voice echoed inside the confines of the SUV. This is what she reduced him to, talking to himself, sitting in his driveway with a hard-on that would make walking the short distance to his front door, stepping inside, and easing the zipper down on his jeans a painful experience at best.

He pressed a fist to his forehead, willing his body to relax. Any more tension and he'd bring on back spasms. And each time that happened, it was a step in the wrong direction, away from complete recovery and away from his goal of returning to work.

Of course, that would mean a step away from Marlee too.

Pushing open the door so hard that it recoiled and swung back at him, he put out one booted foot to hold it open. That stretched his jeans the wrong way and he leaped out of the car before he yelped. The key didn't want to fit into the lock on his front door, and when he finally wrestled that open and slipped inside, it was all he could do to lean back against it as it closed and ease open his jeans for some much-needed space.

He stroked himself once, thinking of Marlee. It was just physical attraction. The woman oozed sex even in her dark garb and stark hair and make-up. She was the absence of color, and yet, he couldn't help but feel drawn into her.

He stroked again, wondering if he needed to end this in that cold shower. Not that he thought it would help. And getting off would feel unsatisfactory unless Marlee was right there with him. What would it be like, taking her hard and fast against this door? Or would they make the few steps to the bedroom and get horizontal instead? His fingers tightened as he pictured what he expected her creamy skin to look like as she writhed beneath him. He hadn't been able to see enough of it in the back seat of her car.

The knob turned behind him and the door he leaned against jiggled. Foolishly, lost in his haze of sexual energy, he wondered if Marlee had followed him home.

"Jake? Something's wrong with your door. I can't seem to get it open."

The door pushed against his back once more, and his sexual fog blew away on a gust of reality. His mother. He reached a hand behind him, keeping pressure on the door, and flipped the lock shut. Then he pushed off and headed for the bedroom.

"I'll be right there, Ma. Just changing clothes."

Not that his mother hadn't seen her share of woodies in her life, both from his father and from the boys as hormonal teenagers, but that was a long time ago. As an adult, it would embarrass him.

He kicked off his boots and pushed his pants off in a quick movement that caused him a pang of discomfort. Dropping the jeans into his laundry basket and pulling on a pair of baggy old sweatpants, he felt things flag and wither. Nothing like the thought of your mother finding you with your piece in your hand to deflate a man.

Checking himself in the hallway mirror, he was relieved to see that things looked almost normal in the worn clothes. He flipped open the lock and pulled the door wide, opening his mouth to greet his mother as she frowned at him on the front steps.

"What is wrong with your door? I know you never lock it when you're home, and the handle turned, but the door wouldn't budge. What's going on?"

She traipsed past him and into the living room, dropping an array of bags on the dining table on top of his schoolwork. He flinched as the neat stacks shifted and mixed. Then the labels on the bags registered and the flinch became a full-on cringe.

Emie turned to face him, her gaze sweeping him up and down as if assessing his current physical condition. Even though there was nothing to be self-conscious about, he felt the blush of embarrassment start at the roots of his overly-long hair. He suddenly wished he was wearing his uniform. At least that gave him the appearance of authority.

"You look good, flushed, but good. Were you doing the exercises the physical therapist gave you?"

He wanted to go with that excuse, but this was his mother. He had a hard time lying to her. Half-lies weren't much easier, but he'd take his chances.

"I just got back from a massage. The therapist, she's very good. My pain lessens and then I can exercise. So yes, in a round-about way, I'm working out."

Ma eyed him thoughtfully. He wondered if she read his mind and could see him the way he'd been only moments ago, engorged and thinking about Marlee.

He shouldn't have thought her name. His body stirred to life again.

His mother, though, seemed satisfied with whatever she saw, and turned to the bags on the table. With a hum of satisfaction, she began unpacking a colorful assortment of items made out of fabric and other stuff.

"I bought you a few things, you know, to brighten up your place. It's so dark and empty and sterile. Look, don't you love this quilt?"

A quilt? It wasn't his style. Color wasn't his style.

"Ma, I know what you're trying to do. Deke's gotten himself engaged, and now you're working on marrying me off." He didn't want to be married. Sex, on the other hand, was something he wanted, and he wanted it again with Marlee.

The twitch in his sweatpants momentarily distracted him from the somewhat convoluted path of his mother's response.

"...and you won't be able to attract a woman by being a hermit, living in a dark cave, and only coming out to growl like a bear through your shifts."

Emie returned to pulling out items, currently holding small framed prints in one hand and a pillow in the other, as if comparing them.

He tried again. "I don't need anything. I don't want anything. My house is fine the way it is." And he had no prospective women on the horizon, unless you counted Marlee.

Another twitch, getting harder this time. He shifted so that his body couldn't be seen in profile by his mother.

She turned to him and frowned. He would have expected disappointment, which in turn would make him feel guilty. But she looked honestly angry, and an angry Emie was a force to be reckoned with, since it happened so rarely.

"Son, I am very disappointed in you. This is not a life that's healthy for you, living alone and isolating yourself the way you do. What about companionship and friendship?

What about having a life outside of work? What about love?"

He didn't want this to become a family bonding moment, and he turned for the kitchen, opened the refrigerator door, and stared inside to buy himself some time. He could hear his mother's toe tapping on the wood floor, all the more amazing since she was wearing sneakers. She must be truly pissed off with him.

His life was fine the way it was. He loved his work, even if the hours were longer than anyone anticipated. He had the wolf pack, and by extension, the girl tribe. He had plenty of friends who stepped up for him, as evidenced by their recent support since his injuries. He had family close by and a community he'd know since his first memories. He had a lot.

And he was lonely. The sudden pang of realization made him straighten faster than he should have, and a shudder of pain lanced through his back and made him wince.

A small hand rested on his lower back almost immediately. He hadn't noticed his mother move across the room to him. His observational skills were deteriorating, another good reason to get back to work as soon as possible. He used to be sharp. He felt duller than a rusty knife now, his thoughts unable to get past the fact that he was lonely.

"You know, you were always the one I worried about the most. You have this over-zealous sense of how you expect the world to be. All you boys have the same strong sense of right and wrong, and that's good. That's the way we raised you. But in you, it's all black and white, with no shades of gray in between. That's not the way the world works, Jake. And you need to get used to it."

Chapter 15

Marlee let the freeway traffic flow around her old sedan as she climbed the hills toward Flynn's Crossing. She was sorry she'd run out of the spa with no explanation, but she'd felt herself spiraling downward into the abyss. The cravings were emotional more than physical. The need for escape, to hide from pain and disappointment, was something she would always fight.

She made the half hour dash to the meeting in desperation, and the look on her face must have alerted the others that something was very wrong. After they recited the obligatory opening phrases and promises of anonymity, they turned to her as one. And they waited.

She didn't even bother with the preliminaries. It burst out of her before she could stop herself.

"I had sex with a man."

Silence. Some of the others looked at her with congratulations on their faces, and most were puzzled at her panic.

"How long has it been, Marlee?"

The de facto group leader's pointed question took her by surprise. Usually, discussions followed a protocol that kept probing about people's personal lives off limits until they were ready to share. Since she wasn't sure how to respond, she kept silent and cursed herself for losing verbal control.

"I had to face my own issue like this, you know." The older woman across the circle shook her head in sympathy, cracking a grin that showed off discolored teeth and ragged gums. "I waited, you know? Like a long time. Like denying myself anything that I found pleasurable meant I was strong. But it doesn't work like that."

Several other attendees had nodded in agreement, moving their stares between Marlee and the other woman as if watching a tennis match to see who would win the point. When Marlee still said nothing, the older woman took a sip of her coffee, frowned her displeasure at the taste, and continued.

"I kind of OD'd on it when I went back to it, and that was bad too. Jumped from one guy to the next, trying to have as much sex as possible to replace the highs from before. But then, I only waited four months."

Cries and gasps rang out from other people, some in censure and others chirping in laughter.

"I know, I know, you're supposed to wait a year and all that. But I was horny, you know?" And she laughed at herself in a rough smoker's voice along with everyone else.

When the noise level died down, one by one, all sets of eyes rested back on Marlee, and she sat as still as possible to avoid squirming under their gazes. No one had said anything, and no one repeated the earlier question, until she felt the weight of it force a defensive answer out of her.

"I waited over eleven years."

She swore everyone in the room stopped breathing and inhaled every available molecule of oxygen in the place. Then they all started talking at once.

"Eleven years? But that's…"

"I couldn't, I just couldn't…"

"Why did you wait that long?"

"Are you sure that was…"

Pushing down her embarrassment, Marlee held up a hand and the voices instantly quieted, eager to hear what she wanted to share.

"After what happened to me, I couldn't. I never felt safe. And I never trusted anyone enough to make an exception." She paused, feeling the red blush creep higher on her face and into her scalp. They had heard her story before, so no one would be surprised. "Besides, it seemed like the appropriate amends, given the circumstances. And what if I replace one problem with another?"

A young African-American man to her right had put a hand on her arm and rubbed it consolingly. "I get it, I really do. But you have to move on. Denying yourself everything makes you miserable, not to mention lonely. It gives away all your power. You have to take some back, girl. You know right from wrong now. You won't walk down that same path again."

Power. Everything always came back to that. She'd thought about nothing but that single word since she turned the key in the ignition.

Had she ever felt powerful? As a child, there was a certain cache being the treasured girl. When that collapsed around her, she didn't know where to turn. Her treasure became buried in a cascade of events no one could control. That had been the beginning of the long implosion of her life. True, she hadn't helped matters by acting out, being a brat and shoving away any hint of reconciliation or support offered to her. The spiral continued until she'd ultimately destroyed the best thing that ever happened to her.

How could she have been so stupid? Nothing had changed the outcome, and eleven plus years of remorse and penance had done little to improve her situation. Responsibility like a heavy set of chains wrapped around her, tightening her fingers on the steering wheel as if that alone would answer her question. When she flicked on the turn signal for her exit and drove through the evening quiet outside Flynn's Crossing, she barely saw the streets in front of her.

Celibacy had become comfortable to her, up until that surprising night. She'd always believed anything making her feel deeply would trigger her dependency. Control was critical to avoid problems.

Thoughts of Jake made her yearn to reconsider her choices. It wasn't simply the way his skin felt under her hands or how his muscles tensed and relaxed as she worked. It was the man and what he stood for, even if he would laugh if he knew how opposite the two of them were. Worse than laugh, maybe. His disgust and disappointment would be a hell of a lot worse. Her stomach flopped and churned, and she forced her fingers to loosen their death grip on cracked plastic as the worn shocks of the sedan creaked into the turn for her apartment building.

Night had long since fallen, and two light bulbs in dirty fixtures gave the parking lot a dusky glow. A few windows lit with the glare of television sets, images dancing on blinds and curtains pulled closed against the squalor outside. If she succeeded in her quest, she'd need to move. This was no place to start the next important phase of her life.

The engine rattled to a stop, leaving the inside of the car unnaturally quiet after the constant din. Glancing around at the parking lot, she noted that every other space was filled. It wasn't until she reached for her purse that she noted the big truck parked across the gate to the dumpster, almost hidden in the shadow of the surrounding wall. The driver sat behind the wheel in near darkness.

Her heart rate picked up immediately, its pounding beat forcing too much blood into her brain and making her feel suddenly woozy. She reacted with the same stealth that had served her well up until point years ago when it didn't. Moving slowly, she pushed down the locks on the passenger side doors nearest the vehicle before doing the same on her side. Breathing through her fear, she slid down in her seat and waited.

The truck's driver door opened, but no light came on inside its cab. A hooded man stood but stayed behind the door. Should she run for the apartment? Beep the horn? Scream for her neighbors? Start the car and race out, even if it meant hitting him in the process?

The man waited with the door between them, and she wiped her hands on her jeans and reached into her purse. The can of pepper spray was probably illegal, but it gave her a small sense of control. When the man quietly closed his door and faded into the shadows, she shrank against the panel furthest from him and uncapped the container, putting a shaking finger on the spray nozzle.

Fear hammered her heart. She tightened her hold on the canister. If he came too close, she was ready. She would not be a victim again.

The man reappeared next to her car, staring at her with eyes she couldn't see in the darkness. Damn the apartment manager for being unwilling to create safety here. The stab of anger made her nerves steady. She could do this. She would do anything to survive.

He shook his head, moving again and more quickly now as he rounded the rear of the car. She lost sight of him and had to slide up in her seat to find him again in her rear view mirror. He rounded to the passenger's side and she fought the dim lights to get a better view of his face.

His hand reached for the door handle and he pulled. The door yanked open against its lock, and surprise made her freeze for vital seconds as he dropped down to peer inside. She lifted the can and felt her finger twinge as she pressed the deeply grooved top. When he spoke, she pressed the rest of the way down in delayed shock.

"Marlee, are you all right?"

Jake's eyes squinted in with concern, right before the cloud of pepper spray blocked her view of him.

Fuck, it hurt like hell, even though he'd ducked to the side and only gotten the tail end of it. Thankful that he'd been wearing a heavy hooded sweatshirt against the chill of the night, he still swore when the spray burned his cheek and ear.

"Oh god, I'm so sorry. Jake, I didn't know it was you. I didn't recognize your truck. Are you okay?"

She pulled her sleeve over her hand and raised it as if she planned to pat the sting off his face, and he ducked further away, considering how fast he could jog back to his car and pour his water bottle over the tortured areas.

"Water. This needs to be rinsed. Cold water." He glanced back at her, noting that she still held the canister tightly in her fingers. In the dim parking lot light, shock seemed to hold her prisoner. "You didn't get hit with any back spray, did you?"

She shook her head slowly from side to side, and then much more quickly. Her gaze dropped to the canister and she let go of it fast enough to send it skittering off into the dark under a neighboring car. He grimaced, realizing that he couldn't let it sit there, waiting for the fingers of a curious child to find it.

She ducked back into the car and reappeared with a coffee to-go mug, twisting off the top. That's all his burning face needed, hot liquid to add to the pain. He grabbed her wrists without thought, closing around them to prevent her tossing the contents in his face.

"Hot liquid is a really bad idea right now, Marlee. Really, really bad." He grimaced, attempting to hold his head at an angle that wouldn't encourage any stray drops to fall near his eyes.

"Oh god, I'm so sorry. This is water. There isn't much in here, but it might help." She wiggled the mug in her fingers, and he realized that he had her wrists in a death grip. Loosening his hold, he took the mug from her hand, leaned to the side, and poured the small amount of its contents across his cheek and ear.

He couldn't say anything. He'd felt the effects of pepper spray before, a rite of passage at the training academy. Over the years on a couple of occasions, errant spray hit him when they were taking down a particularly unruly subject. Since the academy, though, this felt the worst.

"Here, come inside. I can wash it off you. Or you can take a shower. I'm so sorry." She repeated her litany as her fingers closed around his wrist now, her grip unnaturally strong.

Kicking the door of her car shut with her boot, she glanced back at his SUV as she dragged him up the walk. "Is your car locked? I wouldn't want anyone to steal it."

That made him laugh out loud. He was a cop. If someone wanted to steal it, they would truly rue the day. Towing, though, was something else entirely.

"I should move it." He turned back, breaking the hold of her hand by working against those strong fingers. He had a sudden recollection of those fingers working the muscles in his back, gliding dangerously close to his ass as his erection pressed harder against the massage table. That member picked this moment to twitch in his jeans at the memory.

Her fingers yanked the simple keychain and fob free from his hand and she jogged back the short distance to the SUV. He knew what she planned to do, and he thought to intercede, his self-assurance immediately quelled when he rubbed his cheek and fire roared to life once more.

"Shit". Now he had it on his hands too. He put them up in the air, wishing for a cold shower more than anything in his life, as she started the vehicle on the second try, jerked it into gear, and pulled on to a dried out patch that was once lawn. Jumping out, she locked the door and jogged back to him, picking up her purse from where she'd dropped it on the ground as she reached for his hand again.

"Don't touch me." He couldn't control the rough order in his voice. His cheek burned like hell on steroids and now his palms started to itch and torch as well.

The hurt in her expression was instantaneous and hidden almost as fast, but not before he recognized it for what it was. Disappointment.

Jake sighed, pulling in the night air and hoping that the pain would subside. He was almost willing to lay down on the concrete walkway and feel that cold under his cheek.

"It's not you, Marlee. I rubbed my face and now it's on my hands. I don't want to get it on you."

Understanding flooded her expression, and he thought he saw gratefulness too, though it was hard to tell in the dark of the walkway. She turned and hurried toward the building, climbing the stairs two at a time. He followed more slowly, blinking up at the perfect slender curve of her behind as she raced up the steps before him.

Damn, she was something. Maybe they could sort this out, or start over. Like, have a date or something.

Working keys in two locks in rapid succession, she pulled him into her apartment by the sleeve of his sweatshirt, all but flinging the purse across the floor to a folding table in what appeared to be the dining area before reaching for the lower edge of his hoodie.

"Take this off. The bathroom's through there. You can wash your face, or take a shower, or whatever you need. God, Jake, I'm so damned sorry."

She looked full of remorse too. In the sudden bright glow of overhead lights, her skin appeared ghostly white and it wasn't her stark make-up for a change. Shadows dipped and moved across her face, making it look slightly out of balance, as if one cheek was different from the other. Her blue eyes were too wide, and at the corner of one, a tear seemed to hang. He started to reach out before he caught himself and pulled his hands back.

He couldn't stand to watch the misery on her face. He wanted to comfort her and tell her it was okay that she sprayed him pointblank with pepper spray. He'd been worried something was terribly wrong when she didn't get out of her car in the parking lot. He'd moved too fast and scared her, but something else had scared her first.

Spinning away, he moved in the direction she'd pointed toward the bathroom. It wouldn't be hard to find. The apartment was tiny, barely bigger than a large hotel room. He reached for the hem of his t-shirt and realized that he had a bigger problem. He stopped and turned back slowly.

"Ah, this is embarrassing, but I don't want to touch any skin I don't have to."

She frowned at him, then realization dawned and her frown deepened. She stepped forward.

"I can help you. Sometimes I have to help my clients with their clothes before or after a massage. This won't be any different." Hands outstretched, she reached for the t-shirt herself and bit her lip as her fingers scraped his abdomen.

His muscles jumped. He couldn't help it. The shiver of sensation the tips of her fingers caused as they skimmed his skin made everything jump to life. A distraction in his jeans made itself known. How the hell would he get his pants off too? He didn't want to start something he was in no position to finish, or they'd both be burning.

Solution, no shower. He'd wash his face and hands as best he could, get dressed, and go home to a long cold shower. The cold would solve another of his growing problems.

She lifted the shirt, momentarily blinding him. He could hear her breathing, quickened and more labored than when she worked on him. It was fear. That's what it had to be. When his head sprang free and he looked at her, she dropped her eyes and made a production out of shaking out his shirt before hanging it over the back of a folding chair. When she finished, she stood still, her hands hanging at her sides and her face turned away from him.

"I'm sorry, Jake. You startled me. I've had a long day and I saw monsters in the shadows. I'm sorry." She kept her face turned away.

His cheek burned and the tender skin of his ear felt like flames were leaping out of it, but he couldn't bring himself to turn away, not until she looked at him and he could tell her it was okay. Urgency about how she felt and what frightened her took precedence over his discomfort.

"Where did you go? I was worried sick about you. What happened?"

She didn't respond, keeping her eyes downcast with the single bulb in the ceiling fixture shining down on her glossy hair like a crown.

He stepped forward until he was a pace in front of her. Still, she didn't raise her face, and viewed from above, the distinct differences between her cheeks was more pronounced. Why had he never noticed this before? She was skillful with a make-up brush and hid in the shadows, large dark glasses and hats, with hair color that didn't seem to fit her natural skin tone. She could hide her face under a cake of make-up, but the skin on her hands was on display for everyone to see, and it was a different shade.

"Marlee, look at me. Tell me what's wrong. I can help you."

>>>>>

His words rang with commanding certainty, even as his eyes seemed to beg her to comply with gentle understanding. She bit her lip again to keep from speaking, because it would be too easy to spill it all. If she did, he'd walk away in disgust. He might even arrest her.

Opening her mouth to deny anything was wrong, she snapped it shut when she noted that tears now spewed from the angry redness at the corner of the eye where pepper spray must still sting and burn on his cheek. That skin and his ear had turned an angry blistering red. He coughed, sniffing deeply like he had a sudden cold. But rather than dealing with his pain, he was trying to convince her he could help.

In a commanding tone, no less. No way. She'd had it with men who issued orders. That ship had sailed so long ago, they'd used oars to move it.

"You need to wash that spray off now." She advanced across the small space between them and put her hands on his arm to turn him toward the bathroom. "Go. There isn't anything that can't wait until your face feels better."

He grimaced, and the move brought heavier tears to his injured eye and another congested sniffle. The words popped out of her mouth before she could stop them. "I'm really sorry, Jake."

He sighed, a deep sound that made her think of other sounds, moans of pleasure, murmurs of assurance, groans of completion. Her heart chattered, fast, then slow, as warmth dropped from her stomach to the vee of her legs and settled there, throbbing in time to the uneven beats of her heart. What would it be like to wrap herself around his man, and forget about the past, only focusing on what could be the best in the future?

His sea-kissed eyes watched her carefully, or rather, the one that wasn't tearing and now beginning to swell shut watched her. He brushed casually at the tears, then swore as the spray left on his hands made contact. Turning with a sound of disgust, he grabbed his shirt and paced quickly to the bathroom, shutting the door with a heave that echoed twice in the small apartment before silence fell. In the quiet, she heard water begin to run full force in the sink.

Exhaling so hard that she gasped, she wondered why he brought out such a reaction in her. Over the years, she'd been able to fight off any wink of desire so rapidly that she barely recognized it was there. But now, things were different. Maybe her friends in the meeting were correct. Maybe she needed to regain her power by being willing to live again. But was Jake the one for that experiment?

This was wrong. On so many levels, this was wrong. He would not force his way into her life, and yet she looked miserable.

Repeated applications of soap and rinses finally eased the burning sensation on his face somewhat. His hands felt almost normal again, so the pepper spray must be old since it wore off so fast. She'd probably had that spray in her purse as long as he'd had that condom in his wallet. It was a good thing she didn't need to use it on someone who threatened her.

He examined the red-rimmed eye in the mirror, wondering why she felt the need to carry it. He'd seen the fear in her eyes just now. Who was she afraid of?

Only one towel hung on the rack, so he shook his head over the tub and hoped the sting wouldn't return once his face dried. He reached for his shirt lying draped over the top of the toilet and began to pull it on, then reconsidered. She'd seen his naked back, so maybe making himself accessible would calm her. After all, it was just skin.

He opened the door, glancing around the small room until he found Marlee, her back to him, standing at the sink in the kitchen. She didn't seem to be doing anything, her body unmoving and still. When he walked across the space, she raised a hand as if to stop him.

"I'm sorry, Jake. I know you hate that I keep apologizing to you, but it seems that this is what I always need to do. I screw things up. You – ah – you'd be best off if you walked out of here and we never had anything to do with each other again. Okay?"

She still hadn't turned around, so he covered the rest of the distance and stood behind her.

"I think I'm a better judge of what's best for me, don't you think?"

Tension came off her in waves. He didn't touch her. If he did, he might pull her into his arms and demand to know what she was so afraid of. Whatever it was, he could protect her.

She shook her head, the movement releasing the last strands of hair from a clip that had come loose. It clattered to the floor, but neither of them looked down. The curtain of black swung back and forth in a seductive rhythm, and Jake had a sudden vision of it curtaining them as they made love, Marlee riding him with tender passion until they both came hard.

He sucked in air, a constriction in his chest making it difficult to breathe. This woman bewitched him, even as she tried to send him away.

"What do you want from me, Jake? Tell me, what do you want? Why don't you go find yourself some nice girl?"

He wasn't sure why she pushed him away. She was a terrific woman. He enjoyed her, every part that she'd been willing to share. Once she relaxed, she had a quirky side that hit his funny bone in exactly the right place. She intrigued him, and he wanted to know more. She had no business berating herself like that.

"You're right, you're no girl. You're an amazing woman, and you should know better than to think that poorly of yourself." He heard the anger creep into his words, but he was powerless to stop it.

She responded with a huff, spinning around to face him with anger of her own flashing in her eyes. Her eyes snapped, her chest heaved, and if it had been possible, sparks would have been flying from her fingertips. She was magnificent, and she turned him on more than ever before, if that was even possible.

"Is that what you think? That I have self-esteem issues? You know nothing about me, Deputy Jake Kermarrec, nothing at all. And that's the way it should be. I don't do cops."

She shoved against him hard enough to push him back a step, whirling through the small room and throwing open the front door. "Now go. I won't apologize to you ever again. Out, before I call a cop to come arrest you for overstaying your welcome."

Chapter 16

Jake stared at the homework on his dining room table. Minutes passed, then hours. He'd made little progress. In his solitude, his thoughts focused on the mess he'd made with Marlee last night.

"I shouldn't have startled you. Why did you have the spray out in the first place? Have there been problems around here I should know about?"

Marlee shrank back visibly at his question last night. Shaking her head, she said, "I'm bad luck for you, Jake. Look at this situation. Look at the night at the diner."

She blushed at that, and he wondered again at the discoloration on her face. Whenever he thought they were making progress and she was growing to trust him, a new mystery seemed to pop up between them.

"Jake, this – whatever it is – between us needs to stop. We're no good for each other."

Like hell. He wanted to reassure her, even as his cop instinct told him there would be hell to pay for continuing to pursue her. And he'd been honest with her as she wanted to throw him out. He wouldn't force himself on her. But her words cut at him.

"I don't do cops."

They stood at her door, staring at each other, for what felt like long minutes. Her chest had heaved with angry breaths, and her eyes flashed at him in challenge. He was never one to walk away from a challenge.

He dropped his hoodie to the ground and began to pull his shirt on over his head. Putting his head inside meant breaking eye contact, and when his head popped out again, he found that her eyes had strayed lower down his body to settle on his crotch. His very aroused crotch. He let his gaze rove down her body and found that his interest didn't appear to be one-sided.

When their eyes met again, resignation warred with her anger. He found his own anger had dissipated. When her stomach growled, he decided that maybe it was the opening he needed.

"Want to order pizza and talk?"

She blinked at him, and he pulled out his phone.

"Preferences?"

She shook her head, looking more confused by the minute.

"You don't want to get to know me, Jake. You don't."

"But I do."

The fact that he thought she needed close friends, and needed him most of all, didn't need to be mentioned.

Hitting the speed dial button, his call connected almost immediately.

"Hey, it's Jake Kermarrec. Can I get my usual? Make that a double order. And a different address for delivery."

He recited Marlee's address smoothly, his eyes on her. Her eyebrows rose in surprise, as if she didn't expect him to know.

"Yeah, I know. But that's the address."

Pizzas secured, he returned his phone to his jeans pocket and waved to the couch.

"Shall we sit down and wait? They said half an hour, but usually, they're faster."

Marlee seemed to struggle for words, pushing the door shut and wrapping her arms around herself like she was cold.

"No one wants to deliver here. They think it's too dangerous after dark. How did you convince them to come here?"

The fact that this neighborhood had that bad of a reputation raised his level of concern for her safety once more.

"We'll get to why you live here and why you should move later. For now, why don't we sit down, and you can tell me where you went today. You scared people who care about you." He paused, testing the truth out in his mind before adding, "You scared me."

That seemed to confuse her more, so when he reached for her hand and pulled her toward the small sofa, she let him. When she was seated, he headed for the kitchen. "Do you want something to drink? Soda? Coffee?" He opened her refrigerator like he did it all the time and looked inside.

"I don't buy soda because it's a waste of money. I drink water. I can make you coffee or something."

She half-rose from her seat, and he waved her back, searching through the sparsely populated cabinets until he came up with one coffee mug and one drinking glass. Filling each from the tap at the sink, he covered the short distance back to the living area and sat down, handing her the glass. She sipped, her eyes watching him warily.

"I just want to talk, Marlee. Like I said, I want us to get to know each other better. Let's start here. What scared you off today?"

She bit her lower lip, and he was tempted to put his mouth over hers and sooth that spot. But if he couldn't control himself, she'd never trust him.

"You wouldn't understand."

There it was again, that resignation and disappointment. He wanted to make whatever bothered her go away, and replace her sadness with the flash of power he saw in her when she was about to throw him out. And he wanted to see her smile.

"Try me."

Her face lifted from her examination of her water glass and she stared at him without emotion. She seemed to settle and turned away again, staring at the wall.

"It became too much today. I've lost a lot in my life, Jake. My family. Friends. Sometimes, I've felt so desperate that I didn't know if I'd make it into the next day. I was overwhelmed with how friendly people are to me, like you and Gabby. I had to get out of there, to be able to think. I know it sounds crazy, but when people are nice to me, I don't know how to handle it."

He sensed it was the most honest she'd ever been with him, and he wasn't going to dismiss that gift. When he had moved closer to her and wrapped his arms around her, she sighed and leaned against him. Searching for something to comfort her, he said, "Tell me some of your best memories from growing up."

And as she talked about fishing trips and barbeques, a treasured doll and unidentified siblings, he'd held her tighter and felt the tension leave her body. That she loved her mother was never a question, based on her stories. When he questioned her more closely about her father, she changed the subject. Some of the stories sounded vaguely familiar, though he wasn't sure why.

Even as he comforted her, his confusion had grown. Who was Marlee Cruiz, and why did she have this strong pull on him? He put a palm to his face, much the same way Marlee had done with a cold cloth the night before, staring unseeing at the laptop screen, and wondered if he'd gotten in over his head.

Chapter 17

"I can't see my toes."

Marlee smiled up at Gabby, looking past her big belly into her resigned expression. It didn't look like the woman had gained much in terms of pregnancy weight other than a whole lot of baby.

"Your toes look amazing, a beautiful bright pink. If you like, I'll take a picture of them with your cell phone so that you can enjoy them too."

Gabby laughed at that, a deep full sound that cascaded out and boomed through the spa room. Every woman in the place smiled with her, and Marlee let the happiness flow through her and bring her a momentary sense of peace.

This is what pregnancy was supposed to be about, a treasured time of happiness and joy, awaiting the coming of a new being into the sunshine. She knew Gabby had faced her own sets of challenges, but look at her now. Two wonderful sons, marriage to the incredible professor, a career she loved, and a new baby about to make an appearance.

"I don't think this baby is going to wait another month." Gabby shifted, reaching around to rub her lower back. Marlee knew it ached and little seemed to alleviate her discomfort. She noted the sudden grimace of pain crossing Gabby's face before she jerked again, jarring the position of the chair as she did so.

"I can't wait to meet him or her, you know? After all of these months together, I feel like I already know their little personality and quirks, based on their kicks alone. But I swear this baby is going to come any minute now."

Marlee froze in the act of painting on a top coat at Gabby's words.

"Seriously? Because you need to call your husband and make sure he gets here in time if that's the case." Marlee painted faster as she spoke.

Gabby deserved to have Rick next to her when their little one made its appearance. Having the other loving half of the equation present was something every woman deserved.

Her heart stuttered. No previous acquaintance of hers who had given birth had wanted the baby's father there. Two loving parents welcoming their child together wasn't a concept she'd experienced.

"Rick is in class now, though he has his phone on vibrate and he checks his text messages even while he's lecturing. His students all know what's going on. He said they're constantly asking him how the baby and I are doing. Poor guy, no one seems to be concerned about how he's doing." Gabby laughed once more, the pain easing from her expression.

"And how is the professor doing?" Neutral territory once more, thankfully. She waved a magazine over Gabby's toes to dry the last of the polish, giving her an excuse not to look up and experience envy at the true happiness on the woman's face.

"Rick is worried, overwhelmed, busy, and frustrated. But he's also thrilled, and the boys are too. They can't wait to meet their little brother or sister."

"What are they hoping for?"

"I don't think they've made up their minds. One day they want a little brother to play with and, as they say, teach about the ways of the world." Gabby rolled her eyes, a smile on her face. "Other days, they want a little sister to take care of. They've already mimicked something Rick said, that she wouldn't be allowed to date until she was twenty-five."

Dating, something she hadn't even considered. Kids today started so young, from what Gabby and others told her, with middle-schoolers talking about going steady and girls at that age wearing make-up. Childhood passed almost before their age reached double digits. The tremor shaking her hands made her sit back and clutch her fingers together in a tight double fist.

Around them, Bliss and another hair stylist worked, and the part time nail tech chattered to her client, a woman whose hearing wasn't what it used to be, causing the tech to shout. The smells were her everyday world, hair dye chemicals and nail products, shampoos and conditioners, and faint tinges of the scents in her massage creams lingering in the air. Marlee clung to those familiar things to help her settle.

"Oh my god." Gabby's sudden rush of breath and elevation in the chair distracted her from her thoughts. Gabby's eyes grew big and focused on Marlee.

"What's wrong, Gabby?" Marlee stood, taking the hand Gabby extended out to her. The hint of a smile on her face confused Marlee more than informed her.

"My water just broke." Then her face contorted in a rough grimace and she closed her eyes. "And that was definitely a contraction." She shoved her cell phone at Marlee. "Here, text Rick."

Marlee glanced between the cell phone in her hand and her client's face.

"Uh, I'm sure you have time. Just wait until the contraction passes and then text Rick. I'm sure he'll be able to make it up here quickly." Though the almost hour drive from the university was usually no issue, construction on the freeway caused delays frustrating the most seasoned commuter. The fact that Rick would be in a damned hurry didn't help the situation.

Gabby's face and grip relaxed seconds later. She gave Marlee's hand a squeeze and let go. Marlee stretched and closed her fingers a few times and waited for feeling to return. Gabby had a killer grip when she wasn't aware of it.

Activating the texting screen and beginning to type, Gabby sucked in air again less than a minute later and her body tightened as if she was trying to roll into herself.

"Okay, that's another contraction. Those are too close together."

Silence fell in the spa, with the eyes of every woman in the place on them. Bliss hustled over with a stack of towels, setting them down around Gabby's wet chair and gently handing one to her directly. "I think we better get you to the hospital."

Voices suddenly rose all around them, each one with a piece of advice. Some advocated waiting for the husband, and others suggested a call for an ambulance. Someone else wanted to boil water. The clamor rang through Marlee's head, raising her blood pressure and causing her skull to pound. So much experience – or lack thereof – and no one the wiser.

The babble of voices faded in Marlee's ears as Gabby stared at her, sometimes unseeing, and sometimes with intense concentration. She grasped Marlee's hand again, and when her expression focused inward, she squeezed and Marlee squeezed back.

That's what women did for each other at times like this. They supported each other no matter how they got to this point or what later circumstances would bring. This she knew how to do.

"Breathe, Gabby, soft pants, remember?" Marlee panted, squeezing Gabby's hand in time to her breathing, and Gabby followed. When the contraction passed, Gabby dug into her purse and pulled out a set of keys, all but shoving them in Marlee's face.

"I want you to drive me to the hospital. Here. Please, Marlee. I want a friend with me." Her eyes all but begged. "What if Rick doesn't get here in time?"

On cue, her cell phone pinged and she read the message. "He said he's racing to the car and he'll drive like hell. God, I hope he doesn't get into an accident."

Another contraction made speaking impossible for a moment, and Marlee tightened their hands and panted in unison with Gabby. When that episode passed, Bliss shoved a purse and coat at Marlee and put a hand under Gabby's arm.

"Of course she's going to take you. She might not know anything about birthin' no babies, but she can get you there." Her good-humored chortle accompanied a direct gaze into Marlee's face. "You are okay with this."

"I, I – sure."

Gabby pressed her fingers, though this time, it was in apparent gratitude. Taking the woman to the hospital shouldn't be a huge deal. She'd drop Gabby off and give the nursery a wide berth coming back.

From across the room, an older woman in curlers snapped shut her phone and yelled, "They're expecting you, Gabby. Now go make a nice baby for us all to coo over, you hear?"

Marlee gripped Gabby's arm and Bliss took the other side as they moved across the room, followed by shouts of good wishes and encouragement. It was like having a cheering committee for a birthing process, and Marlee didn't know what to make of it. It wasn't as if these other women were close, but they were supportive and sympathetic nonetheless. What a difference when a child was a welcome addition to the community. Not like –

She bit off the thought, unwilling to follow that road to its inevitable end.

Bliss beeped open the door of sedan at the curb, continuing to lead Gabby around the far side to the passenger seat. When she had her seated and clicked the seat belt into place, she turned to Marlee.

"Seriously, are you all right with this? You look like you've seen a ghost."

"Good job, Gabby. Pant with me."

Marlee brushed a line of sweat off her face, wondering how much of her make-up was gone and whether the underarms of her shirt showed the perspiration pooled there from the past hour's ordeal. Gabby, like the trooper she was, gripped Marlee's hand until her fingers numbed during each contraction.

"Marlee, you have been amazing. Looks like you've done this before, huh?" Gabby's eyes focused and the quizzical look wasn't something Marlee could avoid. There would be questions someday, she was sure.

"Ah, Mrs. Chagres, you're doing great. Pretty soon, we'll get this party in full swing. Is your husband on his way?"

From the bedside, the cell phone erupted into life. "Yes, I am on my way, damn it. Damned construction. It held me up. But I'm almost there, thanks to my escort."

Escort was the word for it. When Rick got held up in the work zone, he'd called Jake for advice. Jake made a call to some highway patrol buddies and between them, they got an unofficial law enforcement escort to get Rick up the hill faster. According to Rick, very fast, like ninety to a hundred miles an hour fast. When he reached the county line, Jake and another friend were there to help speed him along as well. It seems Jake was a hero once more.

"You shut up and concentrate on your driving, Dr. Enrique Chagres, because this baby needs a father, as do our boys, and I need a husband, in one piece I might add. Marlee's doing a great job as my coach."

From the phone, Rick's voice sounded like he was underwater as he said, "I'm glad Marlee's there with you, darling. It's good that you have a friend with you."

She was a friend? No, she was just convenient. Friendship with Gabby was for women like Serena and Tess, Marguerite and the other girl tribe members. One of them belonged here.

"Yes, I'm lucky to have her and she's a terrific friend."

Marlee tightened her fingers involuntarily, a prickle of tears burning her eyes. Friends told each other things. Friends explained. Friends were honest.

"You haven't told me how, as Bliss so sweetly put it, you know so much about birthing babies, Marlee."

Gabby's gentle question made her turn, feeling the flush of embarrassment start at the base of her neck and rise into her face. From experience, she knew it made the make-up less effective as a hiding technique, not that she was sure she had much left anyway.

"I, ah, had a number of friends who gave birth when we were close."

Gabby opened her mouth to say more, but a contraction distracted her, and with it, the nurse said, "I'll let the doctor know you're ready to start the fun stuff, Gabby."

From the phone, Rick shouted, "I'm in the parking lot, almost there, baby."

The nurse tapped Marlee on the arm, pulling her attention away from the sudden bustle of activity marking the transition to active childbirth. "You'll need to gown up, my dear. It's time. Just leave your shirt over there and change into a gown. No one will see anything under it, I promise, so don't be worried about running around in your undies."

The pale blue fabric was in her hand before she understood what happened. Take off her long sleeves? She never did that in public.

"Marlee, you better get a move on it. I need my friend beside me, and Baby Chagres is really not going to wait." Gabby extended a hand from her spot on the birthing table, the comfortable chair having been transformed by busy aids in the time it took the nurse to put the gown in Marlee's trembling hands.

"Gabby, don't you want to wait for Rick? I mean, he's almost here and I'd be a poor substitute." She sucked in air because lightheaded sensations of spinning made the room appear like a tunnel and she couldn't focus with the light, even soothing as it was.

"Come on, this is childbirth, not rocket science. You're my buddy and I want you here."

Marlee felt a tear slip loose and cascade down her cheek, followed by another. The trembling worsened until her whole body shook.

"Marlee, what's wrong, sweetie?" Gabby watched her with heavy concern, her face bearing the grimaces of cramps and contractions.

"I'm here – damn, darling, I'm sorry. If I'd known you'd go into labor today, I'd have – "

Gabby's attention turned to the big man charging in the door, his hair askew as if he'd been running anxious fingers through it and exuding so much restless energy that Marlee felt momentarily distracted too. It was the perfect time to make her escape. She turned as husband and wife reunited and he began stripping and putting on his gown. In the hubbub, she almost made it to the door.

"Marlee, sweetie, please stay, at least with everyone else in the waiting room. I want you to meet the new addition to the girl tribe – or wolf pack."

Marlee glanced back with her hand on the door, stricken by the gentle tone and friendly face turned toward her.

"Please, Marlee."

She fled out the door, afraid that Gabby would call her back, or Rick would follow. Tears fell as she put a hand on the wall to guide her. As she ran into people, they exclaimed in surprise or worry, but she pushed on. The wrenching in her gut left her feeling like she'd puke, and she doubled over as if she too felt every contraction as her own. When she hit a wide double door that swung out, she stumbled and fell to her knees.

It was all too close, too fresh, too real.

"Hell, what's wrong? Marlee, tell me what happened. Is something wrong with the baby?"

Strong arms grabbed her and lifted her, cuddling her like she was a child. A hard body pressed against her, leading her on wavering feet as she continued to cry, burying her face in a black sweatshirt. As she inhaled to catch her breath for another round of tears, the warm aroma of spicy male brought on hiccups. Between the tears and hiccups, she felt her head swim.

A hard surface pushed against the backs of her knees and she allowed herself to be lowered gently into a chair, the arms staying around her like an anchor. Keeping her face hidden seemed like the best tactic, even though she wasn't sure what had happened.

Scratch that. She knew who held her. She recognized that scent without question.

>>>>>

A cold breeze blew through the hospital parking lot, and Jake fought the urge to pull his jacket more tightly around Marlee's shivering form. After those initial moments, she refused to be held, and almost refused the jacket until Jake gave her his nasty, no-objections cop face. Her widened eyes made her appear even more fragile, but if it kept her warm, it worked for him.

"If everyone's okay, why did you freak out?"

He kept his tone patient and even, though he wanted to shake her until she spilled whatever was on her mind. What made her race out the doors of the maternity department as if the worst tragedy of the world had just occurred? The fact that everything seemed to be progressing on schedule – though a bit earlier than planned – brought relief to the faces of the girl tribe and wolf pack in the waiting room.

Marlee sniffed, and damned if she didn't look even more beautiful with her face blotchy, her nose red, and her lips swollen from biting them. Every time her teeth snapped at the soft skin, he felt his belly clench and blood sped faster than a runaway semi on a steep grade. If that wasn't inappropriate timing, what was?

The woman in front of him huddled against the hospital's stucco wall, heaving in big gulps of air as if she hadn't drawn breath in a week. As she calmed, she stood taller and he watched in fascination as her mask of calm objectivity slipped further and further into place. Not that he wanted that. He wanted to know the real Marlee.

The urge to pull her in, wrap his arms around her again, and comfort her almost won. She was inconsolable about something, and he planned to know what it was.

"Marlee, tell me what happened." It wasn't so much a command as a request, and her pale blue eyes shifted to him and away so fast he almost missed it. That plumped lower lip pulled into a straight line, but that did nothing to disguise its sensual fullness. His chest felt tight with tense control, because the urge to suck it into his mouth to sooth it became overwhelming. He forced his hands into his jeans front pockets, which only pulled the denim more tightly across something else that was plumped and swollen, and he pulled his hands out again and formed fists at his sides.

Damn, she made him lose all sense. She was upset, and he wanted to push her up against the wall and sink into her, out here where anyone entering or leaving the hospital would see them. He wanted to take her, possess her, and ask questions later.

But he was a cop first. Something scared her, and frightened her badly. He needed to find out what it was.

Marlee pushed away from the wall and wiped her hands against one another as if ridding herself of something grotesque. When she looked back at him, her passive expression and empty eyes would have made him wonder if he had imagined her earlier fear, except for the tear tracks on her cheeks and the faded make-up now revealing discolored uneven skin.

"Thank you for being concerned. It's very kind of you. But I need to call my boss, get my car keys, and go back to work."

A distant tone delivered those polite but unemotional words. He'd heard more excitement in dispatchers' voices when they issued instructions about a crime in progress, and they trained to be reserved. Her eyes watched him, unblinking and staring. She didn't even turn away when an ambulance barreled up to the emergency entrance next door and the paramedics shot out like bullets.

She simply waited.

He ruffled a hand through his hair before realizing he gave away his feeling of frustration. Dropping his hands, he again didn't know what to do with them. He wanted to wrap them around Marlee, pull her in, and toy with that plump lip.

Across from him, Marlee suddenly gave a deep sigh, beginning to strip off his jacket. As her arms came free, she shivered, and he swore once in language colorful enough for her to look up at him and quirk a corner of her mouth up in recognition.

"I don't think that's physically possible. In fact, with my knowledge of anatomy, I can assure you that it isn't." She might be smiling, but it was a sad and knowing look. Extending a hand with the jacket dangling off her fingers, she watched him and waited again. Ambulance doors slammed and she jumped and glanced at it before returning her stare to him.

"Keep the jacket. You're cold."

Her head dipped to one side as her eyes focused more intensely on him. Tipping her head further, she kept the jacket at arm's length, swinging it gently as if trying to tempt him to retrieve it.

"Mine's inside, along with my purse. I plan to go back in, get my things, and leave. I'll call Bliss and get her to pick me up." She hesitated, and for a moment, those too-perfect teeth peeked out and nibbled on her lip, and his blood pressure went up another ten points.

God, the woman had no clue how sexy she was.

"I'll go inside with you, and then we'll go get your car." He left the jacket where it hung.

Confusion ran across her features, and her calm front faltered.

"You don't need to drive me anywhere. I told you, I'll get my keys from my boss. She was going to drop them off for me anyway."

"She did, with me. I drove your car here. You're my ride back now."

If she'd looked scared before, she looked terrified now, and he could only hope he could earn enough of her trust to find out why.

Wrapping an arm around her unresisting shoulders, he led her back inside.

Her jacket and purse were right where she left them, in the room just outside the space filled with the sounds shared by Gabby and Rick as they brought a new life into the world. She said nothing as they left the birthing area. While Marlee used the bathroom, Jake let the gang in the waiting room know they were leaving. If anyone was surprised, they didn't show it. In fact, more than a couple of knowing glances were shared among his friends. By the time Marlee reappeared, he'd formulated a plan.

Marlee insisted she was fine to drive. Jake hadn't said a word, merely walking to the passenger side of the car, opening it, and sliding across until he was behind the wheel. He waited as she debated arguing with him. It wouldn't be any use, she knew. He wouldn't give in. His sea-touched eyes focused on her with unrelenting intensity.

She slid into the passenger seat and shut the door, trying to ignore his stare.

"I'm happy to drive you back to work or to your apartment, but I think maybe you need a break. I have an idea."

She wasn't sure what to say, too concerned that her barriers had crumbled. Was her make-up gone? Could he see everything? Why had she agreed to this in the first place? His friends filled the waiting room, and any one of them would be more than happy to drive him anywhere.

She'd avoided them all by slipping around the first corner before the public area and entering the private entrance to the family area of the birthing center. Admitting to herself that it was okay to linger for a minute, taking in the happy sounds, the coaxing words of a stressed Rick and the sometimes funny, sometimes demanding responses of a straining Gabby, she realized what a unique and wonderful experience childbirth could be. If only – but it did her no good to think about it.

Her fingers clutched the collar of her jacket, and she noted the marks of threadbare stitching and faded wear. She couldn't justify the expense of something new, not when the stakes were so high. Shoving her arms into the sleeves in a way that strained the old seams, she heaved her big purse to her shoulder and spun away, listening to the echoes of joy and pain coming from the inner room.

"Why thank you Jake, it would be nice to relax for a while."

His mimicry of her voice cut into her thoughts. Here she sat, with the man who would never understand or condone her actions, in the seat next to her. What the hell was she thinking?

"I'm sorry. Thank you, Jake, but I think I should go back to work. Bliss will be expecting me."

A grumpy harrumph sounded from the man in the driver's seat. "Like hell you say. It's well past the time the spa closes. You're a million miles away, Marlee. Tell me what you're thinking about."

She shook her head before his words finished echoing against the torn interior header of the old sedan. Shrugging, she watched Main Street slide by as he rounded the turn to the parking lot behind the spa. Jake's big black SUV sat nose out in the middle of the lot, as if ready to pounce at a moment's notice. He pulled into the vacant space on the driver's side, set the car in park, and waited with the engine running.

Why didn't he just get out? He smelled good – oh damn – and his scent filled the car, overcoming the aroma of old vinyl and carpet. Nerves sharpened the twists of each cramp in her gut. She needed to be alone so she could process the day. Her feelings swamped her and she didn't know what to do with them.

"Let's go grab something to eat."

She startled at his words, swinging around to him with her hands gripping her purse strap tightly as her only landline. The patient smile on his face made her want to jump him. He looked delicious, like the most fattening candy or irresistible treat. But he was a cop. That settled things.

Turning back to face front, she tapped her fingers with restless energy. "You have to get back to your friends at the hospital. They want you there to celebrate the new addition. Rick and Gabby will expect you to be there."

"They'll expect you too, you know." Again, the patient tone and seeming ease of his posture made her question why she thought his words sounded strange.

Oh yeah, she wasn't part of the girl tribe. She wasn't the girlfriend of a member of the wolf pack. She didn't belong.

Shaking her head from side to side, she let the air held too tightly in her chest slide out on a sigh. Breathing in again reminded her of the man sitting next to her, and she let her left hand drift to the window crank to roll down the glass. Cool air wafted in, but it did nothing to disperse the warm aroma of sexy male.

"They don't want me there. I merely helped when Gabby needed it. I'm not one of – you." She waved her left fingers at him before clutching the purse again. When he said and did nothing, she turned on him and leaned forward until her focus filled with turbulent blue-green eyes. She had to make her point before he distracted her again.

"Why are you doing this? Get out. I helped Gabby because I care about my clients. You should go."

Jake frowned at her, his eyebrows almost meeting in the center above a nose that looked like it had been broken once. She'd never noticed that about his face before. Of course, she tried not to stare at his face. His knowing eyes always seemed to be watching with too much focus. If he looked too closely, he'd know.

"Fine. Then please tell me why you didn't come through the waiting room and say hello to everyone. Tess, Serena, and Marguerite asked about you, since they knew you were there. Now everyone's curious. So tell me, why did you slip in and out like a thief instead of taking the time to talk?"

"I don't do talking, Jake. I don't spend time with people who are obviously in a different realm than I am. I am not part of your crowd." Though once she would have been. The more he pushed it, the more obvious the wide chasm between the phases of her life became.

"I don't have to go back. Someone will call me when we have baby news. Gabby and Rick will be swamped anyway. Rick's brother and sister are on their way up from Sac, and DK and Vince stopped by school to pick up Jeremy and Will. The boys are evidently entertaining everyone with stories about how they're going to watch over their little brother or little sister. I'm fine not going back." He settled deeper into the seat, his jacket making a rasping sound as it rubbed against a crack in the vinyl.

Her stomach picked that moment to rumble, and she realized it had been almost a full day since she'd had a meal. The power bar and coffee for breakfast didn't count, and by lunch time, she'd been at the hospital, clutching Gabby's hand and breathing with her as if her own life depended on it.

Beside her, Jake heard the sound too, and he smiled. The neon brilliance of his relaxed expression tempted her. When his stomach grumbled too, she caved.

"Okay, dinner. But this time, I'm paying."

>>>>>

A couple of hours later, Jake followed an exhausted Marlee to her apartment, walked her up, and took her keys from unresisting fingers to open the door. Her eyes looked too big for her face as she stared up at him, and when he leaned in to kiss her, she didn't protest for once. Little by little, she was letting him in. Her taste made his blood rise and he probably lingered there too long, but he didn't want to push her. If she wanted him, she'd let him know. When he lifted his head, he gave her a gentle push inside.

"Get some sleep. I'll call you tomorrow. Gabby and Rick want you to come and meet the baby."

She'd nodded, her expression falling into that sad stressed look it held too often. But she'd backed up and closed the door, and when he heard the locks engage, he went back to his car and sat staring at the lights coming on in her windows for a few minutes. Once they went out again, he drove to Mallory's to meet the guys and celebrate.

The pitcher made its round of the table, with Jake voting to stay with soda and Geno opting for a glass of milk. All ribbing aside, he said his ulcer made his life miserable and he'd rather be able to sleep. With all glasses loaded, the men around the table raised them high and clinked.

"To the newest addition to the clan Chagres, Elisabeth Joan," said Deke. The men repeated the toast and took their sips. When glasses met the table top once more, Deke turned and asked, "And so, Dane, are you and Serena next?"

Jake noted the quick stillness, as if Dane braced himself for the question and was deciding how to deflect it. His eyelids lowered without appearing to narrow. Based on body language alone, Jake would guess the answer was they were already in process.

Powers leaned forward, regarding his brother with a direct look. To his credit, Dane didn't squirm. In fact, he barely seemed to breathe.

"Yes, Dane. Please do share with us any secrets you might be keeping. After all, we're all brothers here, right guys?"

As the men around the table agreed and punctuated their comments with good-natured ribbing, Jake felt the hairs on the back of his neck rise. Something wasn't right.

The ribbing died down as the men picked up their drinks, sipped, and regarded the still-silent Dane with mixtures of puzzlement, interest and concern.

Finally, he spoke. "Yeah, actually, I have been keeping a secret. But it's not what you think."

The group fell silent, and Jake found himself leaning forward, intent on Dane's expression and tone. This didn't sound like a man ready to share happy news. Next to Dane, Powers also turned his body to face his little brother fully. At his right, Jake saw Deke lean forward too, his body on alert.

Dane glanced to his left, then back to the right. The scars on his face, the ones he'd won nobly in battle, stood out more starkly on his features, and Jake shifted, his hand reaching automatically for the place where his service weapon usually rode on his hip. His back-up sat in a holster on his ankle, and he re-crossed his legs to bring it closer to his hand. Around him, the other men shifted in differing positions of worry or watchfulness.

"Dane, what's going on?" Jake kept his voice neutral with only enough volume to reach across the table.

In response, Dane turned his head slowly, scanning the room. When he'd made a complete sweep of the right side of the room, he turned and did the same to the left. By now, Powers joined his examination, and within less than a minute, the heads of everyone at the table swiveled in an attempt to understand what they were looking for. Everyone looked, that is, but Jake.

He knew better. Dane was buying time. He didn't want to explain what worried him. Good luck with that. If Powers didn't jump down his throat, Jake would.

Seemingly satisfied, Dane's eyes landed on his beer and he reached for it, taking a long drink before setting the almost-empty glass on the table with a distinct crack. The sound brought all attention back to him, but no one said anything. Dane continued to stare at the scarred wood, toying with the glass in small circles of wet condensation on the table. Jake felt his impatience rise. If no one said anything soon, he was damned if he'd leave this on the sidelines.

Powers stepped in instead. "What the hell is going on?" The growl of his voice allowed for no argument.

Dane glanced at his brother, his eyes narrowing and focusing with a sharpness Jake had seen before. Whatever was bothering the man was serious. He didn't raise issues lightly, given the things he'd seen in the world.

"I think I have a lead."

"I thought the private investigator's advice was that we wait a while before trying to find Amanda again. She disappeared again, and there's been no sign of her. He suggested we wait and see if something new pops up in a month or two. He said that sometimes people allow themselves to come out into the light if no one's inquiring about them for a while. Maybe Mandy will surface." Powers sounded more than a little pissed off and growled his words at his brother.

"I agreed, remember? No, this isn't about Mandy, though I wish it was that simple." Dane paused, a rare flash of uncertainty crossing his face so quickly that Jake thought he imagined it. When Dane stared hard at him, his curiosity grew at the same pace as his concern.

Powers added, "What do you think, Jake? Should we want for a while before ramping up the search for Amanda again?"

Jake kept his eyes on Dane while he answered Powers.

"That's one investigative technique, though staying on whatever trail the PI has now would be a good idea for other reasons. Tell me, if your sister wanted to find you, she'd know how to do it, right?"

Both men nodded. Dane added, "Powers has the same phone number and the construction office knows how to reach him. I've been in and out of the news for the past year, and it's no secret where I live. And Dad's still in the business, so she could always call him. Or go home, for that matter. He will never move out of that house." Dane shook his head, his sorrow quickly masked by a distant glare.

Jake often wondered what his friends' lives would have been like if their mother hadn't died in their teens. A father who was more interested in running his construction company than taking care of the emotional needs of his kids after her death meant both men tended to turn off their emotions as well. That Powers and Dane wanted to be reunited with their sister was clear. But in his experience, a woman who stayed away from her family for this long had reasons she didn't want to or couldn't be found.

"Why don't you leave it alone for a while? Maybe there will be new information, or maybe some of the trackers your PI placed will light up one day. Maybe your sister will simply reappear."

Both men shook their heads, Powers in the negative and Dane to agree.

"That's not the point of what I was about to say." Dane sounded as angry as Powers by now, and the two brothers grimaced at each other, while Geno turned and signaled the waitress for another pitcher of beer.

"What were you trying to say? Spit it out, Dane." Powers' growl cut through the noise around them.

"I think I have a lead on the person who's been stalking us. It's a woman."

Jake sat up straighter. A woman stalker usually meant the issue was sexual or relationship-based in nature. That this could be an issue with these two men, both loners until their relatively recent alliances with their women, struck Jake as improbable.

"How do you know this?" Jake patted his shirt absently until he realized that he wasn't on the job, and the notepad ever-present in his uniform pocket hung in his closet, awaiting the day he could return it to his locker at the station.

"Here." Geno handed across a pen and a stack of napkins as if he understood Jake's motions. With a nod of thanks, Jake turned back to Dane. Powers stared hard at his brother, his eyes slits in an angry face.

Dane glanced around the bar again before leaning forward, pulling every man at the table in closer with his movement.

"I was on Main Street the other day and I felt it again, that sense of someone staring at me. I was in front of the cheese store, where the windows reflect clearly in the middle of the day. And there she was."

Impatience rolled off Powers in waves, and Jake could understand the feeling. Before he could say anything, though, a pitcher of beer landed on the table with a thud. Even Geno poured himself a glass this time, as all eyes stayed on Dane.

Taking a sip before continuing, Dane licked his lips and raised troubled eyes to the group. "This young woman across the street was watching me. I could tell she was staring at me, and staring hard. It wasn't just someone looking at this ghoulish scar. I watched her in the window's reflection, and because she didn't notice that, I had time to get an idea of who she is."

"Who is she?" Powers ground out each word individually, and Jake put a restraining hand on his arm as the man half-rose out of his seat.

"That's just it. I don't know. You know how it is. This is a small town, and usually you can find someone easily. But I don't recognize her, and I asked around casually. I didn't find anyone who knew her."

"What did she look like?" Jake poised his borrowed pen over the napkin, waiting for the answer to his question.

Dane's gaze slipped away as if picturing her in his mind's eye. Sometimes, having a photographer for a witness could come in damned handy.

"Five foot six, slender, dark hair. I couldn't tell anything about her eyes. She wore black clothes with a ball cap."

Jake's heart started to beat an uncomfortable tattoo. It couldn't be.

Dane continued, "Finally, I decided that the best way to get a better view was to turn around. When I did, I met her eyes across the street. She jumped when she saw me staring straight back at her, shoving big sunglasses on her face and turning away. It looked like she panicked."

On the surface, the woman Dane described sounded an awful lot like Marlee. And Marlee's penchant for secrecy was one of the things standing between her and Jake. Did she have something against the brothers and was here to cause them trouble? Somehow, the role of stalker didn't fit what Jake knew about her, though that, of course, was too damned little.

"Why didn't you follow her?" Powers still looked like he would jump across the table at any moment, but his anger seemed to be seeping away.

"I tried to, but traffic was busy and by the time I could cross, I lost her. There were trucks in the way, so I'm not even sure which direction she headed or if she ducked into a shop. I kept looking for a while, with no success."

"You should have called me, Dane." Powers flopped back in his seat now, looking pensive.

"You should have called me." Jake's assertion met with a nod from Geno as he nursed his beer and rubbed his midsection.

Dane waved a hand as he sipped from his glass, setting it down on the table and turning it around in the puddle of moisture on the wood. "I know, but there wasn't time. Jake, you know more people around here than any of us. Black hair, long, pulled back. Black clothes. Do you know who she is?"

Jake stared back at the three pairs of eyes on him, hoping his face gave nothing away. These were his friends, the wolf pack, the men who had his back no matter what.

But Marlee had quickly become the woman under his skin. If it was her, she deserved the chance to explain herself. And she would, but only to him.

"I don't know, guys, but let me check around."

Chapter 18

Jake didn't bother to stifle the groan of pain and pleasure. When Marlee traced his spine with only the sheet separating their skin, it felt like a caress. Her magic fingers dug into knotted muscles, but they were no longer tense from his injury. She made him that way.

For a full hour on Monday, she had all but ignored him, even while doing her job. She'd said nothing. He'd tried to convince her that she could trust him with anything. She wouldn't meet his eyes, even when he ran a hand down her arm and linked his fingers with hers. His massage was great, if the size and ache of his hard-on was any indication.

He needed to know if she was the one stalking Powers and Dane. She wouldn't be – he was almost sure of it. He'd spent countless hours analyzing every one of their conversations, and nothing she said indicated she even knew the men. But Dane's description was too similar to ignore.

Wednesday headed in the same silent direction. Her movements were almost mechanical, except they made him feel so good. As she got into her rhythm, he knew she was as affected by their contact as he was. Her breathing quickened, the heat of her body almost overwhelmed his good intentions, and her scent made him wild. When he lifted his head as she prepared to leave, her eyes were luminescent in the room's dim light. And she still wouldn't talk to him.

But today was Friday, and he casually checked the appointment screen as he hung over the counter while Bliss finished a call. Marlee was off tomorrow. He was going to push it, and they were going to get back on track.

Right or wrong, he was going to learn if Marlee was following Powers and Dane, and if so, why.

By now, he knew her routine. She would strip the sheets, pushing them into the large laundry bag she toted back and forth each day. Disinfectant spray came next. She'd straighten the space, leaving it in pristine condition for her next workday. With little conversation for the women she worked with, she'd load up her bags and walk to her car in its assigned place at the city lot.

Dusk swept toward him, hurried by an overcast sky and a threat of rain by Saturday. He leaned on her car, noting that while it wasn't in the greatest mechanical shape, she kept the body spotless and the interior clean. Maybe he could take it by Big Al for her and have the issues checked out. Hell, it couldn't be that expensive to get things fixed. It was safer to have a driver door in working order, no matter what the cost. Besides, Big Al still owed him.

And Jake had time. He didn't have anything on his calendar until his doctor's appointment at the end of next week. With luck, he'd be released to return to full duty. The idea didn't bring him the joy he'd anticipated when this whole thing started, though. Long hours, a string of many long days in a continuous row, and a load of homework from his last semester of online classes wouldn't give him much time to socialize. And time was what they needed now, he and Marlee, time to work past the wall that seemed to grow taller and thicker as each day passed.

She hid something behind her distant façade and cool objective words. On those rare occasions when she acted out before thinking, her fear and hurt were palpable. Despite his subtle or more obvious questions, she refused to share what bothered her.

He had learned a few things, though. She'd grown up in Oregon. She had siblings, though who they were and how many were mysteries. She liked to watch football, didn't have much patience for reading, and had an astounding singing voice. But when he probed more deeply to learn more, she clammed up and withdrew. Everything in her body language said she wanted to remain untouchable. The fear in her eyes told him she was in trouble.

The investigative part of him wanted to learn how he could help. The man wanted to fix it and make life better for her. And he still wasn't sure if she was the one following his friends or not.

"What are you doing here?"

He'd missed her approach as he stared at her car, his thoughts on how to encourage her to open up to him. In his imagination, she felt grateful and happy that he showed concern. In reality, she did nothing to hide the fact that she was pissed off. Scratch that – it wasn't anger. Panic bit through the cooling air and anxiety rolled off her in waves.

"Hi. I wanted us to talk. How about if we grab dinner someplace?"

Her head shook so hard from side to side that he wondered how it avoided falling off her shoulders. As he stood straight, she pushed him aside and opened the trunk – thought not easily, as the key didn't want to go in the lock – and threw the laundry inside with so much force that the bag burst open and pieces leaked out in the interior. Her racing footsteps carried her to the passenger side, where she popped open the door and slid across, still hanging on to the purse on her shoulder.

"Marlee, come on. We have to talk sometime. We can deal with anything if you trust me. What we have is special."

She froze in the middle of the front seat at his words, letting out a sudden guffaw of laughter laced with bitter undertones. She leaned across the passenger side to look up at him, disbelief the primary emotion in her features.

"Special? You call us special? We had a grope and grunt in the backseat on a dark and lonely road, and we were caught by a cop. I don't call that special. In fact, I call that a sad commentary on how fucked up my life is. We have a sexual attraction, Jake, and that's it. We shared some food, and we've shared some life stories. We fuck because it feels good. Now get off my car. I need to leave."

He winced at her foul language, such a marked departure from her usual careful wording that he blinked and second-guessed himself. Had he read something into this that didn't exist? Was that all their encounters were to her, a dumb fuck? It was a whole hell of a lot more on his side. Anger boiled up inside him and he grabbed the door as it started to swing closed, his butt hitting the seat at about the same time she gunned the engine and shoved the gearshift into drive.

"God, Jake, get out. Please. We are a mistake. We mean nothing. I have places to go. I need you out of here."

Her eyes roamed the dashboard and it took him seconds to realize she fixed her gaze on the clock, which, amazingly enough, carried the correct time. Did she have a date? It didn't fit. If she was involved with someone, she never mentioned it. Was that her secret? He swore he felt her jitters in the frame of the old car.

"Tell me what's wrong. While it wasn't exactly what I anticipated in terms of building a relationship, ever moment I've spent with you has been great. We talk, we laugh, and we have a phenomenal physical connection. I'd like us to do all of it again – and more. I want to take you out to places that are nicer, and take you home, someplace with soft springs." He smiled his best suggestive grin at her.

If anything, she became more frantic. She supplemented her stare at the clock by patting her jacket pocket where he could see the bulge of her cell phone. As the big hand on the old analog clock hit the top of the hour, a futuristic set of bells sounded from that pocket, and Marlee's huge eyes settled on his.

"Please, Jake, get out. This is personal. I have to take this call."

The pleading look she sent him almost made him back out of the seat. But almost was the operative word. He wasn't sure what perverse sense made him decide to stay put, to see what she would do and more importantly, who was on the other end of that call. If she was afraid he would find out something secret, he wanted to know what it was. He leaned back in the seat, running a hand across the back to brush her cheek, and he smiled.

"Shit." Her eyes narrowed on him, and she looked pissed off once more. Her hand dove into the pocket, grabbed the ringing phone, and hit the receive button without taking her gaze off his face. "Hold on, please," she said into the phone, as she cranked off the key in the ignition, shoved open the driver door, and paced away from the car, her purse bouncing against her side.

He thought about getting out and following her so that he could hear what she said, but agitation marked every step she took. Maybe stalking after her would be overreacting. Maybe she deserved her privacy. His life had become full of maybes since he first encountered Ms. Marlee Cruiz.

She paced as far as possible, standing at the edge of the parking garage, shifting from side to side on the balls of her feet as if expecting a fight. Tension made every soft curve of her body hard and her face unyielding in profile. She occasionally spoke into the phone, finally removing it from her face and staring down at it for a long time while she continued to rock in a jittery tempo. Something made her jump as she pulled the phone closer.

Then she suddenly went still. The contrast was sharp enough to make him sit up straighter and focus on her expression. The phone rang again, and she was slow to lift it to her ear as if unwilling to hear whatever the caller had to say. He hoped to read her lips, but she said nothing.

In the next moment, her shoulders sank and the hand she raised to cover her eyes shook. Her body curled in and her arm dropped to cradle her midsection as if protecting herself from a kick to the gut.

The overhead streetlight came on, a bright sudden flash that didn't even cause her to raise her head. He blinked against the sudden illumination. She wasn't talking, not that he could see. He wasn't sure which emotion bothered him more, being pissed that she locked him out of what was happening, or concern that something was very wrong. She sank down on the low wall that marked the perimeter of the fourth floor.

His boots were on the pavement before he sent his legs a conscious message to move. Two people had been seriously injured falling from this level in the past year, and as she slumped to the side, he was afraid she would be the third. Rounding the car, he raced toward her, cursing the distance and the fact that his feet felt like lead weights as his legs pumped in slow motion.

Thirty feet away, she swayed. The fear gripping his heart in a vice made him curse out loud. Twenty feet, and her head shook from side to side, denying whatever she heard. At ten feet, she leaned back, her body following as he cried out.

Closing the last long steps, he grabbed her arms and yanked her upwards against his chest. He didn't give her time to react, and she sucked in air, her hands opening and closing, clutching at his shirt. He grabbed the phone as it slipped from her fingers, rescuing it before it crashed to the roadway four stories below.

Dragging her backwards, he absorbed the weight of her body with a couple of retreating steps. He tried to manage the surge of anger that she could have fallen, at risk because this wall still had no fence to keep people from the edge. Then his need to protect roared up, particularly when Marlee looked up at him with a mixture of confusion, fear, and overpowering sadness, tears painting her face with shiny tracks in the bright overhead light.

Her glazed eyes stared at him, but he doubted she recognized who he was. Even under her pale make-up, the whiteness of her skin startled him. Her breaths labored and he doubted she'd be able to stand on her own. Shock and fear warred on her face, and fear finally won as her eyes filled with new tears and she went limp in his arms.

He didn't examine the ferocious need to protect her. It was his job and his nature, but with Marlee, it was so much more. Tempted to check the call log, he dropped the cell phone into her purse instead, cradling her against his chest. When her tears fell faster and thicker, he wrapped his arms around her tightly and tucked her in close. As he rested his chin on top of her head, he rocked her gently, fighting the urge to ask questions.

The words echoed in her head until she swore they'd drive her insane.

"I found her."

The thought of this made her heart pound like a hammer on an anvil in her chest. After all this time, she was finally close. She wanted to jump in her car and fly down the freeway to park at that distant front door.

The man continued, "I found the other party you were worried about as well." He hesitated, before adding, "He found her too."

The pulsing elation evaporated like mist on a hot day. Her heart accelerated again, but for completely different reasons. The one thing the man had warned her about, finding out more than she really wanted to know, had happened.

He spoke for another couple of minutes, but she couldn't make conscious sense of what he'd said.

Something about trailing the other party, and stalking, and law enforcement. She'd mumbled her thanks as he said he'd call back tomorrow with an update. Her head spun with the implications of what she now knew.

After all this time, she'd found her. Somehow, she'd always believed that no one else cared like she did, so no one else would be following her. But she'd been wrong, maybe dead wrong. Horror was out there. Shivers of regret washed through her, leaving her shaking and numb.

"Marlee, what is it? Tell me what happened."

The deep voice was gentle yet persuasive. The warmth surrounding her felt like a furnace, but nothing would alleviate the ice in her veins. She felt so tired of hopes raised, only to find them dashed a few seconds later.

A careful tug, a benign push, and a voice murmuring in her ear made no sense. The world made no sense. Maybe if she retreated far enough into oblivion, she could make it go away. That quickly, the hunger and craving roared to life.

Oblivion. That was what she needed. The present wasn't something she could deal with, but in the past, she knew how to find the peace she craved. Refusing to think about the words any longer, she slumped down and moaned with need.

"Marlee, please. What can I do for you?"

The voice carried worry, and frustration made the tone harsh. She swiveled in her seat, not comprehending who was speaking. Her eyes focused, and for a moment, she didn't recognize him. She wanted a fix badly, and maybe this disembodied voice could get one for her.

The turbulence in his blue-grey eyes drew her in, sucking her into a deep vortex where she felt his turmoil like her own.

Jake. Jake sat in the driver's seat of her car and maneuvered it down the twists of the parking garage ramp with ease, even as his eyes continued to flash to her. Once on the street, he turned and hit the accelerator, though the car took a few seconds to respond. He swore, and the present came roaring in.

She hadn't had a fix in over eleven years, and she wasn't about to fall off the wagon now.

Jake flashed her another look, angry and confused. Turning on a road that led away from town, he drove faster, and the car occasionally coughed at the unaccustomed speed.

"I need a meeting."

Maybe she mumbled, because his puzzled expression settled on her face and he slowed. She tried again, stronger this time.

"I need a meeting."

He frowned, slowing further until he bumped off on to the shoulder of the road.

As he turned off the ignition and turned to face her, he said, "I don't understand."

"I said, I need a meeting."

He looked like she spoke Greek. His eyebrows shot together as he stared at her. She stared back, unwilling to break the gaze. She was stronger than this. If this is how he found out, so be it. She had more important issues to deal with.

Blowing out a breath, she sat up straighter. Swiping at the tear tracks on her face, she wondered how bad she looked. Any trace of make-up was probably gone and her scars would surely show. It seemed they all showed tonight, on the surface and cutting deep inside. Lifting her chin, she repeated her request.

In the pale ambient light, she saw comprehension spread across his face. He nodded his head, narrowing his eyes as on her as realization dawned.

"What kind of meeting? AA? NA? Something else?"

She shouldn't be surprised that he figured it out. He was a cop, after all. He probably saw people like her all the time.

"NA is best, but I'm not picky. I go to AA meetings too. If they had a twelve step program for being addicted to the wrong guys, I'd try it." She tried to smile.

He didn't smile back, only continuing to stare.

"What happened?"

That's the first thing everyone asked. They wanted to know her story. They wanted to feel superior or to pity her. Or they were secretly afraid that they could be just as addicted to their own substance or practice of choice. She didn't care.

"I got mixed up in bad men and wrong choices when I got out of high school, and it took me a few years to figure out I was on the wrong track. I straightened out, cleaned up, and have been clean and sober for eleven years, three months and six days. That doesn't mean that I don't need meetings anymore. I'll always need them."

He nodded. "Thank you for trusting me with that. It means a lot to me."

She wasn't sure what she felt at the statement, anger that he would feel her sharing was a positive or surprise that he didn't freak out about her sordid past. Mostly, she felt empty.

His intense gaze drilled into her, and she wanted to look away. She couldn't when compassion washed across his features. Raising his arm, his hand slid tentatively along the seat back as if afraid he would scare her. When he reached her, he palmed her cheek, and she wondered again what he could see there.

"What I meant was, who did you speak to on the phone and why did what they said scare you?"

Words roared in her head, and in her mind, she flashed to the three pictures. One, taken almost eleven years ago, had well-creased corners. The second was blurry and six years old, with a coffee stain on the back.

The third one, taken hours ago, lived in her cell phone. Three images, one person. She had a sudden frantic need to stare at the one in her phone again. With it, everything became real.

>>>>>

He pulled up to his front door and let her car die its usual unsavory death as she stared through the windshield. That she'd agree to let him drive her to her meeting was amazing. That she allowed him to accompany her inside and sit beside her, her hand in his, was nothing short of a miracle. She'd shared nothing during that hour of public time, but it didn't matter. She let him into her life a little more. She didn't even complain when she seemed to realize he wasn't taking her directly to her home.

"It's small." She nodded toward the house.

He squeezed the hand he refused to release unless he absolutely had to. Pushing out of the driver door, he rounded the car and opened the passenger side for her. When she hesitated, he knew she was probably thinking this was another bad idea.

"Come inside, Marlee. We can talk. We can sit. We can," he almost said make love before catching himself, "eat dinner if you like. Anything you want."

Her big eyes looked up at him, and he wondered what secrets she still hid from him. The fact that she felt the need to hold back ate at him. He still didn't know who called her earlier. But she stood and let him pull her against his side, walking up the front walk. With a hand that shook, he put the key in the lock and pushed the door open.

She walked in front of him, her head slowly turning as she took in the space.

"It barely looks like you live here."

He nodded at her words. His mother was right. This wasn't exactly a warm and friendly place.

She continued wandering, tracing the frames on the photos of his family as she stared at them. Finally glancing around again, her eyes settled back on him, a tentative smile creasing one corner.

"I like it."

He blinked.

"You never asked."

He blinked again, unsure of where this conversation was going.

"Most people ask, you know, about my addiction. How I got it. What happened. You know." She halted in front of the big front window, staring out into the evening.

He cleared his throat, feeling a constriction almost cut off his air supply. If she told him willingly, would that mean she was opening up to him?

"It's your private business. If you choose to tell me, I will listen without judgment."

She gave a soft huff he took to be unbelieving laughter. Still staring out the window, she crossed her arms tightly at her middle and rocked slightly. He stood at the door, unwilling to break the spell.

"I left home after high school, wanting to see more of the world than the limits my family placed on me. Truth is, I wanted to run away from everyone and everything they represented. So I packed up some clothes and my guitar and hit the road."

"A guitar?"

At his incredulous question, her reflection smiled back at him in the dark window.

"Yes, I played the guitar. Didn't everyone back then? I thought of myself as the next great torch singer. But I wasn't good enough to make it big, so I moved around from city to city, finding places to play and live, more often than not with some man who was interested in sex but not my singing." She laughed at this, and the tone wasn't funny.

It hurt to hear her degrade herself like this, but he asked for it. Restless now, he moved to stand behind her, not touching, but watching her eyes in the glass.

"Fast forward a couple of years. There were lots of men, lots of clubs, booze, and eventually, drugs, not that I imbibed on anything stronger than a joint."

He moved to come closer, but she raised a hand to stop him. While his gut rolled with what she told him, his fists clenched at his sides. He wanted to hold her, to let her know that whatever she had yet to say, he would stand by her. This was his Marlee, and he could accept whatever was in her past.

"Then one night, I was singing in a dive in Chicago, the kind where the patrons are mostly drunk or high or both, the drinks are watered, and the amount of criminal activity in the backroom would make even your cop head spin. I met a guy, and for once, someone didn't want to have sex with me before twenty-four hours had passed. I talked. He listened. He got me a hotel room and a job at a better club, one in which he was part owner. He took me out to dinner. We had dates. He bought me nice things, and I let him. He didn't seem to expect much of me in return, and for that, I was grateful. Do you have an idea where this is going?"

He fucking did, and he didn't like it. It wasn't that he could change anything from her past, but it hurt him to feel the pain it caused her, even reliving it in words.

"Marlee, sweetheart, if you don't want to talk about this anymore – "

But she put up a hand to silence him. "I need to get this out, to clear some of the air between us. Remember when I told you that I would always tell you the truth?"

He nodded, watching her somber face as she nodded back.

"I'll tell you the truth about this, but I still can't tell you everything."

If the pitch and drop of his gut were any indication, he'd be disappointed as hell when he had time to think about this later. Right now, his concentration remained completely on where her story would go next.

"Little by little, Davos got deeper inside my life. I let him. It was refreshing to think that a successful man would want to be with me. One thing led to another, like dates to sex to living together, and then he proposed. I was thrilled. I thought we were so much in love. I was a fool."

Her bitter tone didn't escape him, and this time, he stepped forward and put hands on her upper arms, rubbing gently. She let him, still staring at his face in reflection. He couldn't read her expression.

"We got married. Time passed, and the shine of that love became tarnished. I learned more about my new husband. First, he wasn't a good man, he was a criminal. Second, he didn't love me, but he was more than happy to abuse me. And third, he bought and sold drugs, and he didn't care who got hurt in the process. Including me."

She broke out of his hold and walked to the couch, sitting on the arm and rocking slightly. As he remained where he stood, his mind whirled. He wasn't sure what he'd expected to hear, but it wasn't this.

She stared at the floor, wrapping her arms around herself again. He wished he could make his feet move to sit next to her and wrap her in his arms, but he doubted she'd allow it.

"I could say that he was the one who got me hooked, but in reality, I allowed it to happen to myself. Heroin is a powerful addiction, and one snort led to another. When I was high, the world was happy and wonderful, and I was powerful and at peace. In between, I felt desperate and alone and I'd do anything for a fix. He used sex, cruel and empty sex, as his requirement. He was mean and brutal all of the time. But I did pretty much whatever he wanted, as long as I got my fix. I snorted heroin, and when that wasn't enough, he started shooting me up. That's why I wear these sleeves. I don't want anyone to see the marks."

His body vibrated with the need to hit something, and hard. How could a man abuse any woman, let alone someone as sweet and gentle as Marlee? He didn't blame her. Drugs brought their own special curses on their victims, and addiction to heroin was one of the most powerful and painful.

"Marlee, I don't judge you. Addiction isn't completely understood. I'm sure you know that." He stumbled on his next thought, that as a cop, he was one bad injury away from seeking his comfort in a pain prescription. That's why this accident scared him so badly. He didn't want to need a crutch.

She raised her head then, and he saw tears tracing down her face, removing any make-up that she hadn't cried off before.

"He hit you in the face."

She nodded. "I displeased him often, and he hit me. He's a big man, and he's strong. He never pulled his punches because he thought no one could touch him. This particular time, though, it meant cops, courts, and jail time. He beat me, left me on the floor and walked out." She opened her mouth, her words faltering, and took a deep sniff.

He walked past her and into the bathroom, ripping the roll of toilet paper off its holder so hard that the metal yanked out of the drywall. It felt good to work off his anger on an inanimate object. Stalking back to the living room, he put a gentle hand on her shoulder and placed the roll in front of her.

She laughed, more genuinely this time, and pulled off a few sheets to blow her nose. Two more blows, and she almost smiled at him.

"How did you beat it? The drugs I mean." He wanted to beat this Davos character to a pulp, then use him for target practice.

She hesitated. He wasn't sure if she was searching for the words or deciding how much of the truth to tell him.

"That day, lying on the floor bleeding, was the turning point. I crawled out. I found help. I got clean and sober. They fixed my face where he'd beaten me, put teeth back in my head where he'd knocked them out, and helped me beat my addiction. That's where I learned massage. I am eternally grateful to those people."

When she finished, he sensed there was more she wasn't saying. He waited, hoping she would be willing to share everything, but she stayed silent. As she lifted her eyes to his, he saw the tremble run through her body. Her mouth lifted into a sad smile as she watched him, waiting.

He wanted to pull her into his arms and assure her that this changed nothing between them. If anything, it made her more remarkable. And he needed to find this monster who ruined her young life and demand justice.

"What's the piece of shit's full name?"

She giggled, but it wasn't a happy sound. As she wiped the wetness from her cheeks, the marks on her skin became clearer. "Davos Cruiz, but it's okay. You don't need to beat him up. I divorced him a long time ago. I thought he was in prison." She gave a deep sigh and examined her fingers as her lips trembled, not lifting her gaze to his as he walked across the room.

He stood in front of her, his emotions in shambles. He longed to take her in his arms and comfort her. He still wanted to beat up that useless excuse for an ex-husband, but justice seemed to have caught up with him. As he stared at her imperfect face, the well of feelings he had for her spilled over, and he lifted her to her feet and put gentle hands to her cheek.

He stroked the shaded areas, noting how the bone and tissue below didn't quite match her other cheek. She opened her lips on a gasp when he ran his thumb over them, and her too-perfect teeth peeked out. That the bastard had harmed her, injured her to the point where she needed reconstruction, made him angry all over again.

"Let me see your arms."

She blinked up at him, shaking her head slowly.

"Marlee, trust me, please? You've told me the story. You can show me. I won't judge you." His repeated assurance rang in the sparse living room, echoing back slightly.

She continued to stare at him, giving a deep sigh as if resigned to her fate. Stepping back, she reached for the bottom of her shirt and lifted it over her head in one swift move. Then she stuck out her arms and looked away, tears again running down her cheeks.

"Thank you," he whispered, running his fingers down the insides of her arms while keeping his eyes on her face. But she didn't lift her eyes, as if she expected censure and criticism, so he looked down.

Her skin was smooth and pale, hidden from the sun day after day. In a couple of places, he saw the faintest marks imaginable. They could have been scars from old insect bites or the dots of beauty marks. He pulled her closer and lowered his head, and still, he couldn't tell if these were tracks. It didn't matter. Lowering further, he gently kissed the inside of one elbow, then the other.

Her head came up, her expression one of stunned surprise.

"Jake, it's ugly. My story is ugly. How can you be so accepting?"

As she watched him, he wondered how to tell her. There was a time when he would have judged her as weak. There might have even been a time when he would have said she probably got what she deserved, god help him. She'd smashed his clarity on the issue of right and wrong. For her, there was a middle ground, even as it shifted under his feet. How could he judge when all he wanted to do was protect her and make sure nothing bad ever happened to her again?

As he stared at her, she lifted up on tiptoe and leveled her lips with his. Eyes open, she leaned forward and pressed a gentle kiss to his mouth, one he felt zing through his body and settle in his chest, making his heart pound. Blood rushed in his veins as she shifted away from him, and he dropped his hands to his sides as his eyes followed her progress.

She walked with a measured pace around the small living room, stopping at the window and lowering the blind. Moving to the edge of the couch, she ran her fingers along its arm while she avoided his gaze. There was something about her black jeans and the sleeveless tank top she'd worn under the long sleeves that was an enticing as a designer gown would be on another woman. When she looked up, her smile didn't reach her eyes.

"If you have second thoughts, Jake, I understand. What you've learned about me isn't exactly encouraging for a friendship, even the superficial kind we have."

Her words made him seethe with sudden fury. It was as if she dismissed any feelings between them and categorized them as sex buddies, but nothing more. Hadn't he accepted her past and her present? But she had no skin in the game, because she didn't even come close to understanding him. What she hadn't shared with him yet could probably speak volumes for why she didn't believe they had a relationship.

Why that angered him to the point of boiling, he wasn't sure. If anything, he should be pleased she wanted nothing more from him than the occasional quick roll in the backseat. That her life had been reduced to this was wrong. She deserved more. He only had to convince her of that fact.

"Maybe I should be asking you if you're the one having second thoughts, Marlee. You have no way of being sure of what you're getting yourself into with me. I could be another of your bad boys, you know. Don't be fooled by the uniform."

Too many people were. The emotional rollercoaster his feelings rode took a climb, right before they dove and left him suspended in midair. He wanted to kill the bastard who'd done this to her. He wanted to make fast, hard love to her, not much better than that brute. What kind of man did that make him?

Her laugh sounded forced, almost sad.

"You, a bad boy? Come on. You're the pride and joy of Flynn's Crossing. You save lives while risking your own like it's a standard part of the job description. You're smart and wholesome and way too good to be involved with someone like me."

She looked away, but not before he saw her bite her lower lip. That single movement made every drop of blood drain from his brain, making the immediate hardness in his jeans impossible to bear. He reached for his belt, intending to ease the fit of denim on skin. She turned in time to see his action, and he debated the wisdom of having her here.

He was in an ugly and angry mood, and damned if he wanted to expose her to it. Every time he tried to get closer and learn more about her, she pushed him away. When she shared more, it killed him to know the hell she'd been through. But when she stood in front of him, holding his eyes with hers as she reached for his hands on his belt, damned if he could push her away.

Her fingers tightened on his before taking over. The buckle opened as if by magic, and the sound of the zipper's rasp on its downward slide rubbed his nerves raw.

"Marlee, you shouldn't be here." He heard the strain in his voice, even as her fingers dipped inside his briefs and closed on him. The pressure of touch alone could make him come, and he felt his balls pull up in anticipation.

She paused, a dark cloud crossing her face. "You don't want me here? Don't want what we have together?"

He should have told her that she deserved more, much more than he could give her. His dark and lonely thoughts raced past, and he wished he could man-up and say that. God, he was such a jerk, and he wanted to give in to the rage he felt and shove her out the door.

Instead, he pulled her in, locking his lips over hers as he sucked in the gasp of her shock. One hand closed in the band holding her hair back, giving it a hard yank that must have hurt. He didn't care. She was the drug he craved, and if that made him an addict, so be it.

Her body stilled as he dove in deeper, spearing his tongue into her mouth in an unrelenting tempo. When she suddenly closed her teeth around it loosely, his cock pulsed in her hands. As if reminded, she stroked him firmly, and the moan caught in his throat as her fingers tightened.

How long they stood like this, he wasn't sure. Not that it mattered. His tongue danced with hers, and he sucked it into his mouth. He tangled his hands in her freed hair, wrapping it around his fingers to keep her in place. He had vague thoughts about a condom and the bedroom, before she increased the pressure and rhythm of her hands, and deliberate consciousness left him.

Guiding him with her pressure, she turned him, and he swallowed another groan as her hands trapped him even tighter. His balls felt like they were ready to explode. When her grip fell away, he nearly yelled with relief, only to feel a wave of disappointment that her hands were no longer doing their magic on him.

Tripping over the denim trapping his ankles, he fell back, momentarily surprised when he landed on the softness of the couch instead of hard floor. He blinked up at her, wanting to tell her how deep his feelings ran, while he ached to cover her body with his and make reality disappear.

But she seemed to read his mind. She fell to her knees in front on of him, leaning forward and placing a single hard kiss on his mouth before trailing down his neck with open-mouthed licks. When she reached his nipple, she nipped him through his t-shirt.

His erection jolted in sudden pleasure, and his focus became pinpointed on this woman and the aching release he needed more than his next breath. He wanted to thrust inside her and bury himself to the hilt, unmoving until neither one of them could stand the pressure. Then he wanted to pump into her until she screamed his name and they both came harder than ever before.

He reached for her, intent on shoving her shirt over her heard, ripping off her bra, and diving between her small, firm breasts. But she surprised him again as her mouth continued to travel south, and when she reached his cock, her lips closed around him and she hummed.

The vibration did it, unlocking his inner demons in a way that nothing else could. Control shot to hell faster than an assault rifle on auto. His fingers buried in her hair, lifting it so that it fell across his thighs as her mouth worked him over. Each suck brought him closer to that line of unbelievable pleasure he knew he couldn't help but cross.

He didn't deserve this, even as he roughened his grip on her head and thrust deeper into her mouth.

Her hands seemed to be everywhere, stroking his balls or tugging on his nipples, and he tried to force her to slow down the pace. She sucked again, seeming to swallow him whole. When he couldn't hold back any longer, he heard the pain in his voice as he shouted her name and climaxed in her mouth.

>>>>>

Her core burned and her nipples ached, seeking her own release. She was so turned on, she was afraid she'd jump into his lap and ride him to a mutually satisfactory conclusion. Keeping her clothes on was meant as a deterrent, even as she stripped off as much as possible on his body. Every kiss, every suck, every lick – it was all for Jake. The last time she'd done this, years ago with Davos, it was his punishment forced on her, one of many he doled out.

With Jake, it was her gift to him. Maybe she could say with her body what she couldn't tell him in words. He still didn't know everything about her, but what he did know, he accepted. He even seemed to want to slay dragons on her behalf.

The idea sent a wave of ice-cold dread through her veins. It would hurt Jake to know she still kept secrets from him. It would destroy his career if he became more involved. Others would feel the pain too. Her faults seemed to multiply every day. Sudden sadness at the idea made her gasp as her eyes filled with tears.

Jake's thrusts became less urgent as he softened in her mouth. As if he couldn't bear the idea of letting her go, his fingers caressed her scalp as she too slowed the pace. With a final kiss, she let him fall away and looked up, wondering what she would find in his face.

She'd laid herself bare for him, at least in a sexual way. There wasn't anything she was afraid to do with him, and yet her past kept a distance between them. Allowing him to unlock her heart was easier than unlocking her secrets.

Her heart gave a funny little jump as her eyes settled on his face. His eyes were closed, his expression one of utter peace. To find that with Jake would be amazing, but it was a road to nowhere, and she hated to delude herself. He was a cop. She was an ex-con. She might never be able to share part of herself with him, and somehow, he'd know.

The pumping rise and fall of his chest eased, and as it did, the bliss faded until no expression marked his face. Had he fallen asleep? She didn't think so, since his breathing wasn't steady. As she watched, a frown pulled his eyebrows together.

His eyes remained closed, and she didn't like the look that was coming to his strong features. If anything, it made them darker and edgier than ever. She shifted, hoping to stand without alerting him, but her hair caught in his left hand, and his fingers tightened when she tried to rise.

His eyes snapped open, lasering in on hers without hesitation. What she saw there was a dark and vicious anger and something else.

Loathing. It was on his face. She knew she didn't read him wrong. He hated the idea that he could like what she could do for him. He was probably thinking about all the men in her past. He'd figured out what she already knew.

She would never be good enough for him.

Wanting to dart out the door before he said anything, she tried again to stand, and again, he held her prisoner. The fact that his jeans and underwear were around his calves made him no less formidable. His stare alone riveted her to the floor, and he didn't look in the least bit happy.

"Jake, let me up."

If anything, the thunder in his gaze darkened further. His hand moved, releasing her hair, and he shrank into the couch as if he couldn't stand the touch of strands on his naked skin.

He might have passed out for a while. In fact, he was almost sure of it, his body still twitching like he'd been tasered. He'd floated, unable to resist stroking her soft hair as it twined between his fingers. That she gave him this incredible gift was nothing short of a miracle.

And he'd taken it, probably treating her no better than that son of a bitch ex-husband.

No, she deserved better. She deserved his respect. She'd turned her life into something positive and she stayed clean, even when there were plenty of reasons to bury her suffering. He could read between the lines when she'd told him about the abuse. The scars she bore were more than skin-deep.

What kind of a monster was he? His control issues were past the point of being civil. Blame the accident that might cost him the job he loved. Blame the reality that forced him to see his way wasn't always the only way. Blame him for being an asshole who used her with no more care than the asshole who beat her.

Yeah, the blame was all on him.

His loathing cut so deeply that he flinched. He didn't deserve Marlee, and maybe he didn't deserve to serve if he couldn't understand what motivated the people he tried to help every day. He'd never thought about it in this light before. Here he'd been thinking that he was better, in control. He was probably worse.

Self-anger snapped his eyes open, and the first thing he saw was Marlee's gorgeous face. He wondered what she'd looked like before the doctors fixed her injuries, before she'd been beaten, before she'd been drawn into a life that cut her off from whatever family she had. Her eyes, large and round as she watched him carefully, would be the same. The flecks of taupe seemed to stand out against the pale blue background in stark relief, or maybe he was romanticizing it. He vacillated between self-loathing and stark fear. Because he'd just figured it out.

Scars and all, inside and out, she was the one person who could convince him, without pleading her case, that he'd been dead wrong. Justice wasn't a sharp sword but a dull blade, and sometimes, it did more damage than good as it sliced through to the truth.

His fingers tightened as he frowned at his thoughts, examining her face for her truth. Would she forgive him? If he said the words, would she laugh them off as casually as she did their sexual relationship? When he let her go, the trail of her hair across his over-amped flesh made him recoil.

He hated what he'd done to her. That she felt it was okay to put his needs ahead of her pleasure was a sure sign he'd screwed up. He knew what it cost her to be on her knees in front of him. The position of servitude would be a reminder of the pain of her past. If his self-loathing could grow any deeper, it just did.

He needed to gather his wits and state his case. It might be too early for the words, but he could show her how much he cared. Acceptance came first. She needed to forgive him.

When Marlee leaped to her feet and swayed, his first thought was her safety, and meaning to catch her before she fell, he lunged forward. The tangle of clothes around his legs brought him to his knees, and he cursed as he hit the floor. The jarring brought a spasm to his back, making speech impossible for a few vital seconds.

"Marlee, wait." He panted the words, hoping she heard him.

She never stopped, digging in her purse as she pulled open the door with enough force to slam it into the wall. Rain poured outside, drowning out everything he tried to yell to her.

Through the opening, he could see her yank open the passenger door of her car, and he struggled to stand and pull up his briefs and his jeans. The belt buckle jammed into tender flesh that had only minutes before been so well loved, and it brought him to his knees once more, curling into a fetal position as the bite of metal reminded him that he needed to think with his big brain first after this. The crank and cough of an engine alerted him he was too late. His SUV was parked in town, and he had no hope of catching up to her.

Long after the rumbling faded, he lay on the rug, staring out into the rainy darkness, and wondered how he could make anything right out of this mess.

Chapter 19

The noise of the bar intruded on his pain, but he couldn't stand to be alone in his house. Marlee's unique lavender and vanilla scent filled the space, no doubt left there by her jacket. He'd picked it up off his living room floor, but he was unwilling to return it. Holding it, Jake could relive their last moments together and design a different ending. He didn't want to let that go.

Besides, after driving for hours, he hadn't been able to find her. Today, her car was at her apartment, but she wasn't. He called upon skills from his teenage years and picked the lock on her door, letting himself inside to look around. Okay, that was wrong, but he worried that she'd done something stupid, and he couldn't wait the requisite twenty-four hours to gain legal entry. He'd searched her car too, finding evidence of her tears as she left his house in the wadded up tissues on the floor of her usually immaculate beater. He'd thrown away those and the ones in her apartment, unwilling to look at this reminder of how badly he'd used her.

And those were the rules he broke on just the first day.

"Are you okay beating yourself up, or can anyone join the fun?"

He glanced up from his beer to see his brother standing at the chair across the table. Next to Deke, Rick and Geno stood a pace behind as if waiting for an indication that it was safe to approach. Maybe they were smart to do that, because he didn't feel friendly.

He kicked the chair as he pulled his feet off it – another rule broken in this fine establishment – and let it fall at his brother's feet. The long-time waitress, passing by with a tray full of drinks, gave him a dirty look. It was one she gave out of line patrons, one he'd often followed to see if trouble was about to be caused.

Yeah, maybe he was ready to cause some trouble of his own.

Deke's eyes skimmed him up and down with a frown. "Okay, not feeling exactly friendly, but I don't see a weapon. You carrying?"

He always wore his personal piece, and his big brother knew it. Why he bothered to ask, Jake wasn't sure. He stared back at Deke as he picked up his glass with deliberate slow movements, his eyes never wavering as he took a long drink. Deke cocked an eyebrow at him, and Jake scowled in return.

"I just want to know if I need to intervene, in case you pick a fight or something."

The fact that Deke chose to needle him about this made it all the more painfully obvious, even if the empty beer in front of him didn't flash a neon sign. He was so fucked up.

Deke turned away to Rick and Geno, saying something in a low voice that brought nods from the other men as they turned toward the bar without glancing back. Crouching down, Deke righted the upturned chair and sat on it backwards, cowboy style. He pushed the ball cap back on his forehead as if it was a Stetson, resting his arms on the back of the chair. And he stared.

They were only a year and a half apart in age, but right now, Jake felt ancient, and by decades. He'd made mistakes he didn't even know he was capable of, and now he had no idea how to fix them.

On the second day of Marlee's disappearance, he'd checked the local hospital, running into the same doc who treated him after the accident. Dr. Kinkead listened to his story describing a friend he couldn't find, one that might have been hurt and could have sought help at the ER, and shook his head before Jake even finished spinning his tale.

"Do you have a warrant? A subpoena? You know I can't tell you anything. Patient confidentiality."

"But Dr. Kinkead, she might be in serious trouble." Like, she could have gotten high and wandered into the forest or fallen in a river.

"It's Noah, Jake, and I still can't tell you anything about any patient."

Noah's careful wording made Jake perk up. Examining the man's face carefully, he wondered if he read the situation wrong.

The doctor continued, "But I can assure you that no woman matching the description you just gave me has been admitted or sought treatment through the ER in the last few days. When did you say she went missing?"

Jake mumbled his thanks, grateful to know that at least she wasn't lying there in a hospital bed. She didn't have her car. She wouldn't have gone far. He kicked himself for not hanging on to her phone, to search it for clues. But at least she could get in touch – if she wanted to, that is.

His heart did crazy trippy things, pounding so hard in his chest at times that he wondered if he'd keel over. Then everything slowed to an eerie quarter-speed pace as he replayed their last conversation. It always ended the same, with her eyes welled up and tears falling like rain.

Fuck, he had it bad. If Ma showed up now with a lecture about love and remorse, he'd take out his gun and shoot himself.

Deke continued to stare at him, his expression part humor and part sympathy. Rick approached the table and set a pint of beer in front of Deke, raising an eyebrow to Jake as he gestured with the one in his other hand.

Ah, what the hell. Obviously, his rules didn't work anyway. When the beer made a full, satisfying ring as it hit the table, he reached for it.

"So you want to tell me what has you angrier than a bull?"

Jake glared at his brother over the top of the beer, thankful when his face disappeared into the foam as Jake chugged down half of it. He slapped the glass on the table.

"Isn't there supposed to be more to that? You know, 'angrier than a bull when,' dot, dot, dot?"

Deke snorted a laugh, lifting his own glass and taking a short sip. When he set down the glass and didn't respond, only continuing to stare, Jake shifted in his seat.

"I didn't do anything wrong."

Why he felt the need to defend himself, he wasn't sure. For years, he'd been positive he always lived on the right side of things.

"Did I say you did anything wrong? I'm not even sure what else you've done."

"Wait, what else? What do you know? How could you know anything?"

Deke smiled, raising his glass once more. Jake did the same, surprised to see the clear bottom when he lowered it. Without a word, Geno approached the table with a pitcher, grabbed Jake's glass, and tilted it to fill a perfect pour. Nodding his direction, he left again, and he and Rick stared back at them from their seats at the bar.

"You can't know anything. I didn't do anything."

Exactly. He didn't do what he should have done, which was be honest and caring with Marlee. None of the past two days would have happened if he'd been a man about it. He'd treated her badly instead of treasuring her as he should, and he only had himself to blame when she ran away.

Deke stood up, turning the chair back to the table as he motioned over the two other men. Geno picked up the pitcher as Rick grabbed a basket of pretzels. They approached the table with careful slow steps, as if they were afraid to rile him. It would be amusing, if he felt kindly toward the world today. Which he definitely did not.

Pulling up more chairs and settling in, all three of them took sips of their beer and Rick munched on the pretzels, carefully putting only one in his mouth at a time. Geno topped off everyone's glasses and signaled to the waitress with the empty pitcher before pulling his chair in closer.

"Have any of you seen Marlee Cruiz in the past two days?"

Jake's abrupt question brought frowns to the other men as they shook their heads in denial. Geno added, "I'm not even sure I know who she is."

Rick stopped munching long enough to clarify. "She works at Bliss Spa, and she does massages and whatever else the women do there."

"I've been going to her for my massages, to help my back." Jake heard the growl in his voice, but there didn't seem to be any point in stopping it. They sat down here, so they asked to be part of his bad humor.

He continued, "She's been missing now for two days. I can't find her anywhere."

"Why don't you try to trace her car?" Rick's statement of the obvious only made Jake angrier.

"Because I know where her car is, damn it. It's sitting in front of her apartment. She's not there, but most of her stuff is. The only item I can confirm as missing is her purse."

Deke tilted his head to the side as he examined Jake closely. "And you know this how?"

"Because I checked her apartment already, all right? Fuck." Jake slammed his hand on the table in frustration, causing the others to exchange worried glances.

Straightening as if making the supreme sacrifice, Deke asked, "You went inside her apartment. Um, I'm guessing you didn't have a warrant or anything, since you're still on medical leave."

Jake shook his head.

"Okay, this may be a first. You broke the rules, Jake." Deke leaned back and smiled with admiration. "All I can say is, about damn time."

The fact that he broke not only the rules but also a couple of laws – or more – wasn't lost on him.

Geno tapped a finger on the table, drawing Jake's attention.

"I stopped by the spa the other day, and Bliss was in an uproar. She usually is in an uproar about something, but in this case, it seems that someone cancelled a stack of appointments. That must be Marlee. Bliss can't find her, and she's blaming the man Marlee's seeing. Is that man you?"

When Jake didn't respond, Deke glanced in Geno's direction and gave a small nod. No one said anything, and the silence grew until it seemed to be louder than the noise of the bar. Rick pulled out his phone and tapped in something, staring at it for a full minute without looking up until it pinged. He turned to Deke and said, "Gabby hasn't heard from her, and those two are tight."

All eyes focused on Jake once more, and he fought the urge to squirm or jump up and run. As the stares continued, he felt his anger peak to a new high. They had no right to judge him. Yes, he'd been less than forthcoming about the trash talk happening in his head, but he loved the woman. She was missing, so he was worried about her. What was so unusual about that?

His conscious thought caught up to his emotions and slammed on the mental brakes so hard that he was surprised he stayed seated in the chair and not bucked to the floor.

He loved Marlee. As in, the big L-word. When had that happened? And he'd treated her like dirt.

"Whoa, I recognize that look. It appears that our friend here has had himself a revelation." Rick grinned as he lifted his glass in a cheer.

Deke began to smile too, saying, "Yes, I've been there too. Jake, it looks like it's just struck you."

Only Geno continued to frown. "What is it? I don't get it."

Deke slapped Geno on the shoulder, his laughter ringing out in the bar. The amusement spread to Rick, who shook his head in mock dismay. Deke leaned in toward the center of the table and clarified in a loud stage whisper, "I forget you're a single man, Geno, so you might not recognize the tell. But what Rick and I see is that Jake's got big feelings for Ms. Marlee, and he's just now realized it."

He pulled his jacket closed tighter and wondered if this was a ridiculous venture. He could be stopped for stalking. Worse yet, he probably worried people as they exited the meeting.

The NA meeting would break up in about five minutes, if his one experience there with Marlee was anything to go by. Since she hadn't driven herself, someone might have picked her up to give her a ride. She hadn't seemed overly friendly on that previous night, but she also hadn't been inclined to talk with anyone, him included.

Where could she have gone? She didn't own much, and from what he could tell, she hadn't packed in haste or left in any hurry. Some of her clothes might be missing, but how would he know? She wore black so much, it would be impossible for him to distinguish what she might have taken with her. As to a suitcase, he had no clue.

His SUV sat in the parking lot across the street from the small church housing the meeting. Granted, this was only one of the NA meetings held that evening around the area. Add to that the number of AA meetings and he couldn't be sure he was even at the right place. Marlee could be at any of them.

People in NA had sponsors, he knew that, but he had no clue who to call about Marlee. It could be any of the people currently trickling out of the building. Or it could be someone from somewhere else entirely. A couple of the meeting attendees lit cigarettes as they walked away from the building, and others lingered and talked. If he approached them, what could he say? But he had to try.

He pushed the door open and jumped out, intent on crossing to intercept two people who had smiled at them when he was here with Marlee. As he jogged across the street, both of their heads lifted and they turned to face him, drawing closer together. It wasn't a great neighborhood, but he didn't think he looked like a threat.

Or maybe he did.

"Hi. You might not remember me, but a friend and I came to a meeting a while back, and I was wondering if you've seen her over the past couple of days."

The two frowned at him. The young African-American man tilted his head as if to examine Jake more closely before suddenly breaking into a smile.

"Oh yeah, you and that woman came in kindda late and sat in the back. Never spoke. Don't worry, honey. It's hard for any of us to chime in now and then. How long you been clean?"

Jake shook his head as he spoke. He didn't want to be mistaken for a druggie. He wasn't like that. He would never be that weak.

His thoughts snagged on that. Did he think of Marlee as weak? Her physical strength wasn't in question. But did he consider her emotionally pathetic? Did he think less of her because of her past? Was that one of the wedges he'd driven between them?

His Marlee wasn't weak in any sense of the word, and he felt a surge of pride at that. She'd turned her life around, ridded herself of a wrecked past, and moved on. Her clients respected her, and Bliss trusted her. The girl tribe liked her, Gabby in particular, and these were not women who were fooled easily.

Plus, he loved her. How this had blossomed so quickly or raged inside him with such total devastation that he couldn't sleep or think straight, he wasn't sure. Deke and Rick had assured him this was how the realization about love happened. A lightning bolt came down out of a cloudless sky and left you dazed and scorched, wondering what hit you.

"Let's get going. I don't like this guy."

The older woman pulled on her friend's arm, and the man's smile slipped a little. Jake felt his only opportunity to connect with someone who might know Marlee's whereabouts slipping away too.

"Wait, please, I'm sorry. I'm looking for Marlee Cruiz. She's about five foot six, straight black hair, and dresses in a lot of black and a ball cap. She's been missing for three days now."

The two paused in their retreat, and the unfriendly woman asked, "Who are you?"

"I'm – ," he stuttered, then focused again, "I'm her boyfriend."

"Well, boyfriend, if this woman you're looking for wanted you to find her, she'd let you know. Tell the police. They got ways of looking for people." The black man waved a hand as if dismissing him.

"But I am the police," Jake added, digging in his pocket for his badge. When he flashed it, the woman paled and spun away. He didn't care. Obviously, she had something to hide. The man merely watched him, his expression giving nothing away and no longer friendly.

"Let me give you a word of advice, Mr. Policeman. What happens in a meeting stays in a meeting. If you really are this girl's boyfriend, and she wanted to be found, you'd know. No, I'm not sure you're not just some narc, trying to figure out if she scored and you can bust her." He gave a grunt Jake took for disgusted disapproval and began to turn away.

"Wait, please. I have to find her. I'm worried about her. You see, I love her."

The man looked back at him with a disbelieving expression on his face. He said, "Aw honey, that's what they all say."

Chapter 20

Jake paced his living room, frustrated with the lack of progress in his search for Marlee. Since three days had passed, he tried to file a missing persons report, and his lieutenant had been less than sympathetic.

"Let me see if I get this straight. You can't find your girlfriend, who, if I understand history correctly, is the same woman you banged in the back of a car not so long ago. No one's seen her in town, but no one else is worried. You've been inside her apartment, and other than her purse, nothing seems to be missing. She give you a key to that place, Kermarrec?"

He'd said nothing in response to her question. The lieutenant pinned him with that steely stare of hers and he barely avoided dropping his gaze to give himself away.

She continued, "I checked with her boss at the spa, and she said that Ms. Cruiz cancelled her appointments. Not unusual in that business according to the owner. Operators set their hours and determine their schedule. You got a problem with that, Kermarrec?"

He knew that already too, since Bliss called him to say she knew Marlee accessed the online appointment system, so she was no longer worried. Concerned about why Marlee left without a word as to why, but not worried about her safety. More to the point, Marlee had only cancelled the appointments for the beginning of her workweek. That might mean she would be back tomorrow. Or she would cancel more later today. Either way, he wanted to know where she was.

"Lieutenant, she could be in trouble. She could be hurt." He didn't want to mention her past drug issue. It would be too easy for the lieutenant to dismiss her completely if that was the cause.

"Which brain are you thinking with, Jake? The one between your ears or the one between your legs?"

She raised a legitimate question. He'd thought long and hard about this as he sat outside Marlee's apartment building long enough to make the residents suspicious. When the property owner requested he move on, Jake barely controlled his temper and addressed him with so little civility that the man left mumbling something about police brutality.

If he wore the lieutenant's boots, he'd question his motives too.

"We can trace the GPS in her cell phone. You just have to approve it. Please Lieutenant, I need to know she's okay."

The frown on the face of the woman wearing the stripes deepened until her eyebrows nearly met in the middle. She picked up a pen and tapped a neat stack of papers on her desk, watching Jake carefully. Her expression didn't lighten up, and in that, he read her reluctance to help him and her doubts about his objectives.

"Have her family file the missing persons report, Jake. They're the only ones who can initiate anything at this point. You know the rules."

"But she has no family. At least, she's never mentioned anyone to me."

He didn't need the sudden skeptical rise of her eyebrows to her hairline to know how stupid he sounded. He was a romantic sap for a woman who didn't think enough of their relationship to tell him her life story. As he stood to leave her office, he noted a single brief softening around her eyes, the only sympathy he'd get.

Stretching again, he contemplated changing his jeans for sweats and trying to work out the kinks and pains in his back. Then again, he could get in his truck and cruise Main Street, looking for Marlee. If he ended up outside her apartment again, it didn't hurt to hang around for a while to see if she returned.

Keys in hand, his heart jumped and quickened when a knock sounded on his door. He couldn't cover the distance fast enough, yanking it open without checking the peephole because he was certain he knew who stood on the other side. He nearly said her name on his next breath until he saw his visitors.

"There you are, son. You know, rumor has it that you're chasing a young lady. How do you think I feel, hearing about this from the boys at the bakery?"

Emie sailed into the living room, patting his cheek as she passed. Outside, Deke stood on the steps, his apology written on his face. Even as he too entered with a sympathetic pat on the shoulder, Jake couldn't resist glancing up and down the street.

"So, Jake, when were you planning to tell your old mother about your young lady, hhmmm? Now I've been hearing stories all over town. What's this about you in the back seat of a car in a compromising position?"

His face redden as he continued to stare into the empty street.

Behind him, Ma continued, "Did something happen to your bed? Why did you have to make out in a car? Of course, there's nothing wrong with a good back seat noodling. Why, once upon a time, your dad and I dropped our – "

"Ma!" Jake and Deke protested in stereo. Jake turned back inside, knowing that by now, his face was the color of an uncooked steak. Deke didn't look much better.

"Sorry, Jake. I tried to stop her, but as soon as she heard you were chasing your girlfriend, she insisted on racing over. I drove her so she wouldn't break every speed limit in the county and her neck in the process." Deke paused, and the understanding in his brother's expression unsettled him further. "Any word?"

Jake shook his head. Deke clapped him on the shoulder as they followed Emie into the kitchen. What he really wanted to do was get in his truck and drive until he found Marlee.

Ma rummaged in his cabinets until she came up with a small box he'd long forgotten she'd brought him. Bending into a lower cabinet, the sound of metal on metal action ceased with an exclamation of triumph when she stood with a tea kettle in her hand and turned to smile at them.

"What we all need is a nice cup of herbal tea. You can tell me all about your young lady and what you did to make her run away, and then we'll figure out how to fix it."

"Ma, you promised." Deke gave their mother an angry glare before shooting another apologetic look to Jake. They both knew better. When Emileen was on a mission like this, it was best to ride it out to its logical conclusion.

Turning on the stove under the kettle, she busied herself with mugs and tea bags as she asked, "So, Marlee Cruiz, tell me about her."

Jake dropped on to his couch in resignation and thought about pointing his personal weapon at his mother to convince her to leave him alone. More to the point, she needed to leave Marlee alone. If Ma got to her before he did, who knows what kinds of things she'd spout off. Marlee would be sized up as daughter-in-law material and Ma would be planning the wedding before three minutes had passed.

Funny, but that idea didn't bring a roiling to his gut as he expected it to. Ma would like Marlee, and she'd fall in love with the wounded soul as much as the powerful woman she'd become. Just as he had.

Ma pinned him with a stare that left him no wiggle room to escape. "Exactly why are you breaking the rules for her, son?"

Jake paced to his living room window. There wasn't anything to see outside, and he wished that Marlee would suddenly appear in his short driveway, run into his arms, and tell him why she'd run away.

"Jake? Ma has a point. This isn't like you. I heard you got in trouble with your lieutenant over this yesterday."

It wasn't as if his run-in with the lieutenant had been private. If she knew he accessed official databases to research Marlee's past, to learn where she might have run to, she'd kick his ass first and ask questions later. And he'd deserve it.

Behind him, he heard Ma settle on the couch, the same place where Marlee had made passionate love to him. The juxtaposition of images made his head spin until it settled on Marlee's brimming eyes and look of heartbreaking sadness as she raced out the door.

"Deke, stay out of this. I know what I'm doing. I'm a cop, after all."

"Oh, and that would be your justification for taking the law into your own hands? How many misdemeanors have you committed so far? What's breaking and entering, a misdemeanor or a felony? And stalking her by sitting outside her apartment, making the tenants nervous?"

"Oh, you're stalking her too? Come here and sit down by me and tell me all about it." His mother all but clapped her hands and the delight in her voice resigned him to the fact that tonight, he had lost all control of his family, not to mention himself.

He turned to face his angry brother and his gleeful mother and said the only truth that made sense.

"I'm in love with Marlee. I have to find her, because without her, my life isn't complete."

Deke's face blanked as he processed the declaration. From the couch, Ma bounced in her seat and patted the space next to her. From the kitchen, the teakettle whistled the completion of its task as his mother said, "Come here, dear boy, and sit down. Tell your Ma all about your lady love."

Chapter 21

Darkness swallowed the parking lot as she paid the driver and trudged up the walkway. She'd been lucky to find the gypsy cab hanging around the Amtrak depot in town, hoping for a late night fare. Without him, she would have had to walk the miles to her apartment, and after the last three days, she wasn't sure she had it in her.

The swirl of emotions inside mixed with her empty stomach, leaving her lightheaded. She'd found her, she'd seen her, and if her heart swelled any bigger, her chest wouldn't be able to contain it.

Her daughter. At almost eleven, she had that gangly coltish look of a girl about to sprout another foot in height, the last of her childish pudginess evident in her face and body. Marlee had been like that too, one day a round kid, and the next day, growing into the adult she would become. What she did with her womanhood wasn't something she wanted to dwell on. She wanted better for her daughter. And foster care wasn't it.

She shifted her purse and the small backpack she'd taken on her journey. Once she knew where to find her, she wanted to see her little girl, and she couldn't explain to anyone, particular a handsome sheriff's deputy, why she had to do it. Jake wouldn't understand. Besides, after the other night, he hated her.

After all these years, she needed to make amends to her daughter, assuring that the rest of her young life would be perfect. Marlee would whisk her away and they'd start over with new identities in a new place. It wasn't the first time she'd changed her life. She would do the same for her daughter. That was her plan.

But her daughter appeared to be happy and well cared for. Her clothes looked clean and almost new. Playing outside during recess, she interacted with other kids and laughed, a rich wonderful sound. The memory of that alone would keep Marlee going for days. Her smile was one Marlee recognized, her own smile before her ex beat her face to a pulp. Except for hair that curled more and more copper in her skin, the child got no physical characteristics from Davos. She hoped her little girl got none of his ruthless inhumanity too.

She'd watched until the children returned inside. Then she'd followed her daughter at a distance on the walk home from school. The little girl skipped along with her friends, all of them singing a song Marlee didn't recognize. She thought she could separate her daughter's clear tone among the chorus, but she wasn't sure.

The street she turned into was worn, the houses tired and yards nonexistent. But even if the house seemed dreary, her daughter didn't hesitate at the door. When she'd disappeared inside, Marlee stood behind a tree down the block and stared at it, willing the door to open again so she could have one more look. She couldn't take her daughter away when she was happy and seemed settled. The realization brought tears to her eyes then, and it did again now.

Returning here alone had been her only option now that her quest was over. She felt empty inside. No daughter. No Jake either. Her future was dark, blank. Rounding the corner, she dug inside her purse for her keys as her tears fell, juggling both purse and backpack clumsily in the darker confines near the stairwell.

When she ran into hard warmth, she yelped and dropped her things, putting her hands up to ward off the intruder.

Her breathing hitched as her hands caught on denim and knit. Her body registered instant recognition before her mind could catch up as she looked into sea-turbulent eyes reflecting the weak light. Even as her heart settled into a jungle beat, she opened her mouth to say his name, but she never had a chance.

Jake's mouth rammed on to hers like he wasn't planning to let go any time soon. He sucked her breath away, leaving her spinning, and she didn't care. After everything she'd been through, his welcome home was exactly what she needed. She threaded her fingers into his over-long hair and pulled him closer.

She tasted desperation in the kiss, but she wasn't sure if it came from him or from her. He'd filled her mind as much as her daughter these past days, and in that time, she realized that no matter what, she'd take what he gave her for as long as he was interested. Even if he didn't respect her, she'd take the connection and the gratification of being in a physical relationship more satisfying than any drug. When he left, she'd have those memories to fill the long upcoming years of emptiness.

She inhaled the scent of him, an aroma she'd recognize anywhere, and ran her hands over the muscled back she'd come to know so intimately. She knew she'd left him in a lurch, and undoubtedly his continuing pain caused the tension she felt him holding in every muscle she touched. His tongue wrapped hers in an erotic dance, and she wished she had more light, to see the expression on his face.

Pulling back slightly, she felt his fingers tighten in her hair and push at the base of her spine to bring her closer. She longed to grind against the erection pressing against her, their perfect fit lining things up and making her wish they were inside, on her meager and unexciting bed doing exciting things to each other. But she owed Jake an explanation. After that, if he still wanted her, she'd be more than happy to oblige.

He rested his forehead on hers, his hands tracing her face. When his fingers examined the uneven match of her cheekbones, she flinched and tried to step away, but he held her closer. She heard only rough emotion in his voice when he said, "You scared the hell out of me, Marlee."

It popped out before she could stop it. "I'm sorry, Jake." Then she winced at her stumbling apology.

His head reared back and she waited for him to tell her once more that he didn't want to hear that from her. His eyes locked on hers and she imagined that the dim light must be playing tricks on her, because there appeared to be tears in Jake's eyes.

"No, I'm the one who needs to apologize to you. I didn't realize what I have with you, didn't value it enough, until you walked out on me. I don't blame you. I was a bastard and I took advantage of you. Will you forgive me, Marlee?"

He cursed the darkness, but begging her forgiveness was something that couldn't wait until they were inside. If he frightened her away, he needed to control himself. If she didn't trust him enough to tell him why she ran, he'd learn to live with it and change her mind. He'd replayed her words so many times in his brain that it felt like a tape on auto-replay. "I don't do cops." He'd change her mind about that too.

As long as she let him show her how much he loved her.

Feeling her shiver, he released her with regret and bent to pick up her things. He handed the purse back to her as she watched him, her wide eyes filling her face. When she made no move to take it, he put it over one shoulder, holding the straps of her backpack in one hand. He linked the fingers of his other hand through hers and gave her an encouraging pull toward the stairs, heartened even more when she followed without protesting.

At the top of the stairs, he held her purse open toward her. She stared at him, frowning. Then she reached her empty hand not into the purse, but to his face, tracing lines and creases as if examining them.

"You didn't look this old before."

He grunted out a laugh. What could he say? That the last three days had aged him more than everything he'd seen in over ten years on the force? He went for honesty.

"I was worried about you. I couldn't find you, you weren't picking up your phone, and no one knew where you were." He paused, realizing that he wasn't saying anything meaningful when she looked like she planned to apologize to him again. Giving her a quick kiss to shut her mouth seemed like the best solution.

She tasted like vanilla and lavender, reminding him of his favorite cookies, and he realized that if he didn't get them inside, he'd have another misdemeanor under his belt.

Breaking off the kiss, her eyes popped open and he saw the swirling confusion war with something else before she masked her expression. He regretted that. She no longer gave him her openness, another thing he'd have to earn back. She took the purse from him this time, digging around with her head bent until she came up with the keys and put them in the lock.

When he pushed the door open, she strode in ahead of him, hitting light switches as she advanced across the small space.

It looked just like it had two days ago when he broke inside. The darkness, the shoddy lock on her door, and the meager accommodations reminded him that he didn't want her living here anymore.

"You need to live in a better place, Marlee. That lock wouldn't stop a ten-year-old with an attitude and you didn't see me in the shadows when you got home. This place isn't safe."

She simply stared at him, her face giving nothing away.

"And your car is an invitation to trouble too. The passenger side back door doesn't even lock, did you know that?"

Now she looked suspicious. Dropping her purse on one of the two folding chairs, she glanced around, the first round quick and the second more slowly, examining things closely. When she looked back at him, he could read the anger as easily as a regulation book. She was pissed.

"Did you come in here? Without my permission?"

He realized he was busted about one second before she marched over to him and got in his face, her hands on her hips in rigid tension. He'd cleaned up the place a little, getting rid of the tissues she'd left on the folding table she used in the dining area and the overflowing trash can of them in her tiny bathroom. He didn't want her coming home to reminders.

He nodded.

"And if I check my car, I bet you cleaned that up too. Am I right?"

Figuring it was better to let her have her rant, he simply nodded again.

"And why did you do these things, Jake? You broke into my home. You broke into my car, and don't use the excuse that the door was unlocked. I know it's against your precious rules. So why did you do it?"

Her eyes flashed at him, the light blue simmer like rapids on the river at high water. She didn't bite her lower lip like she did when she worried something. No, her kissable mouth parted on her huffing breaths, the same breaths that raised her breasts to press against his chest on each pass. She didn't back down from his intense stare, and returned it with one of her own. She was magnificent.

That broke him faster than the promise of a lighter sentence to a three strikes crook.

"I was scared, Marlee, scared that something happened to you. Fear makes people do things they wouldn't under other circumstances."

Her face softened slightly, but she shook her head as if she didn't believe him. Glancing away on a deep sigh, she moved to the open door, putting a hand on the knob. She said, "As you can see, I'm fine, Jake. I had to see someone, and I didn't think it was any of your concern if I was gone. After all, we're barely friends."

Her easy dismissal of everything they shared angered him, the feeling rising swiftly on the echoes of his fear the past few days. Marlee was back, but instead of linking her body with his, she pushed him away as if they didn't matter. As if she didn't matter to him.

Realization dawned at the same moment when she tapped her foot in impatience and crossed her arms over her breasts. He wanted those arms wrapped around him, her small perfect breasts pressed against his chest as their mouths locked and did amazing things to each other. If he wanted that badly enough, he had to take a risk, a big one.

He kept his pace slow as he stalked toward her, the confines of the small apartment disappearing at the periphery of his vision. All he could see was Marlee, her perfect unbalanced face, and the guarded expression in her eyes. He hadn't been completely honest with her.

When they stood toe to toe, he looked down without touching her. Their locked gazes were enough connection to say what he knew he had to admit.

"We're much more than barely friends, Ms. Cruiz. I don't know what you're feeling, but I can tell you with complete certainty that I would break every rule for you. I'm in love with you, Marlee, and while you may not return the feeling yet, I swear I'll make you trust me with your secrets and love me as much as I love you."

In a million years, she never thought she'd hear this man say those words to her. Even Davos never uttered them, not when he lied to her while on his best behavior to win her over, and never in the years that followed, when he took his control of her for granted. The last time anyone said anything like those words to her, she'd been a different person, a girl with hidden hopes and anger at the world, and the words hadn't been said by a lover.

Jake continued to stare at her, a mix of emotions crossing his face and making his eyes blaze blue-green with intensity. Remorse. Pain. Love. A hint of anger. Worry. Back to love.

It all came back to love.

If she opened up to him now, he'd push her away. Could she ever be completely honest with him? His life was in Flynn's Crossing, and if she stayed, the inevitable would happen. Her secrets, every single dirty one of them, would come out. It was only a matter of time and circumstance. And he'd realize that the woman he thought he knew and loved lied to him.

Not lied, exactly. More like an error of omission. But that would be the same as a lie to Jake.

Still, when he watched her with such hope, she couldn't help but hope too. Her life had been without that emotion for so long, and if the last few days had taught her anything, it was to grab on to what she could in life and hope that somehow, everything would work out.

If she said it in words without telling him everything, she'd still be denying him the truth he deserved. Loving Jake was part of her soul. Not sharing everything made her feel like a fraud. But the truth would destroy what they had together, and without Jake beside her, her life would be an empty shell.

She took the final step forward and leaned her body against his. Locking her fingers behind his neck, she pulled his face down to hers.

"Let me show you how I feel about you, Jake."

She pressed her lips to his, and in the next second, he yanked her tightly against him and deepened the kiss. Emotions swamped her, making her dizzy. When his tongue wrapped around hers, she forgot about her half-truths. This was simple, about Jake and the way they made each other feel.

His hands were rough and urgent when he pushed her jacket off her shoulders. It fell to the floor, followed closely by his. His fingers tangled in her hair, and she sighed into his mouth when he wrapped an arm around her waist and pulled her against his hard and unforgiving body. She couldn't get close enough. When he snarled in impatience and pushed her away long enough to shed his sweater, she pulled her long sleeves and tank top over her head and tossed them to the ground.

"Marlee, I'm not sure I can be gentle with you tonight."

The need in his voice made her heart beat faster, as his fingers flicked open the clasp of her bra, pulling it free from her body. The sharp gasp escaped her before she could control it, and he stared at her as if this was the very first time. When his hands molded her breasts and toyed with her nipples, she moaned. His blazing eyes tossed like the sea, and she'd happily drown there if it meant keeping him with her for a while longer.

"Jake, I'm not sure I want you to be."

When he grabbed her against him in response, she knew there wouldn't be room for regrets or omissions in their bed tonight. Tonight would be about them, about showing Jake how much she loved him, so that someday, he'd remember the emotions and forget that when she said the words, she hadn't told him everything.

When she took his hands and walked backwards into the bedroom, her face filled his vision. Her eyes glowed an unearthly color, enough to challenge the stars. Her lips parted and gleamed, rich and plump, as if tempting him with a forbidden treat. Each layer of clothes she shed revealed a greater feast for his senses, and Jake wondered if he had the patience to sample and sip instead of gorge himself.

Because he wanted to consume her. He wasn't sure he could hold back, even though it was important, this first night he'd shared his words of love with her, to show her the depth of his feelings. She was his and he was hers, and he treasured that.

Marlee climbed backwards on the bed, her black hair a stark contrast to her creamy skin, and Jake grabbed the condom from his wallet as he dropped his jeans to the floor.

"Only one?"

Her saucy smile made him throb wildly and wish he brought a truckload. He rolled on the protection and gave her a wolfish grin in return.

"There might be a couple more in there."

Her smile widened as she held her arms open to him. When he growled and charged her, she laughed as she caught him. As he reached between them to find her slippery heat, her laughter changed to moans, and damn if that didn't make him harder.

She held nothing back, every moan, every hiss of pleasure, every cry. When she closed her hand around him and stroked, he nearly lost his mind. He was determined to make sure her pleasure came first, and he put a finger inside her and stroked her nub until she came with a sharp jolt, whispering his name in a choked litany.

Knowing about the challenges she'd faced and the tragedies in her life made her unbridled acceptance of their pleasure a gift. She didn't let the past hold her back. He'd like to think that here in his arms, she felt whole and full and complete. When he thrust into her to the hilt, it was because he couldn't hold back either.

"Jake, I love you."

The words were so faint, he wondered if he wished them. He raised his head to look at her face, and she smiled up at him, her eyes shining radiantly in the color of unending sky. She nodded, and that uneven quirk of her smile deepened. This time, he was sure he heard her.

"I love you, Jake."

Then she laughed. The freedom in the sound made his heart open wider. Whatever they'd each done in the past, whatever the future held, didn't matter. Life narrowed down to this one moment, this one woman, and the love soaring in his heart.

"I love you, Marlee."

Her eyes seemed to darken and turn solemn at his words, and she reached up and kissed him hard enough to draw blood. Her moves against him grew more desperate, her pace quickening as if she was afraid they didn't have enough time. And while he wanted to savor, the impatient twist of her hips made him grind against her faster. Each deep thrust echoed in his head with a repetition of a single phrase. You're mine, you're mine, you're mine.

"Yes, Jake. I'm yours."

She gasped and tightened around him, her eyes open as she stared at him in open ecstasy. He couldn't hold back the spasms that rocked through him as the world tilted and exploded. His fingers locked with Marlee's. She was his lifeline to the world.

"We broke the bed."

He'd been unconscious for a while. He was sure he had been, because he had no thoughts for minutes, maybe hours. Being with Marlee was like that. He'd gladly give up all control if he would have more times with her like this.

"Jake, did you hear me? We broke the bed."

He pulled her closer, frowning when she slid away. Wrapping both of his arms tightly around her, he shifted her on top and gripped her hips. When he opened one eye, her body slanted at an angle and she stared at him in a mixture of amusement and dismay.

"Why are you crooked?"

A flash of emotion crossed her face, so out of place with the moment that he opened his other eye to make sure he watched closely. She quickly hid whatever she was thinking, and she laughed, even if it sounded a bit forced.

"I'm not sure what the rental company will make of this. Or how I'll explain it."

She shifted her body over him, and he registered the roll of her hips with an exuberant one of his own. It brought her true smiling attention back to him.

Arching an eyebrow at him, she said, "Did you say something about packing, deputy?"

He grinned at her, understanding perfectly what she meant. If a shadow again crossed her features, he forgot his need to question her about it when she nestled closer, lining up her wet folds perfectly with his hardening cock.

He reached for his jeans and dug in the pocket, pulling out another condom. When he whispered that he loved her and she returned the words, this time, he was sure he heard her. He wrapped his arms around her and let her kiss him into oblivion.

Chapter 22

"It's good to see little Marlee back in town, isn't it Jake?"

At Brew Bank, Stuart filled his mug with coffee while Sarge plated the sugar cookies with exaggerated motions. They knew. Hell, the whole town knew.

Jake and Marlee were an item. When Jake appeared on Main Street, people whispered behind their hands before giving him big knowing grins. He'd hate the attention if he wasn't so delighted with the reason.

Marlee loved him. He loved Marlee. Things were that simple, and life should be pretty much back to normal and back on track.

Except it wasn't. Secrets lay between them. He wasn't sure why he thought he knew this, but his instinct told him he still didn't know everything that he needed to about Marlee. She'd been mysterious about where she'd been for those missing days, other than reassuring him that it hadn't involved drugs and he didn't need to be concerned about it. Whatever it was, she said, was now behind her. He trusted what she said. But the fact that she made the declaration with shadows in her eyes, regret that didn't appear to have anything to do with him, put him on alert.

He knew whatever it was lay in San Jose. She'd shared that much with him, a cab to the Amtrak depot in town, a bus to the train, a train to San Jose. What she did there, she dismissed without explanation, and if she didn't meet his gaze for any length of time when she declared this, he'd have to accept it.

They'd fallen into something of a routine. He came into the spa for his massages, hoping to find release of the knots in his back as she worked on him. The first time he ever turned over on the table and surprised her with something hard enough to double for the nightstick on his service belt, she'd blushed a deep red through her make-up and giggled. Actually giggled.

She made up for it later though.

More and more, she moved into his life. He'd all but convinced her to give up the crappy apartment and live with him. His one bedroom place wasn't cramped by any stretch with her there, since she had little to bring with her. She insisted on her coffeemaker, and once he got used to the ease of dropping a cup in place and hitting the button, he had to agree with her choice.

She loved him. A part of him still couldn't reconcile his current life with where he'd been a few months ago. On Valentine's Day, so many things changed for him.

Change was bound to continue too. His last trip to the specialist hadn't been much better than he last.

"Your range of motion remains limited, Jake, below the department's guidelines. I can't release you for duty. I'm even concerned about putting you at a desk, since we know that sitting is even worse for a bad back. Another two weeks, and we'll reassess things again." The doctor had hesitated before adding, "You might want to consider what other opportunities you'd like to explore."

The statement didn't bring the feeling of doom it once would have. Having Marlee by his side meant the world to him. This profession had been his career, but that didn't mean he couldn't choose something else equally rewarding.

"You're thinking deep thoughts."

Deke dropped into the chair across from him with a mug of coffee in one hand and a large envelope in the other. His expression lacked the usual lazy smile and happy countenance.

"Nothing's wrong, if that's what you're thinking. I mean, the doctor wasn't exactly overjoyed with my lack of further progress, but I'll learn to live with that, if that's where the fates take me. Being in law enforcement isn't everything."

Deke quirked up an eyebrow at that.

"Really? Because I can't recall a time since you hit puberty that you didn't want to be a cop. Why the sudden change of heart?"

Jake let his eyes drift to Main Street, watching the traffic outside and the pedestrians enjoying the early spring sunshine. This sense of watchfulness of his surroundings would probably always be with him. He'd had plenty of time to think about his motivations and goals over the last few months, and some of what he'd learned about himself made him distinctly uncomfortable.

Turning back to his brother, he said, "Do you know why I became a cop, Deke?"

His brother shook his head, settling deeper into his chair as if expecting a long story. But it was simple.

"Dad. Right and wrong. He ingrained that in me, in all of us, and we all took it to heart differently."

Deke nodded but didn't interrupt.

Munching on a cookie and taking a sip of coffee, Jake struggled to find a way to explain himself.

"I saw the way he was with you. He had rules for everything, and you tried to follow them, even when doing the thing he considered right meant that something or someone was wronged. I saw the misery on your face every time, until you started to find a way to make the wrongs right and live in the areas between the rules and reality to put things in balance. Does that make sense?"

Deke nodded without comment, sipping his steaming mug.

Jake continued, "Rock did the exact opposite, said screw the rules and constantly got into trouble. Even Ma would get perturbed with him."

His brother smiled at that. "Perturbed is a big word for a cop. That doesn't sound like something to go in one of your brief and to-the-point reports."

Jake smiled back. "Yeah, well, I've been expanding my horizons since I finished my course work."

"You're done? Congratulations. You didn't say anything. We should get everybody together and celebrate."

He'd kind of hoped Marlee would feel like celebrating, someplace other than the bed or the couch, not that he minded that, of course. When he suggested they go out to dinner, she shook her head so hard that her hair clip fell out. His disappointment must have shone on his face, because later, after a particularly powerful bout of lovemaking that left him seeing stars, she acquiesced.

But he had explaining to do, if for no reason other than to understand things himself.

"The twins, by the time they came along, lived in their own world. They were always tight with each other, and I don't think Dad's displeasure ever penetrated."

Deke shifted this time, a grim line to his mouth. "I always wish I'd taken better care of them, like the oldest should. I'm not sure I understand them, and I know so little about their lives these days."

"You did everything you could for all of us, Deke. I tried to protect Rock and the twins too, but you took the brunt of Dad's anger more times than I can count."

"You still haven't told me how this plays into you being a cop."

Trust his brother to focus on the obvious. Even as he worked to find the words, he knew Deke would understand.

"As you and Ma have pointed out to me more times than I care to count, things changed for me. I screwed up so often, I wondered why I bothered. Then the solution came to me one day, when I'd had my butt tanned by Dad again for some infraction I've long since forgotten. If I follow the rules to the letter, I'll never be in the wrong."

"That explains the rule part, but not why you chose to be a cop."

Jake took another bite of cookie, letting the warm fragrance remind him of Marlee and center him. She was the center of his life now. Everything else dropped in priority.

"Being a cop, I can help people. I can make the bad guys go away. And it's all about the law. Ergo, rules."

Deke nodded in understanding before asking somewhat tentatively, "So what do you plan to do if you can't go back to work?"

Jake shrugged, because he knew he'd wait to cross the bridge when it was in front of him. He had time. He had Marlee. The rest would work itself out.

Changing the subject, he said, "Marlee and I are going to Mallory's for dinner tonight, to celebrate. Why don't you and Marguerite join us? I'm keeping it small and simple, because I don't want to scare her off again."

"Did she ever tell you here she went?" Deke's question, delivered in a too-casual tone that immediately set the hairs at full alert on the back of Jake's neck, accompanied a rapid tattoo of fingers on the envelope sitting between them on the table.

Narrowing his eyes at his brother, Jake shook his head but said nothing. Deke had an agenda.

Pushing the envelope closer to Jake, Deke said, "I took the liberty of hiring a detective to look into the background of your Marlee."

Anger flashed over Jake and he half-stood, ready to take on his brother for intruding where he had no business.

"Calm down, Jake. God, you'd think I said I took a contract out on her. Her background didn't add up. I asked around. She never talks about a past, other than vague references to living in the Bay Area before this. I bet you don't even know where she grew up."

He knew it was Oregon, but that was as specific as she'd ever responded to his questions.

Deke's serious tone finally registered, and Jake dropped back into his chair. "You might not like what I've learned, Jake. You should look at the detective's report."

Jake continued to ignore the envelope, considering the ramifications of punching his brother full on in the nose and damn the consequences. He had no right. If Marlee was ready – when she was ready – she'd tell him whatever was so important herself.

Deke leaned forward, his expression serious and worried. "There are gaps in her history, Jake. Big, mysterious gaps. What do you really know about the woman you call Marlee Cruiz?"

Without another word, Jake stood and left his mug and the bag with his cookies on the table. He picked up the envelope, carrying it as far as the door. Standing there, looking his brother full in the eye, he shredded it into four pieces, dropped it in the garbage can, and walked out.

Chapter 23

When the SUV pulled up in front of the bar outside Flynn's Crossing, Marlee still clutched her purse in her lap. Across the front seat, Jake seemed just as tense. Heating up the sheets was one thing. Going out as a couple was something else completely. She didn't want to disappoint him, and she knew that if she let this go too far, she would.

"Why are we here?" She didn't like bars, and she knew this one by reputation. It was noisy and loud, the kind where everyone was on display. She'd thought being in public would make her confessions easier, but this wasn't the place to tell Jake the rest of her ugly truths.

"I think you'll like it. Look, we've been going out for over a month now, and I think it's time – "

"We don't go out. We stay in and have sex. There's a difference."

Great sex, the kind you can only have with someone you love deeply. You're joined in every way, except she wasn't, because she lived with more than a few half-truths.

Fingers gripping the steering wheel with enough pressure to turn his knuckles white, Jake responded through clenched teeth. "We would go out if you didn't keep saying no. Tonight you said yes, and I won't question what changed your mind." He turned in his seat abruptly, his expression softening as he scrutinized her face. Leaning across the confines of the truck, he traced a finger down her cheek. She would have loved to lean into the caress and unload it all. But selfishly, she wanted a little more time with Jake before she saw the hurt and disgust in his face.

"Please, Marlee, let's go inside, have some dinner, maybe throw some darts or shoot some pool. Don't make it out to be more than it is, a simple date to celebrate a milestone."

His eyes tossed in turbulent colors, and she wondered how he could turn on a dime like that. One minute he was angry and frustrated, and the next, he pleaded with her to ease up like it was the most natural thing in the world. His control never ceased to amaze her. She only knew how to break it between the sheets.

"Please," he said again, bringing his fingers to rest where hers clenched the strap of her purse, squeezing gently.

As Jake continued to watch her, she released the purse and turned her hand over until her fingers twined with his. He gave her a huge smile. If she expected him to crow in triumph, he disappointed her. That made her smile in turn as she reached for the door handle.

He squeezed her fingers again and said, "Let me be a gentleman, okay? My mother would heat my behind with a paddle if I didn't treat a lady right."

She doubted that the diminutive woman had it in her to spank her big cop son, but then again, Emie Kermarrec had a reputation around town of being tough when necessary. The picture in her mind of his butt in that predicament made her smile wider.

"That's my girl." He gave her a quick kiss before opening his door. He ran around the truck and grabbed the door she had already swung open.

"I want us to have a normal date night. No mysteries, no trouble, and no secrets. Just two people who love each other, out having a good time." Jake gave her a little push in front of him as he opened the bar's door.

It was what she expected, noisy and busy, even on a weeknight. Sports blared from big screens mounted around the walls, mostly occupied stools lined the bar, and in the back, the ceiling of the room rose above pool tables and dartboards. Off to one side, a short partition separated the bar area from a dining room, and Jake pulled her in that direction.

"Let's get something to eat first, okay? Mallory's has the best burgers in the area and they serve them with – get this – tater tots. Did you have those when you were growing up? They always make me smile."

The idea that this strong and nearly invincible cop would get excited over something as retro as a childhood food choice made her heart open up a little more. Jake Kermarrec had gotten under her skin, and she had no desire to squelch this little bit of happiness. Soon enough, he'd figure out that he couldn't possibly love someone like her.

"Tater tots, huh? Who knew you could be such a softy? Does your lieutenant know about this?"

He flashed her that killer grin as she teased him, and she let the light of it fill her heart. Soon enough, she'd be telling him the rest of her story, and then he'd be done with her. That thought made her smile dim for a moment. But not tonight. None of the rest of it needed to come out tonight.

The hostess seated them at a table off to one side, and Jake made a big show of pulling out her chair and helping her into it. He flicked her paper napkin off the table and draped it across her lap with a flourish and a leer that made her giggle. She would enjoy this side of him while she could.

As he rounded the table, she glanced up, catching a tender expression on his face. If only she could keep that in place. He liked what they had together. But he didn't really love her as he said he did, since she hadn't told him everything. The woman he said he loved didn't exist.

Pulling out his chair, Jake was halfway into it when a female voice called his name across the restaurant. Marlee felt her heartbeat pick up, because she recognized the owner of the greeting. She didn't want to turn to confirm it, but Jake waved and said, "Hey, it's Serena. She's with Tess. They're asking us to join them. What do you think?"

She thought she'd like to melt into the scuffed wood floorboards and disappear into the basement, if this place had one. The one time she went out with him, and look where it headed. She had to change that direction, because the table wasn't occupied by Serena and Tess alone.

Reaching across, she grabbed one of his hands and squeezed. "Hey, what happened to us having a date night? If we join their party, it's not so much of a date. Please, can we just stay here?"

Jake looked confused, his eyes moving between her and the table across the room. Then his face brightened and she thought she'd won.

"I agree, let's stay here. But they're coming over to say hello. Hey, do you know the guys too? Powers and Dane. They're brothers. Serena is married to Dane, who's a photographer, and Powers runs a big construction company, which is how he and Tess met. You'll like them. They're stand-up guys."

She wanted to assure him that she did know them. She'd been watching them for months now. And they wouldn't be happy if they figured out who she was.

"Hi, how are you?" Jake rose and kissed Tess on the cheek, giving the tall broad man beside her a handshake and slap on the shoulder in greeting. Marlee stayed where she was, trying to pull her ball cap lower on her face. The other man, his long hair pulled back in a ponytail, kept his face averted from her, and she knew why. She'd examined the scar on his face with a mixture of sadness and admiration when she'd spied on him. Serena leaned in for a kiss and a hug next, then turned to Marlee.

"Hi Marlee. It's so nice to see you someplace social. I don't think you've ever met my husband, Dane Ashland.

Honey, this is Marlee Cruiz, who gives me those great massages at the spa."

She tried to hide her face as much as possible, murmuring something vague. Without looking up, she could tell that her lack of interest took everyone's welcoming smiles down a few notches.

Tess added, "Don't forget those wonderful pedicures, too. This is my other half, Powers Ashland, Dane's older brother. Marlee? Is something wrong?"

Maybe if she said a quick hello and made her excuses to find the ladies room, she'd be out of view before they had an opportunity to figure it out. If not, she risked losing everything she'd worked so hard to achieve.

"I, ah, I'm happy to meet you both. If you'll please excuse me, I'm not feeling too well."

She ignored the outstretched hands and leaped up from her chair, letting the paper napkin flutter to the floor. Spinning to escape, she ran directly into Jake's broad chest, bouncing away to free herself as his eyes snapped with disappointment and confusion. Then she tripped on the leg of the chair as she attempted to back away, beginning a slow descent toward an ungainly meeting of her butt and the hard floor.

"Hey, look out. I've got you." Dane's hands closed on her upper arms to steady her, effectively keeping her upright while stopping her retreat. She knew her blush would show, even with her layer of carefully applied make-up.

Dane spun her around and smiled in a teasing manner as he handed her back to Jake. "Looks like this one wants to escape you, my friend. Running away again already. Let me know if he's not taking good care of you. Powers and I will rough him up on your behalf and get him back in line."

As he continued to look at her, Dane's quizzical expression changed gradually, morphing into one of careful examination. His gaze flicked over her features, coming to rest on her eyes more than once. His smile faded into neutral territory.

"Marlee, are you okay? Guys, we may need to leave." Jake's eyes stayed on her face even as he addressed the group.

Dane continued to stare too, which in turn brought everyone else to watch her. She felt her embarrassment change to fear, and with it, the heat in her cheeks drained away, leaving cold panic behind.

"I'm sorry, but have we met? You look familiar." Dane stepped a little closer, and Marlee would have stepped away, but Jake's chest rested against her back, blocking any escape.

Serena stepped forward, laying a hand on Dane's arm as she said, "You've probably seen her around town. You only moved here from the Bay Area what – about eight months ago now, Marlee?"

Powers interrupted the conversation as he moved between Dane and Marlee so abruptly, she couldn't help but rear her head back to look up into his confused face.

"Dane never forgets a face, so if he says he met you someplace, he has. But I know you from somewhere too. Have we met in town?"

A shiver of pure terror moved through her, shaking her bones to the point that Jake pushed her behind him and stood between her and the others.

"She's not feeling too great, guys, so we're going to disappear, okay? Maybe we can sort this out later. Marlee, ready to go?" As he turned her toward the door, she glanced back at the two men standing with puzzled faces.

"Wait. Jake, wait up a second." Dane sprinted forward before they had a chance to cover much ground, and Marlee fought the urge to run.

With a hand on her arm, Dane nodded to Jake as if asking permission before stepping in front of Marlee once more. This time, he examined her face as if cataloging each of her features. She tried to keep her own expression bland, which ended up being easy because she thought she'd hurl from the stress at any moment.

When hands tightened on her arms, Marlee could do nothing but look up into the scrutiny.

Dane said, "You're the woman who's been watching us."

Behind her, she felt Jake stiffen. If she were to guess, she'd expect his face to be closing down, turning into the distanced and objective cop she knew was the core of his being.

Sliding his hands down her arms until he'd linked fingers with her, Dane's face changed with his amazed expression. A tentative smile pulled up the scar on one side of his face, as he said, "Powers, who does she remind you of?"

When Powers stepped forward, Marlee heard an angry buzzing in her ears, and little sparks of black light dove at the edges of her vision. She tried to breath, but her body didn't seem to work right. As the other man stared into her face closely and his eyes met hers, she let the darkness draw her under.

"What the fuck do you mean you think she's your long lost sister?"

Jake knew he was in full-on angry cop mode, his voice menacing without a single change in tone despite the questions he kept shooting at Dane. Powers continued to deny it, even as he shot repeated confused looks at Marlee.

Dane said, "The detective picked up her trail last summer in the Bay Area. He found record of her suddenly appearing, but no trail of how she got there. Then he lost the trail again. That was last summer, which is when she appeared here. Now she's using a different name. It fits."

Powers shook his head, his skepticism burning in every glance at Marlee.

Behind them, Serena and Tess sat with Marlee at a table in a corner of the dining room, hidden from view from most of the patrons. When Marlee passed out and would have fallen to the floor, Jake scooped her up and deposited her there like she was priceless china as the world around them was going to hell. Once he roused her, she wouldn't meet his eyes.

She raised them now, though, when all three men paced toward her. Resignation and acceptance filled her face, and tears made her eyes glow. Jake forced his expression to be noncommittal, because if he gave in to the turbulent feelings he carried inside, he'd pick Marlee up and throw her over his shoulder, caveman style. What he did after that, he wasn't clear.

In unison, Serena and Tess stood, both giving Marlee's arms a squeeze as if to reassure her they would be close by. They each gave Jake a tough glint as they passed by on their way to their men. He got the message. Take it easy on her.

Marlee turned her head away, and a single solitary tear dropped to her cheek. He watched it run down her face, roughly following the discolored line of a scar, no longer hidden so well by her make-up after the emotions of the past half an hour. She didn't look back as he dropped into the chair next to her, taking her free hand in his. Hers was ice cold and shaking.

"Marlee, look at me."

She didn't turn back. In profile, he could see her lips tremble.

"Please, we need to talk."

He kept his tone gentle and his fingers rubbed hers, trying to give her some warmth. He could hear the angry rumbles of voices behind him. If he didn't find out what the truth was, Powers and Dane would burst into this and any chance of knowing from her might be lost.

"Is what they're saying true? Are you their sister?"

She didn't reply, but she loosened the hold on her purse enough for it to slip to the floor between their feet. He reached for her other hand and held on tight.

"You need to know that they've been searching for their sister for quite a while. It's been a struggle for both of them, and for a time, it created a rift between them. They've said that they felt like they were being watched in town. Was that you?"

She gave him a small nod as she stared down as their fingers, his interlaced with hers tightly. He wanted her to know that she could tell him anything. Love was like that.

"Why didn't you talk with them and tell them who you are? Or are you not their long lost sister? Tell me the truth, Marlee. We can handle anything together as long as we share the truth."

She drew in a deep breath, tipping her head back far enough so that he could hear her neck crack. When she opened her eyes, she met his frank gaze with one of her own. While she looked brave, he watched her swallow hard before she said anything.

"Yes, Powers and Dane are my brothers. My birth name is Amanda Ashland. They called me Mandy."

His thoughts swirled. How could she have kept this from him? He'd been talking about love and the future and she hadn't even unloaded about her past.

Her expression changed, bravery ebbing away like a deflating balloon. She tried to extricate her fingers from his, but he was too numb to let go. At the edge of their reality, he recognized that a few feet away, their four friends had stopped talking and stood in silence. When she tugged her fingers from his again, he released her.

"I still don't believe it's her." Powers sounded uncertain and confused. "She needs to prove it."

"How do you expect her to do that? Take a blood test?" Dane hissed the words, but Jake thought it might not be a bad idea.

Serena's voice of reason cut across the angry words. "Marlee, tell us something about your childhood, something you and your brothers would know but wasn't common knowledge."

If she was surprised by the question, Marlee didn't show it. She shifted her eyes to the faces of the men who might be her brothers and said without hesitating, "We took a fishing trip to the mouth of the Columbia. You two threw up. I didn't."

The scenario caught Jake by surprise, and he stifled a chuckle. His Marlee always surprised him when he least expected it. But he might not be able to call her his anymore.

Dane started to snicker, accelerating to a full laugh as he clapped a hand to Powers' shoulder. The older man looked astounded. That, and embarrassed. He shook his head from side to side, and an expression of amazement came over his features. He dug his wallet out of his pocket and pulled something from inside, glancing up at Marlee as he did so and narrowing his eyes. He gave a satisfied shake of his head and handed a creased photo to Jake.

"Look, here's her picture. Granted, it was taken a long time ago, her senior year in high school. Her face, it's a little different. But her eyes are the same. You can't deny it."

Jake took the proffered picture and examined it, even though he knew she was telling the truth. Her words at their first dinner came back to him. Whatever she chose to tell him would always be the truth. She just might not chose to tell him everything. He didn't need to look between Marlee and the photo to compare the two. He'd watched her face for hours, awake and asleep. This is what she'd looked like, before the monster beat her.

Why hadn't she told him? He'd opened his heart to her and told her he loved her. She'd returned the words. But she refused him the comfort of the whole truth. He was beginning to realize the reason might be that he still didn't know everything. If she'd kept something like this from him, what else might she be hiding?

Marlee stared at him, her eyes brimming with unshed tears as she straightened in her chair. He watched her shoulders stiffen as if she could read his doubts.

How could this be real? What he felt for her was real. The way she held nothing back when they made love was real. The way they laughed together and shared each other's pain, those were real emotions. But he couldn't wrap his brain around why she wouldn't tell him, even if she asked him to keep it a secret. She had to know that he'd always keep her secrets safe.

As if recognizing his retreat, she leaned away from him, fixing her hair behind her ears and trying to pull the errant strands into a twisted tail. With her arms in the air, he had an advantage when her phone buzzed loudly in her purse.

He grabbed for the bag, even as she tried to extricate her fingers from her hair and reach for it too. He dug through the purse as she protested, his fingers closing around the cell phone and pulling it out as he rose and put it out of her reach.

The display held a Bay Area phone number, and he decided that this was an opportunity too good to miss. The answers to many questions could be on the other end of the line. Pressing the call button, he barked out, "This is Sheriff's Deputy Jake Kermarrec. Who is this?"

Behind him, Marlee stood and tried to grab the phone out of his hands, but he wrapped his free arm around her and held her close to his side. A din of noise rose close by as if some combination of his friends protested, but he didn't give a damn.

The phone stayed silent, though he could hear heavy breathing.

"I said, this is Deputy – "

"I'm sorry, you surprised me, Deputy. Give me a second." The older male voice on the other end inhaled deeply once more. "This is McClelland. I'm the private investigator hired by Ms. Cruiz. Is she all right?"

Glancing at Marlee who was no longer attempting to retrieve the phone from him, he wondered if that was true. Her eyes had dulled and her skin paled to gray. He acknowledged the man's question and confirmed that Marlee was fine.

"That's good, great really. When you answered, I assumed the worst, that he already got there."

Jake felt his heart rate slow, the way it did whenever the stakes were high. Noise faded away and the voice on the other end became urgent, even as he watched Marlee – or Mandy – grow paler.

"Who already got here?"

"Do you know where Ms. Cruiz is? Because you have to warn her, officer. It was her ex-husband. He grabbed their daughter and kidnapped her."

Jake's brain tried to engage, but it was useless. He couldn't understand. Turning to Marlee, he stated another truth she hadn't bothered to share with him. "You have a daughter."

She looked like he slapped her. She nodded, but as he watched, raw fear filled her features, a hand covering her mouth as tears fell unchecked down her face.

"What happened? Is she okay? Oh my god, Lilliana." She stood in rigid stillness next to him. The fact that she didn't fall to the floor said a lot about how much terror she felt as her expression blanked to nothingness.

Behind them, he heard exclamations from Powers. "You named your daughter after Mom?"

In his ear, the PI kept jabbering.

"Repeat that."

"I said, he left behind a note, I think to let everyone know how smart he thinks he is. In the note, he said that no one would find where he took the girl. And that he was coming for his ex-wife, for Ms. Cruiz, and then no one would find a trace of any of them."

>>>>>

"Lieutenant, I don't give a fucking damn if I'm not medically cleared for duty. I'm on this case, and that's it." The night pressing around them held unseen threats, and Marlee needed protection.

"Kermarrec, let me be crystal clear on this. You are personally involved with the potential victim. You are not thinking clearly. You are not on this case, medical clearance or not."

He wanted to slam his fist into the side of the building, but that wouldn't accomplish anything. He hung up on the lieutenant without signing off. The only thing he could do is stay close to Marlee – or Mandy, he still wasn't clear on what to call her – and protect her.

"What did your lieutenant say? We need to get her somewhere safe. She can't be out in the open like this."

Jake couldn't agree with Powers more, and Dane stood next to them, continuing a scan of people in passing cars as if he knew who he was looking for.

"Do either one of you know him?"

Powers and Dane turned as one and stared at him as if he was crazy. Dane spoke first, shaking his head.

"Look, Jake, until an hour ago, we didn't know Marlee was Mandy. Until then, we didn't know she was married or that she had a daughter. What else don't we know?" His anger curled the last words into a snarl.

Jake felt just as mad. Marlee had lied to him. Okay, not lied, exactly, but she hadn't told him everything. Partners shared things, even the dirty little secrets. It was part of the rules.

She hadn't explained about the daughter. Why had she walked away from the girl? Why hadn't she claimed her long ago? She hadn't explained that either.

He didn't answer Dane's last question, choosing instead to pace over to his SUV. Marlee sat in the passenger seat, with Tess standing in the open door and Serena in the driver's seat. While it didn't look like the women intentionally blocked her in, Marlee – or Mandy – was all but trapped. And he wanted to keep her that way.

"At the risk of repeating myself, we need to get Mandy someplace safe. That psycho can't be allowed to get near her."

"Our house is closer, and he won't know to look for her there," Dane said.

"We should take her to my old condo in Sacramento. The building has security, so no one can get in unless they're announced. It's empty, but at least it's safe." Powers looked like he was ready to yank Marlee – scratch that, Mandy – out of the SUV and manhandle her there himself.

Reaching the SUV, Jake stared at the woman he thought he knew, the woman he thought he loved, until she stared back at him. He knew she kept secrets, but he never believed they were so desperate. Little did he know.

Marlee's tear-filled eyes pleaded with him as she said, "Jake, you need to find her. He's a monster, and who knows what he'll do to her."

He could only guess, because between the PI and the lieutenant, they'd filled in a lot of blanks about one Davos Cruiz, released from prison on charges of assault and drug trafficking and currently in violation of his parole. How he got out of prison so quickly was beyond understanding. That the man was violent went without saying.

"Don't worry, Marlee. Jake will find your daughter. Why don't you come home with us until your ex is caught?" Tess flashed a warning look at Powers as she delivered her invitation.

"Tess, that makes no sense. And I don't want you in danger." Jake heard the fuming frustration in his friend's voice. According to all reports, Cruiz knew Marlee lived in Flynn's Crossing, and a house on Main Street was the last place she should be hiding. Too many people knew who she was.

"It makes perfect sense, Powers. She can't stay at Serena and Dane's, because they're out in the country. Anyone could approach that place unseen."

Jake had to agree with that.

"The condo then."

"By herself in the middle of the city? That makes no sense either." Serena shook her head. "No, I think Tess is right. The police station is only a few blocks away. We'll stay with her. We'll get the word out on Main Street, and this guy is toast if he appears."

As much as he'd like to argue, Jake could see the logic in it.

"Besides," Tess picked up the justification, "Marlee can pick Davos out faster than anyone else, even if you do have mug shots of him. She can watch the street and tell you if and when he appears."

Turning back to the SUV, Tess took one of Marlee's hands and Serena took the other, and between them, the three women shared a look of solidarity.

He wished Marlee would look at him with the same confidence.

Next to him, Dane said, "I still don't like it, but it's the best option we have. Just keep her inside and away from the windows. She can peek through the curtains or something." He glanced up and down the road outside Mallory's as if he expected danger to be lurking in its rural setting.

Jake wasn't sure he wanted her anywhere near Main Street. When this guy showed up – because something told him the scumbag had something to prove – he planned to be there with as much of the local law as he could muster and take him down. He'd reunite Marlee with her daughter.

It was the part about what came after that had him worried.

She hadn't reached out for him once since the bombshell in the restaurant. All but pushing him away, she chose instead to take the comfort of the women while she stared at her brothers like she wasn't sure any of this big reveal was a good idea.

"I need to be in the open."

It wasn't the gravel in her voice that drew all pairs of eyes to Marlee. Her words didn't make any sense. Did she have any idea what she was saying?

>>>>>

Five pairs of eyes drilled into her with varying degrees of anger and disbelief. Marlee didn't care. She hadn't protected her daughter years ago. She certainly wasn't going to fail her now.

Jake stared at her, and she wasn't sure if it was admiration or abomination she saw in his expression. His eyes shuttered and dropped, examining the ground at his boots. She knew that look. Deep in thought, weighing his options. She wouldn't blame him if he ran for the hills and let chance take care of this outcome.

She pushed her way out of the seat, grateful neither of the women seemed intent on holding her back. Covering the distance quickly, she stopped in front of Jake, willing him to look at her. He kept his eyes downcast and she swallowed her disappointment and held her head up, turning to her brothers.

"He has Lilliana. It isn't her he wants. It's me. You see, I did something a long time ago and he's never forgiven me for it."

"I don't like where this conversation is heading." Powers paced a few steps away and came back, rubbing at the back of his neck so fiercely, she was surprised his skin didn't ignite.

"You aren't doing this alone, Mandy." Dane's quiet affirmation of support made her heart ache.

"You damn sure aren't. We're behind you, whatever you need." Powers stopped pacing and stood next to Dane, and the commitment she saw in his eyes made her stronger.

"Friends stand up for friends," Serena added, and she and Tess joined her brothers, all four of them presenting a united front. Her heart cracked open a little further.

Behind her, Jake remained silent. She sucked in a deep breath and squared her shoulders. She would do this without him then. He said he loved her, but she understood his reluctance to say another word. She hadn't been completely honest with him. When she laid all of her cards on the table, she doubted he would understand.

The lightest of shuffles sounded, boots against gravel, and Jake stood behind her. She felt his heart pounding too fast, even as a slight tremor shook them. Was it from her, or from him? His arms didn't come around her as she hoped they would. She felt a fleeting touch she thought might be his lips. Then he stepped away as he said, "I will protect you, Marlee."

No words of love to console her. He didn't attempt to meet her eyes. He put a hand under her elbow as he guided her back to the SUV. Impersonal, as if he didn't want to touch her. Tears pricked her eyes as she realized it was the best she could expect.

Chapter 24

"If Jake says he loves you, he loves you. He doesn't put conditions on his emotions. He needs time to adjust."

Marlee shook her head, knowing differently. While Jake made a good show of being by her side, she felt him pulling away from her emotionally. The glances he gave her maintained their distance and she had no idea what he thought of her now.

Sitting a few feet away, Serena accepted a glass of water from Tess. Marlee received the same. Powers had a soda in his hand, which he regarded with such a glare that she knew he wished it was something stronger. But no one wanted to let their guard down in the least. She didn't blame them.

Tess seated herself on a small sofa to one side of the ornate parlor. At least, Marlee thought it should be called a parlor, the room spanning half of the front of the old Victorian at the end of Main Street. With filmy curtains drawn closed, she could watch the six blocks without being seen.

Patting the sofa next to her, Tess looked at Powers, lowering her eyebrows a tiny bit. It must have served as a glare between them, because her brother sat without arguing and took his girlfriend's hand.

Dane perched on the arm of Serena's chair and took his wife's hand, and together, the four of them looked like a tableau of love and commitment. The fact that Jake stood at the fireplace, his arm on the mantle and his eyes looking everywhere but at her, made their separation more obvious.

"Tell us what we should call you now." Tess asked the simple question and Powers started to argue, silenced by a single look. Under different circumstances, she would have enjoyed seeing her big brother tamed like this.

Taking a deep breath, she decided getting it all out there was her daughter's best hope for survival.

"I guess you should call me Mandy now, though it will confuse everyone."

"They'll deal. You're Mandy. That's all there is to it."

Tess shushed Powers' outburst and he leaped out of the chair to pace.

"Tell us what happened, Mandy, from the beginning." Dane's patience far outweighed their brother's, and his eyes on her face were unwavering, even as he stroked the back of his wife's hand.

"I left Portland the day after I graduated from high school. I couldn't stand it any longer. Dad looked at me with such criticism and hate, and he took every opportunity to tell me I abused Mom's memory by my actions." She looked at the other women as she added, "I did my best to get in every kind of trouble I could think of."

"You acted out, but then, Dad wasn't exactly supportive. There's a reason he had such a hard time, Mandy. You look just like her."

She jumped at that idea. "What?"

Dane leaned in. "You look just like Mom. You were starting to back then. As I look at you now, I can see it. It probably hurt him. Not that I'm taking his side or forgiving him for anything, but I can see how he was probably in pain. And you know Dad. He has no idea what to do with it."

It made sense. It was a running joke, growing up. Mom would take out their baby pictures, mix them up with those of her and Dad, and make them decide who looked similar. Everyone always voted for her looking like Mom.

How different she looked now.

She shrugged off the thought, wanting to get through this. Jake hadn't turned back to the room, and she dearly wished she could read his expression.

"I played guitar at clubs, hitching across the country. I'd find work, and I'd move on when a gig was over." She gulped, tearing off another bandage. "I'm not proud of how I acted, because there were nights I slept with a man just so I had a roof over my head."

From the direction of the fireplace, a sharp inhale drew her attention. Presented with his back, she wondered if she'd ever get to explore those hard planes again.

"I ended up in Chicago. I was good enough to get a following. That helped me find work. And attention. When it came to Davos Cruiz, it was the wrong kind of attention."

In a strangled voice, Jake said, "Skip to the highlights, okay?"

She sighed. If he was upset now, shortly he'd be ferociously angry and without pity. Jake and his blessed rules.

"Davos got me a great gig in a name bar, and he was there almost every night, sitting at a back table. He brought me flowers and bought me jewelry. There wasn't any restaurant too expensive when it came to going out. He even found me an apartment and paid for it. He told me I was special."

No one said anything, and she glanced around. Powers paced, Dane gave her a considering stare, and the two women nodded encouragingly. When she looked in Jake's direction, his tense body smoldered like a volcano about to blow.

"Keep going," his voice commanded her tightly.

She knotted her fingers together in her lap, wondering if he'd even look at her once he knew the whole story.

"One day, he told me he cared about me." From the fireplace, a hiss of anger erupted. "And we got married. It wasn't fancy, just us and a couple of his friends at a chapel in Vegas. I thought it was going to magical, but then things changed."

Powers stopped pacing long enough to say, "You don't have to tell us any more if you're not ready to, Mandy." He was probably afraid to hear what came next. She couldn't blame him.

"Keep going," Jake ordered, earning frowns from her brothers. No matter. She wanted to get everything out in the open. Then she'd take the consequences.

"It started out small enough. When I had trouble sleeping, he gave me a couple of pills. When I couldn't get the energy together to perform, there was a drink to pep me up. Then he invited me to hang out with his buddies, and there was weed making the rounds. It dulled the edges of my days, because by now, he no longer treated me like a princess. Now, he yelled at me, hurt me, and as time passed, fed me stronger and stronger drugs."

She heard a strangled sound from Powers, who paced faster. Dane said nothing, staring in that way he had since they were kids, watching everything carefully. Serena might have had tears in her eyes, and Tess nodded her head in sympathy.

Only Jake remained still. He seemed to find something very interesting in his examination of the mantel, since he didn't turn around or make a sound.

She couldn't sit still any longer, not with the bomb that was about to go off. She began to pace the long room, and it was enough to make Powers sit down by Tess and stare as well.

"There were lots of drugs, and I won't bore you with the details. I learned that he was a dealer and a big fish in the pond. Soon he had me running errands, deliveries and pick-ups, in return for my fix. I started snorting heroin and once that started, I was his. At its worst, he injected me. When I was high, I didn't care what happened because I was numb, and when I wasn't, I needed that next fix more than my life."

It was a sad commentary on her weakness, that she didn't see it coming and couldn't fight it once Davos introduced her to the hard stuff. She felt ashamed all over again, just like she did every time she told the story.

"That's why you wear long sleeves?"

She nodded at Dane's quiet question.

Serena asked, "Can we see your arms now? I promise you, Mandy, we won't judge you. You were in a situation beyond your control."

"You could have called us, any time, and we would have come for you." Accusation and anger mixed in her older brother's words, and when Tess shushed him and told him now was not the time, he sucked in air loudly enough to silence the rest of the room.

"I know, Powers but I was ashamed of what I'd become, and I was weak."

Still, Jake said nothing.

She reached for the bottom of her shirt, pulled it up, and tossed it aside. The tank she always wore underneath hugged her body, and she wondered if her family could see how broken she'd become.

Serena moved first, coming forward and gently touching her forearms. Tess came next. As if fighting his better instincts, Powers followed, examining her arms like a construction diagram, and Dane came last. But he didn't look at her arms. He stared into her eyes instead.

"I think you're very brave, Mandy, because it's obvious you licked this thing. That's not easy. Whatever else happened, you're a hero to me."

She fell into her baby brother's arms and let him hold her while she wept. Tess and Serena wept too, and even Powers gave a sniff.

Jake was as still as a statue.

"But you know we can't see anything, right?" Serena grabbed a wad of tissues and shoved them into Marlee's hands.

"Come on, you don't have to be polite. The tracks are there. That's why I keep them covered."

"No, seriously Mandy. We can't see anything. Look for yourself."

She looked down, knowing they were wrong. But for the first time in years, she really looked. And she found she couldn't see them either. The memory of them would be forever in her mind, but the marks on her skin had disappeared with time.

Too bad the rest of her indiscretions wouldn't disappear so easily.

"How did you kick it? Your habit, I mean. And the guy." Dane took Serena's chair and pulled her into his lap, resting her head on his shoulder.

Marlee paced once more, unable to sit still with nervous energy teeming inside.

"Davos asked me to make a delivery. On the surface, it seemed simple enough. Drop packages with people on a route he'd established."

"And one of your drops was a cop." Jake's statement, the most he'd said to her since they'd settled in this room, told her all she needed to know. If his flat tone didn't warn her, the chill in his eyes when he looked at her said it all.

She'd lost him.

>>>>>

He wasn't sure he could listen any longer. She'd been beaten. That monster hooked her on drugs and abused her. She'd lived in fear, deeper and darker than anything he could have imagined. Restless and hurting, he wanted to punch something. He didn't think Tess would appreciate his destruction of her house.

He headed for the front door and was only a step away when he heard Marlee's raised voice.

"You need to hear the rest of this, Jake. You owe me that, at least."

It wasn't a request but an order, and the resolution in her voice made him stop. When he turned around, her sad face a few feet away was the only thing he could see.

She kept her eyes on his as she continued. "They released me after a few hours, once they realized that I was probably worth more to them as an insider than in jail. They hauled Davos in, but they didn't have enough to hold him. He was furious with me for being, as he put it, too stupid to do a mule's job right. All I had to do was deliver the dope, and I got picked up. But that didn't matter, because it wasn't about me anymore. I found out I was pregnant with Lilliana. Yes, that monster is her father. I had to protect my baby, you see. So I cleaned up."

"You quit heroin on your own?" Dane's amazed question brought a small smile to her face, even as she continued to stare at Jake. He felt like the lowest life form on earth. Why couldn't he be proud of her as quickly and as easily as her brother?

"I can't imagine how hard that was. But I understand your motivation," Serena commented.

The others agreed, voicing their support and admiration. Only he and Marlee remained silent. She lifted her chin as if daring him to say a word.

"Anyway, you can guess the rest. He beat me when he found out about the bust. He broke bones in my face and knocked out teeth. A couple of cracked ribs, bone-deep bruises. I was pregnant then, and I nearly lost Lilliana. I was convicted, because I was, after all, delivering drugs. But as Davos pointed out to me as he kicked the hell out of me, I couldn't testify against him, because he was my husband. And I was afraid he would kill my child."

How many times had Jake been the cop on the scene during a domestic dispute, encouraging one spouse to stand up for themselves in the face of this kind of abuse? He never truly understood the issues involved. Not every situation involved drugs, but in too many cases, the women and occasionally, men, feared that it would only get worse if they came forward.

"Anyway, I got a sympathetic public defender, a young woman who also volunteered at a women's shelter. I was sentenced to minimum security and encouraged to learn a skill I could use to support myself once I served my time. That's when I learned massage and nails. And that's where I gave birth to Lilliana, in the prison hospital. I got to hold her for a few minutes before they took her away."

The women gasped and her brothers exclaimed angrily, but she didn't seem to hear them. Her eyes remained on his, as if she expected him to say something.

And he didn't know what to say. That prison was no place to raise a child? That she should have run away once she knew what Cruiz did? But how could he judge? He'd never been in that kind of situation, and he was learning his assumptions were being challenged at every turn.

"What happened to Cruiz?" His voice sounded tight and strangled, even to his ears. Marlee nodded, as if this was exactly the question she expected of him.

"I mentioned the public defender. She ended up turning into more than my representation. She found a program for women like me, who needed extra help to start in new life. Surgeons and dentists donated their time to put me back together. Counselors helped with my self-esteem, not that this part of the program seemed to work with me."

She gave a self-deprecating bitter laugh, and he wished he could tell her how little she realized about her strength.

"And I got a divorce. She helped with that too, and once I was free, I could tell the cops everything I knew. You see, I was motivated."

"What happened to your baby?" Jake wondered how she managed to stay upbeat at all, with a child left to be raised in foster care.

She gave a twisted grin, one filled with hatred. "That's what kept me motivated, Jake. They gave her to Davos."

The room behind her erupted, but Jake didn't register the words and barely recognized the emotions. The system gave an innocent baby to a known drug lord. What the hell were they thinking?

Marlee nodded as if he'd said the words. Maybe he had, because his blood was boiling, even as he recognized a sense of shame that the legal system he held in such high esteem could make such a mistake. And he wasn't without blame either.

Because he'd never given Marlee the benefit of a doubt, assuming the worst of her because he was the big, bad cop and he knew best. At the moment, he felt like crap.

"Anyway, I testified against Davos, which is why he feels the need to get even with me. He went to prison for a few years, and Lilliana went into foster care. By the time I was paroled, she'd been moved a couple of times and I couldn't find her. I've had a PI searching for the last few months because I finally found they moved her to the Bay Area."

"That's why you went to San Jose." Jake heard the accusation in his tone, but he couldn't help himself. She didn't trust him enough to share something this important, even when she told him she loved him.

Marlee nodded, her eyes distant and sad. "Yes, but I'm not proud of why I went there. I wanted to protect Lilliana now because I couldn't before. I planned to rescue her from foster care, and we'd disappear. I would build a safe life for her, for us. But when I saw her, I realized how wrong that was. She seemed to be happy, maybe even thriving. I don't think the courts would give her to me legally, not an ex-con. But I couldn't tear her away from her life once I heard her laugh."

The room was so silent, Jake heard the thud of his heavy pulse in his ears. That Marlee had planned to kidnap her daughter should have gone against all of his principles, but he understood. You protect the people you love at the expense of everything else. No one else seemed inclined to question her motives either, because when Jake scanned the room, the only thing evident on their faces was sympathy.

"But why couldn't our detective find you?" Powers rose and stood behind Marlee, his hands on her shoulders. She gave Jake one more hard stare before turning to her brother.

"I started using the name Marlee in Chicago. Davos said it sounded like a better stage name. Then somehow, it ended up on our marriage license. When I was arrested, I went to prison under my married name. When I got out, I tried to use my birth name again, but all of my records were under Marlee at that point. I only used Amanda a few times when I came to California. You're lucky he picked it up."

"I don't care how it happened or where you've been in the interim. I'm just glad we have you back." Powers wrapped his arms around his sister, and Jake watched her stand stiffly until something broke inside her and her shoulders shook. Dane rose too and hugged her from behind, and her sobs echoed in the room.

It should be him, holding her and comforting her. It should be him standing by her side as she told her story. It should be him protecting her now.

But he was too much of a coward to admit that he had been wrong. She wasn't weak. She'd done everything she could to protect her child and turn her life around. Her strength awed him. Finding her daughter was the reason she lived in a crap apartment and pinched her pennies. He wondered how he could have been so stupid not to trust his gut and his heart when they screamed she was the one.

Because she was, his one and only. He never loved her more than he did right now, and she wouldn't even look at him as her brothers led her to the sofa. It was as if she expected him to desert her.

And frankly, he didn't even know how to begin to apologize. He waited, hoping she'd lift her eyes, even if she looked at him like a bug she wanted to squash. But she didn't look toward him at all. Neither did anyone else, for that matter. Family circled its wagons around her, and she didn't need him anymore.

He slipped out the door and climbed in his SUV, sitting in the driveway until his hands stopped shaking. Then he put the truck in gear and headed out for a drive that he hoped would clear his head.

Chapter 25

"Shit on a stick, Kermarrec, what do I have to do to get through to you? You're on leave. I consider you a civilian. You are not part of this investigation."

The lieutenant couldn't be clearer, and yet he continued to argue.

"You don't have the manpower to cover Marlee. I have the time, and I can do this. I will do this. She needs protection."

"I repeat myself, Jake, when I say what the fuck is wrong with you? You used to be a by-the-book guy, and now I can't turn around without finding out that you're breaking the rules. Let's not mention the various laws here. At least no one's filed charges against you."

Not yet, anyway.

At least Marlee hadn't turned on him completely. She'd been frigidly polite when she retrieved her things from his house. He didn't know how to break the ice. Dane had shrugged and Serena shook her head, clearly in no better position to advise him. When they drove away, the hole in his chest where his heart broke open gaped wide for everyone to see.

At least that's how it felt. With each passing hour in the four days since he'd learned her full history, he felt more hollowed out.

"Jake, you need to get off this vigilante justice thing and listen to the lieutenant. She told you to stand down, and you'd better listen."

At the other end of the phone line, his friend Lankowski had the courtesy not to tell him he was being an asshole.

"Paul, I can't. Marlee needs my protection. I can watch out for her."

"I thought she was Mandy now. Anyway, remember our training? We don't take the law into our own hands. You find out something, you call me, day or night. I'll have your back, and I can do the legal things you can't right now. Don't blow this, man."

He wasn't going to blow this. After these last few days, even he was thinking of her more as Mandy than Marlee. The woman foolish enough – and brave enough – to walk into personal danger without so much as a whimper had left the sorry parts of her past behind. He was going to protect Mandy and he would take down this scumbag. He'd find her daughter and return her to her mother.

And then he'd drop to his knees and beg that same woman for forgiveness.

He'd break every rule to keep her safe. She insisted on walking down Main Street in full sight every couple of hours, courting trouble. Powers and Dane hadn't been able to talk her out of it. Jake saw the resolve in her eyes her brothers missed. She'd paint a target on her back if it meant rescuing her daughter.

His one shot at changing her mind came yesterday, and he'd tried.

"I don't think this is a good idea. Let the various departments do their jobs to find her. You don't need to make yourself this visible."

Mandy looked at him with hard-worn wisdom and asked him, "Do you still believe you're meant to serve and protect, Jake?"

He nodded, not trusting himself to speak in case he said the wrong thing.

"Then I trust you to protect and serve Lilliana by freeing her. That's all I ask of you. You don't need to have feelings for me, and in fact, I don't expect that you do anymore, now that you know the full truth. I'm damaged goods, Jake, and I can't change that truth about my past. I can only try to do better in the future. So you can stand down."

She walked away from him, head held high, before he had a chance to argue with her. Before he had a chance to tell her he loved her, no matter what.

"I think I see him."

If she was scared, it didn't show in her voice. They could hear her, but she put her foot down when they asked her to wear an earpiece as well. The small mic wouldn't even be there except for the entreaties of her brothers. She barely acknowledged Jake when he clipped it on her. Yet another rule broken, since he'd borrowed the system without permission from the department.

"I hope she tells us where he is." Dane's frustration was barely a whisper through the communications link.

Jake watched her lift a hand to her face as if to cough, as she said, "The big silver truck parked in the block past the bakery. I'm going to see if I can draw him out and get him to follow me."

Swinging his binoculars around from the window to look at the truck, he spotted the driver and didn't need to glance down at the picture in his lap. He'd memorized the face of Davos Cruiz. He might always remember it for the brutality he'd shown Mandy. It was the man, and he was obviously stupid. This was a small town, and as an outsider, he stood out like a flashing sign. Jake took the stairs down from the room above the bakery and slid in behind him as Cruiz followed Mandy up the street. In his ear, Jake heard Powers swear.

The plan was for her to walk three blocks to the Victorian, go inside, lock the door, and call for help. Jake sent the text he'd keyed up for Paul, hoping his fellow deputy was close by and not busy. Then he sent an officer in distress message to the city police, with similar hopes. Until then, he, Powers, and Dane would do their best not to lose track of Cruiz or allow him to leave town.

And even though she didn't ask for it, Jake swore he'd protect Mandy above all else.

She walked up the street toward Powers, seated in the upstairs window of the Victorian. Dane, at the opposite end of Main, would take longer to get here. Jake felt inside his jacket pocket, his hand closing around the grip of his gun. In front of him, Cruiz put his hands in his pockets too, speeding up his steps. He moved quickly for a big man, but Jake knew he'd be faster.

Mandy reached the first alley and paused as if checking for traffic. She waited long enough that had a car been coming, they would have seen it by now. She glanced over her shoulder and stepped off the curb, but instead of continuing straight for the safety of the Victorian, she turned right and disappeared into the alley.

"What the fuck?" Jake tried to keep his voice down, not willing to draw attention to the situation from passersby.

"What's happening?" Dane sounded like he was jogging now.

Powers said, "She turned into the alley, and he's going after her. Fuck, why didn't she stick to the plan?" His voice cut off as he panted into his mic, probably at a run now as well.

Jake accelerated, reaching the end of the buildings and halting to check the status. He took a quick glimpse around the corner and saw Mandy and Cruiz at the far end of the alley. A back street led around Main Street shops until it hooked up with the street by Brew Bank. If Cruiz's plan was to grab Mandy and return to his vehicle to make his escape, they had to cover the possibility.

"Dane, there's a silver SUV three doors down from Brew Bank. It belongs to Cruiz. Stay with it in case he circles around with Mandy." Jake whispered the license plate from memory.

He crept around the corner low to the ground, pulling his weapon and ignoring the pain in his back as he crouched. Cruiz was speaking, reaching out a hand to touch Mandy's face, the side he'd destroyed years ago, and he laughed when she cringed. His muscular frame dwarfed Mandy, like he could easily break her in two with his bare hands. When he ran those hands down her arms, Jake wanted to kill him.

The lieutenant was right. His personal involvement clouded his thinking. His hands shook with rage and he barely kept himself from yelling at Cruiz to leave her alone. Mandy took a step back and away from the big man, and he followed and pressed her against the bricks, laughing the whole time.

Intent on the scene in front of him, Jake took five more crouched steps forward, the pain fading from his consciousness. He didn't want Mandy to see him and give away his position in her surprise. Even at this distance, she looked pale and shaky.

Hold on, sweetheart. The cavalry's almost there.

And in the confines of the alley, the sound of his cell phone ringing echoed in the stillness.

"What the fuck?"

In front of her, Davos swore and grabbed her arm, swinging her around and putting the cold steel of the gun barrel to her temple as he twisted her arm behind her. It wasn't the first time he'd pulled a gun on her or used her as a shield. Years ago, he considered this kind of fear foreplay. And years ago, she'd taken it.

Once he'd moved, she could see Jake walking forward with his weapon trained on them. She'd never thought he looked better, intent on his prey and unwavering. His phone continued to ring in his pocket, but he ignored it.

"Oh look, who do we have here? Is this the boyfriend, Marlee? Oh yeah, I know all about him, a beat-up cop you've been doing to keep yourself busy. Take a good last look at him, because where I'm taking you, he ain't gonna find you."

The resolve on Jake's face tightened, and she recognized that cold stare and slow pace. He'd keep walking until Davos shot them. He didn't realize the man was serious.

"Drop your weapon and release her, Cruiz."

Behind her, Davos laughed, the sound maniacal and unconvinced.

"And who's going to make me? You need me, cop. You need me to find the girl. Isn't that right, Marlee? We're going to be reunited, the three of us, and be one big happy family. I can't wait until I get my girls right where I want them."

She couldn't help the shake of her skin crawling at his words. Instead of scaring her, though, it made her stronger. She would stay alive for Lilliana, and the best way to do that was to keep Davos talking. Maybe he'd give away something that Powers or Dane could use to find her daughter. She doubted she or Jake would make it out of this alley alive. Davos would shoot her once she was no longer a helpful shield, and then he'd turn the gun on Jake. Her cop would try to keep Davos alive to question him about Lilliana's location, and he wouldn't stand a chance.

As she always suspected she would, she'd ruined his life. Even if Davos didn't kill him at this range, Jake's injuries were bound to be career-ending. And that career meant more than anything to him. She'd never told him again that she loved him. She doubted he still felt the same way for her anymore. Blinking back the wave of regrets building inside her, she tried to distract her attacker.

"How is Lilliana, Davos? Did she recognize you?"

He tightened his grip at her questions and raised her arm higher, making her stand on tiptoe to avoid the worst of the pain. He shifted the gun to her back, behind her heart. At this range, the bullet would pass through her and hit Jake.

"Recognize me? Why would she? She got dropped on me when she was a whiny baby. Now she's a whiny, sniveling kid and completely useless to me. I doubt I could even sell her on the market. Oh yeah, guys pay big bucks for a fresh little virgin with her looks. She takes after you, Marlee. Come to think of it, maybe I'll keep her around for a while and show her the ropes, if you know what I mean. Then she'll be worth something."

It was a good thing she hadn't been able to choke down any food this morning, because she surely would have thrown it up. It would have been worth it if she could have vomited in the monster's face.

Jake stood about twenty feet away, close enough for her to see the flare of his nostrils and anger reddening his face. His hands were rock-steady, though, and she realized that whatever else happened today, he lived up his commitment to her. He would protect her to the best of his ability, or get himself killed trying.

"Mandy, listen to me." Jake's voice boomed in her ears, even though she doubted he raised his voice at all.

She nodded, hoping he saw the move of her head because his eyes stayed on Davos.

"Everything I've said to you over the past month is still true. No matter what, I love you. I trust you and I love you, Amanda. I need you to trust me too. Do you understand?"

She nodded again, earning herself a yank by Davos as he laughed harshly.

"Aw, ain't that sweet? The lovebirds are having a heartfelt farewell. Because you see, I don't need her and I don't need you. I'll kill you both without blinking an eye and I'll walk away with the kid. Easy."

Jake didn't seem to hear him, and Mandy watched the intensity of his eyes increase as his focus narrowed. The mix of color turned to a raging torrent of angry blue as his eyes flicked briefly to hers. In that second, she realized what he wanted her to do. If she screwed up, they'd both be dead.

Jake said, "I need you to tell me, Amanda. I need you to tell me – now."

The command in his last word was unmistakable, and she collapsed her legs and fell to the side, pulling her shoulder from its socket as gunfire erupted around her. She screamed as Jake fell to the ground. So much sound filled her ears that she couldn't make sense of it. Something wet and warm seeped around her on the pavement, as the pain in her shoulder intensified.

Jake must have been hit. He might be dead, and she'd never had a chance to tell him one more time that she loved him. He knew her whole truth now, and she could tell him she loved him without holding anything back. For many reasons, now it was probably too late.

Ice running through her veins made her shiver. She wanted to turn towards Jake, but her body wouldn't obey. She knew she was crying, because tears fell in hot rivers down her cheeks. Regrets washed over her and all she could think about was Jake. Shock made the world smaller, and she barely registered the noise surrounding her until she felt a hand clasp hers.

"Stay with me, Mandy. You're safe now. I love you. Stay with me."

Then strong arms lifted her up when her circle of vision got smaller and lips pressed to her forehead as things turned black.

Chapter 26

"You're keeping my ER pretty busy tonight, Jake. Are you sure you're okay? You took quite a fall from what I hear."

Noah Kinkead held on to both ends of his stethoscope and stared Jake in the eye. The truth was, Jake felt like shit, but he wasn't about to pull the attention of the medical staff away from the people who counted.

"When can I see Mandy?"

Noah frowned at his refusal of care but let the moment pass. "The asshole dislocated her shoulder and she tore muscles when she pulled away. She'll need surgery. She's kind of out of it on pain meds. She'll probably be in a hell of a lot more pain after the surgery, because she's refused any ongoing meds. Based on her past addiction, she's afraid to start anything, which I can understand. You're almost as tough as she is, my friend," and he clapped Jake on the shoulder. The movement hurt enough to make Jake wince.

In front of him, Noah gave a satisfied grin as if he knew. "Let me bring you in on a little secret, Jake. Women are tougher than men when it comes to pain. You and I haven't got a clue what it's like to give birth. Women go through all that, love their babies, and turn around and do it again. Mandy will be fine, eventually. Until then, baby her too."

Before the doctor could walk away, Jake asked, "And how's Lilliana?"

Noah turned back with a frown, his expression grim and ugly. "So far, so good. It doesn't look like he assaulted her. At least she was easy to find in the back of his SUV. He kept her drugged to keep her quiet, and we don't know what the long-term effects of that will be. We don't know what kinds of mind games he played with her, tormenting her. Only time will tell. CPS is with her, and they'll care for her after she's released."

Jake had only one brief glimpse of Lilliana as the paramedics removed her from the vehicle and loaded her on to stretcher, rushing her inside the ambulance. She had Mandy's features, a dead ringer for the picture Powers showed them of their sister years ago. Her skin was pale but darker than her mother's, and her brown hair was curly while Mandy's was straight. He hoped those minor coloration differences were the sum total of what she'd inherited from her bastard father.

Noah stood before him, waiting, and Jake didn't want to disappoint him.

"And Cruiz?"

An evil chuckle erupted from the man, and he shook his head. "I have to say, that was some pretty fancy shooting. I never had to treat a GSW to the nuts before. Made my boys pull up so tight they could see what I had for lunch." And he chuckled again as he turned and walked away.

He hadn't intended to shoot Cruiz in the balls, but maybe that was fitting. He intended to drill him in the legs, but the asshole had dropped Mandy and was turning to run, ruining Jake's target. Based on the long list of felonies he'd committed over the last few days, he wasn't going to be needing his balls where he'd be going.

"Deputy? You can see her now."

The nurse beckoned him over and pointed to a room down another long hallway. Passing one, he saw the lieutenant and Lankowski standing on either side of Cruiz, who was handcuffed to the bed and swearing. Both of them stared down at him with such bland lack of interest that Jake almost had to laugh. For a moment, his boss glanced up and met his eye, nodding once before scowling at him.

He moved on before she decided to pull him in for something just on principle.

He rounded another doorway and stopped quickly when he saw Mandy. Gauze wrapped her shoulder and arm, and where the blanket didn't cover her side, he could see the thick band extending around her middle. Droopy eyes looked back at him, but he thought she brightened when she noticed him.

His heart in his throat, he wondered what to say. He'd been dead serious in the alley and meant every word. He loved her still and would always love her. But she might think it was a ploy to get her to move away from his target.

"Hey," he said by way of greeting.

Her blurry eyes settled on him, and she got the sweetest smile he'd ever seen. Reaching out with her good hand, she said, "Jake, my hero." And she giggled.

He smiled, because he couldn't help it. Even wrapped up like a mummy and high as the mountains around town, she was gorgeous. She'd hate coming down from that peak, but he knew she'd weather this as she'd handled every other storm in her life.

When he laced his fingers with hers, she brought their hands up to her lips with a little difficulty and she kissed his knuckles. "You saved my life. You saved my baby's life. You'll always be my hero." She kissed his hand again.

"You're embarrassing me, you know. You trusted me to take care of Cruiz. You're the real hero. I'm in awe of your courage. It must have been painful to dive out of the way like that."

He didn't want to think about what it cost her. He'd heard her shriek as she fell, and it wasn't one of fear. If he'd missed his shots, he could have struck her too. He might never stop replaying that terror in his mind.

"I had to do it, Jake. I had to. Davos is a very, very bad man, and he would have killed you and me and my baby. How is my baby, Jake? How is Lilliana?"

He wrapped his arms around her as best he could and related what Noah told him.

"CPS will take her away again, won't they? I'll never get to be with my baby. Jake, can I see her?"

If she continued to look at him like that, with big trusting eyes like he could slay all her dragons, he'd make it happen no matter what the authorities said. Her brow furrowed and she bit her lip in a way that made him almost forget they were both walking wounded in a public place. Instead, he put his lips on hers and kissed her until he felt lightheaded.

As her head fell back against his arm, she said, "Whoosh, that was a good one. You kiss good, Deputy Jake. I think I'll keep you."

He wanted to keep her too. He wanted to tell her, but he also didn't want to take advantage of her drugged state. He might be better off waiting until she felt better and they could discuss things like two levelheaded adults.

"I love you, Jake."

He gulped at her words, watching her face for signs of the stupor he expected from the meds. But when she opened her eyes, they were clear and focused sharply on his.

"I know you had to say what you did in the alley. I know it wasn't real. But I need to say this. I love you and I trust you. And that's the whole truth. I know it's a lot to ask for you to trust me back, but maybe we can get there with time. Jake, do you think we have a chance?"

His throat closed and he wondered if he would pass out from lack of oxygen. This amazing woman loved him and was willing to give them another chance. He wondered if he deserved her.

The blaze of emotion on her face faded a little, sadness creeping into her brave smile. She nodded as if she expected she knew his answer, and she dropped her face forward and hid behind the curtain of her hair. His hand shook when he pushed some of it back behind her ear.

"I love you, Amanda Ashland. I love you with all that's in me and I trust you with my heart. You'd better believe it, sweetheart, because you're sentenced to life with me by your side."

Her face lifted and her eyes shined up at him, her smile tentative as if she didn't quite believe him.

"Oh, kiss the girl already, would you?"

Dane and Powers stood in the door with big grins on their faces. What his friends said made a lot of good sense.

So he kissed his girl.

Epilogue – Two Months Later

She gripped Jake's hand in both of hers as she waited for the judge's decision. Otherwise, she'd be running sweaty palms down the unaccustomed dress Serena and Tess helped her pick out for court, at Jake's suggestion. She'd long since abandoned her dyed black hair, but she still jumped when she caught sight of auburn waves out of the corner of her eye. Jake assured her it emphasized her resemblance to her daughter even more.

The emergency hearing for her temporary custody of Lilliana lasted all day. It hardly seemed long enough for such an earthshaking conclusion to everything that happened. The system held Davos, Lilliana was safe, and when she asked him to, Jake didn't stand down.

Next to her, he looked composed and handsome in his dress uniform. Jake insisted on wearing it today, to add gravity to her case, he said. She didn't care, as long as he kept holding her hand. The chances of her winning immediate rights were slim to none.

The bailiff came out of the judge's chambers and called out, "Deputy Kermarrec, the judge understands that you would like to speak to the court?"

"Yes, I do."

Mandy looked at Jake in surprise. He hadn't said anything about speaking after the hearing. Jake, her brothers, half the girl tribe, her boss and various other people she knew had sworn their oaths and said their peace, strengthening her case. Emie, Bliss, Deke and everyone else stayed after they spoke, even though they could have long since left the courtroom. Their support amazed and awed her. In the end, though, it would depend on what the judge thought was best for Lilliana. Mandy sincerely hoped that winning temporary custody of her daughter would be the result. Someday, she wanted to make that permanent.

"All rise," the bailiff announced, and Mandy let Jake help her to stand. Her shoulder still wasn't healed, and it would be a while before his back was anything close to normal. The two of them tended to lean on each other. It was fitting.

"Be seated. I've given the matter of custody of the minor, Lilliana Cruiz, thoughtful consideration. It will be a long time before her father sees a day outside of prison. I understand his trial is postponed while he recovers from his – ah – injury. That was some fancy shooting, Deputy Kermarrec. Wish I could have seen it."

Beside her, Jake blushed a little and said, "Thank you, Your Honor," while people chuckled in the seats behind them.

The judge continued, "In light of Ms. Ashland's injury and since she and her daughter have never had a chance to get to know one another, I've decided on the following."

Mandy tightened her hand in Jake's and he squeezed back reassuringly.

"Ms. Ashland, you can have visitation rights for the coming six months, during which time your daughter will live with a foster family."

Mandy felt her heart drop. She didn't want Lilliana with strangers. It would be hard enough to earn her trust in whatever time was allowed.

"I will expect biweekly reports from CPS on her adjustment and her progress in counseling. It's a terrible thing for a child to suffer like this, and I want to make sure she has a chance to heal."

"I do too, Your Honor." Mandy made sure her voice sounded confident, even if she felt anything but.

"I think you'll be satisfied with the foster family, Ms. Ashland. Will you please rise and identify yourselves?"

Mandy glanced around, looking for strangers' faces in the crowd. Her eyes widened when Rick and Gabby stood, smiling at her.

"Dr. Rick Chagres and Gabriela Cooley Chagres, ma'am. We'll be happy to take care of Lilliana until you decide she's ready to be with her mother."

Before she sat down, Gabby winked at Mandy and gave her a big thumbs-up.

"All right then, let's put something on the docket in six months. Deputy Kermarrec, you have something to say? You know that you can't change my mind."

Jake helped Mandy sit before moving forward, stopping when he was in front of the judge.

"Ma'am, you know that Ms. Ashland is my girlfriend and I'm therefore a bit biased about her." The judge smiled as others waiting in the courtroom chuckled.

"Speak your peace, Deputy."

"Your Honor, Ms. Ashland is an amazing woman who has fought hard to rebuild her life and make something of it. She's an upstanding member of this community and an asset to us as a friend."

Behind her, Mandy heard people agreeing, and she felt her heart swell with pride. She could do this. She belonged.

"Yes, Deputy? I'd say take your time, but I'm guessing you would."

This time, outright laughter sounded in the courtroom, and the judge looked like she was enjoying herself. But Mandy wished he would hurry up too, because she wanted to thank Gabby and Rick and set up arrangements to get acquainted with her daughter.

She didn't register Jake's return to her immediately, and she looked up in confusion. While he wasn't smiling, his eyes twinkled in that flashing blue light she loved.

"Your Honor, in addition to Ms. Ashland offering a stable household for Lilliana, I'd like to make you aware of an upcoming change in our living arrangements."

They'd agreed on this, that she would find a better apartment, and she would live there with Lilliana once she had custody. It killed her to think about being apart from Jake, but under the circumstances, it was a sacrifice she needed to make.

"Yes, Deputy?"

When he took Marlee's hands in his and dropped with difficulty to one knee, her heart started beating hard enough to make it difficult to breathe.

"Your Honor, Ms. Ashland will soon become Mrs. Jake Kermarrec, and we'll be supporting Lilliana together."

Around them, applause and catcalls erupted, and the judge appeared to be in no hurry to stop the uproar.

Mandy thought her blood must have drained away completely, because she felt lightheaded and goofy. Jake wanted to marry her. This didn't happen to women like her.

In front of her, Jake kissed her hands and leaned closer, and he didn't bother to whisper when he said, "Amanda Ashland, I love you with everything that's in me. If you're willing, I'd like you to spend the rest of our natural lives reminding me that living only by the rules is never enough. You have to live with love too. I love you. Will you do me the honor of marrying me?"

His face filled her vision. This amazing man wanted her at his side. And she wasn't a fool.

"Yes, Deputy Kermarrec, I love you too, so I'll marry you. But only if I get to make the rules."

She leaned forward as he did, and met his lips in a kiss that surpassed anything they'd shared before. It made her dizzy, and in the noise surrounding them, she heard the sound of something banging.

"Order, order in the court please. Deputy, that was quite a display. I have to commend you for originality. Now, when is this wedding going to take place?"

Jake pulled a piece of paper from his uniform pocket with a flourish, holding it up for their families and friends to see before rising and handing it to the bailiff. Then he returned to pull Mandy into his arms, and she thought he looked like he'd won the lottery.

"Well, well. This is a marriage license. But you haven't answered my question. When will this wedding take place?"

Jake squeezed Marlee against his side and glanced around at their loved ones surrounding them. He kissed her hard once more. His eyes twinkled as he stared into hers and said, "Your Honor, how about right now?"

THE END

Excerpt – Karma Trumps Love's Choice

Eager for the next installment in the Flynn's Crossing series? Coming in February 2015, look forward to the story of Bliss and Geno, **Karma Trumps Love's Choice** (working title).

His gut rotated faster than the top speed of his circular saw. Cautious sips of milk hadn't helped. If his new friends thought it was weird that he drank milk while they enjoyed beer, they were kind enough to keep those thoughts to themselves.

He never should have asked. And then he never should that acted on the response. He figured he'd get a safe read from his sheriff buddy.

"There seem to be a lot of great women around Flynn's Crossing. Anyone I should stay away from?" Geno had asked the question with as much casual interest as he could form.

That had surprised a gut laugh out of Jake.

"You want to know who to stay away from, not who to chase?"

"Well yeah. I don't poach, and I don't want to invite trouble. I figure that you being a cop and all, you'd know who would be trouble."

Jake didn't help him out. In fact, he didn't list the one woman Geno wished he could avoid at all costs. But a promise was a promise. Jake headed the list of available single women with the one woman he couldn't chase, no matter what. Geno frowned and didn't ask anything more, accomplishing the remainder of their ride in silence. Jake never asked him for clarification since, and Geno never offered. If his friend stared at him with a bit of a frown from time to time, he chose to decide it was simply his cop curiosity.

Standing on the sidewalk at the end of Main Street in Flynn's Crossing and staring up at the shop's sign, Geno debated about his approach. It wasn't like he needed a haircut, since he shaved off the little bit of hair left on his head. Otherwise, he'd look like one of those weird monks with a fringe haloing his bald pate. God forbid he needed his nails done. He'd lose his wolf pack membership card if he did that. And a massage was just too personal, particularly if the woman in question provided it.

A body moved behind the blinds of the front window, and he realized he'd been standing and staring long enough to attract attention. The petite form stopped and peeked through the white slats. Big brown eyes glanced down and he spun around before she could see his face. Pretending to examine the store across the street, he caught her reflection for ten seconds before she turned away. The blind rose quickly and without a pause, and the northern California sun, still low in March, lit the interior with a stage set quality.

She always had the most expressive eyes, teasing and laughing one minute, turbulent and snapping the next. Had those changed? Life hadn't exactly been easy for her, and yet, from what he'd heard around town, she handled the curves it had thrown her well. Curves. Her curves. He shouldn't think about them. He imagined those had aged well over the years too.

The buzz of his cell phone, a hard rock melody he'd selected because he could hear it over power tools, gave him an excuse to stand still a while longer and turn back toward the shop. Acting like any other guy who was more distracted by his call and not looking at what was in front of him gave him an excuse to stare once more. All of the blinds were open now, and she was clearly visible, chatting to a woman while she leaned on the front desk.

"Hello?"

"Hey Geno. How are you? How's life in the sticks?"

And of course, the one man he didn't want to talk to now would call when he least needed to be reminded of his promise. The heavy accent and rough cadence reminded Geno he hadn't visited the city where he'd grown up in far too long. And his friend since childhood was going to remind him about that.

"Hi man. Life is good, and this isn't the sticks. How's Boston?"

"The same. Things don't change much around here. Mom sends her love, by the way." The voice paused, as if searching for more idle words to fill the required time for social niceties before he got to the ones he considered important.

"Tell your mother I miss her marinara sauce, and despite following her recipe exactly, I still can't duplicate it."

A genuine laugh filled their cross-country connection. "She'll tell you that it's because you don't put enough love into it."

Geno chuckled in response. Yes, that sounded like Sophia, though how someone could talk about love and extend it to strangers but not be accepting of her own flesh and blood was beyond his understanding.

"You know why I'm calling, right?"

Geno sighed. "I have nothing to report yet, other than her business is doing well. She seems to be settling in Flynn's Crossing for the long haul. Northern California agrees with her, and everyone appears to be thriving."

"Have you talked to her yet?"

"No, I haven't. I'm still looking for the right opportunity. It's not like I can waltz in without raising questions and suspicions." The fact they hadn't parted on

the best of terms didn't need to be brought up, at least not to this man.

On the other end of the phone, frustration all but crackled over the connection. *"What do you mean? She has a business. You need whatever she's selling. It's easy. Walk in there and meet up with her."*

Geno grimaced, watching the woman they were discussing hug her customer goodbye and turn toward the building's interior. *"That would be challenging. I won't get my nails done, and I don't need a haircut."*

"Are you stalling? How hard can this be? If you don't need what she's selling, she probably needs your services. Every woman wants to remodel something. Troll for business, man. Use your connections. Didn't you say that you have friends in common? Or just walk up to her and say hello. She might be surprised, but I doubt she'd call the cops or anything, right?"

"I'll figure something out. I'm going to hang up now, because talking with you always gives me a headache and makes me talk funny."

"I miss you too, man. The bros all say hey and Dad said he expects to see you here for the holidays. Just giving you fair warning."

"Tell them all I miss them too. And I'll think about the holidays." They were months away, and he had plenty of time to come up with a reasonable excuse or two.

His attention froze on the short package of round curves and abundance leaning on the front desk inside, her face animated as big hand gestures punctuated her words. She was just as pretty as he remembered, just as vibrant and energetic as she'd been for all those years growing up. She'd allowed him to bask in the light of her bubbly spirit. If she'd sensed that his friendship was anything more, she never let on. When she left, it was like the sun set permanently in their neighborhood.

Nine years. She had every reason to hate him. He had every desire to love her. A lot had happened, but one thing hadn't changed. His crush on her had grown more intricate, more complicated, and more compelling. And Geno wasn't sure what the hell he was going to do about it.

About the Author

I love to hear from readers, so feel free to contact me through my website, www.yvonnekohano.com, or directly on Facebook as Yvonne Kohano, on Twitter @yvonnekohano, and at yvonne@yvonnekohano.com. Please leave an honest review of this novel at Amazon, Goodreads, or your favorite book discovery site of choice.

A HOLT Medallion Award of Merit recipient in Romantic Suspense, Yvonne enjoys channeling her characters' voices and passions as they overcome real world problems and discover love. Her Flynn's Crossing contemporary romantic suspense series is set in a fictional northern California foothills town not unlike the one where she used to live. Of course, the beauty and wonders of the Sierra Nevada Mountains and the surrounding counties play costarring roles in her work.

The first six books in the Flynn's Crossing series follow the developing love interests of the girl tribe, a group of successful women who work through real world conflicts and challenges to find acceptance and love - with some suspenseful happenings thrown in! In the next six books, the wolf pack of single guys in the area find their true loves, but not without their own issues to conquer. Periodically, Yvonne will be adding seasonal novellas to the series, featuring the first person voice of a character from one of her previous books experiencing an event that we can all relate to.

www.ingramcontent.com/pod-product-compliance
Lightning Source LLC
Chambersburg PA
CBHW021201250626
47155CB00008B/2622